"Whatever are you thinking *now?*" she demanded.

"This." Crispin moved quickly. Their closeness made it no great matter to slide his hand behind her neck, to cup the back of her head through the layers of her thick hair, and draw her the short distance to his body. He took her lips in an open-mouthed kiss that tempted and tested.

She was more than up to the challenge, responding with a fierceness that rocked Crispin to his core. Her tongue tangled with his, she sucked hard on his lower lip, grazing the tender skin with her sharp teeth. At length, she pulled back, a knowing smile on her lips. "Well, I suppose we can all be thankful for small miracles."

"What would that be?" Crispin gave a smile. This was more like it. Women were usually impressed with his kisses. He stepped forward, ready to claim more.

She stepped backward toward her mount. "At least you kiss better than you ride."

* * *

Untamed Rogue, Scandalous Mistress
Harlequin® Historical #1001—July 2010

Author Note

I had a great time with each of the Ramsden brothers. They're all a bit different: there's Paine, the youngest who, by birth order, has the opportunity to dabble in business to make his fortune abroad in exotic India since there's no chance he'll inherit. There's Peyton, the heir, born to be the earl and the patriot. Then there's Crispin, who was born to be wild. He loves horses and women and shuns commitment—until he meets Aurora Calhoun.

Crispin's story was fun to write. My favorite section is the part at the St. Albans Steeplechase. England is mad for horses, and the historical records are quite thorough. I was able to find a list of horses and riders that ran in the 1835 race, and a report of the race itself—who finished and who fell. It's all accurate, so pay special attention to the race and know you're reliving history.

Crispin's tale was meant to be the last, but it's not necessary to read the three stories in order. Be sure to check out Paine's story in *Notorious Rake, Innocent Lady* and Peyton's in *The Earl's Forbidden Ward.* There is also a short story—*Grayson Prentiss's Seduction*—giving Julia's cousin her own romance (available on the eHarlequin.com Web site), which runs concurrently with Julia and Paine's story.

Thank you for all your interest in the Ramsden brothers. I enjoyed getting your e-mails and the comments you left on my blog, urging me to get those Ramsden books on the shelves.

Readers can reach me at
www.bronwynswriting.blogspot.com,
or at my Web page, www.bronwynnscott.com.

Stay in touch!

UNTAMED ROGUE, SCANDALOUS MISTRESS

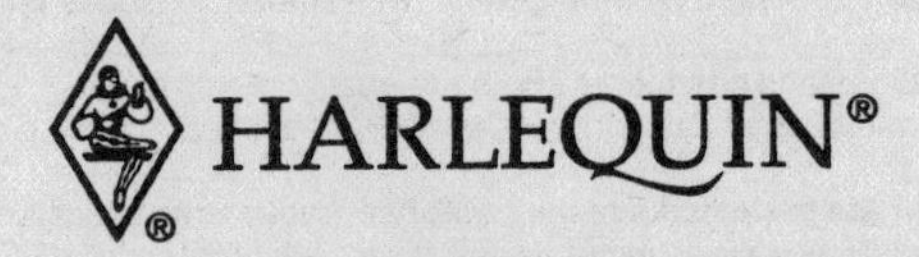

TORONTO • NEW YORK • LONDON
AMSTERDAM • PARIS • SYDNEY • HAMBURG
STOCKHOLM • ATHENS • TOKYO • MILAN • MADRID
PRAGUE • WARSAW • BUDAPEST • AUCKLAND

Recycling programs
for this product may
not exist in your area.

ISBN-13: 978-0-373-29601-9

UNTAMED ROGUE, SCANDALOUS MISTRESS

First North American Publication 2010.

This edition published by arrangement with Harlequin Books S.A.

For questions and comments about the quality of this book please contact us at Customer_eCare@Harlequin.ca.

www.eHarlequin.com

Printed in U.S.A.

Available from Harlequin® Historical and
BRONWYN SCOTT

Pickpocket Countess #889
**Notorious Rake, Innocent Lady* #896
The Viscount Claims His Bride #929
**The Earl's Forbidden Ward* #986
**Untamed Rogue, Scandalous Mistress* #1001

And in eBook Harlequin Historical Undone!

Libertine Lord, Pickpocket Miss
Pleasured by the English Spy
Wicked Earl, Wanton Widow

*linked by character

To Suzanne Ring, thanks for your support of the South Sound Titan's swim club annual auction.

Thank you also for your personal friendship. Your commitment to the community is inspiring.

Praise for
Bronwyn Scott

The Viscount Claims His Bride

"Love, honor, duty, lies and guilt along with a nice overview of the diplomatic machinations between England and Europe following the Napoleonic War all come together in Scott's well-written and moving romance."

—*RT Book Reviews*

Pickpocket Countess

"Scott brings freshness and sassiness to the traditional Robin Hood plot and allows her characters free rein to play their sexy cat-and-mouse game in this fast-paced, sensual and delightful light read."

—*RT Book Reviews*

Chapter One

Early February 1835

Crispin Ramsden never saw it coming. One moment he was trotting peaceably down the dirt lane that led to the turn towards Dursley Park, savouring a countryside he hadn't seen in three years, and the next he was flat on his back, having been unceremoniously spilled from his stallion, who was even now rearing and flailing his dangerous hooves in reaction to whatever had spooked him.

Straining against the pull of a sore hip and buttocks that had taken the brunt of his fall, Crispin levered himself into an upright position to take in the scene. He saw the cause of the accident clearly: a tall, slender youth and his horse, an impressive-looking bay hunter that went at least sixteen hands. Even with a sore hip, Crispin noticed such things. The youth was standing in the road, managing to calm Crispin's highly strung stallion.

'Miraculous,' Crispin called out, hoisting himself to his feet carefully. He'd only ever met a handful of people who could handle Sheikh.

'That's what I was going to say about you.' The

youth turned from the horse and faced Crispin, hands on hips, and Crispin realised his mistake. It was no youth who'd calmed his horse, but very clearly a woman; a woman with long athletic legs shown off to advantage in riding breeches that did nothing to disguise the delicious curve of her rear-end and high breasts that rose and fell provocatively beneath a man's cut-down white shirt.

'Miraculous? I can be.' Crispin sauntered towards Sheikh, doing his level best to not limp, wince or otherwise indicate the fall had left him in need of a hot soaking bath. This woman didn't appear to be the type to appreciate infirmities or she would have run straight over to him first and seen to the horse second. He reached out a hand and stroked Sheikh's quivering flank.

At this close proximity he could make out the long braid of dark hair tucked down the back of her shirt. In fact, it was quite amazing he'd mistaken her for a young man at all.

She shot him a hard look with eyes the colour of summer grass, a deep verdant green. 'I meant it was miraculous you didn't hear me shout when I entered the roadway. I called out twice to warn you of my presence. You had plenty of time to get out of the way. What were you thinking?' she snapped.

He'd been thinking how nice it would be to get home, to see his brother, Peyton, to see his twin nephews, who had been born two years ago, and the new baby, who had arrived a month early in January. He'd been thinking about settling the inheritance that had finally compelled him to stop making excuses and come back to the Cotswolds.

His attention might have been errant in regards to his surroundings, but Crispin Ramsden didn't like being taken to task by anyone and certainly not by a black-haired virago dressed in men's clothing a mile from his home.

Crispin folded his arms over his chest and faced her squarely. 'The better question is—what were you thinking? You're the one racing a horse into a country lane out of nowhere. In case you haven't noticed, this is a public thoroughfare. Any number of people or conveyances could have been on this road and you would have bowled right into them.'

'How dare you impugn my abilities as a horsewoman,' she shot back, boldly stepping forwards so that now they stood toe-to-toe, her dusty riding boot touching his. It was hard to tell whose was dirtier. 'You have no right to pass judgement on my skills when you were as absentminded as the vicar's grandmother. You could have ruined that fine animal of yours.'

Not only were they toe-to-toe, they were nearly nose to nose, give or take a few inches on her side, Crispin observed. He appreciated the benefits of her height. Being a tall man himself, he'd always had a preference for taller women—better compatibility when it came to dancing, which he abhorred, and bed sport, which he liked quite a lot.

He knew he should at least feign attention to the dressing down she was giving him, whoever the hell she was, but it was deuced awkward to concentrate when his mind was giving her a dressing down of another sort. Who could blame him when those luscious breasts heaved with indignation mere inches from his chest? When those grass-green eyes of hers flared with passion for her subject? It was rather difficult *not* to imagine how those eyes might fire with another sort of passion that had nothing at all to do with horses and everything to do with those long legs wrapped about his waist, locked in the throes of ecstasy, and those inky tresses spilled across a pillow, free from their confining braid.

He had himself thoroughly aroused by the time she drew a deep breath and brought her scolding tirade to an abrupt halt. 'Whatever are you thinking *now*?' she demanded, obviously alert to the fact that his thoughts had wandered from her lecture.

'This.' Crispin moved quickly. Their closeness made it no great matter to slide his hand behind her neck, to cup the back of her head through the layers of her thick hair, and draw her the short distance to his body. He took her lips in an open-mouthed kiss that tempted and tested.

She was more than up to the challenge, responding with a fierceness that rocked Crispin to his core. Her tongue tangled with his, she sucked hard on his lower lip, grazing the tender skin with her sharp teeth. At length, she pulled back, a knowing smile on her lips. 'Well, I suppose we can all be thankful for small miracles.'

'What would that be?' Crispin gave a wolfish smile. This was more like it. Women were usually impressed with his kisses. He stepped forwards, ready to claim more.

She stepped backwards towards her mount. 'At least you kiss better than you ride.'

Small miracles indeed! Crispin was still fuming over the encounter by the time he arrived in the drive of Dursley Park. She'd pricked his pride and ridden off without a backwards glance. She could not know, of course, that he took great pride in his horsemanship. It was the one thing he did better than anyone he knew and he knew many fine equestrians.

Her blind arrow had hit the mark perhaps more intensely than she'd meant. Crispin would love nothing more than to find the minx and show her just how wrong she was. However, he was grateful that his stinging pride had given his body something else to focus on the last mile home. It wouldn't do to show up at Dursley Park after a three-year absence with a painfully obvious erection straining his trousers and no good explanation for it.

Crispin jumped down from Sheikh and tossed the reins to a groom who'd come running from the stables the moment he'd been sighted. He mounted the wide steps to the front door, taking a moment at the top to survey the park spread out around him. The place looked the same as it always had: the lawns neatly manicured, the hedges that bordered the gardens impeccably trimmed, flowers blooming when and where they should. He chuckled to himself. Even nature in late winter obeyed Peyton and Dursley Park was clearly Peyton's domain; well-ordered and peaceful.

There was comfort in the knowledge that such a place as this existed in a chaotic world. But that comfort came with a price Crispin knew all too well: boredom. Just as he embraced the comfort of Dursley Park at the moment, he already knew two or three months from now he'd be chafing to get away.

His knock was answered by the butler who immediately ushered him in and went to inform Peyton. It was four o'clock in the afternoon. If he knew Peyton, he'd be in his study. Like the clockwork Crispin had bet on, Peyton emerged from the study ahead of the butler. His brother crossed the entry in three long strides and surprisingly pulled him into a firm embrace.

That was new.

Crispin could not recall the last time Peyton had *hugged* him and this definitely qualified as a hug, not a mere embrace done simply to make a show of expected, scripted affection.

'Crispin!' Peyton said at last, stepping back, his hands still gripping Crispin's forearms as if he were reluctant to let him go. 'Why didn't you tell us you were coming?'

'I didn't know I was coming until I got here,' Crispin said truthfully. He'd thought to come home so many times in the past three years. He'd even mentioned returning in a few of his letters, but then he never had. Something had always come up; some new adventure claimed his attention and he put off returning yet again. After a while, he stopped making any mention of coming home for fear of letting everyone down when he failed to appear.

Peyton nodded, perhaps understanding him as well as anybody did. 'It doesn't matter. You're here now. Tessa will be glad to see you and you have to meet the boys.'

With uncharacteristic informality, Peyton led him to the nursery on the third floor, the noise from which would have made it easy to locate even without a guide.

On the floor in the centre of a large, braided rug, two identical-twin boys wrestled and yelled in their excitement. Not far from them, Tessa sat in a rocking chair, holding a blue-blanketed bundle and watching the boys' antics, good-naturedly putting up with their noise.

'Tess, look who's stopped by,' Peyton called over the racket. 'Boys, come meet your Uncle Crispin. Crispin, this is Nicholas and Alexander.'

Two little dark-haired boys bounded over to them with no trace of shyness, two sets of piercing blue eyes looking up at him in curiosity. The boys were Ramsdens through and through. There was no mistaking the trademark dark hair and the blue eyes for anything less. Crispin dropped down to his haunches and met the boys at eye level. 'Want to see a trick?' The boys' heads nodded vigorously. Crispin made a show of flexing his hands and then slid one hand over the other to create the age-old illusion of his thumb separating from his hand. The boys' eyes grew large and they howled with laughter. Crispin ruffled their hair and stood up. 'They're Ramsdens all right.' He smiled at Peyton.

'Here's the newest one.' Tessa joined them, proudly holding up the blanket bundle to reveal another baby boy bearing the same genetic imprint, this one named Christopher and as healthy looking as the others in spite of his early birth. Crispin laughed and slapped his brother on the back. 'Three boys! It's you, me and Paine all over again. Probably serves you right, you old devil,' he teased, but he could see the obvious pride and love in his brother's face.

'I'll have tea set up downstairs,' Tessa said once the initial excitement of Crispin's arrival passed. She handed the baby to the nurse and shepherded the boys into a quieter activity.

In the drawing room, Crispin studied Peyton while Tessa made general small talk and poured out the tea. Peyton appeared the same as always: tall, fit, in prime health. But if he looked closer, Crispin could see subtle signs of change. His brother's Ramsden-dark hair showed brief signs of silver at the temples. Tiny lines faintly etched the corners of his blue eyes and the brackets of his mouth.

Very small variations on the usual theme, to be sure. He shouldn't be surprised. Peyton would have turned forty-one last August. Forty-one wasn't so terribly old. All in all, Peyton was ageing wonderfully, but Crispin still hated to think of Peyton as getting old simply because it meant he was getting older too. If Peyton was nearing forty-two, that made him thirty-eight and far closer to forty than he'd care to be.

Tessa passed him a teacup. 'Do you still take it plain without sugar?'

'Yes.' Crispin took the teacup, thinking how delicate, how fragile it was. He'd not drunk from such a frail vessel since he'd left home. Dainty teacups were not practical in the places he'd been.

'So you're home to settle the inheritance,' Peyton remarked, referring to the property a few miles away that Crispin had inherited from an aunt on their mother's side. Peyton took a teacup from Tessa. 'The manor is in great shape. I've been over several times to keep an eye on things, but the steward is doing an outstanding job. He's a younger fellow, highly capable and eminently trustworthy. I think you'll be pleased, Crispin. The stables are in prime condition; lots of light and big stalls. There are not any horses there at present, of course.' He smiled knowingly over the rim of his cup, taking a sip.

Crispin shifted slightly in his chair. He'd had months—a year really if anyone was counting—to mentally come to grips with his inheritance. It wasn't that he was ungrateful. Second sons rarely had anything to call their own if there wasn't some kind of settlement from the maternal side of the family. But after all this time, he still hadn't reconciled himself to the notion that he was a landowner with all the responsibilities therein. He'd already decided it would be better to sell the property. A wanderer like himself had no business owning land he had no intention of supervising.

'I'm not sure I'll be keeping the estate.' Crispin steeled himself for a cold scolding from Peyton. Peyton would think him most ungrateful.

Peyton merely raised a quizzical eyebrow. 'Perhaps you'll have a better idea of what you'd like to do after you've seen it. Woodbrook is an attractive piece of property for those who are horse-minded. Regardless of what you decide to do, there are a few papers that need your signature and some other minor points in the will to settle.'

'We can ride over tomorrow and take a look at things,' Crispin offered by way of a subtle apology. The least he could do was go look at the property. Peyton was no doubt disappointed he'd not immediately declared his intentions to set up a home and embark on establishing a superior stable. Such a goal had long been Crispin's dream in childhood, but these days, he had little desire to be tied down in the way such an enterprise would demand.

'Woodbrook is a bit too far for me to stable my horse there on a daily basis, I was wondering if I could put up my stallion in your stables, Peyton?' Crispin shifted to a safer topic.

'Of course, if we had room. However, we're full up just now for any long-term boarding,' Peyton said regretfully. 'But I'm sure we can think of something.'

'What about boarding the horse over at Rory's?' Tessa suggested. 'It's close by.' She shot a look at the mantel clock. 'You could go over and see about making arrangements. Rory will be done giving lessons in a half-hour.' Tessa reached for a scone and added, 'Petra's taking riding lessons over there. You can walk home with her.'

Crispin smiled. 'How is Petra these days? Has she survived her London début?' Of all the Branscombe girls, and there were plenty of them—four counting Tessa—he liked Petra the best. Although there was a large difference in their ages, Petra and he shared an affinity for horses that made for enjoyable conversation. He'd genuinely enjoy the chance to talk with Petra and show off Sheikh.

Peyton grinned. 'You know Petra—she put up with London for our sakes, but was happy to come home. It's where her heart is, quite obviously in this case. She's engaged to the squire's son, Thomas. They'll be married here at Dursley Park this autumn.'

'One down, Peyton. Two more Branscombe girls to go.' Crispin laughed, offering his congratulations. 'If you give me the directions, I'll head over to this Rory's and see about boarding my horse. I'll have Petra back for dinner.'

Peyton rose too. 'The groom can show you the path, it's just across the valley.' He paused and smiled. 'It's good to have you home, Cris.'

'It's good to be home, Peyton,' Crispin said, knowing his simple words to be entirely sincere.

Peyton turned to his wife after Crispin had gone. 'You're quite the minx, my dear.' He smiled and wagged a scolding finger in her direction.

'Whatever can you mean?' Tessa feigned innocence, busy stacking the teacups on the tray.

'You know very well what I mean.' Peyton fixed her with a laughing stare. 'You didn't bother to mention that Rory is a woman.'

Chapter Two

Aurora Calhoun shot a considering eye at the heavy grey clouds looming ominous and low overhead. 'Good work today, ladies, let's get the horses unsaddled quickly so everyone can get home before the rain sets in.'

The five young women in the equestrian arena, all wearing trousers, dismounted and began moving their mounts towards the long stone stable, Petra Branscombe leading the way with her grey-flecked hunter. Petra had ridden well today, taking even the highest jumps with ease. It was a point of pride for Aurora to watch Petra blossom from a horse-mad girl into an expert horse-woman over the past two years under her tutelage. Petra was no longer the quiet girl she once was. Her confidence on horseback had translated into confidence in other areas of her life as well.

Aurora frowned, surprised to see the other horses moving around Petra at the gate. She narrowed her gaze and found the source of the disruption. A man lounged against the gatepost, engaging Petra in conversation. Even at a distance, Aurora could tell the man in question wasn't Petra's fiancé.

Aurora wiped her hands on her dusty riding trousers and strode forwards, ready to protect Petra. Strangers were unwelcome at her riding school and unannounced gentleman callers even less so, not to mention that she'd had enough of men for the day after her encounter with the arrogant man in the road. She wouldn't mind another look at the man's stallion, but she could do without the rider and the hot kisses that went with him.

There'd been a disturbing aura of wildness about the man, a feral quality about his bold, blue eyes, and the unconventionally long dark hair that had hung loose about his shoulders, to say nothing of the fact that he kissed like sin itself. *That* kind of man boded ill for any woman no matter how enticing he was in the moment.

Apparently this was not to be her lucky day. After eight years on her own, Aurora Calhoun knew enough about men to know trouble when she saw it. And she saw it now. The man from the road was leaning against the gatepost and chatting up Petra Branscombe with an obscene amount of familiarity. How had the blasted man managed to find his way to her stables of all places?

'What are *you* doing here?' Aurora approached the man and Petra with firm authority. From the looks of things, she was just in time. Petra was appearing far too at ease with him and it had only been a matter of minutes. Aurora had rather hoped the usually sensible Petra would prove to be less susceptible.

A slow smile spread across the man's rugged features, softening them slightly as recognition struck him. 'So this is where careless horse riders come home to roost.'

Petra knitted her eyebrows, confusion setting in. 'Do you know each other?'

'We met on the Dursley Road this afternoon quite by

accident,' Aurora explained tersely, her displeasure over his presence obvious.

'*Literally* by accident is a more accurate retelling of our encounter,' the man put in, his blue eyes flickering with challenge and something else, quite possibly humour. 'I am looking for Rory Calhoun. I need a place to board my horse. I was told he might have a stall to lease.'

Aurora was torn. It wouldn't precisely be a lie to say *he* didn't have a stall to lease. After all, Rory wasn't a man. She couldn't imagine anything more disturbing at the moment than having this man underfoot on a daily basis. Then again, there was the allure of having that splendid beast of his in her stables where she could study it up close. Perhaps she could even convince him to put the stallion to stud with her mare. She thought the stallion carried Arabian bloodlines. Mixed with her standard-bred mare, she could produce an excellent jumper. In the end temptation won out, but not without some parameters.

Aurora crossed her arms. 'Let's be clear. First, it's not "he". It's "she". I'm Rory Calhoun to my friends, Aurora to the rest. You'd be in the latter group in case you were uncertain on that account. Second, I do have a stall you can lease, but there are some stipulations. Foremost, you cannot interfere in any way with my riding academy. The horses, my pupils, and my lessons are off limits. In fact, I'd prefer that you not schedule any of your time here during the afternoons on lesson days. You can come before or after lessons, but not during.'

'Don't want the village knowing the women ride astride and in trousers?' he queried with keen insight.

'We have trouser days just as we have habit days here at my school. Riding astride is a much safer way to learn the jumps,' Aurora countered fiercely. She did not care to have her methods challenged or her secrets exposed. It was not public knowledge the girls rode in trousers on occasion, or astride. It was one of the reasons she banned unannounced outsiders from practices.

Petra moved past them with her horse, leaving them to sort out the details. Smart girl, Aurora thought. She'd like to leave too. Better yet, she'd like him to leave. Once the girl was out of earshot, Aurora delivered her next dictate. 'She's off limits. I will not have you behaving as you did with me in the road this afternoon. I don't want to catch you with her, not walking with her, not talking with her. Nothing.'

The man had the audacity to laugh. 'That might be a bit difficult. Petra Branscombe is my sister in-law.'

Aurora's mind did the genealogical maths at rapid speed. 'Then that makes you…'

'The earl's brother,' he finished for her.

'The Honourable Crispin Ramsden?' Aurora said drily. It seemed the height of irony that this rough-around-the-edges, broad-shouldered man would bear such a title.

He seemed to think so too. 'Technically speaking.' A slow smile spread across his mouth, highlighting the lips that had kissed hers only hours ago.

Crispin raked her form with a gaze that seared as it travelled down every inch of her in deliberate contemplation. 'I would have thought someone like you would be less tempted to judge, Miss Calhoun. It appears you have already catalogued and classified me. I wonder? Should I do the same to you?' He chuckled at her overt reaction. 'That's what I thought. You don't care to be pigeonholed any more than I do.'

He took a step towards her, his strong gaze holding hers with a teasing glint of challenge. 'So, you think you know all about me after our brief acquaintance?'

He didn't look honourable so much as rakishly unprincipled. Not even the moment he'd taken at some point to pull his long hair back with a leather thong into something more orderly could give him an added measure of respectability. Aurora made a special effort not to back up under the onslaught of his advance. 'I've met men like you before, earl's brother or not.'

He had a seductive smile for her alone as he leaned close to her ear and whispered, 'I doubt it, Miss Calhoun. There are no other men like me.'

Four hours later, Aurora was ready to concede Crispin Ramsden might be right. She'd succeeded in getting him out of her stables, but not her mind. Aurora stretched her long legs out, feet resting on the fender of the fireplace absorbing the warmth of the flames in her converted apartments at the back of the stable. By rights, this was her favourite time of day. The horses were bedded down, their quiet snuffles keeping her company as she ate her dinner. But tonight, the usual peace the evening routine brought didn't come.

She was restless. She'd made endless excuses to herself: it was the rain drumming on the roof that made her restive, it was because she had a new horse in the stables. But she'd been out to check on Sheikh twice now and the visits hadn't alleviated her agitation. Neither the rain nor the horse was responsible for her current state. It was Crispin Ramsden that made her uneasy.

Perhaps it was nothing more than like recognising like. She'd certainly seen more than one set of horses test each other out before mating, nipping and biting. Their methods weren't all that different than Crispin Ramsden's. Aurora thought of Crispin's kisses in the road and blushed, glad no one else was there to see her.

There had been plenty of nipping and biting involved that afternoon.

Aurora bent forwards and stirred the fire, forcing her mind to focus on more pleasant issues. There were tomorrow's lessons to plan. The rain would make the outdoor arena too muddy to be useful or safe. The Wednesday class would have to ride in the indoor arena. Eleanor, one of the girls in Petra's class, had wanted to talk with her after the lesson today, but by the time she'd dealt with Crispin Ramsden Eleanor had left. She'd have to make a point to speak with Eleanor on Thursday when Petra's class returned.

She knew what Eleanor wanted to talk about. The girl's father, Gregory Windham, was a very wealthy gentleman who wanted a title for his daughter. He was dead set on seeing her married to an impoverished baron who led a dissipated life. Eleanor was frankly against the match, but Aurora could feel the girl weakening under her father's pressure.

Eleanor wasn't the only student with needs. Young Mrs Twilliger was new to the area after marrying an intimidating older man who clearly had her cowed. Catherine Sykes was worried to death over her impending London Season this spring, fearful she'd be a wallflower, and Lettie Osborne spent most of her days dreaming up ways to bring the new, single vicar up to scratch.

Whatever their needs were, the riding school was a place to start. Here, Aurora gave them a place in which they could discover their own power and build their confidence. If one could master a horse, one could master a man. That was Aurora's philosophy. Perhaps a lucky few would do more than master a man. Perhaps a few would find a true partner for life if they had the confidence to do so.

It was the same principle with riding. She'd ridden two horses in her life that had been her partners. When she rode, she and the horse were equals. Nothing could compare with that. The other horses had been mounts to be mastered. She could get them to do what she wanted, but ultimately it hadn't been about giving and taking with them, it had been about control.

Aurora understood the enormity of the task she'd set herself. Her girls came here to learn to ride, to learn the art of looking pretty in the saddle, their habits spread out behind them, the traditional teachings of young English womanhood firmly ingrained in their minds. Aurora wanted to change that for them, wanted to show them how to think on their own. On a horse there was no one to think for them; they had to rely solely on themselves. If they could do it on a horse, they could do it in other places in their lives.

She didn't pretend her task was an easy one or an acceptable one by the standards of most people. It had been her experience that the local men wherever she'd been weren't receptive to her lines of logic regarding male and female behaviour. On more than one occasion she'd been forced to leave a village once word got out that she was imparting more than horsemanship to the women she instructed. She wondered what Crispin Ramsden would make of that? Would he be a man who supported tradition or a man who could open his mind to the possibilities of equality between the sexes?

Crispin Ramsden. Again. Apparently she'd not been successful in directing her thoughts away from the earl's brother. She gave herself a mental scolding. This was not the time to be considering any kind of flirtation. There were more important concerns. The St Albans steeplechase was coming up in March. She'd trained hard, her hunter, Kildare, was ready. Kildare was the best horse she'd ever ridden, better even than her beloved first stallion, Darby. If she could win, it would garner a great amount of prestige for her fledging stables, opening the gateway to good breeding opportunities.

There were difficulties to be worked out, not the least was how a woman was going to legally ride in a gentleman's race. She could always hire a rider, but the thought of turning Kildare over to another rider filled her with trepidation. The other option was to risk all and ride in disguise. She'd done such a thing before, but only in small venues with very little at stake.

If she were caught, she'd be disqualified and made the fool. Her stables' prestige would be sacrificed. But where would she find a rider that could work intimately with Kildare in the short time remaining? Rebellious images of Crispin Ramsden and his midnight stallion threatened the edges of her mind. Aurora rose from her chair and stretched. She'd do best to leave those contemplations for another day or she wouldn't sleep at all. It was time for bed. Morning always came early at the stables.

Dinner came early in the country, but it was still half past seven before the Dursley clan was assembled at the long dining room table. As Crispin had expected, Tessa turned his sudden arrival into an excuse for an impromptu dinner party, which explained the slight lateness of the meal. Even on short notice, the Dursley clan managed to fill up the table: Petra and her fiancé, Thomas; Annie, Tessa's youngest sister who was thirteen now; and Cousin Beth, who had run Peyton's household for years before Peyton married Tessa.

'Where's Eva?' Crispin asked, taking a mental roll

call in his head once they were all seated and realising one of the four Branscombe sisters was missing.

'She's in London with Aunt Lily,' Tessa answered from the foot of the table.

'Isn't that a bit early?' Crispin had never liked the Season and it was beyond him to imagine why anyone would go up to town earlier than necessary. That Eva had gone months in advance bordered on the point of ludicrous.

Tessa smiled. 'She'll come out this year. She turned eighteen immediately after Christmas. She and Lily wanted to get a good start on her wardrobe.'

Crispin wondered how his brother did it, acting as a legal guardian for Tessa's three sisters; three Seasons to put together and then weddings to follow if those Seasons were at all successful, extra Seasons to follow if they weren't. Either way, there would be more endless twaddle. The very thought of all that frippery and nonsense was enough to put a man off his oats. Yet, Peyton looked as if he'd weathered the first two débuts quite well. In fact, his brother looked to be a well-satisfied man, sitting comfortably at the head of his table. There'd been a time not long ago that Crispin had doubted Peyton's ability to embrace such a life. Then Peyton had fallen in love with Tessa and that love had changed him, as it had his other brother, Paine.

Crispin took a bite of excellent roasted beef and suppressed a shudder. He was not falling in love. He had no desire to be changed. It was all right for his brothers to change. But he had no intentions of giving up his wandering and adventures. He liked his life just the way it was. All he needed was a horse beneath him and the wide world spread out before him. Women had other expectations.

Still, coming home for a while felt good. Crispin ate

the well-cooked food with gusto and enjoyed the conversation flowing around him as everyone brought him up to date on events in the family. Although there were several family members at dinner, there were others missing besides Aunt Lily and Eva. His brother Paine had taken his family to visit his wife's cousin, Greyson. Greyson was interested in Paine's opinion on some new investments and Greyson's wife, Elena, was expecting their second child in late spring. Petra and Thomas had set the date of their wedding for September particularly out of consideration for them. Crispin wondered if he'd still be here for it.

At last, Tessa rose, giving the signal for the women to join her in the drawing room. Thomas rose too. 'I'll join the women tonight, Dursley, and leave you alone with your brother. No doubt there is still more to catch up on and I don't wish to intrude,' he offered graciously.

'He's a very nice young man,' Crispin commented as the group trooped out of the room.

Peyton nodded with a smile. 'We couldn't be more pleased for Petra. They're very happy together and well-suited.' Reaching for the decanter, he poured them each a glass. 'Cheers, brother.'

'Ah, this is the good stuff.' Crispin drank down the brandy with relish. 'I can't remember the last time I had brandy of this calibre.'

'The perks of being home,' Peyton offered cryptically. 'Did you work out an arrangement with Rory?'

Crispin chuckled. 'Tessa could have told me Rory was a woman and a sharp-tongued one at that. A little forewarning wouldn't have gone amiss.'

Peyton grinned. 'Aurora Calhoun is strong minded.'

'To say the least.'

Peyton poured them each another glass. 'Tessa likes

her. She and Petra helped her get the riding school started a couple of years ago.'

Crispin eyed his brother over the rim of his snifter. He wasn't surprised to hear that Tessa had championed the unconventional Miss Calhoun. Tessa might look like an English angel on the outside, but he knew his brother's wife well enough to know it was merely a façade. 'Do you know what goes on out there?'

'You mean the riding astride and wearing trousers part? Yes, I am quite aware of it, although I must caution you that it is not common knowledge. Don't tell me you're shocked? You're the most untraditional person I know besides Tessa. I would have thought you'd applaud her. A woman's lot alone in this world is almost impossibly difficult, yet, against all the insufferable odds, Aurora Calhoun has found some degree of success. As much as she can hope for, I think, given the circumstances of her gender and situation.'

Peyton's remark was quite telling. Crispin took a moment to digest the layers of his brother's comment. His brother was devoted to his wife. He would tolerate his wife's eccentric friends for her sake. But Peyton's comment implied he did more than tolerate Aurora Calhoun; he respected her and, for that reason, was willing to make exceptions on her behalf. Such a concession from Peyton made the interesting Miss Calhoun all that more intriguing.

'I don't care what she does. She's entitled to her own eccentricities,' Crispin said shortly, realising it was true. It wasn't the unconventional nature of her school that bothered him. It was simply *she* who had him all churned up inside for reasons he couldn't quite put his finger on. She definitely stirred his blood.

'I rather thought the two of you would be good

friends. She knows horses as well as you do,' Peyton was saying. 'That black of yours looks exotic. She'll be interested to hear about him. For that matter, I'd be interested to hear about him too.'

Peyton fixed him with a friendly stare and Crispin knew what was coming next. Inquiries about the 'exotic' nature of the stallion were Peyton's prelude to the bigger question. Whatever else changed about Peyton, this one thing would not: Peyton would always be his older brother.

'So, Cris, before we rejoin the others, why don't you tell me what you and my government have been doing for the last three years? The short version, of course.'

Crispin grinned and drew a deep breath. It was good to be able to talk with someone who appreciated the depth and importance of his work. This was something Peyton understood with extreme clarity. 'Let me start with the Eastern Question…' he began, his passion for his work evident in his recitation of events and astute analysis of the many evolving situations on the Continent.

At last, Crispin leaned back in his chair, balancing it on its two hind legs, and drew his report to a close. 'And that, dear brother, is the short version. I haven't even begun to tell you about British interests in America. There's another powder keg just waiting to ignite.'

Peyton nodded noncommittally at the implied reference to a future posting. 'Well, you've done your duty for Britain. Perhaps it's someone else's turn this time.'

'Perhaps,' Crispin replied vaguely, knowing the direction of his brother's thoughts. Tonight was not the time to discuss his next assignment. When the posting came, Crispin was almost certain it would be an assignment to the American South, a place he was itching to explore on a personal as well as political level. Such a posting would make the sale of Woodbrook imperative. He'd be in America a very long while, more of a relocation than a temporary assignment. Crispin reached for the decanter. There'd be time to quarrel with Peyton over that later. Tonight he simply wanted to enjoy the peace of being home.

'The long and short of it is, I am running out of time.' Gregory Windham leaned forwards across the cherrywood desk in his estate office, pushing a small leather pouch of coins across the desk's highly polished surface to the man on the other side. The blacksmith, Mackey, had been the one villager he'd been able to actively recruit to his side. The others remained quietly neutral with regards to Aurora Calhoun. Damn them.

His *laissez-faire* strategy had not worked. He'd patiently waited for Aurora Calhoun's own unique situation to work against her. He'd originally thought the local gentry and the villagers wouldn't tolerate such a 'modern' woman; a woman who ran her own business and sauntered around in men's clothing. But Aurora had proved wily in that regard, keeping her trousers and lifestyle heavily obscured from the local populace. It had not helped matters that everyone knew she was an especial friend to Dursley's countess and Dursley's ward.

Aurora had lived out of sight and out of mind and the villagers had been happy enough with that. Such contentment needed to change. The villagers had to be rattled out of their complacency. He needed to force Dursley to make a stand. Dursley might quietly countenance such a friendship for his wife if no one complained about it. But the earl was also a traditionalist at heart. Windham thought it would be rather interesting to see what Dursley would do if there was a fuss over Aurora Calhoun.

It was time for a more direct approach if he meant to succeed in launching himself as a respectable horseman and sending Aurora Calhoun down the road of ruin. He tapped his long fingers on the desk.

'The St Albans steeplechase is a month away. That race is mine to win. I won't have her and that hunter of hers interfering.' He possessed a stake in the well-favoured horse, The Flyer. The stake had been an expensive purchase, but money was no object. The Flyer might not be *the* favourite in the race, but the horse was poised to be a contender if not a winner in the prestigious steeplechase.

'What do you propose we do?' The big man across the desk hefted the coin pouch in a meaty hand. 'I could make items disappear around the stable, or plant a burr in a saddle…?'

Gregory Windham dismissed those suggestions with a wave of his long hand. 'Those are the second-rate tactics of an amateur.'

He pointed to the bag of coins. 'Take the money and buy drinks tomorrow night at the tavern. Tell everyone what really goes on at the riding school of hers.' It was time to reveal his daughter Eleanor's confession and lift the veil of obscurity Aurora kept around her lifestyle at the stables.

The big man thought for a moment. 'I'm scheduled to go shoe her horses this week. Won't it look odd if I'm spreading those rumours and still doing business out there?'

'You won't be doing business there any longer.' Gregory Windham drew out another pouch and slid it across the desk. 'This should more than suffice to cover your losses in that regard.' He held the blacksmith's hard eyes with a cold gaze of his own. 'There's more money for you when she leaves town and even more when the horse I've invested in wins St Albans.'

The blacksmith grinned. 'I'll be a rich man by the month's end.'

And Aurora Calhoun will be ruined, Gregory Windham thought silently as his henchman departed. It was no less than she deserved. The woman was a threat to all he'd spent years accomplishing. He'd used his money to buy his daughter a titled match with a baron and to establish a small but prime stable a nobleman would respect.

He was hovering on the brink of acceptance into the ranks of the peerage. His future grandson would have a title. Even now, Eleanor rode at Aurora Calhoun's academy solely because the earl's ward rode there. Originally, it had been a good social-climbing opportunity. Now, such an association endangered his dreams. Eleanor had become obstinate over the match, spouting too many philosophies she hadn't learned at home. Windham knew exactly where she'd learned them. They were the same philosophies Aurora Calhoun had spouted when she'd rejected his attentions the one time he'd thought to recruit her to his side. He'd offered her the position of his mistress. She had all but bodily thrown him out of her stables.

Gregory Windham shifted uncomfortably in his seat. Just recalling how that hellcat had railed at him, spitting furiously at his offer, brought his arousal to life. His cheek had borne a bruise from the flat of her hand for days. She'd been magnificent in her anger, her eyes like emerald flames, her dark hair loose about her, an exquisite flowing curtain.

It would bring him great pleasure to subdue the wildness she exuded. Wild things were meant to be tamed. Aurora Calhoun, that tease of a siren, was going to pay. Women had a place in this world. He would make sure Aurora Calhoun knew hers.

Chapter Three

Crispin blew in his cupped hands and rubbed them together vigorously as he entered the relatively warmer interior of the Calhoun stables. Mornings were colder in England than he remembered and certainly colder than the ones he'd most recently experienced in the south of Europe. Crispin strode towards Sheikh's stall, anxious to see how his horse had fared during his first night in his new home.

Horses whickered as he passed and a few poked their long faces out into the aisle. Even though it was early, the horses were alert and had already been fed. One stall was empty. He recognised it as the stall belonging to Aurora's horse. Perhaps she was out on a morning ride, although Crispin thought it was too foggy yet for that to be a safe option. He'd been glad he'd walked across the valley this morning instead of riding. It would have been too easy to overlook a rabbit hole or a soft piece of land; too easy for a horse to take a misstep and be rendered lame or worse. Well, if Aurora was out that was her business. At least her absence meant he wouldn't have to encounter her.

Crispin slipped a halter over Sheikh's head and led him into the wide aisle of the stable for grooming. Crispin picked up a curry brush and began the morning ritual. He liked grooming Sheikh as much as Sheikh liked being brushed. Not usually a patient horse, Sheikh stood exceedingly still for brushing. Crispin found the ritual soothing. He could lose himself in thought, letting his mind wander freely. The stables were a place of peace for him, any stable. The smell of horses and leather tack were familiar no matter where.

He finished grooming Sheikh and quickly saddled him. Through the stable windows, he could see the fog starting to lift. He was eager to get back to Dursley Park and the hot breakfast that waited. Beside him, Sheikh shook his mane. Now that grooming was done, he was ready to be off too. Crispin fished in the wide pocket of his greatcoat and pulled out a few slices of apple. Sheikh snapped them up as Crispin led him out into the morning.

The fog had definitely lifted, Crispin confirmed. He could actually see the indoor arena across the stable yard now. The faint sound of a horse's nicker drew him that direction. He knew what he'd find inside before he and Sheikh arrived at the door. Aurora had not opted for a dangerous, foggy ride. She'd brought her horse to the arena for a morning workout.

Crispin manoeuvred himself and Sheikh into the shadows of the wide doorway to watch her practise. The arena was set up for jumping and she was executing the fences expertly. She finished the last jump in a corner and made a clean cross through the centre of the arena to the opposite corner and started again.

Magnificent, Crispin thought, his gaze focused on her hands and thighs, appreciating the subtle pressures each of those parts used to communicate with the horse.

Her movements were so completely synchronised with the flow and bunching of the horse's body that it seemed she barely moved at all. Crispin had no idea how long he'd stood there, but at last Sheikh gave him an impatient nudge and Crispin withdrew from the scene. He didn't worry about being heard. From the look on her face when she'd drawn close to the entrance where he stood, Crispin knew she was in another place altogether. Her thoughts were entirely with her horse; when to move, when to ask for the leap in order to get the most height for the jump.

Where had she learned to ride like that? Surely such skill was not acquired haphazardly.

The question plagued him all the way home across the valley and at the breakfast table until he finally blurted it out to Peyton and Tessa. It was a complete non sequitur. They'd been discussing a bill in Parliament and he'd set down his coffee cup and said suddenly, 'Where did Aurora Calhoun study riding?'

Tessa looked at him rather startled. 'I think she said somewhere in Ireland,' she replied vaguely; too vaguely for Crispin's tastes. After making a career out of reading people, Crispin knew without effort that Tessa was withholding details. If Peyton knew the specifics he did nothing to fill in the gaps and the conversation quickly reverted back to the bill under earlier discussion.

But Crispin wasn't willing to give up his inquiries. Once he and Peyton set out on their short jaunt to Woodbrook, he tried again. 'I happened to catch part of Aurora's workout this morning when I was saddling Sheikh. I'd be interested to know where she was trained.'

'Then you should ask her,' Peyton said levelly in a

tone that suggested that topic of conversation was closed. Peyton was more eager to discuss the merits of Woodbrook, which he promptly began to do the moment the first property marker came into view. He continued to elucidate the fine points of the property right up until they dismounted in the stable yard and Crispin could see for himself what an excellent inheritance he'd acquired.

Peyton had not exaggerated. The manor house was a modest, twelve-room affair, hardly more than a cottage compared to the grandeur of Dursley Park. But to Crispin the stone manor was plenty.

'What would I do with twelve rooms?' Crispin remarked halfway up the stairs to see the other six, all presumably bedrooms.

'You could marry and fill the house with children,' Peyton laughingly suggested. 'Within three years, you'd be enlarging the place, declaring how you'd outgrown it.'

Crispin knew Peyton meant well, but all the same, the thought of being somewhere for three years, let alone a decade or a lifetime, sent a quiet shudder up his spine. Children couldn't be dragged around the world every year or so to satisfy his whim for adventure. Children needed the stability of a permanent home, of permanent parents. His own childhood was a testament to that. With two absent parents, Peyton had been the closest thing he and Paine had had to a father growing up. In his darker hours, Crispin often thought it was his worries of turning out like his parents that kept him from pursuing a family of his own, although his brothers had certainly proved such worries to be groundless. Both of them had become model family men.

Crispin made a quick tour of the upstairs rooms and

returned downstairs. 'Perhaps Paine and Julia could make use of the manor.'

Peyton shook his head. 'There's plenty of room at Dursley Park for them when they visit. Tessa has a whole wing set aside for them these days. Besides, they spend most of their year in London. Paine's too busy with his banking investments to make use of a country house on a more regular basis.'

They walked out to the barns, which were just as impressive as the house. There was no outdoor work area for horses yet beyond a paddock, but the room for establishing a training arena was readily available in the wide, open spaces around the barns. Crispin could easily imagine setting up an equestrian centre here. The old dreams came to him as he walked the wide aisle of the barn, counting stalls. He had Sheikh to stand to stud for a pricey fee and to race. He could build a legacy from Sheikh.

Peyton stayed close, continuing his verbal tour of the facility. 'There's stalls for fifteen horses. The windows provide good light.' Peyton pointed overhead. 'There's plenty of hay storage in the lofts above. The tack room can easily support all the riding gear you'd need for that many horses. The roof is fairly new. There aren't any serious repairs you'd have to make. All of your attention could be on improvements and additions.'

Peyton had been a dangerously compelling diplomat in his day, knowing exactly when to push, when his opponents were most open to persuasion. To be honest, that was precisely where Crispin was now; wondering, in spite of his earlier inclination to sell the property, if this place was what he needed to conquer his wanderlust or even if he wanted to conquer the wandering spirit that drove him.

Crispin let a hand drift idly across the half-door of a

stall. Commitment begot commitment. It wouldn't stop at committing to the stables. There would be grooms to employ who would count on him for pay and for work. There would be social obligations. The community would expect him in church and at their gatherings. Women would expect him to marry, if not someone from London because of his family, then certainly a lady from their part of England. Peyton was right. Manor houses were expected to be filled.

He was too much of a realist to believe he could stop at just one commitment. One commitment was merely a gateway to other commitments he felt less compelled to make. The commitments would not happen overnight. They would form a slippery slope that would erode slowly over the span of several years. It would occur gradually so that it didn't appear to be a life-changing overhaul, but single small steps taken in isolation from one another until, one morning, he'd wake up and realise it was too late to go back.

Crispin tamped down hard on the old dream of his own stables. It was a startling discovery to find the dream was far more potent than he'd realised. He'd come home, thinking to sell the property. He would stay with his original plan. He had his work. It was only a matter of time before a summons arrived from London. He would not give in, he would not change his course, no matter how much Peyton talked.

They emerged out into the daylight, Peyton's well-rehearsed tour complete. To his credit, Peyton pressed for nothing. He merely gestured down the road where a rider had turned into the drive. 'I've invited the steward to go over the books,' he said simply.

Crispin fought back a chuckle. Of course Peyton had invited the land steward. His brother had this visit orchestrated perfectly for maximum effect. All the same, Peyton would be disappointed. He wasn't going to stay. He couldn't. It just wasn't in him.

Several hours later, Crispin knew one thing. He needed a drink and he needed a drink *alone*. He'd been surrounded by a horde of well-meaning people since his return home. For a man who was used to operating solo and keeping his own counsel, such attention was unnerving. Well, he had to rephrase that. He'd been surrounded by *Peyton*. In all fairness, Tessa, Cousin Beth, Petra, Annie, the twins and the new baby had all kept at a respectful distance. They'd done nothing more than make him feel welcome.

But Peyton knew what he wanted from Crispin and he was wasting no time in trying to extract it. Crispin could see his brother's vision clearly. His brother wanted him to embrace the stables, settle down, take a wife and raise a family. For Peyton that had been the clear road to happiness once he'd found the path. Crispin understood it was only natural for Peyton to want that same happiness for him. However, Crispin doubted that path would work well for him. Crispin understood too that Peyton was trying not to be oppressive, certainly a harder task for him than for others. Peyton was well used to being obeyed. But Peyton could not make him into a man he could not be.

He and Peyton swung up into their saddles, thanking the steward for his time and his conscientious adherence to every detail. They turned their horses towards home, riding in much-appreciated silence; Crispin's head was full to bursting with all he'd learned.

Crispin was amazed Peyton had stayed quiet for as long as he did. He'd bet himself Peyton wouldn't make it a mile before asking what he'd thought of the manor. Tessa's influence must be powerful indeed, Crispin mused. But he could see the effort the restraint cost his brother. Peyton's mouth was tense; on two occasions, Crispin felt Peyton was on the verge of bringing the subject up, but then thought better of it.

They reached the fork in the road, one turn leading to the Dursley Road and the other going on a short distance to the village. 'I think I'll stop in for a pint or two,' Crispin said off-handedly.

'I'll come with you,' Peyton offered, making a quick check of his pocket watch.

'That's all right. I'd prefer to do some thinking in private.' Crispin hoped Peyton understood. He needed a kind of privacy he wouldn't find at Dursley Park and he'd have no privacy if he turned up at the inn with the earl in tow.

'And dinner?' Peyton asked cautiously. 'Shall I tell Tessa to expect you?'

Crispin nodded his head. 'Probably not. I'm not sure how long I'll sit and think.'

'It's no trouble to set an extra plate if you change your mind,' Peyton said graciously. Crispin could see that his absence wasn't what Peyton had hoped for, but that his brother guessed at how monumental the day had been, how many things needed thinking over.

Once inside the inn, Crispin lost himself in the crowd, taking a small table by the window. Word had not yet spread of his return and he was thankful for the anonymity. Around him, the work day was ending. Large groups of local workers filed in for a pint before heading home for the evening.

Crispin studied this crowd unobtrusively. These men worked the fields as hired labour or in various other occupations in the village. They were journeymen and artisans, a few apprentices among them. They would drink and go home to supper and wives. The rougher crowd, those without familial commitments, would come in later after the supper hour and stay until closing; drinking, wenching, perhaps brawling if it suited them.

The men here now, though, would be the men he'd fraternise with if he took the manor. They'd be the men who would work his stables. They'd be the men who he'd drink with on occasion. Their lives would be interwoven into his.

Crispin took a swallow of his ale, trying to imagine his life as a gentleman landowner. It seemed so far from the things he'd told Peyton over brandy the other night as to be laughable.

These men didn't care about the nationalist revolutions sweeping Europe, about water-routes to faraway places they'd never visit, about fighting over lines on a map. Their lives were about wheat crops and sheep, cattle and corn. If he threw his lot in with them, his life would be too. Everything to which he'd devoted his life in the first twenty years of his adulthood would cease to matter—every nebulous peace he had brokered, every boundary dispute he had negotiated, would carry little weight in that new life. It would be tantamount to erasing who he was and remaking himself in a new image. The soldier, the warrior-diplomat, would not fit into this new world of quiet landownership.

The thought sat poorly with Crispin. He rather liked himself just as he was. Of course, there were plenty of people who didn't. The *ton* didn't know what to make of him. He was too bold, too loose with the rules of proper society for many of the matchmaking mamas to trust him with their daughters. Yet, he had a certain appeal with his brother's connections, his brother's wealth, and his brother's affection behind him. Any woman who married him would be well looked after under the Dursley banner. Proxy polygamy, he called it. The only reason anyone would marry him would be because they were marrying Peyton by extension. If he stayed in England, he'd have to decide in whose world he fit.

Without appearing to eavesdrop, he listened in on snatches of nearby conversations, trying to put himself in the frame of their world. Could he come to care about the issues they cared about? Could he empathise with the problems that plagued their lives?

Snatches of one conversation rose over the rest. 'The Calhoun woman was in today to buy some shovels. It's not natural, a woman buying tools. There's strange things going on out there,' a beefy man said loudly, drawing all the room's attention. Crispin tensed. In the silence of the inn, the man let his news fall on expectant ears. 'I've found out that the girls in her stables ride in trousers *and* they ride astride.'

Shock and outrage exploded at the announcement; questions were shouted over the din. Crispin stifled a groan. That could hardly be what Aurora wanted. But what followed was worse. Crispin slouched anonymously in his chair and listened.

The big man, named Mackey from what Crispin could gather, hushed the upset crowd. 'Aurora Calhoun needs to go. She's no good for our village, teaching our womenfolk to ride astride. Who knows what kind of ideas she'll plant in their heads next? We don't want our women turning out like her.' There was a loud roar of agreement. 'One of her is enough. She's had two years to prove she could fit in. We've left her alone and look how she's repaid us! The only thing she's proved is how out of place she is.' There were other comments too. 'We should have paid more attention…' 'Should have known it wasn't natural from the start…'

Good lord, the man was creating a witch hunt. Crispin half-expected the men to pick up torches and march out to the stables then and there. Crispin had heard enough. He'd end up fighting with someone if he stayed. Crispin slapped a few coins on the table and made a quiet exit, opting to exercise his authority when cooler heads prevailed, including his.

Dusk was in its final throes when he swung up on Sheikh. He could still make dinner at Dursley Park, but he wasn't ready to go home. More to the point, he wasn't ready to go to Peyton's home. He couldn't expect Peyton to keep silent about the manor forever. But Crispin wasn't ready to talk about it yet, at least not with his brother. He could only think of one place that might suit his needs. In the fading light of day, Crispin turned Sheikh towards Aurora's stables.

The stable lanterns threw a welcoming light into the yard and the fresh smell of evening hay assailed his senses the moment Crispin led Sheikh through the stable doors. Horses neighed, acknowledging Sheikh's presence among them as they passed stall doors. Crispin stopped outside Sheikh's stall and removed the saddle. With one hand, he stroked Sheikh's long neck, soothing the horse. With the other, Crispin groped for the kit holding the brushes. The kit should have been right behind him on the nail hook outside the stall where he'd left it that morning.

'Are you looking for this?' The voice startled him. Crispin whirled around; releasing a breath when he saw the voice belonged to Aurora.

She held the kit out to him. 'I didn't mean to give you a start,' she apologised, taking one of the brushes and moving around to Sheikh's other side. She began to curry the horse.

'You've had a long day. I noticed Sheikh was gone when I came back this morning. You must have been here early and now it's dinner time,' Aurora commented.

'Peyton and I rode over to see some property,' Crispin said, surprising himself with the truth. He could have answered the question just as easily by saying he'd waited until lessons were done. Such an answer would not have given away any particular information about his whereabouts and it certainly wouldn't have invited any further conversation. His chosen answer, on the other hand, invited all nature of possible comment, none of which Aurora opted for.

'Your brother is eager to see you settled,' she said, meeting his eyes for an instance over Sheikh's back.

Of all the things she could have said, he'd not expected that. He'd expected the usual; 'Do you mean to settle here?' 'Where is the property?' 'What do you plan to do with it?'

'I suppose he is,' Crispin replied, bending over and clicking to Sheikh to lift his hoof.

'How do you feel about that?'

Crispin answered honestly. 'The property is enticing, but I'm not the right man for that kind of life. I'll sell the property outright and then I'll be on my way.' He finished picking the hoof and stood up, stretching his back. Aurora was nearly finished brushing Sheikh's opposite flank.

'I know what you mean,' she said casually. 'I've been here longer than I've been anywhere else. I'd always taught on a property owned by someone else. But Tessa talked me into leasing this one. Actually, in all truth, Tessa wanted me to buy it, but I couldn't go that far. A lease was as permanent a commitment as I could make.' Aurora stopped brushing and shook back her hair, which had fallen forwards over her shoulders as she worked. An awkward silence fell between them as if they both suddenly recognised they'd said too much to someone they didn't know.

Crispin met her eyes over the back of Sheikh and nodded in the awkward quiet; a wealth of understanding passing between them in that single look. He could well imagine all the trappings of permanence to which she referred, trappings that went beyond owning the actual structure.

Buying the property would have meant applying for a loan. She wouldn't have had any money of her own. She would have had to have relied on Peyton's support. Support Peyton would have provided based on the comments Peyton had made at dinner, but she would have been indebted to him. She couldn't have left until that obligation was fulfilled. Once again Crispin's hypothesis proved true. Permanence bred obligation. It was odd to think how much this stranger's situation paralleled his own in spite of its own unique circumstances. It begged several questions.

How had a strikingly beautiful woman come to own a riding academy in the unlikely middle of sheep country? How was it that a stranger he'd never met until yesterday could sum up in a sentence his precise feelings over the property? She could empathise with him on this issue while his brother, who knew him better than anyone, could not.

Aurora cleared her throat in the silence. 'It's late and I'm sure you haven't eaten yet.'

Ah, the audacious woman was dismissing him. Of course. She'd want to get to her own meal. It had been a long day for her as well. She'd been up jumping before he'd even arrived that morning. It had been a long time since a woman had dismissed him.

'I'm sorry to keep you. I'll just see to Sheikh and be going.' Crispin piled the brushes into the kit, disappointment unexpectedly swamping him. He hadn't been ready to leave the stables. Or perhaps he hadn't been ready to leave her. They'd got off on the wrong foot yesterday. This brief exchange had been a pleasant contrast, but perhaps that was too much to hope for. Perhaps she was merely being nice.

'No, don't go.' Her words rushed out. 'I was going to suggest, before you interrupted me, that you stay for dinner.'

There was that sharp tongue he remembered. Crispin stifled a laugh on behalf of the truce they seemed to have struck. But he noticed she couldn't help sneaking that small rebuke in—'before you interrupted'. What might have been an invitation had now been turned into a suggestion, which everyone knew was just a step below a command. He was very familiar with 'suggestions'. Peyton made a lot of them.

But she wasn't Peyton and Crispin found he'd like nothing more than to have dinner with the intriguing Aurora Calhoun, who was less like his brother and perhaps more like him; a wanderer, a straddler of worlds. A kindred spirit? It was far too early in their acquaintance to draw that conclusion. There was too much unknown about her for him to make such leaps of logic. Still, it couldn't hurt to find out and Crispin intended to explore the potential.

Chapter Four

What was she thinking to invite the earl's brother to dinner? Because that's what he was, when all was said and done. Men with that kind of power were dangerous to her freedom. One word from him and Dursley could shut her down with a single sentence dropped at a dinner party.

She needed Crispin Ramsden to keep his distance. But, no, she'd invited a potential danger right to her dinner table. It didn't matter that he wore plain clothes and didn't put on aristocratic airs. It didn't matter that she wanted to see if he was worthy of riding Kildare. He was still brother to the earl.

In retrospect, she was amazed she hadn't seen the resemblance instantly. He had the earl's raven-black hair, the earl's dark-blue eyes, but not the earl's urbane demeanour and that made all the difference, distinguishing them from one another in spite of their inherited physical similarities.

Dursley carried his confidence like one born to it. Everything Dursley did was done with a polished veneer of sophistication. Not Crispin. He exuded a rough worldliness. She was certain his blue eyes had seen things that would render most men cynical about the world they lived in. The tanned skin of his face and hands suggested he was a man who knew how to work. The rugged planes of his face and the breadth of his shoulders affirmed this was a man used to hard living. He was no pampered prince of the *ton* regardless of who his brother was.

That was why she'd invited him to dinner. Like her, he knew a world outside the circles of rarefied society, he'd lived in its milieu and, like her, he'd been a participant in that world beyond the drawing rooms. When their eyes had met across the back of his stallion, she'd felt a connection; two wayward souls contemplating the merits of landowning against the odds of their natural tendencies. It would be somewhat comedic if the connection hadn't been so strong.

Aurora laid out the dinner things, setting the earthenware plates down on the plank table with a harder thud than she'd intended. She tried to remember anything, everything, Petra or Tessa might have mentioned in passing about Crispin. There was very little she could recall. She could hear his boots coming down the short hall from the stables. In moments he'd be there in her meagre rooms, thanks to her impetuous offer, and she would have to live with it.

'Smells good.' Crispin ducked into the room under the low-beamed door. He was all male, all six foot two and change of him. He positively radiated potent masculinity and Aurora wondered what other impetuous decisions she might be tempted to make before the night was over.

Crispin had taken time to wash off at the pump outside in the yard. Leftover droplets of water glistened at his neck where his shirt opened in a V, offering a small glimpse of his chest. She smiled at the interesting dichotomy he posed; a man who cared enough to wash before dinner, but had no use for the finer rules of gentlemanly dining that demanded he eat with a waistcoat and jacket on. Aurora doubted one ever caught Dursley dining in his shirt sleeves.

'Stew and fresh bread,' Aurora announced, placing a pewter plate laden with slices of dark country bread on the table. 'Sit down, I'll have the stew on in a minute.' She was suddenly conscious of his eyes on her, following her movements. She told herself it was to be expected. Her quarters were small—where else was he supposed to look? It was only natural to be interested in the one moving object in the room. That object just happened to be her.

Crispin straddled a bench on one side of the table and politely tugged off his boots to save the floor from dirt. 'You live here instead of the house?'

Aurora put a pitcher of ale on the table. He was referring to the cottage at the end of the drive. She'd never lived there even though it was part of the lease. 'I like being close to my horses.'

She turned to the fireplace and the hob where the stew pot hung, feeling his eyes peruse her backside. 'The cottage is too much work for me to keep up and run the stables on my own.' She set the stew down and began ladling it into bowls.

Crispin nodded. 'I like these rooms. They're cosy.' His gaze stole past her to the small bedroom. Aurora wished she'd taken time to drop the curtain that separated the bedroom from her main room. She wished she could read his mind as well as she was following his gaze. What was he thinking about her invitation to dinner? Was he thinking it was an invitation to something more? Did he think because he was the earl's brother and she a woman without rank that he was entitled to something more? Aurora rather hoped not, but her experience with Gregory Windham had proved that hope was often misplaced. She was now fully regretting her impromptu decision to invite Crispin Ramsden to dinner and the finer philosophies that might have motivated it. She had convinced herself last night this wasn't the right time for a flirtation. She should have stuck with that. But those resolutions had been quickly trampled.

'This is good,' Crispin said between mouthfuls. 'There's nothing like hot stew on a cold night.'

Aurora watched him thoughtfully throughout the meal. He ate much like regular people ate, people who were conscious of the cost of food and the effort it took to prepare a meal. He used a piece of bread to sop up the remaining stew, making sure not a spoonful went to waste in his bowl. It was odd to think of him as a man who knew hunger, who knew of the simple things it took to survive the day when he could have chosen otherwise. His brother's table was always set with plenty.

Aurora had not meant to pry, but the question was out of her mouth before she could stop it. 'What do you do, Crispin? I mean, where have you been for three years?'

Crispin set down his bread crust and fixed her with his sharp gaze, a small smile playing at his lips. 'How badly do you want to know?'

Aurora smiled back, recognising the game afoot. 'Ah, so it's to be twenty-questions?'

'Precisely. I'll answer your questions, but you need to answer mine.' Crispin reached for another slice of bread and buttered it.

'I work for the British government when they have

need of me. Before that, I used to be in the cavalry. I found I didn't enjoy the life of a half-pay soldier. It was too dull for me. I saw some action in the early twenties after Napoleon's defeat. But then my regiment came home and I spent far too much time being Dursley's brother.' Crispin swallowed some ale. 'There wasn't much to do as Dursley's brother, as you can imagine. Peyton doesn't need any help and, frankly, I'd rather be my own man. I didn't relish the idea of being defined as the "spare". I was at a loose end. So, Peyton introduced me to some friends at the Foreign Office and off I went to look after British interests abroad.'

'Where did you go?' Aurora asked, feeling as if she'd been told everything and yet nothing.

Crispin winked across the table. 'Princess, I could tell you, but then I'd have to kill you.'

'You were a spy?' she asked evenly, deciding to push the boundaries of his disclosure.

'More like the government's best-kept secret,' Crispin corrected with equal seriousness. 'Suffice it to say that I've been places that don't exist on maps. I wasn't responsible for the kind of diplomacy that goes on in the glittering mansions of Vienna.' He drew a deep breath and steered the conversation away from himself. 'Now, it's your turn. Where did you learn to ride?'

'Ireland,' Aurora said shortly. She'd expected a question along that vein, but, like Crispin, she wasn't ready to divulge all the details. 'Now, as for my next question—' she began, leaning forwards on her elbows. But Crispin had no qualms about interrupting a lady.

'No, Aurora, finish your answer,' Crispin said shortly, arms crossed over his chest. 'You have to say more than that. Where in Ireland? I saw you jumping this morning when I came to get Sheikh. No one rides the way you do without extensive training.'

He had been watching. She'd thought she'd glimpsed someone at the entrance to the arena, thought she'd felt his presence. When no one had materialised, she'd chalked it up to silliness on her part. Of course no one could really feel another person's presence.

'I lived near Curragh in County Kildare. My father was head groom to a wealthy family.'

'You don't have an accent,' Crispin said pointedly as if judging the truth of her answer.

'Accents can be bred out of you.' Among other things. Once upon a time there'd been such hopes for her, thanks to the status of her mother's family. A moment of foolishness had dashed those hopes. Aurora rose from her bench and began collecting the dishes. The conversation was heading in a direction she was distinctly uncomfortable with. There were things Crispin didn't need to know about her. Those things could make no difference now. She'd negotiated her own peace with the past and accepted the consequences of her decisions, as lonely and as costly as they were.

She reached to take Crispin's bowl, but his hand shot out and his fingers closed around her wrist. 'Why did you invite me here, Aurora? You won't tell me anything about yourself, so, clearly, getting to know each other was not the purpose.'

Aurora tried to pull away, but his grip held firm. 'You're hardly the epitome of a forthcoming gentleman,' she replied tartly. 'You can't or won't tell me anything about yourself either.'

'Perhaps that gives us something in common.' Crispin's voice was husky. 'Two people with mysterious lives.' His eyes moved to her mouth and back to her eyes.

Aurora's temper rose. 'Did you come here to seduce me?'

Crispin laughed softly. 'How could I do that? I had no idea I was coming to dinner until you invited me.' Silence rose between them. Aurora was acutely aware of the crackle of the fire, of the light drum of rain on the roof, of the intimate play of firelight on her walls, the only light in the room.

Crispin released her wrist and ran the back of his knuckles gently down the side of her cheek, skimming it low where cheek met jaw line. 'Would it be so bad if I did?'

'Did what?' Aurora's concentration waned, heat surging in her belly at the stroke of his hand against her cheek. She could not delude herself now. She had not asked him here for Kildare. She'd asked him here for herself.

'Seduced you, hmm?' His tone was languorous. He shifted on the bench, straddling it to draw her down to him. She went willingly, cognisant of her growing need. She'd been alone too long. It had been ages since she'd taken a lover. No one had compelled her. Even the ones that had were few and their appearances in her life had been irregular at best. Men were a luxury she could not afford. They'd shown themselves to be fickle companions on the path she trod.

Why not play his game a while? It's just one night and he's already said he's not planning to stay around. It won't upset your plans, a wicked voice in her head prompted. It was the perfect night for love, or what temporarily passed for it: English rain on the roof, a fire in the fireplace, a handsome man who knew the rules of this sort of engagement, a man whose hot kisses in the road had already proven he was a master of pleasure, a man who was the master of his own destiny just as she was of hers.

Crispin's lips replaced his hand against her cheek. He trailed a line of gentle kisses to her mouth where all gentleness ended. Intuitively, he seemed to know she would not tolerate being seduced. Seduction implied that she was somehow not an equal participant in the activity, that she needed to be led. Aurora revelled in the aggressive action of his mouth on hers.

She pulled his shirt loose from the waistband of his trousers and pushed the linen up, her hands running underneath the fabric, caressing the expanse of chest beneath the cloth. The man felt magnificent, all sculpted muscle beneath her fingertips.

He gave an appreciable shudder as her hands ran over his nipples. 'Perhaps I should be asking you the question. Did you invite me here to seduce me?' Crispin said.

Aurora gave a throaty laugh and repeated his earlier words. 'Would it be so bad if I did?'

'No,' Crispin breathed against her neck. 'It wouldn't be bad at all.'

But Aurora had no illusions about being in charge of the seduction. Crispin Ramsden was very clearly a man used to being in charge. He would let her participate; in fact, he gave every indication so far of liking a partner who was actively involved, but he would call the shots. Still, Aurora thought she'd see just how far she could go before he rebelled.

She shifted back on the bench and stood up, tugging on the neck of his shirt. He had little choice but to rise and follow her. Once on his feet, Aurora tugged him closer, pressing a full-mouthed kiss on his lips. She reached a hand between them to the front of his breeches. Her own aroused state grew at the feel of him, hard and ready behind the cloth.

'God, Aurora,' Crispin growled at the intimate

contact. He propelled her backwards until she made contact with the wall. He grabbed both her hands and raised them over her head, manacling them in position with his strong grip. His eyes were dark and wild now, his hair erotically loose about his shoulders. There was an immediacy to his actions that warned Aurora they weren't going to make it to the bed. He was going to take her rough and fast against the wall.

A tremor of anticipation, of pleasure at the very thought of his impending actions, surged through her, firing her passion. The core of her was weeping already. She rattled her arms beneath his grip, wanting her hands free to touch him, to push his shirt off his shoulders, to drag his pants down his hips.

'Not yet, my impatient one.' Crispin was all seductive huskiness. His free hand deftly slipped the buttons of her shirt free. He pushed the folds of her shirt aside, only momentarily foxed by the presence of her thin chemise. He would have to let her arms go now, she thought gleefully. But Crispin surprised her. He bent his mouth to the chemise and held a bit of it between his teeth and ripped with his hand. The fabric gave easily, releasing her breasts to Crispin's hot gaze. He cupped them, one at a time, his breath coming in gratifying rasps. His arousal was full and complete. Only then did he release her arms, letting her work the fastenings of his trousers as he worked hers.

Aurora kicked out of her breeches, feeling his naked member brush against her thigh as she did so. She bit her lip to keep from crying out, so intense was her longing. It was time. Her body knew it was time. No part of her wanted to wait a moment longer. Crispin was lifting her, his hands fitted beneath her buttocks. She wrapped her legs about his waist, gripping his shoulders for balance. Crispin took her weight easily.

'Oh, God, you're so ready.' Crispin's member teased at her entrance, testing, planning its entry. She moved slightly, forcing him inside, taking all of him without a qualm. He slid deeply. For a moment, Aurora savoured the feeling of fulfilment his presence brought. Then he began the exquisite rhythm. This time she did cry out as he pleasured and tortured by turn. The roughness she'd anticipated came and she welcomed it. His mouth seized hers in a bruising kiss even as his body claimed hers against the rough-hewn wall.

Crispin was her only source of stability. She clung to him, feeling her body's passion crest, feeling his own need peak alongside of hers. He shuddered his release into her shoulder moments after she gave voice to her own. She was drained, so completely sated that coherent thought eluded her. The wildness of the interlude had gone, replaced by something more peaceful.

She tried to tactfully disengage her legs, sure that even Crispin's strength must be waning beneath the extended weight of her, but Crispin murmured a soft denial in her ear. Still buried deep in her, he carried her, carried them, to the pine-framed bed just beyond the doorway. He lowered them down on the soft blanket. She could feel his member stirring inside her, could see his body towering over her, possessive and primitive in the echoes of firelight from the other room. Her breath caught; her desire rose again.

'This time, we'll go slowly,' came Crispin's whispered promise in the firelit darkness.

Slowly or roughly, on top of her or underneath her, the night could not outlast Crispin, nor the insatiable desire he raised in her and fulfilled repeatedly until dawn when at last Aurora fell asleep, deeply and wholly sated with a pleasure beyond any she had felt before.

She had to admit privately as she drifted off to sleep that when Crispin Ramsden had boasted there weren't men like him, he just might have been right.

Crispin dozed beside Aurora, more awake than asleep, savouring the languorous peace that held him in its thrall. The intense night of love-making had left him feeling unusually complete. The concerns he'd carried throughout the day were securely tucked away at the back of his mind. His thoughts were centred on the black-haired beauty breathing softly next to him.

She had been boldness personified the prior evening, matching him relentlessly in their passionate explorations. No lover he'd ever taken had been as compelling, as beguiling. Aurora moved against him in her sleep and Crispin felt himself harden yet again at the merest touch.

Perhaps what made her so appealing was that she'd established herself as his equal thus far. Last night she had taken what she needed and given him what he needed in return without him having to ask. There had been women who'd purported to be capable of such loving, but all had fallen short when put to the test.

That test wasn't complete, Crispin reminded himself. There was still the morning to contend with. He'd bedded women too who had no expectations of further commitment in the night, but who were suddenly struck with a need to attach themselves to him come the morning.

His gaze drifted the length of Aurora's form, half of it under the warm plaid blanket, the other half encased only by his arm. He knew her, and knew her not. He could no more predict what Aurora Calhoun would do when she awoke than he could predict next month's weather. The woman in his arms was a marvellous mystery. In most cases, he'd be happy to let a woman's mysterious history lie untouched. Not so with Aurora. He found he wanted to know everything about the groom's daughter from Curragh.

Aurora gave the semblance of waking, her body stretching against his. Crispin decided to encourage that behaviour, his curiosity getting the better of him. What would she do when she awoke? He didn't want to wait any longer to find out. Neither did his rising member, which apparently had a mind of its own and was fairly certain what it thought Aurora's response would be. Crispin pulled her firmly against him, letting his not-so-bashful erection greet her buttocks. He pressed a gentle kiss to her shoulder, his hand tenderly massaging a naked breast.

'Good morning,' Aurora murmured in appreciative, husky tones. She turned in his arms to face him, her hair spilling thickly around her in a morning mess of tumbled curls. He watched her study him through sleepy green eyes, the beginnings of a smile flirting on her lips. Then she tugged at him, pulling him on top of her, her legs parted, ready to take him into her. 'I want you, but we'll have to be quick. The horses need to be fed.'

Crispin laughed softly. 'They can wait a few minutes more, Princess.' He entered her, finding her slick and eager even after their night. He quickened at her welcome, his body throbbing with the intensity of his need. This coupling would indeed be swift and urgent. Such an outcome would please them both. Crispin could sense the fervent urgency in her body as well. She was impatient in her desire to achieve her ecstasy, like a child who couldn't wait for Christmas morning. Beneath him, she cried out.

'Almost, hold on, Princess,' Crispin groaned, his own pleasure about to overwhelm his sensibilities. Somewhere in his passion-addled mind a distant jangle of sound registered. He crested and let his release swamp him.

With a surprising amount of haste, Aurora squirmed beneath him. 'The horses are fine, they can wait,' Crispin repeated.

'I know they can,' Aurora said tartly. 'But the blacksmith cannot.' She gently pushed him aside and leapt out of bed, grabbing up clothes from where they'd fallen the previous night.

Crispin rolled over and folded his arms behind his head, appreciating the view of Aurora dressing at rapid pace. She struggled into her boots and strode out of the rooms into the stable. Crispin gave full rein to the smile he'd sought to suppress. He let out a low whistle and raised his eyes to the low-beamed ceiling. He could not recall having ever been thrown over for a horse or a blacksmith before. It was quite a novel experience really. He couldn't blame her. In her position, he would have done the same. Clearly, this was his kind of woman.

Chapter Five

Reality pierced the morning and Crispin suddenly remembered. The blacksmith wasn't coming. The realisation served to hurry Crispin out of bed. He dressed hastily. If that wasn't the blacksmith, then who was it in the stable yard? Recalling the conversation from the tavern made him worry for Aurora's safety.

Crispin moved into the dim hallway between the apartment and the stable, still tucking his shirt into his breeches. If he had to make his presence known, he didn't want to do it half-dressed and broadcast to everyone where he'd spent the night. Until then, he'd wait and watch. From his vantage point in the hall, he had a good view of Aurora in the yard.

'Where's Mackey?' Aurora stood her ground, arms crossed, disgust evident in her expression. Crispin could see that Mackey had not come. Instead, he'd sent one of his assistants, a drunken lout named Ernie who still looked hung over.

'He sent me to tell you he's not coming. He said to give you this.' Ernie fished a crumpled sheet of paper out of his pocket with grimy hands.

Aurora scanned the note, fighting to keep her temper in check. Mackey wasn't just not coming today, he wasn't coming again, ever. Well, she'd see about that.

'Shall I tell Mr Mackey anything?' Ernie sneered.

Aurora's gaze hardened. 'I'll tell him myself. Now, get off my property.' She turned hard on her heel and swept past the hallway where Crispin stood, not seeing him in the dim light of the passageway. She threw open the first stall door she came to and swung up bareback on the sturdy gelding. Her intentions were clear. Crispin could read her thoughts plainly. If she went cross-country, she'd beat the worthless Ernie back to the forge and get Mackey out of bed with a wake up he wouldn't soon forget. Crispin couldn't allow that to happen. Such an action would be more damaging than helpful.

Aurora flew out of the stables, urging the gelding to full speed. Concern spurred Crispin into motion. She had no idea what she might be riding into. She hadn't heard the anger directed at her last night at the tavern, but he had.

Crispin flung open the door to Sheikh's stall, not bothering to go back for a coat. 'Come on, boy, we've got to stop her.' He led the stallion into the aisle and leapt up on to the Arabian's lean back. Aurora hadn't taken time to tack up, so he couldn't either.

He sighted her veering off the Dursley road and followed, pushing Sheikh into a hard gallop. Aurora's gelding might not be fast, but she had a head start. Crispin had ground to make up. With sure feet, Sheikh overcame the distance.

'Aurora, hold up!' Crispin shouted over wind and hooves, pulling alongside the gelding.

The gelding slowed slightly in response to Sheikh's presence. Crispin grabbed for the reins and missed. 'What do you think you're doing?' Aurora railed.

'Saving you from yourself,' Crispin shouted, angrier than he'd recognised. 'You're a stupid fool if you think you can ride into the village and call the blacksmith to account.'

'Why is that?' Aurora's eyes flashed a lethal green. She urged the gelding to more speed. Crispin matched her.

'Because they mean to pillory you. Your secret's out. Mackey told everyone who would listen last night. I was there at the inn when it happened.'

That brought her to a full stop, the gelding's sides heaving from exertion. 'What secret is that?'

'The girls ride astride,' Crispin replied, choosing not to acknowledge the implication of her response. She had more than one secret. He wondered what they were? He would have to tread carefully if he meant to unearth them all.

'How did he know?' Some of the fire had gone out of Aurora's eyes, replaced by a sense of betrayal. 'Who would have told him? None of the girls would have. We're all sworn to secrecy. They know it would be the end of the academy.' She shot him a chilled look. 'Was it you? Did you tell him?'

It had not crossed his mind that she would suspect him. The idea that she would was a slap in the face of his honour. 'It wasn't me,' Crispin said defensively. 'It doesn't matter who told him. What's important is that you don't go charging into town and live up to their expectations. They're ready to think the worst of you and ranting at Mackey will only prove it.'

Aurora looked out over the fields, away from him. 'I haven't a choice. If I don't confront him, it will only serve to encourage him and others. They will think they have power over me, that they control what I do.'

Crispin stared at her. Had she not heard what he'd said or understood its importance? 'I hardly think it's a question of supply and demand. It's larger than that. Someone means to see you run out of business and out of town if possible.' He related what he'd heard at the inn.

Aurora snorted and fixed him with a baleful stare a lesser man might have shrunk from. 'Do you think I don't know that? Do you think this is the first time something like this has happened to me?'

The weariness in her voice cooled Crispin's anger. 'If you know what people are up to, what will shouting at the blacksmith solve?'

She didn't have a ready answer for his question. 'It will make me feel better.'

Crispin nodded. 'Breakfast might make you feel better too.' He was starting to feel the chill in the air now that the heat of emotions had been banked. He turned the horses in the direction of the stables.

Aurora put up one last effort at resistance. 'Breakfast won't solve the problem.'

Crispin grinned. 'No, it won't, but I always think better on a full stomach. I imagine you do too.'

Crispin stood at the hearth, making breakfast, intent on the cast-iron frying pan he held over the fire and presenting Aurora a glorious view of his backside encased in tight, buttock-hugging riding trousers. This morning was her turn to do the perusing, but the opportunity was lost on her. She might have found the sight arousing if she hadn't been so angry. Empirically, there was something positively alluring about a man cooking breakfast. She was just too upset to appreciate it at the moment. Her mind was reeling with questions and conclusions. The battle had begun. She knew this pattern well, but what had provoked it? Crispin was wrong about one thing—it *did* matter who'd told Mackey.

Aurora drummed her fingers on the table, trying to follow the twisting paths of her thoughts. Who had spilled the secret to Mackey? On his own, Mackey wasn't ambitious enough to care what went on at her stables.

'Someone's behind Mackey, using him,' Aurora spoke her thoughts out loud.

'A phantom puppeteer?' Crispin asked.

The very notion gave Aurora chills. 'It's the most likely reason.' She shrugged, trying not to let it show how much the idea bothered her. 'Mackey has no reason to know such a thing or to share it. Someone has given him a reason and the information.'

'Any ideas who might want that information spread around?'

'None comes to mind,' Aurora said quickly. It wasn't true. One *did* come to mind, but surely he had come to terms with her rejection long before this? Surely he would not stoop to such levels?

Crispin turned towards the table with the frying pan in hand. 'I've managed a fry-up of sorts.' Crispin scooped eggs and sausage from the pan and popped them on to two wooden plates. 'There's toast too.' He reached for the slices of bread he'd placed on a rack in the hearth, juggling them so as not to burn his hands as he placed them on the plates. 'And coffee.' He retrieved the tin coffee pot from the embers of the fire where he'd left it to heat.

'Delicious.' Aurora took a bite of the eggs, more than half-expecting they wouldn't taste as good as they looked, but they did. 'Where did you learn to cook like this?' It was better talking about food than potential enemies.

'The military,' Crispin said between bites. 'Most useful skill a soldier can have besides knowing his weapons. A soldier can't fight on an empty stomach, although most quartermasters I've known have been hard-pressed to believe it.' Crispin winked. He bit into his toast and sobered, returning to the earlier conversation.

'You should tell Peyton.'

Aurora shot him a hard look. 'If I went running to the earl every time someone troubled me, I'd never convince anyone I was anything more than the earl's lackey. How could people take me seriously as a horse breeder, a horsewoman, if I couldn't manage my own business? I would think you of all people would understand why I won't mention it. You don't strike me as the type to let your brother fight your battles.'

'Touché.' Crispin tossed her a wry smile. 'Still, don't let pride get in the way of your security.'

Aurora sensed a stalemate and tacitly returned to her eggs, but Crispin wasn't content. 'Are you sure one of the girls didn't let it slip?'

Aurora shook her head. 'I am sure.' She gave him a hard stare. 'It is unconscionable to doubt my students.' Even as she said it, an uneasy suspicion crossed her mind. Her students *would* keep the secret to the best of their abilities, but she didn't expect them to withstand extreme punishments or worse in order to protect it. They were gently bred young women after all and had little experience with the darker side of life. Except for Eleanor Windham. The poor girl! Could Gregory Windham have extracted such a confession from her, his own daughter?

Crispin leaned across the table, answering her with equal steel. 'In my experience, Princess, secrets are leaked by those on the inside. Very rarely does an outsider stumble upon a secret and expose it. Don't be naïve, Aurora. In all likelihood, one of your girls told someone. Don't ignore the reality simply because it is unpalatable.'

Aurora rose from the table, pushing her unpleasant thoughts to the back of her mind. 'You presume too much on too short an acquaintance, I think, Lord Ramsden.' She gathered up the plates. 'Thank you for breakfast. I am sure you have responsibilities elsewhere that demand your attention.'

His hand seized her wrist. 'I will not be dismissed so easily.'

'Unhand me.' This was how it had all started last night; a quick touch, a little flirting, and she'd talked herself right into bed with the earl's brother. Now she had Sir Lancelot in her kitchen wanting to do good deeds.

'We're not finished. If you won't talk about the potential danger you're in, then we can talk about last night.'

Aurora groaned. The only thing she wanted to talk about less than the stables was last night. Conversations that began with 'about last night' never went well.

'What is there to mention?' Aurora sat down hard on the bench. 'I thought we were doing rather well not mentioning last night at all.' That was the way she preferred it at least, which was one reason she so seldom took a man to her bed. Worthy men always wanted to complicate matters afterwards with feelings of obligation. With feelings of obligation came feelings of ownership. Aurora fought back a shiver. She did not belong to any man. Not any more. Not ever again.

'What is there to mention?' Crispin repeated coolly. 'Surely it hasn't escaped your notice that we didn't take any precautions.'

Aurora looked him firmly in the eye, her tone brisk. 'I did not consider you a traditionalist in that sense. There won't be any complications. You needn't worry. Now, if you'll excuse me, I have classes to prepare.' She moved to go past him.

He put a staying hand on her arm. 'This discussion is not over,' Crispin said warningly. 'Peyton has set up a meeting with my steward today, but I'll be back and this discussion will be continued.'

Mackey finished his report and Gregory Windham rubbed his hands together in satisfaction. 'And the rest? Was your man, Ernie, able to scout out the stables last night?'

Windham preferred to believe that his indirect attempt to stir the villagers against her would be all that was required. However, in the event that failed by the month's end, he needed a back up. He'd hired Mackey's assistant to find out the night schedule of the stables in case more direct intervention, such as an injury to Aurora's prize horse, was needed. Such drastic measures were only to be used in desperation. He didn't want to risk anyone being caught in the act and have them lead the authorities back to him.

Mackey shuffled his feet. 'Ah, no, sir. She had company at the stables last night and we weren't able to get close without fear of being spotted.'

Windham steepled his hands, pretending apathy. 'Oh? Who might the visitor be?'

'Ernie says it was Crispin Ramsden, sir. Dursley's brother. I've never met him before, so I have to take Ernie's word on that,' Mackey hedged.

'I'd heard rumour he was home. You could have waited until he left. I pay you enough to wait all night if need be. Everyone has to go home some time.'

Mackey coughed, embarrassed. 'That was the problem, sir. He didn't go home. Ernie said he stayed all night.'

Envy shot through Windham in hot bolts. The

Jezebel! She'd shunned his offer only to take Dursley's rakehell brother to bed instead. It sickened him to think of her with another, doing the things he'd dreamed of doing to her.

Windham carefully schooled his features to not give away any hint of his inward turmoil. Ramsden certainly complicated matters, especially if he was welcome in the hoyden's bed. Yet, this last transgression provided another nail in the proverbial coffin, proof that Aurora Calhoun was no better than she ought to be. It was his experience that women living alone without a man's guidance were prone to illicit behaviours. He would make sure that was the village's experience too. When he finished with her, no man would want her again except for him and she would be glad to welcome his attentions. When she was broken, finally, she would see that only he could save her.

'Did you know?' Crispin fixed Peyton with a challenging stare over the decanter of brandy in the empty dining room. He'd dined at Dursley Park that evening, but the excellent food and company had done little to appease his dark mood. The day had gone steadily downhill after leaving Aurora's.

The meeting with the land steward had been less than satisfactory.

'That the estate was entailed?' Peyton clarified. 'Yes, I knew. I hardly thought it mattered since I assumed you'd be taking the property on permanently. If you kept the property, the entailment is irrelevant.'

'You knew I was thinking of selling. I told you as much over tea,' Crispin ground out. 'You could have mentioned that little detail then.' Entailed property was under legal restrictions with regard to how it could be treated or managed. Entail regulated what could be sold and what remained intact. In this case, the inheritor of the property was not allowed to sell it in whole or part. Such a restriction put quite a crimp in Crispin's plans.

'But that was before you'd seen the property,' Peyton dismissed the complaint easily.

'Yes,' Crispin groused. 'Before I'd seen it, before I was treated to your exquisite tour and well-calculated visit with the steward. You thought you could change my mind.'

Peyton shrugged. 'I thought *you* would change your *own* mind if presented with the right arguments, if you could be persuaded to see past your own stubbornness.'

'My dreams aren't yours, Peyton. They never have been. I am not a landowner like you or a banker like Paine,' Crispin said in a dangerously quiet voice. He didn't want to fight with his brother, but neither did he wish to build up Peyton's hopes with half-truths.

'What are your dreams, Cris? Surely you don't expect to work for the government the rest of your life.' Peyton's tone was hard with hurt.

'No, but I do like to travel. There's an exciting world out there, full of changes, and I want to be part of that. I'd prefer to consider the subject closed before I say something I'll regret later.' Crispin drew a deep breath. 'So, speaking of changes, is there another blacksmith in the area?'

Peyton raised an eyebrow. 'What's wrong with Mackey in the village? I've found him quite adept.'

'Let's just say I don't like his attitude,' Crispin answered.

Peyton thought for a moment. 'Thomas's father uses a smithy closer to Woodbrook, named Durham, I think. You can ask Thomas tonight for his direction.'

Crispin rose and took the opening. 'I will, then I think I'll head down to the inn for a pint.' He could not believe his small bit of good luck. Peyton wasn't going to call him on the carpet for not coming home last night. As well he shouldn't. His brother had to learn he was a thirty-eight-year-old man, not an adolescent with his first beard any longer.

At the door to the drawing room Peyton reached out a staying hand. 'By the by, Cris, you didn't say anything about Aurora's stables. Are they to your liking?'

'Yes.' Damn. He wasn't going to get off as easily as he thought. He heard the unspoken question behind his brother's casual query, but Crispin offered Peyton nothing more. If Peyton wanted to play lord of the manor, he would damn well have to ask the hard questions if he wanted answers.

When Crispin volunteered nothing more, Peyton meted out careful words. 'She is Tessa's friend. I would not want any awkwardness to drive a wedge between them. Even so, I would caution you. Aurora's past is full of shadows. She is a hard woman to know, I think.'

'I know someone very much like that: myself.' Crispin gave a wry grin, silently acknowledging that Peyton could have said much more. Once upon a time, Peyton *would* have said much more.

Crispin had made his way to the inn shortly after their brotherly exchange in the hallway. The other blacksmith's name was indeed Durham and Crispin planned to put that piece of information to good use. He ordered a pint at the bar and sauntered over to insert himself into the large group of people surrounding the blacksmith who'd disparaged Aurora the night before.

'Are you the local smith?' he asked as the loud conversation waned for a fraction. Crispin took a swallow of ale from his tankard.

'I am. My name's Mackey. You have a horse that needs shoeing? I shoe everybody's horses around these parts,' Mackey boasted. Someone gave a nervous laugh. The man was awfully bold. Crispin attributed his boldness to his ignorance. The man was new to the area since he'd left three years ago. It was obvious to Crispin the man hadn't attached a name to his face.

'Then why didn't you shoe Miss Calhoun's horses this morning?' Crispin asked bluntly. 'Is it the shoddiness of your work that causes her to seek out Durham? I'd like to meet this Durham fellow. My stallion will be needing shoes soon. Sounds like he might be quite the smith if she's willing to make the effort.'

His tone was friendly, but the implication of his comment spread through the room on a wave of whispers. If Dursley's brother was going to use Durham, perhaps Dursley's patronage would shift too. And if the Ramsdens used Durham, maybe the rest of them should as well.

Mackey's eyes narrowed—the insult was not lost on him. He understood the risk to his business even if he didn't understand with whom he spoke. 'If you understood anything, you would understand that I don't care to do business with "Miss" Calhoun. That woman is a slut in trousers.'

There was an intake of breath and the space around Mackey widened. Many might agree with Mackey when it came to Aurora Calhoun, and Crispin knew for a fact that they did. He'd heard the cheers when Mackey had made similar comments the night before. But to make those comments to the earl's brother's face about a woman rumoured to be the countess's friend was to invite trouble.

Old timers in the village who'd watched him grow up knew Crispin Ramsden was a good man in a fight and the speculation about what he did during his years abroad only heightened that belief.

'You slander a woman whose only crime is to make her own way in the world,' Crispin said calmly. True, he didn't know Aurora that well in their short association, but that much he felt sure of and his gut instinct was seldom wrong.

The blacksmith grunted, rolling up his sleeves with a snort. 'Ah, a Lancelot is among us.' He spat on to the floor. 'Who do I have the honour of pummelling tonight?'

Crispin grinned, setting aside his coat. He didn't usually enjoy throwing his title around, but tonight was an exception. 'Crispin Ramsden. *Lord* Crispin Ramsden.'

To cover his surprise, Mackey snarled, 'That explains it, then, why you're willing to take a beating for the whore. You're defending her because you're infatuated with her. Rumour has it you spent the night between her legs.' Mackey swung a giant fist at Crispin.

Crispin neatly dodged the blow and came up lightly on the balls of his feet, his fists up and ready. 'I'm defending her because a lady should never have to beg.'

Crispin planted the man a facer and the fight was fully engaged.

A few broken benches later, Crispin shouldered into his greatcoat, tossed some coins on the bar for the damages and headed out into the night, leaving the blacksmith passed out under a table. He swung up on to Sheikh's back. It was late. He'd stable Sheikh and be on his way back to Dursley Park. Aurora would be asleep. In spite of his promises to continue their conversation from the morning, he wouldn't bother her.

That was the plan at least, but it was a hard plan to follow when his mind seemed obsessed with conjuring up images of Aurora as she'd been last night, all hot passion in his arms, her dark hair hanging down her back, her hands on him, her body answering him with its pleasure.

This was turning into one devil of a homecoming. When he'd stood atop the stairs at Dursley Park, thinking how serene and orderly everything had looked, he had no idea such turmoil would lurk beneath the surface: an estate he couldn't sell, a village looking to run an independent woman out of town, the very same passionate, stubborn woman who had landed in his bed. Crispin smiled to himself, remembering last night. He'd made his bed, he'd happily lie in it… And he'd thought he'd be bored.

Chapter Six

'Rory, can I talk with you?' Eleanor Windham asked tentatively on her way to the tack room, a saddle in her arms after lessons.

Aurora turned from the horse she was currying with Petra. She smiled fondly at the girl. 'Of course, Eleanor. Come to my apartments after you've put your saddle away.'

The girl nodded gratefully and hurried off. Aurora was glad Eleanor had persisted in speaking with her. She'd known Eleanor wanted to talk, needed to talk, but she didn't relish the upcoming conversation. Eleanor's situation was a difficult one. It would take an inordinate amount of character and courage on Eleanor's part to change the outcome. Additionally, she suspected Eleanor held a certain amount of hero-worship for her, that the girl saw her life as being considerably more alluring than it was. If Eleanor thought she was going to tell the girl to run away and forsake the marriage Windham had arranged, the girl would be disappointed.

Aurora had tea going by the time Eleanor had put away her tack and come to the apartments. 'Now, tell me everything.' Aurora offered her a mug and motioned for her to take a seat across from her.

Eleanor gratefully took the mug. 'I can't stay long, though. My father will be angry if I'm late.'

If Gregory Windham hadn't been so concerned with losing a chance for his daughter to ride with the earl's ward, Aurora knew he would have withdrawn Eleanor from the riding school out of spite if nothing else after her pointed rejection of his indecent proposal.

'He watches me all the time now.' Eleanor nervously sipped from the heavy mug.

Beastly man. Such controlling behaviour had been at the core of Aurora's dislike. Couldn't the man see that managing his daughter in this strict manner was having the opposite effect? The harder he tried to rein her in, the harder Eleanor strained to get away.

Aurora's temper began to simmer. She wanted to march straight up to the Windham place and give Eleanor's father a rather large piece of her mind, the piece that demanded women not be treated as chattel. Yet that would do Eleanor no good, nor would it help the other girls if she got herself expelled from yet another village.

With a calm that hid her inner turmoil, Aurora said, 'Does this have to do with the engagement?'

Eleanor nodded, her face pale. 'My father and the baron feel a woman's place is in the home.' She looked down at her hands and shrugged. 'It's understandable, of course, there's a lot to be done. I have my trousseau to put together. There's linens to be embroidered and invitations to be penned.'

'You don't have to excuse them, Eleanor,' Aurora said softly, but there was unmistakable steel to her voice. 'A woman's place is where she wants it to be. If embroidering your trousseau gives you pleasure that's fine, but if it is an activity that is used to make you a captive in your own home, then that's wrong. There's no excuse for it.'

Eleanor looked up and offered a wan smile. 'Perhaps I am being too emotional. My father says that I am. Perhaps I haven't given the baron a fair chance. It's true that I hardly know him. Perhaps when I am mistress of my own home, with my own family to look after, things will be different.'

Aurora put down her mug and reached for the girl's hands. 'That's an awful lot of "perhapses".' The baron was much older than Eleanor, an heirless widower with a less-than-pristine record about town. 'Don't you think you should find out if the two of you are compatible before the wedding instead of after?'

'Father and the baron think whatever rough edges exist between us will be worn away with time,' Eleanor offered the empty platitude.

Aurora could hear the doubt in the girl's voice. Tessa had told her how Eleanor's father had scoured London for an unmarried peer of any rank who'd be willing to take an attractive daughter of a wealthy gentleman off his hands. The Windhams were landed gentry, but nothing more; they'd coveted a title for generations. Now they would have it, at the expense of Eleanor's happiness.

'What do you think, Eleanor? Do you think that is true?'

Eleanor's usually soft gaze hardened with something akin to bitterness. 'What does it matter what I think or if I think? If I disagreed, what could be done anyway? It's a woman's lot to be thankful to marry at all. I'll have to make the best of whatever my marriage brings. At least for once I will have done something to please my father.'

Eleanor's despair swamped Aurora. She knew that

feeling of hopelessness all too well. She knew how overwhelming and complete it could be, this giant abyss that swallowed you up whole, body and soul, until you forgot who you really were. But what could she say to the girl?

Difficult was an incredibly inaccurate word to describe her own journey away from a marriage that had nearly destroyed her. In good conscience, she could not advocate running away. Eleanor was clearly desperate and would jump at any option. In her desperation, Eleanor wouldn't see the long-term costs such a choice entailed. Yet, she did not want to let Eleanor down. To tell her to give in to the marriage, to give up being true to herself, was counter to everything she'd taught her students.

A little of the bitterness receded and Eleanor pushed back a length of blonde hair that had come loose. 'Tell me what to do, Rory. I want to be like you. You go where you want, you do what you want, you live on your own, with no cares, no responsibilities beyond your horses. No one owns you. Tell me how you did it.'

Her passionate outcry invoked a level of panic in Aurora. She had to be honest with her. She'd not told her students much of her own story. Indeed, she seldom told her tale to anyone. Eleanor had to be made to see the grim realities of Aurora's own choices.

'No, you don't want this, Eleanor.' Aurora shook her head emphatically. 'There's a price for my freedom. Choosing to be on your own is not an easy sop to your problems. You're not just on your own, you're alone, Eleanor. Alone.' She never misrepresented her choice as an easy elixir to the choices women faced. Leaving Ireland and her father had been the most harrowing choice she'd ever made.

'I know that doesn't mean anything to you right now,' Aurora continued. 'I didn't fully grasp what being alone meant when I first decided to leave Ireland. For me, it meant a chance to start over, to be my own person.' Aurora shook her head. 'I learned there's no starting over, Eleanor. There's only going forwards. I will never marry. I will never have a husband. I will never have children. There's no man who wants a woman who has put herself outside society.'

'But you have Tessa and Petra,' Eleanor protested.

'For now,' Aurora said quietly. 'Eventually I will move on, that's the nature of my life.' She didn't bother to elucidate the finer points as to why she'd have to move on or that in most cases it was an issue of force.

'You have your horses,' Eleanor continued to argue.

'For now,' Aurora repeated. 'I will have them for as long as I can afford to care for them and for as long as I can ride them. Some day, I'll be too old.'

She met Eleanor's gaze squarely, wanting the girl to see the naked emotions in her eyes, wanting her to see that she spoke a deep personal truth. 'That some day scares me, Eleanor. There will be no pension for me when I'm too old to work, no family to take me in, no husband to guarantee my financial security. You're right. I have my horses. My riding is all that stands between me and abject disaster. It's a very thin bulwark, Eleanor, and I know it will not last. I know what awaits me and I would not willingly send you down that path.'

'You're saying you would have chosen differently if you could do it again?' Eleanor knit her brow, clearly perplexed by this surprising disclosure.

'I didn't get to choose,' Aurora replied evenly. Jonathon had decided to discard her. It had not been her choice at all. She had loved him and he'd only thought he loved her. To be fair, he had loved her, just not enough.

'Then what I am to do?' Eleanor asked.

'I can't tell you what to do.'

That made Eleanor angry. She rose in a huff, tears threatening. 'It's not fair. You tell us to be true to ourselves. You tell us to be masters of our futures and now you sit there and tell me to accept this marriage. You taught us to think for ourselves!'

'Yes, Eleanor. I've taught you to think for yourself. You should no more look to a man's opinion to decide your future than you should look to mine,' Aurora answered her firmly, sternly, rising to meet the angry girl. 'I've taught you to trust yourself, to trust in your own strength. One doesn't have to forsake society to be strong. You're a far stronger young woman than the one who first came to me. Embrace that strength now.'

The reference to her growing skill brought a smile to Eleanor's face. 'I could hardly ride when I first started coming here.' Her rage started to ebb as Aurora's words penetrated her thoughts.

Aurora nodded. She remembered vividly Eleanor's father marching the timid girl into the stables and demanding she be given training. The boorish man had originally liked that the instructor was a woman. No inappropriate, unvetted male would be working with his daughter, laying his hands on her. All that had changed once she and Windham had taken each other's full measure and found the other lacking.

Eleanor was calmer. She wiped at an errant tear on her cheek. 'Thank you, Rory. I understand things better now. You've given me some hope. I must go home and think what to do.'

Aurora walked Eleanor to the stable yard and saw her off in the pony trap, then was surprised to see Tessa riding down the drive. She smiled, glad to see her friend.

Tessa hadn't been out since the newest baby had arrived and Aurora had missed her visits.

'Hello, Tess. What brings you here today?' The sky was overcast and Tessa could have picked a nicer day to come over if this was a social call. Aurora hoped her friend didn't bring bad news. 'I think I saw Petra still in the stables.'

'I'm sure you did. I can hardly pry her away from Peyton's stables when she's not over here.' Tess swung down from her saddle with ease and hugged Aurora. 'It's been a long time. It feels good to be out on my own a bit.'

'I can imagine.' Aurora smiled. 'You look wonderful. Motherhood agrees with you. I would never guess you'd just had a child and a third one at that.' Tess really did glow, Aurora decided, taking in her friend's appearance. Her dark-blue habit showed off her eyes and her figure to best advantage. Tessa Ramsden was clearly a happy woman.

Aurora did not begrudge her friend an iota of that happiness, but a twinge of regret kicked at Aurora's insides. She would never be a happy mother, escaping for a few hours from a house full of boisterous boys. Aurora tamped it down. She was being maudlin because of her discussion with Eleanor.

'Let's go inside. I have hot water on already for tea. We can chat while Petra finishes up,' Aurora offered. 'Tell me what the boys are up to.'

They made small talk about the nursery antics of the Ramsden twins until Tessa's tea was ready. Then Tessa settled herself in a chair and got straight to business. 'Was that Eleanor Windham I saw leaving?'

'Yes, she's distraught over the engagement.'

'Understandably so.' Tessa sighed into her tea. 'That

man her father has picked out has little regard for anyone, not even a wife. He'll get an heir on her if he can and tuck her away in the country while he goes straight back to London to spend her fortune.' Tessa's tone was brittle.

'At least he'll leave her alone for a good part of the year.'

Tessa raised her eyebrows. 'That doesn't sound like you, my dear, willing to settle for a marriage of absence.'

'I told her the truth, that this life of mine is not as desirable as it might look from the outside, and gave her the usual talk about her rights; that her opinion matters, that she's entitled to her own life.' Aurora shook her head. 'I do not know if Eleanor has the fortitude for making such a choice.'

'Few of us do.' Tessa nodded in agreement. 'I could have Peyton talk with her father. If it's not too late, I could send her to London to stay with Eva and Aunt Lily. With the right kind of Season, she might find someone she cares for and who might also appeal to her father. Her father's idea of combing the marriage mart was a bit heavy-handed. With Lily's guidance, the search might go better.'

'That would be most kind, Tess.' Her friend's offer was heartfelt, but Aurora doubted it would make a difference. Eleanor's arrangements were too far gone for Windham to back out now. Still, she would not cheat Eleanor of a chance, no matter how slim.

Tessa poured another cup of tea. 'Now that's settled, I came to tell you that Peyton and I are throwing a party, a small ball.' She drew an invitation out of the small bag she carried. 'It's in official honour of Petra and Thomas's engagement and it will be a chance to celebrate Crispin's homecoming. He's been gone so long there are lots of new faces to meet, especially if he's going to take over Woodbrook.'

Aurora focused on the invitation in her hand, the heavy cream paper, the crisp black ink in Tessa's precise hand. Better to look at the invitation than to give anything away in regards to Crispin. The last thing she needed was Tessa playing matchmaker. 'You don't want me there. This will be a formal affair. I'm not sure your guests will want to fraternise with the local riding instructor.' She usually eschewed formal invitations to Dursley Park. Dressing up and pretending to be someone other than the head-groom's daughter hadn't worked out for her in the past. She had no desire to repeat such foolishness.

Tessa shrugged as if oblivious to any of the rumours that swirled around Aurora. She wasn't, of course. Tessa knew exactly what the neighbourhood thought of a woman setting up on her own. It was only through Tessa's tenacious sponsorship that the school had become acceptable. Aurora knew too that many of her pupils came from families who hoped for a chance to enter the earl's social circle by riding with Petra, his ward. That dangling carrot and the effort she'd taken to keep any breath of scandal from her name had worked wonders. Now, the episode at the inn threatened to undo her hard-won peace.

Tessa leaned forwards reassuringly. 'I want you there, Rory. Petra wants you there to celebrate her engagement and surely Crispin would appreciate you being there.'

Aurora snorted at the last. 'Why would he care? He hardly knows me.' Surely Tessa didn't know what had transpired between her and Crispin.

Tessa fixed her with a knowing gaze. Aurora knew she'd come to the heart of the visit. 'I am told Crispin broke Mackey's nose at the inn last night. He threw in a black eye for good measure.'

Aurora took a sip of tea to disguise her surprise. That was bad. Clearly Tessa attributed the brawl to her and that was worse. 'Men tend to brawl.' Aurora shrugged, hoping she sounded compelling in her apathetic response. 'Perhaps Mackey spilt his beer.' So, that's where he'd been last night. Not that she'd expected him to return last night, she hastily reminded herself. They had no claim to each other beyond their one night.

Tessa arched her brows and Aurora knew her ruse of objective nonchalance hadn't worked. 'It wasn't about beer, Rory. I have it on good authority it was about you. I must say, my dear, you do have quite an effect on men.'

Aurora choked on her tea. So much for hiding her surprise. How could she have misjudged him so badly? She'd thought she understood Crispin Ramsden. She never would have taken him into her bed if she'd thought he'd feel compelled to brawl on her behalf. She'd wanted a lover, not a hero.

It was the height of hypocrisy to warn her off confronting Mackey and then go and do the very same thing himself. He could be quite sure there would be a reckoning when he returned to the stables. Whatever possessed him to behave like that?

Tessa studied her over the rim of her teacup. 'Crispin's more of a gentleman than he leads most of us to believe. If a lady's honour were at stake, he would not hesitate to defend her. He was raised by Peyton, after all.' She set her cup down. 'What's going on, Rory?'

'Mackey announced to everyone at the inn that my students ride astride and wear trousers.' Aurora explained.

Tessa reached for her hand with a comforting squeeze. 'I'm so sorry, my dear. I know how hard you've tried.' She paused and then asked quietly, 'Do you know who told him?'

Aurora nodded and confessed her suspicions. 'I think it was Windham. It's unlikely Mackey would discover anything like that on his own. I fear Windham may have bullied the secret out of Eleanor. I know she wouldn't volunteer that information readily.'

'Is that all?' Tessa probed gently. 'Is that the sole reason Crispin broke Mackey's nose? Goodness knows it's enough.'

'It's the most significant, but Mackey also refused to come out and shoe my horses.'

'That must be why Crispin wanted the name of another blacksmith at dinner the other night,' Tessa mused in a considering tone. 'He's certainly put himself forwards as your champion in such a short time.'

Aurora experienced a moment of panic. It was bad enough to discover Crispin had broken a nose over her. 'Tessa, I don't like where your thoughts are headed. This is not the time for me to be pursuing a relationship. You know how important the race at St Albans is to me. I cannot afford a distraction.'

Tessa laughed. 'I am sure you're the only woman who has ever referred to Crispin as a distraction. Most of them find him to be something more.'

Aurora shot her a stern look and Tessa stood up, correctly assessing that Aurora could not be pushed further on the subject. Tessa brushed at her skirts, 'Right. Well, I'll go fetch Petra and we'll be off before the rains come.'

'It was good to see you, Tess.' Aurora hugged her friend again.

'I'll see you this weekend for the horse fair,' Tess replied. 'And you have to come up to the house for dinner soon. The table seems empty with Eva gone.'

Aurora gave a non-committal nod, seeing the invitation to dinner for what it was. She would have to make it very clear that she had no permanent designs on Crispin Ramsden no matter how many noses he broke.

Aurora waited until she heard Crispin moving about in the stables later that night, helping Sheikh to bed down. She squared her shoulders and marched out to meet him. There was no sense in waiting. She began without preamble, 'I don't need a man to defend me.'

Crispin turned to face her with equal solemnity, unbothered by her blunt approach. 'I disagree.'

His cool response fired her anger. How dare he stand here in *her* stables and second-guess what *she* needed? He should not have insinuated himself into her affairs. He should not have tried to manage her business. He should not have told her to do one thing and then gone and done another. There were so many things he should not have done she could scarcely list them all.

'Why should I worry about making a spectacle of myself when I have you to do it for me?' she stormed. 'You had no right to go down there and beat Mackey to a bloody pulp because he didn't show up, no right at all when you'd counselled me against taking action.'

'I didn't punch him because he missed his appointment. I told him you were thinking of using the smithy closer to Woodbrook.' Crispin's voice was calm, neutral against her indignant tones. 'I suggested that if the smith, Durham, was to your liking I might shoe Sheikh there as well. I think it made him nervous to think that he could lose the Dursley patronage and in turn lose some business in the village.'

'Why did you punch him?' She'd already heard Tessa's answer to that, but she wanted to hear Crispin say it.

He fixed her with his blue stare. 'He called you a

whore in no uncertain terms.' Crispin's gaze did not waver from hers.

Aurora fought the urge to flinch. She'd been called such harsh names before, but that didn't make them any easier to digest. She paced the short length of the room. 'He's entitled to his thoughts.'

'Not when he voices them out loud,' Crispin retorted.

'No, *then* he's apparently entitled to your fist in his face,' Aurora argued fiercely. She had to make this man understand that one night did not entitle him to any claims or require any obligations.

'Why are you defending him? Do you want him to turn the village against you? Do you not care that you're slandered?' Crispin's cool demeanour was fading.

Aurora wanted to blurt out it was the only option open to her under the circumstances. She'd badly misjudged Dursley's brother. She'd thought the rumours of his devil-may-care lifestyle meant he had little regard for responsibility, that he'd be less like Dursley. If she'd known he'd react this way, she might have found the fortitude to resist. She did not need a responsible man in her bed no matter how virile he was. The very thought was nearly as disturbing to her as the growing situation in the village.

'Let me be clear, I don't welcome your interference, no matter how well intended it may be. Did you stop to consider that by standing up for me you proved to them that I was all they believed? You cannot defend me and not expect people to think there's something between us.' Aurora slapped her hand against her thigh in agitation. 'Why couldn't you leave well enough alone?'

Crispin studied the woman pacing before him. They weren't exclusively talking about the situation with the blacksmith any longer. Leaving well enough alone extended to the nature of their liaison. They'd tacitly decided there were to be no expectations, no obligations, and now there were, put there by others who would make assumptions about their relationship. He could see the world through those jaded, conservative eyes. In their narrow minds, it would be quite a coup for a woman like Aurora to keep the earl's brother in her bed.

Regardless, he'd not been raised to allow a woman to be treated with the disregard Mackey had shown Aurora. Even amid the shambles of his parents' marriage, there had been some semblance of courtesy between them as a matter of honour.

'Are you going to answer my question?' Aurora snapped.

'Not to your satisfaction, at any rate. I will not apologise for acting chivalrously on your behalf,' Crispin said staunchly.

'Chivalry is dead,' she ground out before turning on her heel and stalking out of the room.

Crispin watched her go, chuckling softly under his breath. He understood why she was angry, although he disagreed with her sentiments. What he didn't understand was why she was so adamant about being left alone even at the cost of her own reputation. Anger was often a convenient mask for fear, but he had no inkling what she might be afraid of. For that matter, he had no inkling as to why he'd behaved as he did on such short acquaintance.

True, Aurora Calhoun was a rare beauty and a confident lover. Both were appealing qualities to him, but those qualities alone did not make her unique. He'd had plenty of affairs with attractive, assertive women before. There was something deeper that drew him to her, that nebulous connection of understanding that had driven him to her two nights ago instead of going home to Dursley Park. In all his experience, he'd never felt such an immediate and intense connection to anyone. It was both novel and frightening. But he was not one to shrink from an adventure and that was exactly what Aurora Calhoun was proving to be.

Chapter Seven

She was supposed to be mad, Aurora reminded herself two days later, cantering side-saddle beside the Dursley carriage on a well-dispositioned sorrel mare from her school string. But it was hard to remember that when the weather was fine and she was on her way to a horse fair.

The reason for her hard-to-remember anger rode casually beside her, chatting easily with the occupants of the coach and acting as if they hadn't quarrelled at all. He should be apologising.

To her.

He'd overstepped his boundaries and interfered unnecessarily. Such a breach of their arrangement had to be addressed. One night didn't entitle him to any claims. But it was difficult to hold on to that reasoning when Crispin looked so handsome with his dark hair sleek and pulled back, accentuating the striking planes of his face, and his clothes so well turned out. He didn't look like the dusty traveller she'd met in the road with his rough clothes. Today he was dressed like a lord in clean buckskin riding breeches, white linen and an expensively tailored dark-blue riding jacket that left no doubt as to the natural excellence of his physique.

He'd be an incredible specimen of manhood if it hadn't been for the little issue of his over-protective, misguided 'chivalry'.

'Sheikh's a prime-goer, no doubt about it.' Crispin was saying to Peyton, who rode inside the carriage with Tessa, Thomas and Petra. Inside was where Crispin was supposed to be as well. She'd ridden the sorrel mare expressly for that reason. She'd thought to avoid his company.

'I had to win him twice. The nomad chieftain who'd wagered him had second thoughts about parting with him, after he lost of course. Seems our nomadic friends have different notions of fair play than we do.'

'Did you steal him back?' Petra asked, looking pretty in pale blue and leaning out the window. Aurora hadn't meant to be sucked into the story, but it proved irresistible. She leaned forwards to hear better in spite of her resolve to the contrary.

'No, we had a knife-throwing contest and I was much more prepared, shall we say, for that competition.' Crispin gave a light chuckle that belied the underlying danger of the situation. Aurora could well imagine a darker scenario than the one Crispin alluded to.

'Then the horse is an Arabian,' Peyton put in.

'Yes, and about nine years old, just coming into his prime. I was thinking of racing him. The larger Arabian nostrils enhance his ability to breathe. That gives him an advantage in endurance races. He's ripe for steeplechase and for stud.' Crispin shot her a naughty look and Aurora flushed, letting her horse fall behind the carriage while she fought images of a stallion of another sort who seemed quite ripe for stud too. It appeared horse and master had a lot in common.

She didn't have her privacy for long. Crispin's horse soon dropped back to join her. 'You were supposed to be riding in the carriage,' Aurora said without preamble.

'So were you.'

'That's why I didn't,' Aurora's answer was short.

'You wanted to avoid me,' Crispin said. 'I guessed as much.'

'You're a wicked man to upset a lady's manoeuvring.'

'You're still upset about the other day,' Crispin charged.

Aurora kept her gaze straight ahead on the back of the Dursley carriage. 'You over-reached yourself.'

'I don't feel the need to apologise for defending a woman's honour.' Crispin's answer was simple. 'However, I do regret any inconvenience my actions may have caused. It was not my intention to imply that something untoward existed between us.'

Aurora struggled not to grin. 'You're absolutely right. That's definitely not an apology, not even close, but it's probably the best I'll get.' Her anger was vanishing rapidly.

'Probably,' Crispin affirmed, then adroitly changed the subject. 'Are you looking or buying today?'

'Buying, I hope. I need a good jumper for intermediate riders. My girls' skills are growing beyond the school horses I have.'

They made no move to catch up with Peyton and Crispin was happy to have Aurora to himself. When had he ever found a woman so compelling? Crispin was well aware how mundane that question really was. In their days apart, he had become more certain that he'd never encountered a woman that held anything like the level of Aurora's appeal. However, he was usually quite careful not to give women a chance to become too alluring. A quick bedding sufficed to quell any penchant for attraction that he might be tempted to feel for a woman. Not so with Aurora.

His regular method of disposing of potential attachments had soundly failed in her case. The early physicality between them had merely served as a gateway to increased desire—a desire his body had recognised immediately and his mind was only now beginning to acknowledge; he was definitely interested in what lay beneath the surface of Aurora Calhoun's lovely face and exquisite body. Today, that exquisite body was neatly showcased in a dark-green riding habit and proving that Aurora was as capable on a side saddle as she was riding astride.

'I wouldn't mind picking up a horse with Irish bloodlines.' Aurora's conversation broke into his daydreams.

His mind was decidedly not on horses at the moment. Crispin dragged his thoughts away from peeling Aurora out of her riding habit and applied himself to the conversation. 'The lines of an Irish draughthorse give a hunter a strong chest for jumping.' Maybe his fascination with Aurora was due to their mutual interest in horses.

Aurora gave a smug laugh. 'That's a pretty good answer for someone who wasn't paying attention. Just where were your thoughts, Crispin Ramsden?'

'I was admiring how lovely you look today.' Crispin opted for the gentleman's version of the truth.

'In my habit or out of it?' Aurora gave a coy sidelong glance.

'Well, out of it, if you must know.' Crispin leaned towards her and said in a low voice, 'What's the point of imagining you in it when I can see that for myself?'

* * *

The fair was early in the year, but no less attended because of it. Dedicated horse lovers had thronged to the wide, flat plains of the fairgrounds, eager to see a fine display of horseflesh outside of Tattersalls and Newmarket. Crispin deduced almost immediately as they strolled the venue that the event was definitely designed to appeal to a higher calibre of horse aficionado. The men who had horses to sell here were professional breeders. This was not a random event open to all and sundry, but a well-planned affair for an exclusive group.

Aurora must have guessed in advance. It explained why she'd opted for the habit instead of her usual attire. She must have known some modicum of social conformity was in order. The habit wasn't all that Crispin noticed about Aurora. She moved with grace and confidence, not the least intimidated by the wealthy surroundings or the elite calibre of horseflesh. She could have passed as a peer's lady. Indeed, when she walked next to Tessa it was hard to tell which one was the countess. He would not have guessed it of her, although seeing her today, the demeanour fit her perfectly. It was no sham, adding to the beautiful mystery of who was Aurora Calhoun?

The fair offered a perfect opportunity to delve into that mystery, to remind Aurora of his interest in her, and Crispin did it most subtly. His hand provided a gentle pressure at the small of her back, guiding her through the rows. He took every opportunity to murmur comments in her ear or to touch her arm. The public would see nothing untoward in these small gestures, but Aurora would not mistake the attentions his body paid hers. He would make sure of it.

Crispin stopped to watch her assess the legs on a bay

hunter. She ran an expert hand down the fetlock and picked up the hoof to inspect it. Daughter of an Irish groom? Her expertise certainly suggested it. He thought of her comment about accents being bred out of you. What of her mother, then? Perhaps a woman of some rank who had the misfortune to fall in love with a man of inferior station? Aurora had clearly been educated in horses and in much else that women of common birth did not bother with. She had enough knowledge of bookkeeping and finances to run her own business. Both skills suggested education in mathematics and literacy.

'What does this horse eat?' She stood up and faced the owner squarely.

'Clover, alfalfa.' The owner shrugged.

'Too much clover, is my guess. The colt's diet is too rich for him. His hooves look like they've been struggling with laminitis.'

The owner looked as if he were about to argue with Aurora. Crispin bent swiftly and examined the front hoof. Setting the hoof down, he brushed his hands off on his trousers and met the man's gaze with an even stare. 'The lady's right. That's my assessment as well.'

'Well, he did have a bout of it this winter. The new stable boy overfed him,' the owner offered as an excuse. Crispin nodded congenially, his point having been made. With a hand at Aurora's back, he ushered her on to the next stall.

'He wasn't going to admit it,' she fumed under her breath.

'All's well that ends well, Princess,' Crispin murmured in her ear. 'There's other horses. We both know you were right and he knew it, too, even if he didn't want to acknowledge it.'

He spied a stand selling sweets and steered them

towards the booth. 'What do you like?' Crispin asked, gesturing to the vendor that he'd take a bag of peppermints.

'You should guess.' Aurora tossed her head.

'Hmm. Toffee?' Crispin guessed.

'Too sticky.'

'If practicality is your consideration, I'd say licorice drops,' Crispin guessed confidently. 'A most practical sweet if ever there was one; good for the digestion, freshens the breath and not sticky.'

'You're teasing me.' Aurora pretended to be offended.

'Just guessing, but I'm right.' He grinned triumphantly. 'I'll take a bag of licorice and some toffees…' he turned to Aurora with a wink '…for the twins.'

She made a face of mock disapproval. 'Very sticky business. I don't think Tessa will approve.'

Crispin shrugged carelessly and laughed. 'I'm their uncle. It's my job to spoil them with treats their mother doesn't allow.'

He paid out the coins for the treats and they strolled away to find a place to indulge in the sweets. 'How did you get to be such an expert on uncles who spoil nephews?'

'My father's sister, Aunt Lily, had a very nice husband who did his best to look out for us.' Crispin led them over to a wide-trunked tree, away from the crowd. He opened one of the bags and offered it to her, watching her enjoy the treat. He helped himself to a peppermint.

'I can't remember the last time I had sweets.' Aurora giggled and then covered her mouth with her hand self-consciously.

'Nor me,' Crispin admitted. 'Sweets weren't a priority in the places I've been lately.'

'Being home has its luxuries,' Aurora said.

Crispin let his eyes linger on her lips. 'It certainly

does. You're not still mad at me?' His voice was little more than a whisper.

'No, not really. Why?' she breathed softly in anticipation.

'So I can kiss you.' Crispin feathered a kiss against the column of her neck, feeling her pulse ignite with desire.

'Do you think my favours can be bought for licorice drops?' she flirted in hushed tones.

'Can they?' He subtly backed her around the tree trunk.

Aurora's eyes fired at the tantalising banter. 'Kiss me and find out.'

This time his kiss took her lips, his tongue tangling slowly with hers, savouring the heat of her mouth, the sweet licorice on her breath. His hand slid behind her neck, cupping her head, the pad of his thumb stroking the curve of her jaw. His need for her spiked. He'd give anything for a bed to lay her down on and relieve them both of their heightened desire. Had it only been three days? It felt like an eternity since he'd bedded her. His body ached with deprived passion.

She moaned beneath his mouth, as frustrated as he by the futility of their situation. The tree might hide a stolen kiss, but Crispin knew better than to risk anything more, although all his instincts clamoured for him to pull up her skirts and take her.

Her hands were at his trousers. He covered them with his own. 'We must not risk it. Besides, we haven't found you a horse yet,' he joked in husky tones that indicated the solution was as unsatisfying to him as it was to her.

'I'll never get my reward at this rate,' Aurora grumbled good naturedly a few hours later. She'd found only one horse worthy of her academy by the middle of the afternoon, a sleek Hanoverian warmblood perfect for intermediate riders, but as they came up on the last roped-off section on the outskirts of the grounds Crispin heard Aurora suck in her breath and exclaim, 'That's the one!'

He followed her gaze to the knot of horses in the section and immediately knew the horse to which she referred. A chestnut stallion stood out from the rest, his mane braided tightly to show off his long neck. Even at a distance, the presence of thoroughbred blood was obvious in his lean body.

Aurora wasn't the only one drawn by the horse. A small group of people had gathered around. A few were asking questions about the other mares, all nice-looking horses with an air of above-average quality. Most were interested in the stallion.

Aurora broke from his side and shouldered her way to the front of the decidedly male crowd. Crispin uttered an oath under his breath and made his way forwards to Aurora's side in time to hear the owner say, 'Perhaps one of my mares would suit a lady such as yourself better. This stallion is a man's horse.'

Crispin stifled a groan. Aurora would not stand for that. True to form, Aurora's dark head shot up from her examination of the chestnut stallion. 'I assure you I'm man enough for the horse,' she said coldly.

'He's not for sale,' the owner said pointedly.

'Not for sale to me? Or to anyone?' Aurora queried, unwilling to be denied and far too savvy to be dismissed with such a comment. 'I rather doubt we're all assembled here to stare at a horse that is unavailable.'

Crispin fought the urge to intervene, but he'd learned the hard way what Aurora thought about chivalry. He might still have to step in, but not yet.

'Not to you. I don't sell to women,' the man said

bluntly, turning towards another interested customer. 'His dam is from a thoroughbred line and his sire is a Cleveland Bay. He's six years old, a good jumper.'

Not to be ignored, Aurora moved around to the horse's mouth and pulled back the horse's lips to see the teeth. 'Six, you say? More like eight,' she interjected into the conversation from which she'd been excluded.

The man whirled on her. 'Are you calling me a liar?' A hush fell over the gathered group.

'I'm merely calling you mistaken,' Aurora retorted boldly. 'It makes me wonder what else you have mistaken.'

Crispin put a warning hand on her arm. 'Aurora, please, have a care,' he murmured.

Someone moved towards them, parting the crowd, drawing Aurora's gaze. For a moment, Crispin thought he felt Aurora step closer to him.

'Miss Calhoun. Of course it is you causing this flurry of conflict.' The speaker who'd emerged from the crowd was a tall, slender man with fading brown hair and cold grey eyes that assessed Aurora with unswerving scrutiny.

'Windham,' Aurora said curtly.

'You must be Crispin Ramsden.' The man turned his attention to Crispin. 'I've heard a lot about you.'

'I cannot say the same for you.' Crispin met the man's icy glare evenly. Whoever this man was, he made Aurora uncomfortable.

'My daughter rides at Miss Calhoun's academy. Surely you're not thinking of purchasing this animal for your students to ride?' Disapproval was evident in his voice, his gaze returning to Aurora again with something akin to disdain. 'I must inform you that the horse is not for sale because I have already purchased it. I am merely here to pick the beast up.'

'How much was the horse?' Crispin asked the owner, who reluctantly named the price Windham had paid.

'I'll give you triple,' Crispin said confidently.

The crowd gasped.

Windham interrupted. 'The horse is sold, Lord Ramsden.'

But the owner was greedy and Windham had already lost. 'I'm sorry, sir, the price has just gone up.'

The little knot of people murmured over the exchange and began to drift away, sensing the excitement was over. Windham fixed his anger on Aurora. 'I hope my daughter is not being treated to unladylike displays during lessons such as the one I witnessed back there.'

The man's eyes could freeze hell, Crispin thought wryly, treating Windham to an assessment of his own and finding him lacking in any personal warmth. Beside him, Aurora did not back down to the none-too-subtle scolding. 'I assure you, Mr Windham, your daughter is not being "treated" to anything unfit for her,' Aurora answered squarely, but Crispin had to stifle a chuckle. He was quite sure Aurora spoke the truth and even more certain that Mr Windham and Aurora would absolutely disagree on what exactly constituted 'unfit' for Eleanor.

Her sharp answer earned a flicker of surprise in Windham's grey eyes. 'Well, I should hope so.' It sounded as if he held little hope at all of that being the case.

Crispin made arrangements with the horse trader and turned to go. Windham still lingered, his hand reaching out to grab Crispin's arm as he passed. Crispin tensed and shot the man a pointed look. 'Take your hand off me,' he growled.

'Pretty expensive ride you bought yourself. Hope it's worth it,' Windham spat derisively, his gaze flicking to Aurora. Not even the most forgiving of gentlemen could overlook his intended meaning. Crispin bristled, his fist tensing. If this hadn't been England, he would have gone for his knife already.

Peyton materialised beside him, a restraining hand on his shoulder. 'You forget yourself, Windham,' Peyton said with the steel command of a man long used to being obeyed. 'Cris, we need to go. Tessa and the others are waiting at the carriage.'

Gregory Windham clenched his fists in frustrated silence. How dare the earl intervene! How dare Dursley choose to champion the no-account Aurora Calhoun over a fellow gentleman. There they'd stood arrayed against him, Aurora between the two all-mighty lords with that haughty tilt of her chin, saying nothing while Dursley's rakehell brother simply outbid him on the horse.

Windham understood now there was a glaring oversight in his original plan. Provoking the villagers against Aurora Calhoun wasn't enough. Today's demonstration proved it. She didn't need the villagers to provide her with services. Anything she lacked, Ramsden would see that she had it. If he was to succeed, he needed to go directly to the parents of her students. He needed to ruin the riding academy by removing the students. Ramsden could do nothing about that.

Windham grimaced. When he was done with Aurora, he might go after Ramsden too and pay him back for his shabby treatment of a fellow gentleman today. This was far from over.

Chapter Eight

'You can't punch them all.' Aurora flopped down into one of her worn chairs, fixing Crispin with a stare. Dusk approached outside. Crispin had stayed after they returned to help her feed the horses for the evening and to make room for the big hunter to be delivered tomorrow.

He pulled off his boots and took the other chair. 'What is Windham to you, Aurora?'

'That's a cheap strategy, answering a question with a question,' Aurora commented, trying to divert the conversation.

'So is evasion,' Crispin replied. 'The man's dislike of you is palpable. I'm not convinced people randomly hate at that level of intensity without reason.'

Aurora drew a deep breath. The subject was deeply uncomfortable. 'He thought he fancied me. He asked me to be his mistress.' Gregory Windham was a man of intense extremes. Many people described his tendencies as merely puritanical. She'd go much further and describe them as cruel.

'You rejected him and he didn't take the notice well,'

Crispin surmised grimly. 'Could he be behind the occurrences in the stables?'

Aurora bit her lip. 'I hope not,' she said quietly. It was her greatest fear that the culprit was Windham. He was a formidable enemy, secretive and dangerous. There was no limit to the lengths he would go and she wasn't certain she could fight him under those circumstances. She suppressed a shudder.

'I didn't mean to bring up any unpleasantness,' Crispin said.

Aurora shrugged, wishing she could just as easily shrug off Gregory Windham's threatening presence. 'Thank you for what you did today. I will pay you for the horse.' It galled her that business had to be done that way, a man's way, but it had almost been worth it to see Crispin tread on Windham's arrogance.

Crispin grinned. 'Who says I'm giving him to you?'

'I do.' Aurora smiled, dispelling the gloom of the prior conversation.

Crispin held her gaze for a moment and Aurora could feel desire flickering to life in her core. It was positively unnerving to think he could stir her passion so thoroughly with a single look.

To her surprise he rose. 'I should be going. I'll be down in the morning. I confess to being eager to see what the big horse can do.'

Ah. The horse. Her surprise was replaced with understanding. He could not initiate love-making tonight without worrying that it might be seen as claiming his dues for payment on the hunter. The gallantry of his choice touched her unexpectedly.

Aurora stood and went to him. 'Don't you dare look at me like that, Crispin Ramsden, and think you can leave.' He couldn't initiate love-making, but she certainly could.

She ran a hand along his chest, watching his eyes darken with anticipation. 'Why don't you stay so you can be here when the horse arrives?'

She could see him struggle to hold on to his restraint and she enjoyed having the upper hand at the moment. She had no illusions about that lasting. 'Aurora, I didn't come here expecting to stay. I would not want you to think I had made such presumptions.' They both knew precisely which presumptions he meant.

'No expectations,' Aurora whispered huskily. 'This is not about owing, Crispin. This is about wanting.' She slipped her hand to his trousers, cupping him boldly through the cloth.

'No expectations,' Crispin repeated, his voice hoarse with mounting desire, although it was clear to both of them his body had plenty of those at the moment.

'No obligations.' She pressed her body against his, her hands grabbing his cravat and pulling him towards her.

'Surely we need one or two rules?' Crispin queried, his hands resting on her hips, his need to demonstrate a modicum of restraint satisfied and discarded now that they had reached an understanding.

She gave a seductive smile. 'You have to learn, Crispin Ramsden, when you're dealing with me, there are no rules.'

Crispin gave a throaty chuckle. 'Princess, what's the fun of that? Without rules there's nothing to break.'

Crispin woke in the night, instantly alert. Beside him, Aurora slept peacefully unaware, but years of military training taught him such a response could only mean one thing—an intruder. In immediate reaction, his hand crept over the edge of the bed to his boot. He deftly withdrew the thin blade from its hidden sheathe inside the leg of the boot and listened to the night sounds of the stable: the horses shifting in their sleep, hay rustling with their movements.

Perhaps the sound had been nothing more than a restless horse. Crispin strained to listen through the usual sounds of a stable at rest. Then he heard it: booted footsteps. Someone was in the stables.

The audacious bastard.

Crispin rolled out of bed in a fluid motion, blade at the ready, navigating the dark room from memory. He gained the corridor joining the stables to the apartments, flexed his hand around the hilt of his knife and advanced. Crispin entered the stables and made out the outline of a figure. 'Halt where you are and drop any weapon,' Crispin demanded in commanding tones.

The man took one look at Crispin in the dim light and bolted for the turn that lay between them and his freedom.

Crispin ran towards the intruder, racing to the only exit, but his speed was hindered by his bare feet. Still, at the turn, Crispin made a valiant effort and launched his body at the man. They both went down, but Crispin's hold was tenuous on the ankle he'd managed to grab. The intruder wiggled and scrambled like a man possessed, screaming at the top of his lungs in his attempt to wrest free of Crispin's hold. Fear can be a powerful ally at times and it gave the man an extra dose of strength. Crispin's hold on his foot slipped, the man yanked and scrabbled to his feet, running and stumbling the length of the stable, yelling all the while.

Crispin gave chase, but at the door he had to desist. Bare feet would be no match for the shod intruder over outdoor terrain. 'Dammit,' he swore, leaning against the door frame to catch his breath.

Lantern light fell over Crispin and he turned to find

Aurora standing in the middle of the aisle, a dressing robe hastily thrown on, her dark hair loose and tousled about her. 'Whoever that was, he was screaming like an Irish banshee.'

In spite of the circumstances, Aurora put a hand over her mouth and started to laugh, then raised her eyebrows. 'Oh, my, now I can see why.'

Crispin drew his brows together in consternation. Laughter seemed a highly inappropriate reaction to his efforts. He'd tried to stop an intruder for her after all.

Then he followed Aurora's gaze down his torso and realised what the intruder had seen. The hilarity of the situation was not lost on him. Crispin lowered his knife, relaxing his hand. 'Considering the circumstances, I'd scream too.' He grinned at Aurora. He was completely stark naked.

'He was nude! He had a knife and he was nude!' Ernie repeated for the countless time, shifting nervously from foot to foot, relating his horrific encounter with Crispin Ramsden the night before.

'So you've said.' Gregory Windham drummed his fingers anxiously on the scarred dining table in the private parlour he'd reserved at the village's Bull and Boar tavern. He listened impatiently to Ernie's garbled accounting of the bungled outing, keeping one eye on the clock. He was expecting important guests at three. Ernie needed to leave before they arrived.

Ernie was patently incompetent, but Mackey had declined to be involved in any further episodes at the Calhoun stables after Ramsden's arrival, citing some damnable ethics about breaking and entering. Ernie didn't suffer from any such malady, but Ernie was a fool.

'If you'd been caught, you could have jeopardised all

our plans. You must be more careful next time.' He slid two coins across the table to Ernie, who took them reluctantly.

'We agreed on more,' Ernie stammered.

Windham fixed Ernie with an unpleasant stare. 'I pay for success. Now go. I have other business to attend to.'

Ernie would still have his uses. Ernie would be the perfect scapegoat if anything went wrong. A slovenly man whom most villagers generally viewed as lazy, people would have no trouble believing the worst of him. It would be a simple matter to lay all the trouble at his doorstep if the need arose. Until then, Windham needed better henchmen.

It was just as well that he was about to marshal new troops to his cause this afternoon. These respected citizens would be henchmen and not even know he was using them for his personal gain.

The men arrived at three o'clock sharp, eager to fill their plates with Windham's largesse. A full buffet lay spread before them in the private parlour, bottles of wine neatly decanted at their tables. Windham had spared nothing in return for their attention.

Before today, these men knew each other by name only and only because they lived in the same area. After today, Windham would give them something more upon which to further their acquaintance. Their daughters and wives rode at Aurora Calhoun's riding academy for women. He wanted to put a stop to that. If he told these men what he knew, what he suspected and what he'd seen at the horse fair, Gregory Windham felt certain he'd achieve his goal. They would conclude as he had: a woman like Aurora Calhoun was dangerous and must be stopped.

'Gentleman,' he began once they'd helped themselves liberally to the wine, 'thank you for meeting with me. We do not know each other well, but we all have something in common. Our women ride at Miss Calhoun's stables and I think there are some concerns you need to know about if the women we care for are to continue associating with Miss Calhoun in that venue.' He watched the men exchange looks. One or two heads nodded. Gratified, he continued. 'There are rumours that the women wear trousers to ride, and that they practise riding astride.

'Now, I am not one to put too much credence into fantastical gossip, but neither am I one to overlook reality when it slaps me in the face. Miss Calhoun makes a regular practice of wearing trousers herself. She rides astride in public places. Based on these displays, it is difficult to believe there isn't any truth to those rumours.' There was an outbreak of murmured agreement and vigorous head nodding. Gregory Windham put up a hand to forestall comment just yet. He had more he wanted to say.

'I might not even be worried about such riding practices if they were limited to the stables,' he said with a feigned amount of magnanimity. 'What worries me most is how these behaviours are spilling over into other practices that extend beyond the stables.' He went on to recount Aurora's confrontation with the horse trader. 'I do not think this occurrence is an isolated incident. I think Aurora Calhoun not only acts like a man, I think she incites the girls at the riding academy to do likewise. My Eleanor, a quite biddable girl most of the time, has actually voiced her resistance to the match I've arranged with Baron Sedgwick. She's become uncontrollable these days and I can only attribute such behaviour to Miss Calhoun.'

Mr Twillinger, an older man in his fifties, spoke up. 'I've recently re-married—a man must have his heir, you know. I'm not getting any younger and I want a son to leave the business to, but my wife has other ideas. She wants to travel and spend time in London. She's young and I expect a little flightiness from her until she learns her place, but egads, she wants to look at my ledgers and help with the finances! I have to draw the line somewhere.'

Gregory Windham nodded his sympathies. Alfred Sykes and Latimer Osborne spoke up, voicing similar thoughts about their daughters.

'I do not think we're alone, gentlemen,' Gregory put in when the men had a chance to share their own misgivings, adding fuel to his carefully stoked fire. 'I've discovered there are tradesmen in town, like Mackey the blacksmith, who are uncomfortable doing business with Miss Calhoun.'

'What shall we do?' Alfred Sykes asked.

'It's very simple. We pull our daughters and wives out of the riding academy. Miss Calhoun cannot spread her poorly conceived ideas about women's entitlement if there's no one to listen.'

There was a thoughtful pause and Gregory held his breath. Then Mr Twillinger, the businessman of the group, nodded his agreement.

'I like it. Straightforward, but effective. Although, for it to work, we've all got to do it. It's got to be like an embargo. It won't work if only a few drop out.'

'We've got to be subtle,' Mr Sykes put in. 'We should pull out gradually so that it's not obvious. We need to avoid offending Dursley.'

'If we're successful, we might not only shut down the academy, we might even run her out of business.' Mr Twillinger rubbed his hands together.

'And good riddance that will be.' Windham nodded with puritanical solemnity. He'd worked diligently over the years to secure the family wealth. His credo had always been 'do it to them before they do it to you', and that was precisely what he intended to do to Aurora Calhoun.

He'd worked too hard arranging a marriage for his daughter that finally catapulted him into the ranks of the peerage. An upstart female with odd notions of feminine propriety would not ruin his plans now. The strategies he and the men devised tonight would be the next step. He thought about the inquiries he'd sent off after Mackey's run in with Ramsden's fist and a thin smile spread across his usually dour face. Soon, he'd know all Miss Calhoun's secrets.

Chapter Nine

It was happening again. Aurora set aside the tack she was repairing and sank down on the hard wooden bench in the tack room, her mind still on the break-in. Nothing had been taken or damaged as far as she could tell, but her sixth sense suggested something had happened. She just didn't know what. Something, somewhere in the stable, had been jeopardised.

All for the sake of getting to her. Aurora put her head in her hands. The last two days had been quite taxing. She and Crispin had spent the day after the break-in sorting through the tack and saddles looking for potentially damaged pieces. Nothing had turned up so far. Crispin must have caught him almost immediately.

That raised another concern. Crispin had awakened, but she hadn't, not until the intruder had started his unholy caterwauling. It galled Aurora to think she would have slept through all of it. If she'd been alone, would she have awakened in time or would she have discovered the treachery only after it was too late? If she'd been alone, would she have had the strength to subdue the attacker?

She liked to think she'd slept so deeply because of the rather vigorous 'activities' she and Crispin had engaged in beforehand, but even that road wasn't safe to travel. If that was the reason, then Crispin was definitely becoming a distraction she could ill afford, especially if it put the very safety of her horses and students in question.

The only bright spot during the last two days was the arrival of the two new horses. She and Crispin had put them through their paces in the arena and managed to take them out on a cross country ride. The big Cleveland Bay and the Hanoverian warmblood had proven to be worthy additions. Even now, she smiled at the memory of the wind in their faces, racing across the fields, jumping stone fences and tumbled-down portions of walls. The impromptu steeplechase and what had followed afterwards beneath a wide-spreading oak tree had both been exhilarating.

She and Crispin. That phrase had cropped up in her thinking quite often since his arrival. She really needed to do better. There was no such thing as she and Crispin. She did herself no great service in pretending there was. It would be too easy to think she could lay her burdens on his broad shoulders. He'd been there when the intruder struck purely by luck. She could not assume he'd be around for ever. Indeed, he'd made it clear he did not intend to be around more than a few months, let alone for ever. He would go and she would be left on her own to fight her own battles alone. Again. *The way she liked it.*

Aurora set aside the broken bridle pieces. She'd fought this battle before on her own. This would not be the last time. It would happen again and again until men were no longer threatened by a woman's abilities, but this time it would be different. This time, they wouldn't run her out. She had her own land now, her own stables. True, Dursley held the lease, but there was protection in that. This time she wasn't an itinerant instructor relying on others' land and horses for her lessons. This time, men might forbid their daughters from practising with her, but she had other outlets now. She could breed horses, sell horses, train horses. Oh, yes, this time, thanks to the backing of Tessa and Peyton, it would be different. No one would be able to push her out, to erase her presence. They would have to acknowledge her existence and her ideas. This time, she simply wasn't going to go away.

Aurora clung to that bittersweet thought and headed to her apartment. It was time to get cleaned up for dinner. Tessa had invited her to Dursley Park for a quiet family evening. Of course, it wouldn't truly be quiet, not with the twins around. None the less, the thought of being surrounded by Tessa's family brought a smile to her face and a flutter to her belly. Crispin was part of Tessa's family and Aurora had no reason to believe he wouldn't be there.

Aurora poured cold water into a basin and splashed her face, hoping to drive some common sense into her head. She had to stay focused where Crispin was concerned. He'd turned out to be far more dangerous than she'd imagined. Beneath his rugged exterior and his reputation as an adventurer, there'd been a gentleman. Not the kind of gentleman one was used to seeing, the kind that dressed up in fancy clothes and emasculated themselves with stiflingly proper manners, but a gentleman all the same. He'd stood up for her. At the horse fair, he'd treated her with all the respect due a lady and yet had left her breathless with the evidence of his desire in ways a gentleman seldom dared.

Aurora shivered, not so much from the cold washing water, but from the memory of his touch. At the horse fair, his light touches at her back, on her arm, his low voice murmuring at her ear, had all been intoxicating. In some ways, those caresses had been more provocative than the intimacies they'd already shared, recalling to her the possibilities of what could be.

What *could* there be? She strode to the trunk at the base of the bed and pulled out the gown of plum merino wool she saved for visits to Dursley Park. She dressed quickly, letting the pragmatic side of her mind cool her passions. Beyond the passions they'd already shared in bed, there was little else that could come of being Crispin Ramsden's lover. She'd known from the beginning there was nothing to expect other than mutual physical pleasure. What more did she think there was?

Aurora did up the tiny buttons that secured the high neck of the gown. It was easier to think there wasn't anything else when he'd merely been an adventurer, the type of man who loved and left when hearts were broken. She could understand that man. She didn't understand the man he'd revealed to her by accident or intention, the man who was both rogue and gentleman. Rogues didn't have expectations, but gentlemen did and that was far more hazardous than any trouble she could have foreseen the day he'd ridden into her life. In that regard, she could only disappoint him.

Crispin Ramsden did not disappoint, Aurora thought, sliding into the shadows of the hallway outside the Dursley nursery to watch the enchanting scene unfold. Inside the warm yellow room, Tessa's two little boys clung to the back of their 'pony', squealing loudly and often while Crispin 'cantered' about the nursery. Aurora put a hand to her mouth to stifle the laughter that bubbled up within her. Not laughter *at* Crispin, but a laughter that wanted to burst forth and join in the fun, a laugh of pure joy. However, she knew her presence would break the spell so she remained in the hall, watching.

'You're a better pony than Daddy,' Alexander exclaimed, tugging on a handful of Crispin's long hair. 'You have a mane.'

'Again! Again!' Nicholas yelled.

'I told you to cut that hair, Cris. Consider it penance,' Peyton ribbed from the rocker where he held the littlest Ramsden with the consummate ease of a loving father.

Crispin shot Peyton a long-suffering look and took off around the rug for another circuit, the boys yelling gleefully on his back. 'Who would have thought two year olds could wear one out so completely in such a short matter of time,' he complained playfully. It was clear to Aurora that he didn't begrudge the boys a minute of his time. He adored the little scamps and when they got older, she didn't doubt their uncle would show them a trick or two. *If he was around,* she silently amended. Peyton and Tessa had waited years for him to come home. Who knew how long he'd stay? Crispin had been plain spoken about the fact that he had yet to make up his mind about the property or how permanent his situation here would be.

Crispin collapsed on the floor and rolled the boys off him. 'The pony's tired. The pony needs to rest.'

'And boys need their supper if they want to grow up strong.' The nurse bustled forwards to gather up the boys.

This was the perfect time to announce her presence. Aurora moved from her dark alcove, but Crispin's words stopped her and she slid back into hiding.

'I envy them, Peyton. They've got a great father in

you.' Crispin stretched out on the floor, trying not to lie on top of soldiers and blocks.

'They've got two good uncles in you and Paine,' Peyton replied, shifting the baby to his other arm.

'That's amazing considering we didn't have much of a father to model ourselves after.' There was a mournful sarcasm to Crispin's tone.

Peyton gazed down at the baby boy in his arms. 'Tess says that loving isn't something you learn. She says it's something you feel. The longer I know her, the more I think she's right.'

Aurora shifted uncomfortably in her hiding place. The conversation was intensely private. She felt like a spy with her inadvertent eavesdropping. Crispin was such a complete man in and of himself that she had not stopped to ponder about his family beyond Peyton and Tessa. To hear him speak of his parents was deeply personal and, she sensed, quite rare. She should announce her presence, but her curiosity over what Crispin might reveal next kept her rooted in the hall. There would be no more disclosures.

At that moment the twins broke back into the room. 'Get up, horsey!' they yelled, mobbing Crispin on the floor. He promptly seized them and began a loud tickle-wrestling match that drowned out Tessa's arrival in the hall.

Aurora jumped at Tessa's light touch on her arm.

'I didn't mean to startle you,' Tessa said, following Aurora's gaze. 'Ah, that explains what you're doing out here.' She gave a low laugh. 'It always moves me to see Peyton with the children. It's a side of him no one gets to see but me.'

Light from the nursery illuminated Tessa's face. The love encased in that expression for Peyton was humbling. Aurora could not fathom the depth of trust, of respect that must flow between them for that much love to flourish. To open oneself up to such a possibility was to open oneself up to incredible risk, a risk she'd only taken once and for which she'd suffered greatly.

'Crispin is good with the boys,' Tessa continued. 'He's a natural father, only I suspect he doesn't know it yet. I hope time with the twins will help him recognise that side of his life while he's here. Peyton's greatest wish is for Crispin to take on Woodbrook and build a family there.'

It had been on the tip of Aurora's tongue to ask if that was also Crispin's wish, but the boys' squeals escalated and Tessa gathered up her skirts and waded into the fray.

'Oh, dear, boys, let your uncle come downstairs.'

Crispin looked up through the mess of hair hanging in his face. 'All right, you heard your mother.' Crispin sat back on his heels and set Alexander on his feet, smoothing down the boy's wrinkled smock. Aurora's throat knotted at the kindly gesture. She thought of Tessa's remarks. Crispin as a father? Why had she not seen it before? Of course Tessa was right. Crispin's patience with the horses, the way he doted on Sheikh, taking great pains to personally see to Sheikh's care, all spoke to the amount of devotion Crispin possessed—an amount of devotion he went to great lengths to hide. Aurora rather doubted overt devotion worked well in his occupation.

She felt his eyes move past Tessa and catch her staring. She blushed furiously, glad that the high neck of her gown served to hide a bit of the flush.

'Good evening, Aurora. You're just in time for the fun.' Crispin rose from the floor, his hands going to his hair in a hasty attempt to retie the leather thong that had come loose. He was dressed casually in a shirt, dark-blue waistcoat and breeches, having made no attempt to dress for dinner although Peyton had. Against Peyton's subtly polished veneer, Crispin was wildly handsome. Even Crispin's sensuality was bold. No one could look at him and doubt this man enjoyed bed sport or that he could deliver everything his wicked eyes blatantly promised, just as they were doing now at the sight of her.

Aurora's blush heated. Did he not have a care for others in the room? No one but Crispin would even contemplate seducing a dinner guest in the nursery beneath the watchful eyes of his brother. She shot him a look of censure for what little good it did. His hot, roaming gaze was giving notice, making her feel as if her wool gown was of the thinnest gauze. He wanted her and he intended to have her before the night was out.

Dinner was no better. Aurora tried to keep her mind on the excellent meal laid before her, but apparently no venue was sacred to Crispin when he had seduction on his mind. There was the usual assortment at the table—Petra and Thomas, Annie and Cousin Beth, Tessa and Peyton—but Crispin was heedless of their presence, or perhaps they were all incredibly naïve. Or perhaps she was incredibly randy.

'Aurora, is your mare in season?' Crispin asked from across the table where he was treating her to the spectacle of his hand absently caressing the stem of his wine glass.

Aurora choked on her wine. Why wasn't anyone else choking? She scanned the table, half-expecting Peyton to raise a scolding eyebrow. No one appeared the least bit shocked. Did no one see what he was really asking? 'I expect two of them to be in season soon.' Aurora held his gaze, determined to play his game to its fullest.

'There's only one I'm interested in,' Crispin replied easily, his foot suddenly rubbing against her ankle. Aurora stifled a jump. How would she explain to everyone why she'd suddenly leapt up from the table?

Petra innocently entered the conversation. 'Aurora's got a quarterhorse mare that would be excellent with Sheikh.'

Petra's comments were the perfect distraction. Aurora shot Crispin a wry grin. She could not sit there and let him get away with this one-sided game of his. Besides, games were more fun when shared. It was time to go on the offensive. Hands were off limits since they were across the table, but she had her feet and her mouth.

She caught Crispin's eye and took a bite of the succulent game hen, making sure to flick her tongue across her lips. During the fish course, she kicked off her slipper under the table and gave him a dose of his own medicine that turned his eyes to blue flame. While they waited for the fruit platter, she decided using hands wasn't a foregone conclusion after all. She just couldn't use them on him. She coyly toyed with the high buttons at the neck of her gown, absently unbuttoning and re-buttoning them. When the fruit platter came at the end of the meal, she bit into a huge strawberry and let the juice stain her lips before she licked it off.

As soon as it was decently permissible, Crispin pushed back his chair. 'If we're not standing on formality tonight, I'd like to take Aurora to the portrait gallery and show her a few of the ancestors.'

Even Aurora shot him an incredulous look. Had she really reduced him to such levels? Who would ever believe Crispin had suddenly developed a love of art? But Peyton merely nodded. 'I don't think you've ever seen the family paintings in all the time you've been here, Aurora. Be sure to see the one of our great-uncle and his stallion. You may have heard of him, he won a few races in his day.'

Crispin came around to her side of the table to escort her and Aurora had enough wit left to say, 'The stallion, Count Dashing? I do know him. He's the stuff of local legend.'

Crispin marched her out of the room, his hand on her back warm and firm, his voice taut with desire at her ear. 'You are a minx of the highest order.'

'Developed a penchant for portraits?' she teased sotto voce.

'Where else were we to go? I could hardly say I wanted to show you my bedroom. As for my penchants, my only penchant right now is getting you out of that dress and all those damned buttons.'

'Will that be before or after the portrait viewing?' Aurora was all coolness in response to his heated replies, sweeping into the darkened gallery ahead of him, enjoying his aroused discomfort for the moment.

'Shut up and kiss me,' Crispin growled, his mouth seizing hers with hungry force, his efforts backing her to the nearest wall. The wall was hard and unyielding against her back, much like the planes of Crispin's body pressed against her front. She welcomed the roughness of the moment, the claiming and spending of all the pent-up frustrations and desires. Had it only been two days since he'd been in her bed? It seemed an eternity. The games were finished. There was only the blunt honesty of their mutual need, hot and physical.

Crispin had her skirts up, his hand at the juncture of her thighs, searching, finding entrance. She bucked hard against his hand, instantly alight at his intimate touch, her need for him something wild and primal, threatening to rage out of control like some uncontainable fire. 'Don't make me wait, Crispin,' she sobbed, her hands frantically fumbling with the fastenings of his breeches. She wanted him hard and fast, deep inside her, but Crispin had other ideas.

He swept her up in his arms and carried her to the wide viewing bench set in front of a series of portraits. Skirts went up, trousers came down and he covered her completely with his length. She welcomed the heat and weight of him, all muscle and strength as she settled him between her legs. Aurora supposed the velvet of the bench cushions allowed a modicum of comfort, but in truth the feel of the fabric against her bared skin served to heighten her desire to a fever pitch. Crispin surged into her and she cried out, becoming living flame beneath him.

Such ecstasy should be illegal. She shut her eyes tight, attempting to find an anchor against the onslaught of his passion, suddenly aware that his passion could easily consume her, suddenly fearful that she would let it.

'Open your eyes, Aurora. There is nothing to fear here,' Crispin coaxed in husky tones, reading her mind far too easily for her sense of security. Then again he seemed to make a habit of it. 'I want to see your satisfaction in your eyes. Don't cheat me, Aurora.'

He thrust hard and her hips instinctively reared up to fully sheathe him. At the last moment, her eyes flew open, her body deciding against the wisdom coached by her mind as Crispin filled her with seed and pleasure.

In the aftermath of their passion, Crispin whispered temptingly, 'It is not enough to have you clandestinely in the dark, Aurora. Stay tonight.'

'Someone has to watch the stables,' she protested.

'I'll send men to watch the stables,' he countered

easily. 'Stay. I'll come to you, love you properly in a bed as you deserve and we can talk. We need to talk.' He kissed her deeply, his body moving against hers, an intoxicating form of persuasion. But there was no question of accepting.

How easy it would be to fall for the allure of his power. The world was his to command. If she let him, he could fix even the more complex issues that plagued her. As potent as the implicit offer was, Aurora knew she could not set aside her principles, not even for a night. Her answer was simple and immediate and difficult. 'No, Crispin.'

'You're stubborn,' Crispin growled, his body not ready to take no for an answer.

Aurora gently pushed at his chest and began to wriggle out from under him before she lost her resolve. 'It's not just the stables. I can't ask Tessa to countenance the nature of our relationship beneath her roof. She is a respectable woman, Crispin. After all she and the earl have done for me, I would not shame them.'

Crispin sat up on his knees, pushing his hair back from his face with a grin full of mischief. 'If you insist on us being respectable, you leave me no choice. I'll have to escort you home.'

Aurora tossed him a coy smile in return. 'I guess you will. You're quite the gentleman.' But she knew without words there'd be nothing 'respectable' about Crispin's idea of an 'escort' home.

Hours later, her gentlemanly escort lay beside her, breathing evenly in his sleep, an arm draped lightly about her hips, apparently not as disturbed by what transpired between them this evening as she was. They'd not got to the talking. She'd seen to that, sensing the impending hazards that surrounded such a conversation, but her strategy had not succeeded entirely.

She did not understand what had happened; only that something had changed. She'd understood the passion in the gallery when it began. It had been straightforward and honest; two people hungry for the pleasure the other's body could provide, but it hadn't ended that way.

Crispin had demanded a more personal connection right at the end, a look into her eyes, a look into her soul—albeit only a glimpse, but a look none the less. She feared relinquishing even the barest of peeps, dreading that it would become a slippery slope into revealing far more than she intended, far more than what was necessary between two people who were interested only in a short affair based on physical pleasure.

That was it.

She had her answer. In the morning she'd remind Crispin this, whatever *this* was between them, was only about sex. For reasons he need not be apprised of, that was all it could ever be. She had to say it first before he could talk about whatever it was he'd wanted to talk about last night.

Crispin's hand flexed gently around the curve of her hip and Aurora's hard-won contentment with her solution faded in the wake of another thought. What if she was wrong? What if there could be more? But she knew better, didn't she?

The temptation she'd felt in the gallery to give in to Crispin's strength and lay her problems on his shoulders surfaced again. Dangerous optimism rose in her mind...*maybe this time it would be different*. There was no reason to believe Crispin was another Jonathon, but he was a man and at their core weren't all men the same? She'd do better to stay her course and stand her principles than to go risking them on a man like Crispin Ramsden who'd been clear from the start that he was going to leave.

Chapter Ten

Aurora did everything she could the next morning to ensure that she maintained the advantage. She woke first and dressed quickly to avoid any temptation of a morning bedding. She busied herself with morning chores in the stable, forking hay for breakfast and organising the tack room.

All her planning was for naught. Crispin found her anyway, mucking out a stall. He grabbed a shovel and joined in, making it clear he would not be ignored. Good lord, the man was redoubtable. He stopped at nothing when he was on a mission. And he clearly was now.

'You left before we could talk.' Crispin tossed a shovelful of dirty straw into a big bucket set in the aisle.

'I didn't want to wake you.'

'Of course not. If you woke me, you'd have to talk to me,' Crispin snapped, flinging another shovelful with extreme vigour, confirming her earlier instincts. Crispin was turning out to be far more the gentleman than she'd counted on.

Aurora leaned on her shovel. She needed a get-away until his chivalric ardour cooled. 'I need to see to the horses. If you could finish here, I'll move on to Kildare's stall.'

'You're not leaving this stall until we talk,' Crispin said hotly, his frustration with her attempts at evasion obvious. But his demand sat poorly with her.

Aurora squared her shoulders and faced Crispin. 'Why are you doing this?'

'Doing what?' Crispin drawled.

Good lord, he was actually going to make her say it. 'Acting like a gentleman who has compromised a lady.' She blew out an exasperated sigh. 'It was just sex. I thought you understood that.'

Just sex? That was usually *his* line. Crispin took a moment to let the novelty of having his own words flung back at him wash over his brain. What a fine bit of irony this was: to finally meet a woman who wanted no claim on him and to discover that the arrangement was not wholly satisfying in that regard.

'Well, we've been having a lot of "just sex".' Crispin set aside his shovel and leaned against the stall wall, arms crossed, looking hard at Aurora. The interesting parallel between mucking out stalls and the nature of this conversation to 'muck out' their relationship was not lost on him.

'Very nice sex too,' Aurora said in clipped tones, implying that she felt it should stay that way too.

'That's not the point. The point is that we've not been taking any precautions.' He'd mentioned it before after the first time and had let it go with her hasty assurance that there'd be no risk, but that had been just the once. Odds were they were safe on that account. Since then, it had been significantly more than once. He was running out of fingers and toes.

'Ah, so you've turned out to be more like Peyton than I suspected,' Aurora said with a hint of sadness. Was that regret he saw momentarily in her eyes? It was there for a brief moment. Regret that he was like Peyton? Or something else?

He bristled a bit about the Peyton remark. Perhaps that's what she'd been angling for, something to start a fight with, to distract him from his purpose. 'There's no shame in being like Peyton. My brother is a very noble man,' Crispin said, but there was no fighting force to his statement. He would not quarrel over her supposed barb. He was certain now the comment was meant as a red herring. The regret he'd glimpsed was intended for something else.

Crispin redirected the conversation once again. 'We must face facts, Aurora. We have risked a child on more than one occasion.'

There was that soft sadness again in her tone when she answered. 'And if we have? What do you propose we do? Should we marry and make each other miserable for thirty or forty years, pretending we're something we're not?' She smiled gently at him to dull the underlying sharpness of her words. There was a quiet serenity to her beauty in that moment, a marked contrast to the Aurora he knew in trousers, who commanded every moment with her overt strength and tenacity. But this serenity had power too, the power of a woman who knew her level and was comfortable with it.

If worse came to worst, perhaps that would be enough for him. He shifted his stance against the wall, trying to fight the rising anxiety her words conjured in his mind.

'I can see it already.' Aurora picked up on the slight shift. 'Just the thought of marriage makes you edgy. You've got your back to the wall, figuratively and literally.' He couldn't deny there was a note of smugness when she spoke.

He'd conveniently pushed such thoughts away while he'd grappled with his duty. He'd always been so careful in the past, vowing to himself that a child would never suffer for his momentary pleasures. In that regard, he'd never be like his parents. But with Aurora he'd been careless, not once, but numerous times. He would not doom a child of his to bastard status no matter what it cost him.

Aurora began pacing slowly in the aisle. She shook her head. 'No, I will not let you torment yourself, Crispin. There is no need for concern. There won't be a child. Ever.' Her eyes were fixed on his face. He knew she was looking for his reaction, perhaps waiting for him to smile with unabashed relief.

Indeed, he should be *vastly* relieved. He waited for relief to surge through his body with its sudden burst of adrenalin. He'd escaped the parson's mousetrap, but he felt an inexplicable sadness far removed from what he'd expected to feel.

'Why?' he asked numbly, watching Aurora's pale face, noting how she fiddled idly with a halter left hanging on a peg outside the stall. Whatever she was going to tell him seemed to cost her greatly.

'I took a bad fall jumping several years ago.'

A terribly bad fall, Crispin thought, if it had left her insides so ruined.

'I'm sorry,' Crispin said simply. He'd seen bad falls, horrible riding accidents. He didn't need details to know all the nuances she referred to.

She shrugged, her gaze seemingly intent on the buckles of the halter. 'I'm not. It was a blessing in other ways. It showed me my worth and I saw the world for what it really is. Without the accident, I might never have understood my true strength.'

'So you left Ireland and came here?' Crispin risked, probing further.

'Yes, there was nothing left for me there. That's why it can only be just sex between us. Surely, some day you'll want sons of your own and a wife who can give them to you.'

Crispin chuckled. 'What would I want sons for? Peyton and Paine have supplied me with enough little boys to keep me more than busy.'

Aurora gave him a strong look. 'Men have a way of changing their minds about those things.'

'Has a man changed his mind about you?' Crispin said boldly. 'Is that where this concern comes from? Did a suitor jilt you?'

'Not a suitor, Crispin. A husband.' Aurora let the truth out. Perhaps such a truth was the only way to make him understand. 'Crispin, I'm divorced.

'Jonathon was the son of an Irish baron. He needed heirs.' She sat on the hay bale, Crispin hanging on every word.

'How does a groom's daughter come to marry a baron's son?'

'My mother was the daughter of an earl and, bastard or not, I could outride everyone in the county.' Aurora shrugged. 'I might have aimed higher than a baron if I'd been born on the right side of the blanket. Even so, Jonathon had dreams of building a renowned stud line from Darby.'

'So your horse became your dowry?'

'In a manner of speaking. My grandfather's connections and Darby's potential recommended me to Jonathon. His father hedged a bit in the beginning. He wanted something better for his heir. But Jonathon professed it was a love-match and practical too, once it was known my grandfather approved of the match. The two of us didn't care what anyone thought. We were quite blind to the realities surrounding us. We were in love.'

'You sound as if you doubt that.'

'We were young. He had turned twenty-two the spring we married. I was nineteen. We knew about passion. We sneaked off on our own every chance we got, but what did we know about love? Turns out we didn't know very much. I fell six months after the wedding and we were divorced six months after that. True love didn't last the year. Now, if you don't mind, I really must get busy. I've got lessons later today and I want to put Dandy through the jumping course again before they arrive.'

Crispin would not allow her to dismiss him. He did not want her to think she'd succeeded in scaring him off. There was no reason to be put off by her disclosure. He'd meant it when he said he did not plan on wanting a family of his own. 'I'd like to watch. Dandy is dragging his left leg over the jumps. He's bound to knock a pole off if we don't get his hind legs cleaned up,' Crispin said, knowing Aurora in all her astuteness would understand the implied message: he would not be frightened off that easily.

Some of the tension visibly went out of Aurora. It was a small note of satisfaction that she'd wanted him to stay in spite of her verbal efforts to the contrary.

She stepped towards him and kissed him on the cheek. 'We understand each other, then? Just sex?'

'Just sex,' Crispin affirmed.

'Promise?'

I promise.' *For now*, he amended silently, seized with

the childish urge to cross his fingers behind his back. There was more he wanted to ask, but he settled for the knowledge he learned today. He let her move on to another stall. He was beginning to understand what drove her to create limitations to their growing relationship. He wished he'd learned as much about himself.

He'd broached their discussion, hoping to be relieved of a burden he'd thought he wasn't ready to assume, only to discover he was disappointed to be relieved of it. Now he had no excuse to pursue something of a more permanent nature with Aurora. If he wanted something permanent, he had to own up to it himself. Is that what he wanted? He'd only known her a short time, but he could not imagine riding away from Dursley Park and leaving her behind not knowing when he'd return.

Would she go with him? She had her own place, her own business. She'd worked too hard to achieve those goals to simply throw them away and wander the globe. Could he stay for her? The property at Woodbrook seemed to offer a perfect solution. They could move her venue there. At Woodbrook they might stand a chance of being themselves. Goodness knew he was stuck with the place. The blasted entail was proving impossible to break.

Crispin laughed out loud in the empty stall. What was the matter with him? He was usually so decisive. What did he want? More importantly, could he trust himself with it if he reached out and grabbed it with both hands? He had not come home looking to fall in love, but he recognised the signs. Good God, if this was what falling in love did to a man, it was no wonder men fought it to the last. And yet, if a woman like Aurora Calhoun waited on the other side, it might be a fight worth losing.

* * *

Aurora reached out and seized the fence railing with both hands, fighting back her anger and frustration. She didn't dare give vent to it out here in the stable yard where everyone could see. Stoically, she watched Catherine Sykes's pony trap rumble down the road, carrying a tearful Catherine away from the riding lessons that had given the shy girl so much confidence.

Catherine had come early before the other girls arrived, accompanied by her father, and told Aurora she'd be discontinuing her lessons. It was time to go to London and prepare for her débút. Her parents wanted to go in advance of the rush and see her well settled before the true competition for husbands began.

The girl had trembled and valiantly fought her tears. Aurora had given her what encouragement she could with the girl's father standing there. She'd given Catherine's father the name of a riding instructor in London and told them they must call on the earl's aunt and Eva during the Season. Catherine must tell Eva she was a friend of Petra's. If anyone could get the lovely, but shy, Catherine Sykes to blossom, it would be Eva.

Aurora had said all the right things and meant them all sincerely. She'd known this moment would come. It had been Catherine's parents' plan all along to see their daughter launched in London. Catherine was of course very lucky to have parents with enough wealth to manage a London débút for their daughter, but she hadn't expected it to come so soon. Aurora thought she'd have Catherine for another month, maybe two. She'd never guessed they'd want to go early. From the looks of Catherine, pale and teary, Catherine had not guessed it either.

Something was afoot. Aurora watched Petra and

Eleanor stop in the drive and exchange a few words with Catherine. They'd driven over together in Peyton's old gig. They pulled into the stable yard. Eleanor went immediately to change while Petra jumped down and came to stand by her.

'Rory, Catherine says she's leaving for London,' Petra said quietly.

Aurora nodded.

'I was surprised they were going up so much earlier than planned,' Petra pressed. 'What do you make of it?'

Aurora just shook her head, not wanting to burden Petra. 'Her parents have her best interests in mind.' But silently she thought with a sinking feeling, 'I wonder who I will lose next?'

It was a good thing the St Albans steeplechase was only a few weeks away, the first part of March. Then it would be spring and she could turn her attentions to breeding one of her mares. Maybe Crispin could be coaxed to letting her use Sheikh for that purpose. Maybe it was even a good thing the students were starting to leave. She had no illusions that Catherine's departure was an isolated incident. Someone was encouraging the girls to withdraw. It had happened before too. First they left with legitimate-sounding excuses, then the excuses became more vague and far-fetched. If there were no students, perhaps the subtle and not-so-subtle attempts at sabotage would stop. The students would be beyond her abilities to influence. She could be left on her own with her horses.

Aurora tried to see the situation positively, but throughout lessons, she couldn't help but wonder who had betrayed the academy's secrets? Was Crispin right? Had it been one of the girls who unwittingly exposed the secrets?

She eliminated Petra immediately. Catherine Sykes was also an unlikely candidate for the dubious position. Letitia Osborne was a born gossip. It was possible the girl could have said too much at a church circle, but she doubted Letitia's gossip would have spurred anyone to the vandalism and damage that had taken place. Whoever was responsible for leaking the secrets had told someone who would have been appalled at the disclosure; *and* had the ability to organise this revenge.

She kept coming back to Eleanor Windham. She watched Eleanor take a clean jump over the modified brick wall in the arena. The girl had betrayed her not on purpose, she was sure, but it was likely the girl had been forced to it by her father, even threatened. Eleanor was being forced to marry Baron Sedgwick. It was not impossible that she'd been forced to spill the academy's few secrets. Who was there to help her? She and her father were the only ones beside staff who lived in the big manor house. Aurora was certain the staff were either blindly loyal to Windham or sufficiently cowed not to risk their positions by aiding Eleanor in any way. No, when Eleanor wasn't here at the stables, she was most assuredly on her own. Betrayer or not, Aurora's heart went out to her. Who knew what else the girl had been forced to endure?

'I will not endure silence from you, girl,' Gregory Windham fairly shouted down the long dinner table. The candlelight on his face made him look like a long-faced ghoul.

'My apologies,' Eleanor said stoically, keeping her features blank. She'd learned long ago hiding any emotion was the best way to avoid trouble with her father. She didn't need trouble now. She needed to convince him of her abject obedience. She needed to have the freedom to roam the estate if her plan was to succeed. Being confined to her room was not a setback she could afford. There were three months until the wedding, but she could not wait until the last minute.

'I just told you that lessons would have to cease at Miss Calhoun's,' her father repeated.

'Yes.'

'Don't you have an objection to that?' he baited dangerously.

Oh, she had objections all right, but to voice them would be folly. 'If you believe it to be best for me to leave the academy, then I will.'

'Would you like to know why?' he pressed and then went on, not waiting for an answer. 'I've received word today that she's Irish, half-Irish.' He spat the words with all the disdain he used for those who weren't English. 'And a divorcée, cast off by her husband as an unsuitable wife! No wonder, when she's carrying on with Crispin Ramsden without so much as a blush for her behaviour.'

It had been on the tip of Eleanor's tongue to say that Aurora believed a woman's prerogative was the same as a man's. And truly, who was she to blame? Crispin Ramsden was about the handsomest man Eleanor had ever seen. If he'd looked at her even once, she'd have been carrying on with him too. But all thoughts died and she answered her father evenly, 'That's despicable. Such licentious behaviour is not to be tolerated,' because that's exactly what her father wanted to hear.

Her father gave a cold smile. 'Always remember, my dear, that it's never too late to repent. Aurora Calhoun could be saved with the right discipline to show her the way.'

Eleanor shivered. She wondered if the community even guessed at the depths of her father's discipline. He might be the biggest supporter of the church. His money might have bought the bell, the new elegantly carved pulpit and the silver communion chalice, but she doubted the community would be so welcoming if they understood his perception of Christian justice.

She regretted ever telling him about the situation at the stables, although it had been inevitable. She was not so foolish as to lie to her father and to think she'd escape punishment. If Aurora ever found out, Eleanor prayed she'd understand. Aurora was strong and she had the Ramsdens in her corner. Eleanor hoped it would be enough to protect her.

Eleanor knew what she had to do for herself, to save herself from marriage to the corrupt Baron Sedgwick. She was not naïve enough to think the choice she made had consequences for herself alone. Aurora would bear the consequences too. Once she was gone, Aurora's stables would be the first place her father would go and there would be hell to pay.

Chapter Eleven

Dandy refused the jump for the fourth time. Aurora reined him sharply in a circle and turned him to try the approach again. It had been a terrible week. First Catherine Sykes had left. Then there'd been a letter waiting for her from Letitia Osborne's father, informing her that Letitia had been called away to nurse an ailing cousin. Now, Dandy balked at the simplest of jumps.

Crispin crossed the arena, taking Dandy's bridle in his hand. 'Easy, boy, what's going on this morning?' He ran a soothing hand down the horse's long face. 'He's definitely out of sorts.' Crispin had made it part of his morning habit to stay and watch her work out the new hunter after taking care of Sheikh. He knew Dandy as well as she did.

Crispin checked the horse's eyes and nose for any discharge. Finding none, he bent his ear to Dandy's belly, listening for any telltale signs of stomach trouble.

'Well?' Aurora asked, sharp in her impatience.

Crispin shook his head and moved to the horse's hindquarters. He ran an experienced hand down Dandy's left leg. Then the right and back to the left. 'Slide down, I think I have found something.'

Aurora didn't like the sound of that. She swiftly dismounted and bent down with Crispin. 'The left leg feels hot to me,' Crispin said. 'I'd bet he's got a bit of inflammation.'

Aurora felt the left leg and had to concur. The leg was warm to the touch. 'I checked him out this morning in the stable. There was no sign of this.'

Crispin nodded. 'It could be that the trotting and the warm up aggravated it. Let's get him back to the stables and get a poultice on it. Chances are a week of rest will clear this up.'

Aurora would normally agree. Horses got sore legs. It was not unusual. There were several common reasons for it: rocks in shoes, sharp debris in pastures, an overly strenuous workout. But none of those seemed to apply in Dandy's case. He'd only been out in the pasture for a few hours yesterday and she checked the pasture daily for any unwanted rubbish or potential danger.

They headed back to the stables. Crispin gathered liniment and bandages from the tack-room shelves. Aurora cross-tied Dandy in the aisle and took a moment to investigate Dandy's stall. Too many things had happened lately for her to dismiss Dandy's injury as a normal occurrence.

With a shovel, she sifted through the hay. She hadn't removed the old hay yet from yesterday. She'd planned to do it after Dandy's morning workout while he ate.

Something glinted in the straw. Aurora bent down to examine it. 'Crispin!'

'What is it?' He materialised almost instantly in the stall, kneeling down beside her.

'Glass. There was a sliver of glass in the hay.'

'Any idea how it got there? A broken lantern, perhaps?' Crispin suggested, but they both knew Aurora ran a strict, clean stable. It was unlikely a shard of glass would accidentally find its way into one of her stalls.

'Whoever did this did it when I left for dinner,' Aurora supplied, the next realisation following immediately on its heels. 'That means the stables are being watched.' Someone knew her comings and goings.

Aurora rose and left the stall. 'Let's get Dandy taken care of.' She drew a deep breath, fighting the tears that threatened. Doing something would help. If she could just concentrate on the task at hand, she could push away the horrors that threatened to overwhelm her. It was all suddenly too much—the effort to set the village against her, the students leaving, the attempt to hurt Dandy and possibly her. If they hadn't caught the injury when they had, she could have been thrown during practice.

Someone desperately wanted to strike out at her and they were willing to put horses and people in jeopardy to do it. If only she could prove that it was Windham! But evidence of his involvement had proven elusive.

Aurora held Dandy's halter while Crispin swabbed the back leg with liniment.

'Ah, I see it now. Here it is, come have a look, Aurora,' Crispin called. 'The lighting in the arena wasn't bright enough for me to see. There's a thin cut on the inside of the leg.'

Aurora moved to Crispin's side and examined the slender line nearly obscured by the hair on the leg until one really looked. She stood and sighed, returning to her position. 'It's never been this bad before.' Her voice was far shakier than she'd anticipated.

'What's never been this bad?' Crispin looked up briefly.

'Attempts to run me off.'

'Oh?' Crispin reached for a roll of bandages.

'Students have left before, a few townspeople have

made it socially difficult for me to do business, which resulted in me not being able to offer lessons, but no one has ever struck out so maliciously with attempts.' She tried a little humour. 'Usually the vicar visits and politely explains things to me long before it gets this far.'

Crispin didn't laugh. He held her gaze with his steady blue eyes, his mouth set in a grim line. 'Students have left here? I didn't know.' He firmly tied off the bandage and stood. 'Why didn't you tell me?'

'What would you have done? Some of them were bound to leave at the end of spring. They simply left earlier than expected.' Aurora set to shovelling clean hay, safe hay, into Dandy's empty stall. 'No one will admit it's for any other reason.'

'I would have liked to have known.'

'It's not your problem. It's mine. I'll be here long after you leave.'

'Who says I'm leaving?' Crispin took the shovel from her. 'Here, let me do that.'

'Are you staying? I had not heard.' An irrational bit of hope leapt in her. Had she misjudged that about him too? The adventurer had turned out to be a gentleman. What else might she have been wrong about? Was it too much to hope that he might be enough like Peyton to give up his wandering ways?

'I haven't decided. I just don't like others making my decision for me,' Crispin said tersely, shovelling the last of the hay into the stall.

If his words dashed her hopes, it was no more than she deserved, Aurora scolded herself. She knew better than to hope for such a thing. Staying would complicate things immensely.

For starters, it would violate the whole temporary premise of their relationship. He would be expected to marry and start a family regardless of what he attested to today. Even as a second son, he would need to look far beyond the likes of her as a suitable wife. She was another man's cast-off, an untitled Irish woman whose only recommendation in life was that she could sit a horse like no other.

She was certain it would be far worse to watch him move on to another woman under her very nose than it would be to kiss him goodbye and watch him ride out of her life, out of England off on another adventure. At least then she could console herself with her memories of their brief affair.

She cleared her throat, struggling to maintain her self-control. 'We'll need to watch for fever and signs of further infection.' She attempted to sound matter of fact.

She was usually not so maudlin. The morning had been full of unpleasant surprises, that was the only reason her thoughts were wandering so far afield.

'He'll be fine, Aurora. I think we caught it as soon as we could. This time next week, he'll be taking those jumps again,' Crispin reassured her. He looked past her towards the apartments. 'I could use some tea and toast and I think you could too. Breakfast seems to have passed us by.'

Perhaps breakfast was only Crispin's effort to keep her busy and her mind distracted from unpleasantness, but Aurora set to her task of heating water in the kettle and slicing bread, grateful for the activity. She could hear Crispin putting the medical supplies away in the tack room and fought against the comfort such an image invoked and the impossibility.

Crispin came in time to set out the plates and they assumed their usual positions across from each other at the little plank table. 'I'll set up a cot in the groom's room,' he said after a few bites.

'Why?' Aurora was entirely caught off guard. Admittedly, her brain wasn't functioning as it should this morning, but she couldn't work out why he'd do that.

'I'll sleep down here until the situation is resolved,' Crispin offered offhandedly.

'That's not necessary,' Aurora replied coolly. It was becoming too easy to rely on him, to take his presence for granted. It would be all that more difficult to give him up when the time came. 'Dandy will be fine, as you've said. I've nursed more than one horse through a sore leg.'

'That's not the situation I'm talking about, Aurora.' Crispin's tone was stern, his blue gaze steady and serious over the chipped mug of tea.

She tried a coy smile. 'I thought we'd resolved that situation earlier this morning.'

Crispin shook his head slowly. 'We did. I'm talking about the threats being made to your stables. I do not want you down here by yourself. You've deduced the stables are being watched. Perhaps my presence will prevent any further invasions.'

'I am capable of protecting my horses. Now that I know they're in jeopardy, I can be on better watch. You needn't go to such lengths,' Aurora argued. Having him underfoot every night would create an illusion of permanence on temporary conditions, a very potent and unrealistic combination.

Crispin laughed. 'You're the most stubborn woman I've ever met.'

'I prefer independent,' Aurora countered, a smile working its way to her lips against her will.

'Fine. Independent,' Crispin acceded. 'Independent or stubborn, either way, you're blind to the real concern. I am more concerned about your safety than the horses. Whoever is behind these attacks might try to harm you next once it's obvious that their efforts to run you off have failed.'

'I know how to use a gun.'

'Then that will make two of us in a fight,' Crispin said. 'Hopefully it won't come to that.' He set down his mug and rose. 'I have business of my own this afternoon, but I'll see you tonight.'

Aurora humphed. That was one way to win an argument—simply leave. She couldn't argue against an adversary who wasn't there, but in truth, she would be foolish to refuse his assistance. It had crossed her mind that the attacks were following a pattern of escalation, growing steadily more perilous. The organiser of these assaults was apparently not willing to stop until he attained his goal. If lesser methods of intimidation did not work, the signs seemed clear he would take greater measures. Today it had been Dandy, the horse Windham had lost at the fair. Tomorrow it could be Kildare. Windham meant to do well at St Albans and he understood Kildare posed a threat to that success. He also saw her as part of that threat.

If the ringleader was Gregory Windham, it was almost assured something more drastic would occur than Dandy's sore leg. Aurora shuddered to think what that might be. If she had to choose between facing Gregory Windham's perversities alone or suffering through the temptations presented by Crispin Ramsden's brand of chivalry, the choice was obvious.

'Windham is the obvious choice.' Crispin walked with Peyton in the long portrait gallery of Dursley Hall's main wing.

'So you know about Aurora and Windham?' Peyton asked casually, stopping to take in the portrait of a young Lily Ramsden, his father's sister.

'She told me after the episode at the horse fair.' Crispin smiled at the portrait. 'Do you think Aunt Lily and Eva are doing well in London?'

'I'm certain they are, if Eva hasn't driven her batty yet with fittings at the dressmakers. I've never seen a girl love fabric like Eva.' Peyton chuckled. 'Tessa assures me it's quite natural though. Perhaps you'll look in on them while you're at St Albans? Tessa and I won't be going up to town until May for Eva's official début on account of the new baby.'

'Why would I be going to St Albans? As for London, May is too soon for my tastes. I was hoping to delay an appearance until the races started in earnest.' Even then, he'd hoped to get no closer to the Mayfair mansions than Newmarket.

Peyton gave him a quizzical glance. 'Forgive me, I assumed you'd be going to St Albans with Aurora in a couple of weeks for the steeplechase.'

'Why ever is she going up for that?' Crispin didn't bother to pretend he knew anything about it. What else had the minx elected to keep from him?

They kept moving down the line of pictures marking in paint the stamp of the Ramsdens in Cotswold history. 'I think she means to compete from what Tessa tells me.'

'She can't. Only men can enter,' Crispin shot back without thinking.

Peyton held his gaze. 'I don't believe that small distinction has ever stopped Aurora Calhoun in the past.'

Crispin recalled the intense workouts he'd witnessed on the big hunter, Kildare, whom only she rode. He highly doubted Aurora would let anyone else ride that horse. He was starting to see their first encounter in a new light. She'd been out practising cross country the day she'd nearly slammed into Sheikh on the Dursley Road.

They stopped again, this time in front of the portrait featuring Count Dashing. 'Did you show her this one?' Peyton inquired obliquely.

'Ahem. No,' Crispin said sharply, wondering how his brother had managed to get the conversation so far from his original intent. 'As I was saying earlier, Windham is the most likely culprit behind the attacks.'

'You're most likely right,' Peyton averred. 'I am sure you know by now that he'd asked Aurora to be his mistress. He was distraught to say the least when Aurora jilted him. The man went a little crazy in my estimation. A distasteful business all around.'

'That's what bothers me,' Crispin replied. 'Windham doesn't seem like a man who'd ever seek out a woman of Aurora's background. She's—well, to put it bluntly, she's too wild. Not his type at all.'

Peyton faced the portrait of Count Dashing. 'Windham likes to tame wild things. You should visit his stables some time and see how it is. I suspect the very characteristic you mentioned is the reason he was attracted to Aurora.'

Crispin read a wealth of meaning behind Peyton's careful words and bland expression. He'd known men like Windham before—cruel, with a hidden sadistic streak that ran deep, thoroughly corrupting those it came in contact with.

'It occurs to me that I should pay Windham a call,' Crispin said at length.

'That might be a good idea. He'll be going to St Albans at any rate. He and Baron Sedgwick have plans to make a name for themselves. They have a silent share in one of the horses racing. The Flyer, I think the horse is called. He's owned by a Mr Weston. A strong goer, from what I hear, but not the favourite. Still, I think

Windham believes the horse could finish in the top three or better.'

'Aurora's Irish jumper would put that notion at risk,' Crispin said slowly, a variety of scenarios suggesting themselves all at once in his mind. 'This puts an entirely different construction on Windham's motives.' Crispin had seen Aurora's carefully trained horse and he'd seen Aurora's unique skill. Woman or not, he had no doubts that she would be a top-level competitor. Windham had more reasons to see her out of the way than merely being a wounded suitor.

It explained the dangerous levels he was willing to go to and it confirmed that those dangers had not yet reached their zenith. More importantly, it confirmed he'd been right in his supposition that Aurora would be the next target.

'I'm going to see Windham this afternoon.' Crispin did not want to hesitate now that he saw the game in its full scope.

Peyton nodded. 'Do me a favour, the gypsies have arrived. They're camped on the western corner of the land. Stop in and welcome them. I haven't been able to get out and do it myself.'

Crispin smiled. For seventeen years, ever since Peyton had taken over the title, gypsies had been welcome on Dursley land, their presence livening up the drab end of winter. 'I'd be glad to.'

'And one more thing, Cris—don't punch Windham. At least not yet.'

Chapter Twelve

Crispin had long recognised that horses spoke to you in their own language if you took time to listen. He'd also learned that how a man took care of his horses was a fair measure of his merit. Both of those items were in abundant evidence at Gregory's Windham's stables.

The stables were immaculate with an aura of almost unbelievable sterility, but that did not make the stables a horse-friendly place. The head groom was a strict, dour man who ruled everyone and everything with the power of a whip, which he was wielding with great liberty in the paddock upon Crispin's arrival. Sheikh threw up his head, immediately sensing the underlying evil of the place.

'Shh, boy,' Crispin crooned, recognising the necessity of getting Sheikh away from the setting. He caught a young stable boy by the arm. 'Watch my horse. Take him out into that quiet pasture over there and let him graze.' He flipped the boy a gold coin that widened the boy's eyes considerably. 'I'll explain to your master what I instructed you to do.'

With Sheikh taken care of, Crispin headed back to the

paddock where the grey stallion was still getting the better of the head groom and his lunge whip, but not for much longer. This had been a protracted fight from the look of the stallion. Foam flecked at his mouth and spotted his coat. There was a welt or two from the sharp-tipped whip and Crispin felt his anger rise at the obvious mistreatment of such a fine animal.

If it hadn't been for his promise to Peyton, he'd have stepped into the paddock and given the man a taste of his own medicine. It was a quick experiment to learn exactly how a lunge whip felt and the results were usually lasting. As it was, Crispin opted merely to voice his opinion. 'You might do better to coax him with an apple.'

The head groom turned to face him at the paddock railing, sniffing his disapproval of the stranger. 'An apple will teach him he's the master.'

'It will teach him that this is to be a partnership between horse and rider.' Crispin climbed the paddock railing without invitation and lightly vaulted to the ground. He reached into his pocket for the apple he always carried for Sheikh. 'Step back, please,' Crispin instructed.

He approached slowly, holding the apple out in front of him, talking softly and low the whole while. The stallion backed away instinctively, but Crispin stayed his course and continued to advance. When the stallion had nowhere else to retreat, he laid back his ears. Crispin kept up his low toned patter.

The horse began to trust him. Crispin nodded his head in encouragement when the ears relaxed. The horse's neck inched forwards towards the apple. Crispin took the last step and offered it in the flat of his palm. The horse lipped at the fruit cautiously. With his other hand Crispin stroked the horse's long neck, working his way to the horse's back. 'That's right, boy, don't be afraid. I won't hurt you,' he crooned. To the head groom's dismay, a few of the stable hands who'd stopped to watch gave a smattering of applause.

'It don't take much to bribe a horse with food. That's a cheap trick and a short fix,' the man growled from his post on the paddock fence.

Crispin shot the man a baleful look. He checked the bridle, dismayed by the damage the bit was doing to the horse's mouth. If that kept up, the horse would be ruined in short order and a ruined horse was often a mean horse, forced out of necessity to defend themselves. He checked the legs for other damage. Finding none, Crispin swung up gently on the horse's bare back.

At his weight, the stallion fought, but Crispin stayed him with the pressure of his thighs. After a few rambunctious circles, the stallion took his weight and presence. The stable master spat on the ground as Crispin rode the horse by in a steady trot. The others applauded again at the horsemanship on display.

'Hey, mister, need a job?' an onlooker called out in appreciation.

'You can have old Stanley's,' another called out to the chagrin of the head groom, who was apparently 'old Stanley'.

'He doesn't need a job,' a new voice called out. Crispin spied Gregory Windham hailing the group, crossing the yard in wide strides. 'That's Lord Crispin Ramsden,' he said casually, coming to lean on the fence. The man was very good at dissembling. If he didn't know better, Crispin would have thought the man was looking forward to this unexpected visit from a local friend. 'No doubt he's here to make a nuisance of himself in our stables.'

Crispin trotted the stallion over to Windham and slid

off the big grey's back. 'This could be an excellent horse if Stanley over there doesn't ruin his mouth first. You'd do better to use a snaffle bit on him for a while at least. I might tell him to lay off the whip a bit too.' He didn't expect his advice to make any difference. Still, for the horse's sake, he'd make the effort.

'Come to see the competition? Flyer doesn't board here,' Windham said in low tones, leading the way to the stables, away from the others at the paddock. Out of earshot of any unwanted listeners, all trace of friendship vanished. 'Miss Calhoun still thinks she can enter that hunter of hers in St Albans?'

'Still? You mean after your underhanded methods of seeing her bow out?'

'Now, see here, Ramsden, I haven't an inkling of what you're talking about.' Windham made a show of chagrin at the charges.

'No need to dissemble, Windham, I know all about you. The glass placed in Dandy's stall, the night-time visits to destroy bridles, the attempts to create an accident at Aurora's stables.'

Windham took a different tack. 'So she's duped you too.' Windham stopped and gave a pitying shake of his head. 'She wants to turn you against me because she doesn't want me to compete against her in London. Don't feel bad, she's quite a temptress. I was taken in once by her as well.' The man was a consummate liar. Another, less-experienced, soul might be taken in by his commiserating bonhomie, but Crispin had seen Windham's cold disregard at the horse fair and he could feel the man's vindictiveness permeate the stables. These horses lived under a reign of fear. Aurora had not misled him about Windham's true nature and what he required in his employees.

'Man to man, I must say she can be quite, ah, "compelling", if you know what I mean and I rather think you do.' Windham had the audacity to wink conspiratorially.

Crispin's rage boiled. How dare Windham stand there and suggest he'd shared intimacies with Aurora of which he'd never had a glimpse.

'All that dark hair of hers, those bedroom eyes begging for it. I don't think I've ever seen eyes so green before, green like the Irish land she comes from. I imagine…'

Windham didn't get to finish. Crispin shoved the man against the stable wall and held him there. 'I know what you really are. You're a piece of filth dressed up in fine gentleman's clothes and a criminal to boot. If anything goes wrong at the stables again, I'll personally come looking for you.'

'You can't prove it was me, Ramsden.' Windham's cold eyes blazed with naked hostility.

Crispin roughly released him, thoroughly regretting his promise to Peyton. 'I can try. Your minions will talk and in their eagerness to purchase their own freedom, they'll be more than happy to turn you in.'

'Perhaps you'll be happy to buy your own freedom with your silence when I'm done with you,' Windham snarled.

'Are you threatening me?' If this had been one of his 'diplomatic' missions in the uncharted areas of Macedonia, he'd have drawn his knife by now.

'Absolutely,' Windham snarled.

Crispin nodded his head. 'Then have a good day. I'll find my own way out.'

Crispin's mood improved greatly once he had swung up on Sheikh and headed to the gypsy camp where he was greeted warmly with kisses from the old women who had known him in his younger days when they'd first come to Dursley land.

'We will have music and dancing tonight,' the caravan leader, Tomaso, said. 'You must come.'

Crispin grinned. It struck him quite suddenly that he knew exactly what he and Aurora would do tonight. Gypsy fiddles would be just the thing to take her mind off her recent troubles. It also struck him that the gypsies might know of her. Surely she'd accompanied Peyton and Tessa to the gypsy camp in the last three years?

'Aurora Calhoun? The Irish girl with the horses?' Tomaso gave a wide smile. 'Do we know her? We brought her. She and the big horse of hers travelled with us for a spell before the countess decided to convince her to stay.'

That settled it. He would bring Aurora and they would dance under the stars and they would forget about Gregory Windham for a bit.

'The gypsies are here?' Aurora exclaimed over his news, a huge smile wreathing her face. 'That's better than anything I've heard today.'

Crispin would have thought he'd brought her a diamond bracelet. He couldn't imagine any woman in London reacting with such pleasure over a visit to a gypsy camp.

'Give me some time to wash up and change.' Aurora was suddenly a whirlwind of activity, slipping into the bedroom and shutting the partitioning curtain between them, but not before Crispin caught sight of the rather fancy green gown laid out on the bed.

'What's that thing on the bed?' he called. It looked very unlike anything Aurora would possess.

'Oh, that…' Aurora groaned from beyond the curtain. 'Tessa brought it down. It's for their ball.'

Crispin managed a groan of his own. He'd forgotten about it. 'That's not until later this spring, isn't it?' He remembered now Tessa mentioning something about a ball for Petra and Thomas.

'Yes, it's the first of April and I'll need time to alter the gown.' Aurora's voice was muffled in the cloth of her shirt. Crispin imagined her shirt sliding over her head, her slim torso, and the curve of her waist slowly coming into view as the shirt worked its way upward. His body stirred at such imaginings.

He'd slake those needs later. For now, he needed to subdue them. 'I'm going to check on Dandy one more time before we go and make sure the Dursley men are in place for the night,' he improvised swiftly, giving his body something else to do besides thinking of Aurora Calhoun naked behind the thin barrier of the curtain.

Aurora was waiting for him when he returned, clad in a multicoloured gypsy skirt and open-necked white blouse favoured by the Romany women. Her dark hair was loose down her back, falling in long inky waves. A bright green silk scarf was tied about her waist. The relief he'd acquired from checking on Dandy was short lived. God, she was beautiful. No London débutante could have looked finer in her silk gowns and jewels than Aurora did in her gypsy garb.

'My very own gypsy princess.' Crispin grinned appreciatively at her. 'The gypsies told me you travelled with them for a spell.'

She nodded. 'Safety in numbers.' She gave a wry smile. 'They were camped near the village I was working in at the time when it became apparent that the village felt they would be better off without me. The gypsies were kind enough to take me up with them. It was the fourth place in four years I'd been forced out of.'

Crispin shook his head. 'There will be none of that talk tonight. Tonight is for fun.' He waggled his dark brows playfully and was rewarded with Aurora's laugh.

'So it is,' she said, slipping her hand into his, looking up at him with dancing green eyes that tempted him beyond measure. She winked at him and he knew all thoughts of silk gowns and impending balls had fled her mind.

'What are we waiting for? Come on, let's go to a *real* party.'

They travelled in simple style, bareback on one of Aurora's sturdy geldings. The horse was strong and well trained, taking them both up for the short trip to the gypsy encampment. Aurora rode behind him, arms about his waist, her body pressed warm against his back, and he felt like a king with all the riches of the world laid at his feet. What more did a man need than a good horse, a beautiful woman and a knife in his boot just in case?

Dinner and darkness were in progress when they arrived, the bonfire sparking in the oncoming dusk with its orange flames. A great cheer went up and they were immediately surrounded by those happy to see them. Over the heads of the others, Crispin briefly caught sight of Aurora being bustled off to the women, exchanging kisses and hugs after a year apart. Tomaso swept Crispin into the group of men who were already busy talking and drinking, clucking disapprovingly over his attire. 'I have things that will fit. You cannot wear an Englishman's clothes tonight.'

Crispin easily slipped into the loose trousers and shirt worn by other men in camp, feeling a certain freedom come over him. He'd worn a variety of costumes during his time abroad; the flowing robes of the Bedouin in North Africa and the loose clothes of the Macedonians. It helped him understand the people he worked with better. He became them. Tonight was no different.

He tightened the wide sash at his waist and felt his gypsy soul awake, the part of him that begged release from the strictures of the English world. He had not realised how much he'd suppressed this feeling since his return home. It had been a simple matter to subdue it amid all the daily business of the Woodbrook entailment, the horses at the stables and, of course, Aurora.

Someone shoved a tankard of ale into his hand and he drank deeply, pushing the thoughts away. He didn't want to think that this was how it started—losing one's true self in the mundane worries of everyday living until one forgot who one's true self was altogether. Eventually there would be nothing to remember.

Dinner was ready to be served and they joined the women. His change of attire was met with hearty approval. 'Aurora, come feed your man,' one of them called out.

Aurora swayed through the crowd with a bowl of stew and a loaf of bread on a tray, fitting in effortlessly with the life of camp. How many women did he know that could do that? Would want to do that? Even the courageous Tessa, who'd lived most of her life in St Petersburg, Russia, had succumbed to the allure of a house of her own, a family and all the consequence Peyton's title afforded her. Of course, he knew Tessa loved his brother without question. Her marriage hadn't been driven by convenience, but still, Peyton hadn't asked her to travel the length of the globe with him, offering her no promise of stability.

Aurora found a blanket for them to settle on and eat. 'Everyone is doing well this year,' she said excitedly, sharing with him news of the friends they'd only just discovered they shared. She dribbled a bit of stew on her chin and Crispin reached to wipe it off with a faded cloth.

'Gypsy camp agrees with you.' He grinned at her obvious happiness.

Aurora tossed her head back and looked up at the night sky where early stars twinkled. 'What more does anyone need? If we could all leave each other alone to live our own lives, we could live simply.'

'You'd need your stables, surely,' Crispin probed delicately. His body tensed, waiting for her response, not realising until that moment how many hopes he'd hypothetically pinned on her answer.

Her gaze was still riveted on the spangled sky. 'I need my horses. They're portable,' she corrected.

'And the stable? What function does that serve?' Crispin dared, encouraged by her answer.

'It's my protection from the rules, from society. That's what I tell myself anyway. It makes me feel better, makes me believe in my own independence, but in truth, I know Peyton and Tessa are my protection. I only dared setting up the stables because Tessa could guarantee me some longevity. I understand my situation right now is unique in that respect. I do not expect to encounter it again should I ever leave here.'

'So you're here for the duration, then?' Crispin's spirits sank a bit.

'I don't think of anything in terms of for ever, Crispin.' She turned her eyes from the sky and met his gaze sharply. 'It's too hazardous to one's well being to think that way. It only leads to disappointment.'

'And yet you want to be acknowledged as a horse

breeder. Don't you need a stable to do that?' Crispin carefully dropped the information he'd learned from Peyton that afternoon. 'It's why you're going to St Albans, isn't it?'

That startled her. 'I only need my horses to be a breeder. It would be possible to hire on to someone's string without owning a stable.' She studied him. 'How did you know about St Albans?'

'Peyton mentioned it this afternoon,' Crispin said. He discreetly opted to keep his thoughts on her breeding ambitions to himself. Not many men would elect to hire a woman on their horse string, no matter what her breeding record was like, but perhaps he could help her with that. There were some men of power, rare as they were, who would make exception for a woman of skill, especially if she had the backing of an influential man. It was possible he could help her take the next precarious step in her dreams at St Albans, but first he had to convince her to let him come too.

'Peyton tells me you plan to enter the steeplechase at St Albans as a rider.'

'Yes. I want to show everyone the kind of horse I am capable of training. I'm the best rider to do that.' There was a hint of defiance to her tone.

If Peyton had hoped he would dissuade Aurora from that course of action, his brother would be disappointed. After his unsatisfying 'discussion' with Windham, Crispin could not in good conscience argue against her going. He would not unwittingly assist Windham in achieving his goal of having Aurora out of the way.

'When do we leave?'

Surprise registered on her lovely face. She'd been expecting a fight. 'We?'

'That's right—we. I am going too. I need to check in on Eva and Aunt Lily,' he glibly borrowed from Peyton.

'Then I suppose 'we' will leave the last week of February.' Aurora smiled. She stood and shook out her skirts. 'Now, "we" will dance.' She reached for his hand and pulled him up, leading him to a circle of dancers. The fiddles had started up and a round dance was underway, women dancing in a circle inside the ring of men.

Usually Crispin abhorred dancing, but this kind of dancing was different. It wasn't done in a ballroom to the synchronised organisation of an orchestra with expected patterns and rules. This kind of dancing was what man was born to do, wild and free under the sky and stars. This kind of dancing took his soul and loosed it. He gripped the shoulders of the men on either side of him as they executed something akin to a Cossack step.

Aurora was before him, her hips swaying, her feet moving in a rapid step, a tambourine someone had given her in her hand. The circles broke apart and she danced for him alone now, her eyes locked on his, her body proclaiming the lush promise of her passion in the undulating of her hips. She reminded him of the veiled houris he'd seen in the pasha's courts in Constantinople.

Then it was his turn, time for the men to dance for their women. How he danced; a sinuous masculine yet provocative set of moves he'd learned in the severe, stark regions of Macedonia, a dance the young men did to impress the village girls at the spring festivals. He'd originally learned it to please the villagers, but tonight, he felt the real message of the dance, of the wild turns and jumps designed to impress a woman with his strength and his prowess. Tonight, he was a man who wanted to prove himself to his woman.

His woman. Crispin spun with the other men, the

phrase pulsing through him with strength and power. His woman. Aurora had become his woman. He was going to St Albans to protect her, to assist her in her dreams. Not just ownership, but partnership. Windham would not lay a hand on her as long as he was capable of preventing it because she was his.

The realisation was as stunning as it was true. When had it happened? When had they moved from lonely strangers with separate plans merely looking for a temporary respite from their usual solitude to *this*? Perhaps this was what he'd been thinking this morning, only then he'd tried to couch his need in terms of responsibility. It hadn't worked because it hadn't made sense. But this made sense.

He collapsed, breathless from his efforts, at Aurora's feet.

'Your man dances well.' A woman laughed nearby Aurora. 'He must be a stallion in bed to dance so well.'

In the firelight, he saw Aurora blush becomingly.

His woman.

Her man.

Did Aurora recognise it too? The one thing that they'd not expected to happen had. No matter how much she protested it was all 'just sex', it wasn't, not any more—perhaps it never had been. They just hadn't seen it. If he had any reservations about whether or not he was falling in love, the evening seemed to have settled them. He was in love with Aurora Calhoun. Now, he needed to work out what to do about it. Until then, he could not declare his feelings without scaring her off.

Chapter Thirteen

Crispin's head lay in her lap, the firelight playing across the sharp planes of his face, his eyes laughing up at her while she ran her hands through his dark hair, ink black against the flames. 'I haven't danced like that for at least a year.'

'Tessa told me you abhorred dancing.' She had pulled most of his hair free in her stroking and it lay loose now, framing his face, adding to the wild handsomeness that defined him.

'It's true. I abhor *ballroom* dancing,' Crispin amended easily. 'But not this kind of dancing. This dancing is real, a true expression of feelings. It *means* something.'

What would he say if she pushed him? If she asked him what his dancing tonight meant? Would he be forced to mouth words he didn't mean or sentiments he didn't feel?

She opted to savour the moment for what it was and said nothing. What did she want to hear anyway? A lie? A promise that could not be kept? And for what purpose?

The dancing gave way to quieter entertainment. A

fiddle played a slow ballad and somewhere around the campfire a woman's voice took up the words of the song, a tune about young, unrequited love. The song was followed by another, wrapping the night in tranquil peace, lulling the audience towards sleep. Aurora felt herself start to drop off, her head falling forwards.

'Come on, sleepyhead, time for bed.' Crispin sat up and drew her to her feet. 'Tomaso says we can sleep in his *vardo* tonight.'

Tomaso's *vardo* held very little beyond a big box-framed bed and a large trunk for clothing, but the bed was all that mattered to Aurora. She undressed quickly, eager to be under the covers, more than a little self-conscious over the fact that she had nothing to sleep in and more than aware of Crispin's keen gaze following her every move.

It was silly really to feel such shyness now. They'd been naked together before, they'd explored each other's bodies in the dark, but never had it been so blatant. Now, the lamp was still lit and the heat of the moment had yet to come.

'You're staring,' Aurora commented, folding her skirt and laying it on top of Tomaso's scarred trunk.

'Do you mind?' Crispin was still clothed, having only managed to take off the soft shoes Tomaso had loaned him. He came up behind her, enveloping her completely with his body. His arms wrapped around her, gently cupping her breasts, his lips warm against her neck. 'You're beautiful and it struck me while you were undressing that I've yet to make a complete study of your body.'

The bed was behind them. He turned her towards it and smoothly lowered her. He followed her down, making no move to undress himself. Aurora watched him intently, waiting to see what he proposed, all her sleepiness evaporating in the wake of this new, slow seduction of his.

He started at her breasts, a warm hand on the flat of her stomach while his mouth suckled. She felt her need rise, her core running hot, but it would be a while yet before he gave her satisfaction. His mouth traced a path of kisses to her belly, his hands splayed on either side of her hips, kneading lightly. One of his hands stopped suddenly. His thumb retraced its path and she knew what he felt. He looked up at her, lifting his face from her stomach. 'The accident?' he asked quietly.

She nodded. The scar was eight years old and had faded considerably. It could still be felt from a certain angle and perhaps even seen with the right light, but she hadn't looked at it for years, hadn't consciously felt for it. In its time, the scar had been ugly, surrounded by puckered skin and swollen bruises. It had been repulsive. Once, she'd believed it would never heal. She hadn't been the only one who felt that way.

Crispin shifted his position, trying to make the scar out in the minimal light of the *vardo*.

'Don't, Crispin, it's of no account.' Aurora tensed, fighting the old sense of embarrassment. The scar was repugnant, it made her flawed. Jonathon had not been able to stand the sight of it.

'I've seen far uglier wounds,' Crispin cajoled, still fascinated with studying the area.

'I assure you it has taken a long time to get it looking this good.' Aurora rolled to the side, attempting to dislodge Crispin. This time he acceded.

He crawled back up to the pillow and stretched out beside her, drawing her against him, buttocks to chest, a safe harbour in the night. 'Tell me about the accident.'

'I told you already. I fell off a horse,' Aurora prevaricated.

'I want all the details.' He tenderly pushed aside a strand of her hair and nibbled idly at her ear.

'You don't want to know.'

'I do. I am tired of other people knowing more about you than your lover does.' His hand closed possessive and warm about her waist. Her lover. The words were delicious and perhaps this was one secret she didn't need to keep, at least not from him. In the dying light, she decided to take a chance.

'It was at a fall hunt, towards the end of the day. There were five of us who were feeling reckless and wanting to give our horses their heads. I was unduly proud of my horse, a big chestnut hunter named Darby.' She stopped here to gather her thoughts. As a rule, she didn't think of Darby if she could help it. She'd loved Darby. Together they'd been invincible. Everyone in the county admired Darby and it had been a point of pride to her and her father that she sat the mount so well.

'We decided to have an impromptu race on the way home, our own rough steeplechase. The first one home got to claim a forfeit from any of us.'

'For whatever reason, I was determined to win. Like a true steeplechase, there was no set course, only the goal of arriving at the finish first. I'd ridden these lands since I was old enough to take a pony out. I set out at a full gallop, cutting straight across country even though the direct path I'd chosen was littered with stone fences and country stiles. Most of the fences had low spots and I easily jumped them. Only one in our party dared to pursue my route. The others took their chances on easier ground. I led him a merry chase, but as we neared the end, I thought to pull away and I dared a high fence I knew his horse would not take. Darby had yet to be bested by any fence and I was confident all would be fine.

'Well, it wasn't.' Aurora shifted against Crispin, trying to subdue her rising emotions. 'Unbeknownst to me, the ground was grossly uneven on the other side. There was no way to plan for that landing. Darby cleared the fence barely, but he could not get his feet firmly on the ground. We went down and he rolled heavily on top of me.'

'You must have been terrified.' Crispin drew her tight against him, offering her the comfort of his body.

'I was unconscious. I'd hit my head upon landing. It was perhaps a blessing. The rider with me pulled me out from under Darby and got me home. The doctors say I was lucky my lungs weren't crushed or that a broken rib didn't puncture a lung or that I didn't suffer a hoof to the head. There were so many things that could have gone wrong if Darby had landed differently.' She paused and drew a deep breath. 'My da long thought it was Darby's last gift to me that he landed as he did, almost like he'd done his best to protect me.'

'When I could be moved, a month later, my da took me home to our place, but it didn't take me long to work out nothing was going to be the same again.'

Crispin's hands were absently moving in gentle circles on her abdomen. 'You're alive. You're riding. That in itself is an accomplishment. You didn't give up. I know plenty of men who wouldn't ride again after such an episode.' He paused. 'Is this why you want to ride at St Albans? To prove something to yourself?'

'I ride for the stables, to show people I can breed a champion,' she said staunchly, not wanting to admit that Crispin had hit the nail dangerously close to the head.

They lay quietly together. She could feel the rise and

fall of Crispin's breathing against her back. 'You know, Aurora, I have a scar too. Do you want to see it?'

She felt the warmth leave her back, felt the mattress ease as Crispin stood up, leaving her deprived of his presence. If anything could distract her from the maudlin thoughts her recollection had roused, it would be the sight of Crispin Ramsden taking off his clothes. She rolled over to face him, determined to take advantage of the light as he had.

Crispin drew the shirt over his head, revealing the muscled planes of his chest, the tapering waist with its sculpted abdomen, the dark arrow of hair tempting the eye to follow it down where it merged into the hidden confines of his trousers. He knew she was watching and he smiled wickedly, working the loose trousers with deliberate slowness.

'Where exactly is this scar at?' Aurora teased.

'You'll see.' He stepped out of the trousers and let them fall to the floor.

'No underwear?'

'No point in it. Just slows me down.' Crispin gave a throaty chuckle.

'Now about that scar?' Aurora said.

'Here, on my thigh.' Crispin presented her with an excellent side view of his well-sculpted buttocks.

She'd half-expected not to find anything, but he'd not teased her. A thin white line ran from his buttock around to his hip. 'That's a convenient scar to show the ladies,' she joked, reaching a hand out to trace it with a finger.

'Getting it wasn't convenient, I assure you. That's courtesy of a Turkish blade and being outnumbered three to one up in a mountain village near the old town of Negush.'

'I've never heard of it.' Aurora reached for his hands and drew him back down to the mattress.

'It doesn't matter.' Crispin came willingly. 'The point is, it's only a scar and I lived to tell about it. Just like you.'

It was on the tip of her tongue to say too bad everyone hadn't felt that way, but such a remark would invite more questions, questions she didn't want to answer, questions that would make no difference in the end except perhaps to ensure that there was an end to her and Crispin. Frankly, she'd rather forestall the inevitable for as long as she could.

'We've shown each other our scars, what should we do next?' She boldly wrapped her hand around his shaft, thumbing the sensitive head in a languorous caress that won her a growl of approval from Crispin.

With the morning came reality. The magic of the night spent under gypsy stars was gone. Crispin was dressed again in his regular clothes and she was anxious to get back to the stables. Dursley men had watched the premises while they'd been away, but she had horses to exercise and it was time to get ready for the trip to London. They said their goodbyes to the gypsies, thanked Tomaso for his *vardo* and set off on the gelding for home.

At the stable, Crispin busied himself with tasks for the horses, leading them out to the pasture, mucking out stalls.

'Do you mean to stay all day?' Aurora commented when it became apparent he had no intention of leaving.

Crispin leaned on a mucking shovel. 'I suppose I do. Sheikh needs a good ride. Perhaps you'd like to saddle up Kildare and join me.' He gestured towards the hunter she meant to take to St Albans.

The ride was a good idea, but she sensed he had

something more than a workout for the horses in mind. Her suspicions were borne out halfway through the ride when they drew up to the top of a hill, stopping to let the horses rest and take in the view.

'We should talk about St Albans,' he said without preamble.

'You don't have to come. You spoke in haste last night,' Aurora offered quickly.

'I mean to come. That's not what we need to talk about,' Crispin countered. 'You're mad to ride in the steeplechase. It's a gentlemen-only event. Even if you win you can't claim the prize. If you're discovered, you'll be disqualified.'

'I'll ride under an assumed name. I'll pass myself off as male. I'm tall enough and weight can be added to the saddle. I've done it before.'

Crispin shot her a quelling look before returning his gaze out over the rolling Cotswold hills. 'Why am I not surprised? Are there any rules you haven't broken?'

'I suppose there aren't. I'll be fine.' Aurora knew she had to tread carefully here. Crispin was getting possessive. She'd sensed last night that something had changed for him in their relationship in spite of his promises to the contrary.

Crispin shook his head. 'A local steeplechase or race day at a fair is one thing. Something as prominent as St Albans is very different. For one, Gregory Windham will be watching you. Surely he suspects you don't have a rider.'

'Perhaps I intend to hire one once we arrive,' she answered easily. 'There will be a lot of jockeys hoping for work.'

Crispin looked dubious. 'Windham's not stupid. He'll suspect something; to say nothing of the danger you are placing yourself in. What's to stop Windham from committing some nefarious act during the race? You can't really believe he'll play fairly once the race starts?'

No, she didn't believe that. Steeplechases were notorious for their 'anything goes' atmosphere. Most steeplechases didn't have any places set aside for spectator viewing except for the finish line. As a result there were plenty of places a rider would be unobserved. 'I'll be prepared. I can handle a gun if need be.'

'It's far too perilous of an undertaking, Aurora. Let me ride for you. Kildare's big enough to take my weight and there's still time for him and me to train together.'

Aurora studied the broad-shouldered man beside her. He refused to meet her eyes, keeping his gaze focused on the landscape before them. It was an impossible offer, but no less touching for its improbability.

'I'll consider it.' What else could she say?

Crispin gave her a brief nod that suggested he understood such an answer was the best he'd get for now.

'There, I think that's all of it.' Tessa folded the last garment and laid it in the full travelling trunk. She stepped back from their packing labours and smiled at Aurora. 'I envy you your adventure a little. I wish Peyton and I were going with you.'

'No you don't, Tess. You're not ready to leave the baby.' Aurora smiled at her friend's half truth.

Aurora looked around Tessa's rooms. The rooms were hers only nominally. Everyone knew she and Peyton shared a chamber. But the rooms had served as an excellent staging area for packing Aurora up for St Albans and they'd spent the last two days fitting an unbelievable amount of clothing into two travelling trunks.

'I still don't think I need all of this,' Aurora protested. She'd planned to take one small trunk with her riding clothes and equipment, but Tessa had been appalled. She had insisted on loading up a trunk with several carriage dresses, riding habits, afternoon gowns and even a ball gown.

'I hope it's enough.' Tessa studied the array of gowns carefully stowed in the trunk.

Aurora thought she must be joking. They'd only be gone two weeks total, but when she turned to tease her friend it was obvious Tessa was quite serious.

'I don't intend for this trip to get out of hand,' Aurora said solemnly. Even as she said the words, Aurora knew it was already so far out of her hands, out of her control and it had been since the moment Crispin declared he was going with her.

Now, instead of going alone with her anonymous horse, Aurora would be arriving amid what amounted to fanfare. She was travelling with all the prestige and comfort the Dursley name could marshal. She would arrive in the earl's big travelling coach with Lord Crispin Ramsden as her escort and Cousin Beth as her nominal chaperon (Peyton insisted on an outward show of propriety). Instead of wearing her old worn gowns and trousers, she'd be dressed in the height of fashion in Tessa's altered dresses. Instead of staying in one of the cheap coaching inns in St Albans, she'd be lodging at Coleman's Turf Hotel, sponsor of the steeplechase.

In the end, she'd acquiesced to their plans. How could she fight them all? There was only one decision left to make and she would put it off until the very last.

'Have you thought more about letting Crispin ride Kildare?' Tessa asked, straightening up the odds and ends left strewn about the room.

'It's my race. I can't let the Ramsden clan shoulder my entire burden.' Aurora tried to side-step a direct answer.

'They're a managing sort. When they aren't managing someone else, they're trying to manage each other,' Tessa said fondly.

Aurora didn't share Tessa's easy nature on the subject. 'I will not be managed. I cannot afford to be.'

Tessa stopped sorting the stockings they'd discarded earlier and faced Aurora with a stern look of authority. 'You're not going to want to hear this, but please listen to me. I know what you want. You want a world where women can be equal. I do too. The world is not a fair place. We're changing it for our daughters and their daughters to come, but, Rory, the world won't be changed by next week. You are practical about most things, so be practical about this. If you race and are discovered, you will not gain the acclaim you seek for your stables. You will get the exact opposite—scandal—and that scandal could ruin your chances permanently.' Tessa shook her head. 'You have a capable champion in Crispin. I don't understand why you hesitate. Set aside your stubborn pride, Aurora.'

'I've come too far to stumble now.'

'That's exactly my point,' Tessa said sharply. 'Letting Crispin ride doesn't detract from all you've accomplished. Let him be your partner in this.' She softened her tone. 'You don't have to decide tonight. Come, it's time for us to go to bed. You'll want a good sleep to start the journey tomorrow and Peyton and I want to be up to see you all off.'

Four days to St Albans, counting the one night in London. She would make her decision by the time they arrived, Aurora promised herself as she got ready for bed in a guest room at Dursley Park. She had four days to decide if she could trust another man with another of her most precious dreams.

Chapter Fourteen

Four days later, after an overnight stop in London to carry out Crispin's supposed duty to Eva and Aunt Lily, Aurora, Crispin and Cousin Beth approached the medieval marketing town of St Albans.

The town was a direct stop on the London Road and their journey had been punctuated by an increased amount of coach traffic. 'The town is all inns!' Aurora exclaimed, straining to take in the sights as their carriage passed through town.

'I've heard it mentioned that the town averages about sixty travelling coaches a day. When I made arrangements for rooms, I was told the town could accommodate up to one thousand lodgers,' Crispin supplied, taking a glance out his own window.

'Looks like they'll need all the rooms they can get. The streets are full.' She could hardly keep the excitement from her voice. St Albans was not an old race. It was only five years old, but the race had gained steadily in prestige as organised steeplechases gained popularity as a legitimate sport. Now, she was here, ready to prove herself and her horse. Kildare would have his chance to race in the most prestigious steeplechase currently run on English soil. Soon everyone would see the kind of horse she could train. Soon everyone would see what a woman was capable of doing. Soon, if all went well, the ghost of Darby and the accident that had irrevocably changed her life would be laid to rest.

The going through town was slow, the streets choked with pedestrians and other coaches, some passing through, but most of them arriving for the big event four days away. If it was this busy now, Aurora could imagine how congested it would be as the day of the race neared and was glad they'd arrived early.

Their coach passed the abbey church and the four-hundred-year-old clock tower, making its way to the other side of town and Coleman's Turf Hotel. The Turf Hotel was located on the far edge of town close to the heath known as Nomansland where much of the steeple-chase would take place. The hotel itself was a large, imposing, plain-fronted brick building that ran the length of a town street. Much of its size came from the result of its proprietor, Thomas Coleman, purchasing an adjacent house and turning it into stabling that held up to thirty horses.

The hotel was especially designed to cater to the horseman's needs. Not only was there stabling, there was an exercise yard for the horses as well. Dandy and Kildare and the carriage horses would be well taken care of during their stay. She could see why Crispin and Peyton insisted upon staying here instead of taking rooms at a smaller inn. The quality of care the animals would receive far surpassed anything a crowded coaching inn could offer.

Still, mixed with her excitement was a healthy amount of trepidation. Staying at the Turf Hotel meant staying in the centre of activity. She would be visible, doubly so since she'd be on Crispin's arm. He was not a man to be overlooked in a crowd.

Aurora scolded herself. These megrims were unworthy of her. She was being silly. She'd come here to be noticed, perhaps not as the woman on Crispin's arm, but none the less she'd not come to fade into obscurity. Being with Crispin would get her the notice she desired and the acceptance she might have struggled to gain otherwise.

Of course that acceptance would not be automatic. It hinged on two factors. First, Kildare had to place well. Second, the decision of a rider. She was no closer to that decision than she had been when she took her leave of Peyton and Tessa. Fortunately, Crispin had not pressed her for an answer. He'd been content to avoid that subject during the long hours of their journey.

The carriage pulled to a halt, waiting in line with other arrivals to unload new guests at the hotel. Aurora was glad for the last bit of respite the delay afforded her, one last chance to marshal her courage. She was not oblivious to the orchestrations going on around her. The campaign being waged on her behalf was becoming clear little by little. The fine address, the fine carriage, the fine clothes packed in her trunk—all attested to the fact that the Ramsdens had decided to promote her cause.

She shot a covert glance across the carriage where Crispin sat reading, oblivious to the thoughts running through her mind. This campaign was not Peyton's idea. He'd always been a quiet champion, counselling caution. She knew he supported Tessa and thus her indirectly, but he would not choose to proactively launch her in this manner. Left to his devices, Peyton would choose to be more minimal in his approach, starting small, confident of local success before laying siege to St Albans in such a public venue. No, this campaign on her behalf was being waged by Crispin.

'Why are you doing this?' Aurora queried.

Crispin looked over the pages of his book. 'Doing what? Reading? Most people read to pass the time on a long journey.'

Aurora kicked him playfully, earning a smile from Cousin Beth, who discreetly kept her eyes on her knitting. 'Don't be obtuse. I mean coming to St Albans and throwing your lot in with me.'

Crispin grinned. 'Because I like a challenge.' He shut his book with a resounding snap. 'It looks like we're here.' The carriage lurched forwards to a vacant spot in front of the hotel.

He jumped out the moment the carriage came to a halt and reached in to hand her down. 'Come on, Princess, let us take this town by storm.'

'By storm' was a gross understatement, Aurora decided as the days before the steeplechase slid by in a vibrant kaleidoscope of experiences. The hotel was finer than any she'd seen. The proprietor's reputation for fine organisation was quite accurate and extended beyond the stables. Each room had hot-and-cold water and the dining room served excellent meals with equally good wine. For the men there was a billiards parlour. For the ladies, the hotel provided maids to help with gowns and dressing.

Aurora protested that she didn't need the extravagance of a maid, but Crispin insisted, saying that such a luxury would be expected of a woman travelling under the Dursley aegis. The trunk full of gowns barely filled the dressing room assigned to her, but there they hung pretty and pressed under the care of a pert lady's maid named Polly, who turned her and Beth out to best advantage for the lavish meals served in the dining room.

Crispin had the room next to theirs, but Aurora already anticipated she'd be spending more time in his room. To her credit, Cousin Beth understood both her public and private role as chaperon and said nothing about the implicit arrangement. From the looks of the populace in town for the race, they wouldn't be the only ones reinventing the rules of propriety in the privacy of their own arrangement. It was clear that there were a wide variety of women and relationships present. Some men had brought wives, many had brought mistresses. This was a small town, after all, and the strictures of London did not apply for the duration of the event, but Crispin had smiled patiently at her and then gone about the arrangements in a manner that pleased him. That meant two rooms.

As for Crispin, he was proving to be at ease in their surroundings. They'd no sooner been seated in the hotel dining room for dinner the first night when they were approached by two old acquaintances of his.

'Ramsden, is that you?' Two gentlemen stopped at the table to shake hands with Crispin. 'How are you, Captain?'

Crispin stood up to greet them. 'Baring, Captain Fairlie, it's good to see you.'

Fairlie? The name caught Aurora's attention. One of the first things she'd done was to request a roster of the registered horses as soon as she'd unpacked. Captain Fairlie owned one of the horses who'd be racing, a mare named Norma.

'Allow me to introduce Miss Aurora Calhoun and Miss Beth Ramsden, my cousin.' Crispin gestured towards them both.

'Ah, you must be associated with the Calhoun

stables,' Mr Baring said. 'I saw your horse in the stalls, Pride of Kildare, is that right? Looks to be an excellent jumper, very powerful shoulders,' he complimented.

'Thank you. We are hoping he'll do well,' Aurora replied before turning her attention to Captain Fairlie. 'Your horse, Norma, is entered, I see. Are you riding her yourself?'

'No, I've managed to convince Captain Becher to ride her for me.'

'That will even the odds quicker than anything.' Crispin whistled in appreciation at the mention of the renowned steeplechaser. 'Becher is an outstanding rider.' He glanced over at Aurora. 'Fairlie here has his hackles up with the odds setters. He thinks Norma should be the favourite, but they've all decided Poet should have that honour on account of having won last year.'

'Well, we'll see what Poet can do this year. Jem Mason's not riding him this time.' Fairlie rubbed his hands together in anticipation. 'It's good to see you again, Ramsden, you've been gone a while. I'm sure we'll see you around the stables these next few days. We'll have a pint and catch up.' Fairlie and Baring nodded towards her. 'It's a pleasure to meet you, Miss Calhoun. Best of luck to your horse.'

They were the first of many guests to stop by their table. By the end of the evening, all of the entered racers had put in a brief appearance; John Elmore, the owner of Grimaldi, Mr Frith, Mr Weston, the major owner of The Flyer, Mr Bevans, Mr Parker, even Mr Anderson, The Poet's owner, passed by the table to number among the growing list of their acquaintances.

'*Captain* Ramsden, is it?' Aurora quizzed him when the tide of gentlemen seemed to have ebbed later in the evening. There was always a rash of "captains" at a steeplechase. Military men usually proved to be exceptional riders in the sport. But with Crispin, she suspected the title was more literal than figurative as it was in the case of Martin Becher. Becher's 'captaincy' came from heading up a local group of yeoman.

Crispin shrugged. 'Captain Lord Crispin Ramsden, technically, but that was ages ago, practically another lifetime. I was in the cavalry, I think I've told you that before. I was very young then.'

Aurora tossed him a small smile over her wine glass. 'Of course you were in the cavalry. The way you ride, I expect you could have routed the French all on your own.'

Crispin met her eyes steadily. 'I thank you for the compliment. It is the perfect segue to talk of other things. Dare I ask if you'll permit me to ride Kildare on your behalf?' His voice was low, not wanting to risk being overhead by nearby diners.

Aurora looked down at her plate, her hand idly playing with the stem of her glass. 'I have not decided.'

Crispin might have said more, but at that moment another old friend stopped by the table to greet him. The reprieve wouldn't last for ever.

Aurora watched Crispin talking with the newcomer and wondered why she prevaricated. If she rode, she risked everything if she was discovered. She didn't need to ride to accomplish her goal. She wanted the stables recognised, not be a topic of scandal. It had not escaped her attention that when Crispin had introduced her, the men had assumed she was perhaps a female relation attached to the stables. No one had assumed she owned the stables. They'd find out eventually. The vagueness would work for now, but how long did Crispin think they could keep up this ruse?

They finished the excellent meal of jugged hare and Crispin offered to walk outside with her after Cousin Beth returned to their rooms. Together, they strolled to the stables. The stalls were much quieter now. Only stable boys and grooms were about, settling the last of the horses for the evening. They found Dandy and Kildare housed next to each other and doing well in the new surroundings. Kildare nuzzled Aurora, looking for an apple. She rubbed his long face, gently stroking his white blaze.

'How long do you think we can fool them?' Aurora said quietly.

'Fool?' Crispin reached out to stroke Dandy's neck.

'I noticed at dinner that your introduction of me was rather vague.' She added quickly, 'I didn't mind. I understood the necessity for it, but if we're successful and they come to the stables for training, or for stud, they'll figure it out quickly enough.'

Crispin sighed beside her. 'There's ways to prolong it. Have you ever thought of creating a fictional head of the stables? Someone who's abroad and has left the stables in your capable hands?'

Aurora shook her head at that. 'I won't front a lie.'

'Perhaps there could be a real person who could stand as nominal head and who wouldn't interfere with your daily running of the whole enterprise,' Crispin continued, undaunted by her refusal.

'I don't know who that would be. I can't ask Peyton to do it.'

'No, not Peyton. He doesn't have the right sort of connections that would do you any good. You need a man with connections to the horse world.'

What she needed was a man like him. It had become apparent in numerous ways over the past four days that she needed him, not just as a presence in her bed, but as a presence in her life. He managed to succeed where no other man in her life had. He was her partner, not her guardian, not her protector.

He did not seek to take away her autonomy, but to assist her. Life with Crispin was easier than life had been alone. He did not ask her to lay her burden down, he merely asked her to share it. Did he recognise how potent his actions were? Was he aware of the temptation he created? Did such choices mean he'd decided to stay?

'Penny for your thoughts,' Crispin said. 'I can see your mind is whirling with plans.'

'Are you suggesting you might be the man to head the stables?' Aurora ventured, knowing he wouldn't guess the depth of courage it took to ask the simple question.

'I might be. What would you say to that?'

Could she ask him to stay without feeling that such a request was tantamount to trapping him? Until she had those answers, she could not be sure of her answer.

'You don't have to be alone any more.' Crispin reached for her, cupping her cheek with his hand. 'I'm here now.' He kissed her softly.

Yes, you're here now, she thought, giving herself over to the warmth of his kiss. And now would have to be enough.

They spent the next two days exercising the horses, taking turns riding Kildare over the heath in Nomansland in the early morning, studying the steeplechase. In reaction to the outcry the previous year over the lack of challenge in the jumps, this year's hurdles were much more challenging, too challenging in Aurora's opinion.

Her biggest concern was at the start, which featured a wide brook near the bridge at Colney Heath.

'Coleman should start on the other side,' Aurora said their second morning after Kildare had struggled with the brook, only truly clearing it after he'd been warm and in full stride.

'He means to start from the London-facing side.' Crispin shook his head. 'Perhaps if we look for a different approach,' he suggested.

'We've looked. The other riders have looked,' Aurora argued as two riders drew near to them. She recognised the horses as Mr Baring's Caliph and Mr Elmore's renowned grey, Grimaldi.

'Are you discussing that improbable brook?' Caliph's rider, a Mr Christian, said with obvious frustration.

'Yes, it's no good,' Crispin concurred. 'It's possible if we came at it from the other side, but the horses won't be warm enough to master the brook so early in the race with the way the course is laid out.'

'Well, come with us this afternoon and lend your voice,' Christian said. 'We're meeting with Coleman to go over final details. Perhaps if we're all of one mind, we'll be able to sway him.'

The afternoon meeting resulted in a successful verdict. Aurora felt an enormous relief when Crispin reported that Coleman finally relented and changed the direction of the start.

'I'm sorry you couldn't be there,' Crispin said after sharing his news. He was busy stripping off his cravat and shirt in preparation for a hot bath. 'I did nothing more than spout your wisdom.'

'Thank you.' The compliment mitigated her disappointment. It had galled her beyond the pale that she should be so completely shut out of a discussion that affected her so greatly. Instead of arguing on behalf of her horse's safety, she'd been relegated to a hotel room where she'd had to sit and chew her nails for two hours while men deliberated.

She had put the two hours to good use, however. She didn't lack for anything to think about. There was Crispin's tentative proposal about the stables, and the decision about Kildare to consider. Aurora raised the lace panel of the curtains gilding Crispin's front and centre hotel room that overlooked the busy street below. He had not failed her.

'While you were gone, I had time to think. I decided I would withdraw Kildare if the start was not changed,' she said quietly from the window.

'You wouldn't have been alone. I think Elmore might have withdrawn Grimaldi. The horse is getting too old to take chances,' Crispin affirmed, his voice coming in muffled tones from the bathing room.

Aurora could hear the running water splashing in the tub. The hot water had turned out to be an incredible luxury and a most-needed one after long hard hours in the saddle.

Aurora turned from the window in time to catch Crispin's return to the bedchamber unabashedly naked. 'Forgot my towel.' He held up the thick white towelling.

Good lord, he was a gorgeous man, so perfectly put together. She could hardly be blamed for staring. With those long legs and powerful thighs, he was Adonis and David all rolled into one.

'There's room for two in the tub.' Crispin grinned, divining her thoughts. 'Come on, I'll help you with your buttons.'

His hands were slow and warm at her back, taking their own time with each of the tiny buttons that ran the length of the bodice on her borrowed dove-grey afternoon gown, performing a little seduction of their own as Crispin went about his task.

'Why did you decide you'd pull Kildare out of the race?' Crispin whispered against her neck, another button falling loose.

'I've already lost one horse to foolishness. It seemed the height of folly to repeat such an error, especially when I could prevent it by simply pulling out.' She was nearly lost to his touch, but she couldn't give in yet. There were things that needed saying.

'You were thinking about Darby?' Crispin coaxed, pushing the gown from her shoulders, the buttons undone.

'It's hard not to think about Darby. Kildare is his brother,' she said, breathlessly. It was one of her last secrets. 'Kildare is younger, of course, but they share the same sire. He was two when I left Ireland with him.'

No wonder she was so damn determined to ride, Crispin thought, his hands ceasing their caress at the news. She might not admit it, but he could see how this was some kind of penance for failing in the past, some kind of catharsis. He understood what it cost her to consider withdrawing Kildare from the competition.

Aurora stepped out of her gown and shed her undergarments. 'The water's getting cold.'

They were getting pretty good at this particular dance, the one where someone said too much and they backed off by returning to practical conversation. He slid in first and helped her into the big tub, sitting her between his legs.

She leaned her head against his chest and moaned her delight at the hot water.

Crispin picked up a washcloth he'd dropped into the tub earlier. 'Shall I help you with your bath, madam?' he crooned against her ear.

'That promises to be very wicked.' She laughed, a low intimate chuckle for him alone. He felt his member rise and knew she felt it too.

'Perhaps after you help me with my bath, I'll help you with something else.'

Crispin ran the cloth over her breasts in a gentle, kneading caress and then lower between her legs, massaging her core decadently until she arched against him, finding her pleasure. He revelled in her pleasure. Never had a woman's pleasure been as satisfying to him as it was to watch Aurora and know he'd been the one to bring her such bliss. He loved her passion, he loved her body, how it ignited at his touch, how his ignited at her merest suggestion. Most of all, he feared he loved her.

Aurora rolled in his arms, splashing water over the sides of the tub. 'Your turn.' Her eyes were green fire, promising all nature of pleasurable wickedness.

'Hold on to the sides of the tub, I don't want you to drown,' she instructed, managing to straddle him in the confines of the bath.

He did as he was told. He needed his hands for balance against the slippery surface of the tub, but the inability to use his hands to touch Aurora, to palm those breasts that she boldly presented to him at eye level was an exquisite torture that heightened his already intense desire. She bore down upon him, sliding on to his shaft, using the water to ease her way.

He could not recall ever being taken in a tub before. Or, for that matter, ever really being taken, not fully, not completely in the way Aurora took him now, moving her hips in soft tormenting circles while he surged inside her. God, if men knew what riding astride could do for their love-making, they would ban habits and side-saddles immediately. Crispin arched into her. She slid her hands up his chest, thumbing his nipples with her nails until he groaned his ecstasy.

He wouldn't last much longer. She sensed his impending need to climax closing in on them. He would not be alone; her need was close too. At the last minute she leaned over him, taking his mouth in a bruising kiss while his desire claimed them both.

He was hard pressed to get out of the tub, let alone to get dressed for the formal dinner and dancing that would take place downstairs that evening in celebration of the race tomorrow. But he would be expected and most definitely missed.

Crispin managed to struggle into his clothes alone. Aurora had removed to her rooms. He could hear Polly, the maid, singing next door. He'd like to send Polly away and help Aurora with her *toilette* himself, but only a husband could claim such a position. A husband or a man of certain rights. Since Aurora was neither wife nor mistress, he could claim neither. It was unlikely to change. Neither of them were the marrying type and he would not demean her by asking her to be the latter. She was far too independent to be any man's mistress.

But their situation did not change the fact that he cared for her, deeply. Their arrangement had long since stopped being about 'just sex', no matter what she told herself. He finished dressing in black evening wear and went next door to fetch Aurora. It was time to go downstairs and endure the evening's festivities.

He was not ready for the woman who met him at the door. Aurora was stunning in a ball gown of pale rose satin, her dark hair piled high on her head and looped with pearls. She might have been gracing the finest London ballrooms.

She put out a hand and drew him inside. 'Come in for a minute.'

She fussed with his cravat, making unnecessary adjustments. 'I have something to say before we go down. I told you earlier that I'd decided to pull Kildare if the start wasn't changed.'

He nodded encouragingly, sensing how difficult this conversation was for her, but uncertain where she meant to go with it.

'I decided something else as well while you were gone this afternoon. I decided you should ride Kildare tomorrow.'

Chapter Fifteen

Did no one guess at the fiction Crispin Ramsden played out before them nightly? Gregory Windham scoffed in the shadows of the Turf Hotel ballroom. He watched Aurora waltz past in Ramsden's arms, Ramsden smiling down at her, laughing, totally enchanted with the whore in his arms. Admittedly, she was a fetching bit of temptation tonight in pale rose silk trimmed with dainty cream lace and matching silk ribbons. The temptation lay in the vision of happiness and innocence she presented. None of it was true, of course. He had the papers to prove it just waiting to be revealed. Whatever Ramsden had talked himself into believing regarding Aurora Calhoun's virtue, he would soon be disabused of it as publicly as Windham could manage.

As for Aurora, she'd get no better than she deserved. Unable to arrive until today himself, Windham had set his men to watching her progress from afar this week, watching her glide through society on Ramsden's arm, letting the magic of his name open doors for her. It was disgusting.

He saw the way Ramsden's coterie of friends, men

of some influence in the horse community, made exceptions for her, treated her as something of an equal. His men's reports were full of examples of her excellent riding in the practices and the remarks others had made about her sound horsemanship.

It galled Windham to think that while Ramsden's name had opened doors for her, she'd actually proven worthy of the respect accorded to her—or so those bloody sots thought. Windham doubted they'd feel so inclined once her plan to ride Kildare was exposed.

Unfortunately, there had been no signs that she intended to ride that big hunter of hers herself. He'd been certain she'd attempt some foolish disguise. That was when he'd planned to make his move. He'd uncover her deception and more, but so far, she was foiling his plans. However, she'd made no overtures to hire a jockey and now with the race scheduled for tomorrow, it was virtually too late. Did she mean to let Ramsden ride? Ramsden was in his element, surrounded by former acquaintances from his military days and his skill on horseback was commendable, on par with the renowned Captain Martin Becher himself.

Windham didn't want Crispin Ramsden to ride. Not only did his presence in the race diminish Flyer's chances to place well, but it took away an opportunity to place Aurora Calhoun in the eye of a reputation-ruining scandal. There was absolutely nothing illegal about Ramsden riding. He could hardly raise a hue and cry about a legally qualified rider. Men were supposed to ride in steeplechases. He couldn't bear the thought of Aurora coming out of this unscathed. With Ramsden aboard, her horse could likely win and he'd have no way to protest against such a legitimate win. Ramsden had to be removed and he would be, shortly.

The thought brought a cruel smile to Windham's lips.

An accident was already arranged. He was just waiting for Ramsden to spring the trap. An accident would serve both short-term goals and long-term. It would get Ramsden out of the race and it would suggest to Aurora that the man she cared about was not untouchable. What might Aurora pay to keep Ramsden safe? What might she do?

He felt the familiar tightening of his body in anticipation, his mind filling with images of a penitent Aurora on her knees, begging him as she should have begged him before. She should have been glad of his notice—jubilant, in fact. She was of no rank and Irish to boot. She was far beneath the notice of a man like him, a man with breeding and wealth, able to give her all she could want, all she could expect in return for the simple act of being his.

'I thought you didn't like ballroom dancing.' Aurora laughed up at Crispin, who gallantly navigated them through a lively gallop. She was thoroughly enjoying herself tonight. Now that the decision had been made, she felt an enormous burden removed from her shoulders.

Crispin grinned gamely. 'I don't like it, but that doesn't mean I'm not good at it.'

The night had a festive air to it. The lobby of the Turf Hotel had been transformed into a ballroom, the furniture pushed back for dancing and the dance floor was crowded with all those who'd come to St Albans for the races. The music ended and Crispin escorted her over to a group of people, acquaintances of his who'd now become acquaintances of hers over the days in town. Other women might dream of silk dresses and London balls, but this was all she'd ever dreamed of since she had left Ireland; acceptance among other horse enthusiasts. Crispin had given her that. Never mind that her presence at Crispin's side had ensured much of that acceptance. He'd paved the way most assuredly, but he'd done so in a manner that allowed her to speak her mind among his group of friends and his friends had not rejected that input.

Whether he knew it or not, he was slowly eroding her reasons for keeping her emotional distance from him. The biggest reason of all was simply that she refused to give a man control of her life. But clearly, Crispin had demonstrated he didn't want to dictate terms. The one time he'd tried to do so had merely been out of a sense of obligation. He wanted to be her partner in this venture. The very thought was as intoxicating as it was novel. She didn't want to contemplate how long that would last. She'd meant it at the gypsy camp when she'd told him she didn't believe in for ever.

Crispin leaned close to her ear. 'I'm going out to check on the horses. I'll be back in time for the next waltz.'

Aurora nodded and watched him go before turning her attention to a discussion of tomorrow's field of horses and whether or not last year's victor, The Poet, would be as competitive this year.

That discussion passed, the next dance passed. Crispin hadn't returned. Maybe he'd stopped to talk with a groom at the stables. Or worse. Maybe one of the horses had come down with something. That started the first wave of worries. Maybe something had happened to him. True, they'd not caught a glimpse of Gregory Windham all week, but he could have arrived undetected this afternoon or he could have been here all along and chosen to keep to himself, although she could hardly imagine Windham choosing such an option. The man was too status hungry to remain a wallflower.

'Miss Calhoun, is everything all right?' one of the young men with John Elmore's entourage inquired.

'I'm worried that Lord Ramsden hasn't come back.' She started moving towards the door before she'd even completed the sentence. The young man—Jeremy, she thought his name was—followed close behind, stopping to say a few words resulting in a small parade of men gathering behind her.

The stable area was empty, the stable boys and grooms having gone to their beds earlier in anticipation of the long day tomorrow. Aurora's concern rose. There was no one about whom Crispin might stop and talk with. If no one was about, it would be far easier to perpetrate a crime.

'Crispin!' Aurora called out into the stable at large. There was no immediate answer. She turned down the aisle where Kildare and Dandy were housed. She lifted up her skirts and barely refrained from breaking into a run. 'Crispin!' she called again. Did she imagine she heard a moan? Good lord, surely it wasn't coming from inside the stall where he could get kicked or stepped on by a thousand pounds of horseflesh?

Careless of the ball gown she wore, Aurora opened the stall door and stepped inside, slippers crackling on straw.

Her eyes adjusted to the darker interior and she found him at once propped against a wall, obviously injured. Kildare pranced nervously, keeping his distance from the faces that crowded the door of his stall.

'What happened?' Aurora knelt beside him, hands immediately searching his body for injury. She quickly undid his shirt, noting with quiet horror the bruising around his ribs. Out of the corner of her eye she noted Captain Becher had slid into the stall to quiet Kildare.

Crispin grasped her hands and managed hoarsely, 'Windham is here.'

'Did he do this to you?'

'Seven of his men did this.' Crispin winced as her hands ran over his ribs.

'I don't think anything's broken.' Aurora breathed a sigh of tentative relief. Bruised ribs were bad enough, but a broken rib could endanger a lung.

One of the men who'd followed Jeremy squatted down beside her and affirmed her assessment. 'He's bruised badly, though. He'll need to get those ribs wrapped.'

'How are your legs?' Aurora asked, fearing the men had tried to cripple his knees.

'My knees are all right.' Crispin grunted, struggling to rise. 'I'll be fine.' He was already chafing at being treated like an invalid, but he was clearly not fine. Two men helped him outside the stall. If he'd been fine, he would have dragged himself back to the ballroom. Aurora could see that he was pale, that it cost him a great effort to speak and that the blows to his ribs were causing him not only discomfort, but pain too.

'The horse is fine. I smelled his food, it's fine, too,' Becher said, stepping out behind them and dusting off his hands. 'Do we know who might be responsible for this?'

Crispin sank down on to a hay bale in the aisle. 'We have a good idea, but he owns a share in one of the horses racing and I hesitate to name names out of courtesy to the owner. I don't want a scandal to implicate the innocent.'

'Shh, don't talk so much,' Aurora admonished.

'I doubt he'll be a part-owner much longer,' someone said gruffly. 'This is not the behaviour of a gentleman. We'll handle it discreetly, non-violently, if you give us a name.'

Aurora could see Crispin thinking it over. After a moment he said, 'No. This is a personal affair and I'll handle it in a personal manner.'

'Are you certain? This attack cannot go unaddressed. This impedes Kildare's chances tomorrow,' Becher put in. 'Ramsden can't ride. It's out of the question with his ribs in this condition.'

Crispin protested. 'If they're wrapped tightly enough, I can do it.'

Becher turned a disbelieving gaze on him and shook his head. 'You're tough, but there is no way you can take those jumps safely. The impact of the landing alone would be enough to cause severe pain, to say nothing of the jarring speed of a canter over several miles.'

Crispin tried to rise. 'Miss Calhoun's horse deserves to race.'

'Race, yes, Ramsden, but not to risk serious injury. That's precisely what that horse will be risking with you on his back. You won't have all your abilities to guide him safely through the course,' Frith put in.

'There's no time to get another rider,' Crispin argued, his gaze flicking meaningfully towards her. Aurora read the message hidden there for her. This was her chance. She took the opening, praying that the entrée Crispin had helped her carve out this week would be enough.

'I'll ride,' she said firmly. 'It's my horse, after all.'

That silenced the group momentarily. A few exchanged looks. 'Well, I dare say Miss Calhoun could ride,' Captain Fairlie suggested in a hesitant drawl. 'We've all seen her during the workouts. She's as capable as you are on that horse, Ramsden.'

Aurora shot a sharp look at Crispin. He was nodding, the others were nodding as the suggestion took root. 'There's none better,' Crispin endorsed.

'Except for the obvious factor. She's a woman. It is distinctly illegal,' Frith pointed out.

'She'll have to ride as a man,' Baring said. 'We might all privately agree that she's capable, but the public won't understand.'

Frith spoke up again. 'Remember, the man who did this knows Crispin is hurt. He expects Kildare will be forced to withdraw. Will he expect Miss Calhoun is riding if the horse stays entered?'

Crispin shook his head. 'Whoever is behind this could not expose her without great expense to himself. He won't dare risk it. I'll make sure of it.'

It was all settled when the group finally managed to carry Crispin up to his rooms and wrap his ribs. Aurora would ride and Crispin's friends would see to all the necessary arrangements that would keep her and their little secret safe.

Aurora gingerly slid into bed next to Crispin, careful not to disturb his injuries. 'Why didn't you tell them it was Windham?' She asked the question that had been in the forefront of her mind since she'd found Crispin in the stall. She'd been entirely surprised when he'd chosen not to disclose the name.

'Lots of reasons.' Crispin shrugged in the darkness. 'For one, I didn't want to expose The Flyer. It's not their fault. Windham is acting entirely of his own accord and I didn't want them lumped in with his shenanigans. They're hurting for money; if they lose Windham's share right now, they'll be hard pressed to keep their stables. They shouldn't be punished for Windham's transgression. More importantly, I wanted to keep you safe, at least as safe as I can. If word got out tomorrow morning that Windham had attacked me or harmed Kildare, who knows what he might do in an attempt to save face. He would most certainly challenge the identity of Kildare's rider and if he were successful in his petition, we'd look as dishonourable as he does.'

'You were thinking fast. I would have blurted it out without a second thought.' What Crispin said made sense and she was grateful for his cool head.

'I had more time to filter the situation than you did,' Crispin remarked wryly. 'There's not much else to do in a stall with your ribs crushed. Between how to manage the attack and all the things I'd like to do to Windham when I get my hands on him, I was pretty busy.'

The last part got her attention. 'Crispin, what are you planning?' Caution infused her voice.

'Don't worry. I simply intend to extend some neighbourly goodwill towards Windham tomorrow. He'll have an excellent view of your victory tomorrow, sitting right next to me. I'll be keeping my friends close and my enemies closer and only he and I will know the difference between the two.'

'How do you think you'll manage that? You are hurt. You have to recognise you have some limitations right now. You can't go charging after Windham with your fists.'

'I have something better than fists in this case. I have information.'

Aurora sighed. The man was impossible, but he had her trust. If he said he could manage Windham long enough for her to ride, she believed him. 'I didn't want my dream to come true this way. I wouldn't have seen you hurt.'

'I'll be fine. Tomorrow, you'll be fine. You'll have to add weights to your saddle to make the twelve stones, but you'll be fine.' He laughed a little, remembering too late that it would hurt.

Aurora didn't laugh. Tomorrow she'd be fine. Flyer's

rider had no interest in seeing her hurt on the course and, in fact, was not even aware that it was his mount Windham owned a share in. She didn't have to worry about foul play in that regard. 'I'm not worried about the race. I'm more concerned about after the race.' Thwarting Windham tomorrow would not curtail the private vendetta Windham waged against her. In fact, she was sure it would only serve to inflame him further.

'The cares of tomorrow can wait until then, Aurora. Rest assured, whatever they are, we'll meet them together,' Crispin murmured.

And for once, Aurora let herself believe it.

The race wouldn't start until noon. That left him plenty of time to effect his plans with regard to Windham. Crispin had woken sore, but in good spirits. Aurora had helped him dress. Then she and Beth had gone down to breakfast and out to the stables with one of John Elmore's crew for a race-day inspection. Crispin thought it a good idea that as many people as possible see Aurora as the genteel Miss Calhoun in her skirts walking through the stables to squelch any potential speculation.

He wouldn't see her again until after the race. He wished he could be there to boost her up on to Kildare and give her all sorts of last-minute advice she didn't need, but he had a job to do. Crispin turned on his heel once Aurora and Beth were out of sight and walked back into the dining room, intent on hunting down his quarry.

Windham was eating eggs and ham. Best of all, he was eating with a group of people, gentlemen who'd come to watch and wager on the race. A crowd served Crispin's purposes perfectly. The snake was trapped.

Windham was pompously listing Flyer's attributes

when Crispin approached the table. 'Good morning, Windham,' he said loudly with an enormous amount of bonhomie. He slapped the man hard on the back for good measure. 'Thought I'd find you here.'

Windham's genuine look of surprise to see him up and walking was hugely gratifying. 'Ramsden…' he managed to splutter, his face visibly paling. The table was staring at Windham now, waiting expectantly for introductions.

Crispin elected to help him out. The more people who saw them as 'acquaintances', the tighter the corner he could back Windham into. 'I'm Crispin Ramsden from Dursley,' he introduced himself to the group at large. 'Windham and I are practically neighbours. We bid on the same horse a few weeks back.' He was all jovial friendliness. He could tell many of the people at the table were impressed with Windham's connection.

'I've come to ask your help on a matter, Windham, and to extend an invitation to sit in my box at the grandstand. I've reserved excellent seats at the finish line. We'll be able to see the winner the moment a hoof crosses the line.' The group was looking at Windham with envy now. To be invited to sit with Ramsden and to have such prime seats was an entirely desirable proposition.

As Crispin anticipated, Windham had no choice but to accept. Only a fool would publicly reject the generous offer. Crispin put an arm about the man's shoulder in an ostensible show of friendship, but his grip was iron as he sought out a quiet corner for their 'discussion'.

'What is the meaning of this farce?' Windham dared some bravado once they were alone.

'Men you hired attacked me last night. I have warned you on prior occasions I would not tolerate any harm being done to me or to those under my protection,' Crispin growled, careful to reveal the tip of a knife beneath his sleeve. 'Don't think sore ribs will stop me from using this. You will listen to what I have to say.'

'You cannot prove it. You'll never find those men. They're long gone from here.' Windham paled further, swallowing hard at the sight of Crispin's blade. He summoned his last trump. 'Why all the effort, Ramsden? I've already succeeded in winning. You're out of commission. Kildare cannot enter the race unless you mean for your Irish whore to ride. I will expose her to the race committee and you'll be unable to do anything about it.'

Crispin gave a glacial smile. 'I believe you have a stake in Flyer and a daughter about to marry a baron. I doubt either of those parties would like to know the shenanigans of which you are capable. Baron Sedgwick cannot withstand such a scandal. There are other rich girls for him to marry whose fathers are hungry for a title.'

Cold calculation spread across Windham's frightened features. 'You bastard. How dare you threaten my daughter's wedding.'

'That ploy won't work with me. From what I've heard, she'd welcome the scandal if it saved her.' Crispin was all icy politeness. 'I believe we have an accord. For the sake of your reputation, you will sit with me in my box, surrounded by my friends. They don't know what you've done, not yet anyway. That will be for you to decide. You will say nothing in regards to Kildare's rider. With luck, you'll toast to Kildare's victory at the end of the day. In return, I'll let you run back to Dursley with your tail between your legs just like the cur you are.' Crispin smiled wolfishly. 'Come, my dear friend from Dursley. The race awaits.'

* * *

Waiting had never been her strong suit. Today, her patience had disappeared altogether. Aurora paced the confines of her room, checking the clock hands again and again only to be disappointed in their progress.

At ten-thirty she allowed herself to dress. She'd dismissed Beth and the maid, wanting privacy as she gathered her thoughts, to say nothing of her anonymity. She wanted to dress as a man alone. She bound her breasts tightly with strips of white cloth until they were flattened enough to pass scrutiny. She buttoned her shirt and turned from side to side in the mirror to survey the effect. It would pass. No one would know. *Unless she fell and was carried off the field unconscious and some well-meaning soul searched for injuries.*

Aurora closed her eyes tight against the memories of Darby, of the day she'd fallen so terribly. She could not afford the distraction. Hastily, angry with herself, she reached for her riding trousers and pulled them on. Of its own volition her hand skimmed the scar below her waist, a lasting reminder of her folly. The gambler's hope rose in her mind. *This time it would be different.*

She tucked her hair firmly up underneath a knit fisherman's cap and placed her riding cap over it, her confidence returning. Darby would not want her distracted with the past. If her da were here he'd be telling her to clear her mind of nothing but the course. This was not a case of history repeating itself. Aurora tugged at her jacket. She was Aurora Calhoun, a woman who had succeeded under extraordinary odds. She'd survived an accident that could have rightfully claimed her life. She'd survived a husband who'd cast her off and put her outside acceptable society. She was strong. She would not fail now.

Aurora shot a glance at the clock. At last it was time, time to make her appearance in disguise and lead Kildare through the throng gathered outside the Turf Hotel to the starting line at Colney Heath. She was surrounded by Crispin's friends and quietly assured in cryptic comments from a stable boy who didn't understand what he was relating that Crispin's plan was going according to schedule. But, in spite of Crispin's thoughtful assurances, she still expected to hear Windham's voice ring out with some charge of fraud as she passed through the streets on Kildare.

There were no such charges and she reached the starting line without any fuss. She shielded her eyes against the bright sun and scanned the grandstand for Crispin's box. A little smile played on her lips as she located it. Crispin sat there, surrounded by his racing comrades and a tense Windham sitting on his right. So that's what he'd meant about keeping his friends close and his enemies closer. She'd have to get the details out of him later. Crispin would prevent Windham from exposing her and in turn Crispin's friends wouldn't let Windham hurt Crispin. Windham could hardly do anything to Crispin with so many of Crispin's loyal friends present. It was good to have one less thing to worry about.

Beside her at the start, Captain Becher flashed a quick wink, his humour much improved over Norma's five-to-one odds. Beneath her, Kildare pranced in excitement. Kildare knew with a competitor's intuition that he was about to race.

Aurora leaned down to pat the stallion's neck, a million thoughts jostling through her mind. Today was both for the past and the future. Today was for putting the ghosts of yesterday to rest and reaching for the bright promise of tomorrow. If her father knew, he'd be proud; proud of Kildare and proud of her. A bugle trumpeted, calling the horses to readiness. Aurora turned her thoughts to the course, seeing each jump, each turn in her mind. There was no room for thoughts of anything else now.

The bugle trumpeted again, blowing the notes that heralded the start. Aurora tensed, gathering the reins to her. Kildare bunched his muscles beneath her and they were off.

Chapter Sixteen

The whole field surged as one, horses jostling, riders looking for space to make their own. Becher pushed Norma to the front, a lead pack containing Parasol, Norma and Grimaldi separated from the others. Aurora felt Kildare fight the bit, wanting to catch the leaders. She held him back, preferring to run strong with the middle horses. A few fell back, wary of the early first jump.

Aurora flew over the first jump, feeling Kildare take the difficult leap over the brook easily. She gave Kildare his head, wanting now to catch the leaders as the pack thinned and Kildare settled into his natural stride. Anything could happen in a steeplechase. It was one of the fundamental underpinnings of the very nature of the race. Her father had taught her at his knee how very quickly the race could change.

This steeplechase was no different. Little over a mile from the starting line, Parasol led with John Elmore's prized Grimaldi in second when the first accident hit. Aurora was riding in fourth, three lengths behind the leaders, and saw it all clearly. To her horror, Grimaldi stumbled after the fence and fell, effectively scratched from the race. With a quick glance, she saw Grimaldi's rider, Billy Bean, rise, shaking intensely from the impact and trying to dust himself off. Grimaldi was already struggling to his feet and limping. They would not rejoin the chase.

There was naught she could do for them and she focused her attention on the next fence, a hedge of sorts with a sloped landing on the other side. Parasol held the lead alone and two horses lay between her and Parasol; Becher on Norma and Mr Weston's Flyer, the same horse who had the dubious pleasure of being partly owned by Gregory Windham.

Aurora risked a backward glance under her arm. Plenty of strong horses lay behind her: Shamrock, Bittern, Captain Bob, Caliph and Laurestina ran in the last big group; closer still by only a few lengths were Poet and Cumberton. They were surging, making their move. The withdrawal of Grimaldi had inspired them to greater lengths. With Grimaldi and Billy Bean out, there was hope to overcome the favourites. It was tempting to urge Kildare to faster speeds to put a larger distance between her and the upcoming riders, but she cautioned herself against it. If they caught her, so be it. There was still two miles to go. She would wait. She would want that speed closer to the end.

The accident with Grimaldi was not to be the only incident that day. With two-thirds of the race completed and Poet pounding furiously behind her, Aurora took a fence and heard the horrific scream of a horse in pain. She threw a backward glance to see The Poet staked on the jump at a queer angle that chilled her blood. Her glance was enough to tell her the horse would not recover. Bile rose in her throat at the thought of the beautiful champion being destroyed.

It was almost her undoing. Memories of Darby, of her own fall, threatened to break loose. Tears stung in her eyes, blurring her sight. A fence was almost upon her and she blinked furiously to clear her vision. She searched her memory for the jump. It was a particularly tricky one, higher than it looked. To clear it safely, she had to start the jump earlier than might seem wise. She and Crispin had talked this fence over extensively. She thought of Crispin, waiting at the finish line, of how he believed in her. She could not fail now on grounds of sentimentality. She gathered her courage and Kildare soared.

They cleared the jump, but she knew it was due to her horsemanship more than Kildare's size and speed. She could feel the big hunter tiring beneath her. He'd needed her coaching, her careful timing, to make the leap. The natural talent of the horse would not be enough on a leap like this.

Such circumstances were to be expected with under a mile to go. This part of the race was designed to show off a rider's capabilities more than the horse's. Her strategy was paying off. She was glad she'd held Kildare back from surging after Grimaldi's stumble.

Norma, Flyer and Parasol still remained ahead of her, but the gap was closing. Parasol and Flyer battled each other for the lead, trading places several times. That could work to her advantage. They would tire each other out and leave an opening for Kildare. The last quarter-mile would tell all.

Aurora had a large stretch of flat plain ahead of her and she speeded up slightly, closing the distance between Kildare and Norma. Close up, Norma was sweat-flecked, but still running strong. Aurora wondered how the horse's jumping muscles felt. Did the mare have the strength for the last jump, a high water fence? The mare didn't have the deep chest Kildare had inherited from his Irish draughthorse ancestors.

The finish line loomed in the far-off distance, Coleman's grandstand filled with spectators came into view. Aurora assessed her choices for the last half-mile when two things happened. Slightly ahead of her, Norma stumbled on the flat, losing her footing, and the renowned Becher fell, rolling away from the oncoming racers. It wasn't a harmful fall, and, while it might buy her a few extra seconds, Aurora knew Becher would be horsed in minutes and following in her wake.

She urged Kildare onwards, making the most of the opportunity the brief mishap had afforded her. Norma would have to work hard to catch Kildare. Aurora was two lengths behind the duelling Flyer and Parasol. Parasol was running a spectacular race, having led since the first mile except for Flyer's off-and-on challenge for the lead.

Aurora was close enough to see the two horses now, Parasol sweating vigorously from the efforts. The last jump approached. That's when the second item happened; the amazing Parasol refused the jump. Flyer took the jump and Aurora took it immediately afterwards while Parasol's rider wheeled the snorting horse around for a second try.

The race was all about speed now and whatever the rider had saved for the finish. Aurora lifted her rear from the saddle, hoping to spare Kildare the extra weight, her thighs pressed tight to his sides asking for all his reserves, her body off the saddle and leaning low over Kildare's neck.

Competition fuelled her. Her kind feelings for Mr Weston aside, Aurora wanted to beat Flyer. She didn't want to lose to any horse, let alone one the despicable Windham had sponsored. Ahead of her, Flyer began to slow; the big horse was built more for power than speed and had spent his reserves competing with Parasol. Elation fired her blood. Kildare had enough left. It was only a matter of mathematical inevitability and they would overtake the fatigued Flyer.

Behind her, Parasol vied with the return of Norma. They were both strong horses with smart riders. She passed Flyer as early cheers went up from the grandstand. She heard the hooves of Parasol and Norma overtake Flyer. For a moment it was a three-way sprint, but Parasol had already run her race. Parasol fell off and Kildare sprinted hard, matching Norma stride for stride.

Adrenalin thundered through Aurora's veins. Her arms were damned tired, her legs ached from the strain, she could hear Kildare's breathing coming heavy and fast. A smile took her face from the pure joy of the race. She was flying, she was living her dream. Beside her, she heard Becher let out a whoop as they cornered the last flag. Aurora went to the right of it, Becher to the left. Did she imagine a slight cut of the corner on his part? It was too close to tell.

The yells intensified from the grandstand. Five lengths to go! Aurora kept her eyes fixed on the finish, perfectly sighted between the ears of her hunter. She fought the temptation to look over at Becher. Did she have a nose? She wouldn't win by much more than that, but neither would he. Try as she could, Norma could give him nothing more.

They crossed, so close together the victor wasn't clear to Aurora. Four lengths behind them Parasol finished, and then Flyer crossed the line another several lengths behind Parasol. Aurora pulled Kildare to a walk and let the valiant stallion cool off. Becher was swamped with admirers and a jubilant Captain Fairlie.

Up in the starter's box, Thomas Coleman and the other race officials conferred over the results. She was careful to stay apart from the interested crowds, although the feat was difficult since she and Kildare were involved in the astonishing finish.

Becher seemed to understand her apprehension. It wouldn't do now to be discovered. Becher edged Norma towards Kildare and while it brought the crowds, it also brought Becher close enough to act as spokesperson for both of them. Over the heads of the crowd gathered about them, she finally saw the only spectator she cared about seeing. Crispin made his way through masses, shouldering over to her and taking Kildare's reins. A quick glance at his grandstand box told her Windham had been effectively trapped there by conversation. She was safe for the moment.

'Captain, why don't we get these horses to the stables where we can wipe them down and take care of them,' Crispin called up to Becher.

Glad for any reason to be away, Becher nodded and they led the horses to the safety of Coleman's stalls. The walk to the barns was sheer torture for Aurora. Still filled with the exhilaration of the race, she wanted to throw her arms around Crispin and celebrate, but her disguise made such a display impossible.

The crowds stayed at the grandstand, wanting to hear the results of the close race. They had the stables to themselves. The instant Aurora had Kildare at his stall, she slid off into Crispin's arms and kissed him soundly, letting all her enthusiasm claim the moment. 'We did it!'

Crispin's arms were tight around her, without regard for his bruised ribs. 'You were magnificent.' He grinned broadly, his enthusiasm equalling hers. 'I wish I could have seen the whole race. I saw you coming over the last jump, though, and you looked great. I knew you had it then.'

She nodded her head vigorously. 'I knew it too.' The words came out in an excited rush. 'It was only a matter of time before I took Flyer.'

Crispin laughed. 'Then I saw how close Norma was and I started to worry. Parasol came out of nowhere, not even a favourite, but I could see even at a distance she was too tired.'

They talked over the last bit of the race in each other's arms, springing apart only when they heard rapid footsteps approaching the stall. 'Milord, news from the grandstand!' an eager stable boy called.

Crispin stepped outside the stall. 'What is it?'

The boy was breathless, having run across town with the message. 'The race has been contested.'

Aurora felt a moment's trepidation. After all that had happened, had she been found out? Had someone not kept the secret?

'It's Becher!' the boy said. 'Someone contested his last turn. He cut the flag. He went left when he should have gone right. He strayed off the path. If it's true, he'll be disqualified. That means your horse will win, milord.'

The boy turned around and ran into the chest of Captain Martin Becher. 'Is that so?' He seemed unbothered by the claims, slapping his riding gloves against his palm.

The boy blushed and stammered, 'That's what they're saying down at the course.'

Becher flipped him a coin. 'Get along with you, son.' The boy ran off and Becher looked past Crispin's shoulders to find her in the interior of the stall. 'I think it would be best if that disqualification didn't happen,' he said quietly.

Aurora nodded. If she was the sole victor, there

would be a lot of attention sent her way and questions about the unknown rider who'd substituted for Crispin Ramsden the morning of the race. There would be enough attention as it was, but if the famous Becher won, much of that attention would be deflected.

Aurora changed quickly into a dress, ready to assume her role as the representative for the Calhoun Stables, and the threesome headed back to the grandstand. The race site was still abuzz with activity. They made their way to the starter's box where Coleman and the officials still agonised over the final standings. 'We have news to help your deliberations,' Crispin called out in jovial tones.

Coleman climbed down. 'What do you know?'

Aurora squared her shoulders and said authoritatively, 'The Calhoun rider says Becher didn't cut the flag. He stayed on the path.'

Coleman nodded. 'We're leaning that way ourselves. Several other observers say they saw no proof of taking the flag improperly.' He thanked them and climbed back up to the box. Moments later the bugle blew to signal for silence.

'We have the results of the race,' Coleman's voice boomed out over the quiet crowd. 'In third place, The Flyer, owned by Mr Weston.' Polite applause and congratulations met the announcement. Weston gave the crowd a wave. Aurora shot Crispin a confused look. Flyer should have been fourth. 'In second place, Parasol, owned by Donald Seffert.' The applause increased for the magnificent horse. 'In first place, for the first time since the running of the St Albans steeplechase, we have a tie. Seeing that there was no violation of the course, the officials cannot determine a clear victor. With great pleasure, we award first place to Norma, owned by Captain Fairlie, and first place as well to The Pride of Kildare, owned by the Calhoun Stables.'

The crowd applauded and yelled wildly, caught up in the excitement of the tie. Captain Fairlie helped Aurora up to the blocks set up as a stage for the presentation of the cup and wreath of roses.

Aurora thought it was quite ridiculous that it was all right for a woman to claim the award, but not be able to actually earn it. However, she smiled brilliantly to the crowd, who thought her only a pretty representative of what must surely be her father's or brother's enterprising stables.

'We didn't anticipate such a finish,' Coleman began, speaking out over the crowd. 'Coleman's Turf Hotel will of course provide a second cup in due time. Congratulations to our victors. We'll celebrate with a post-race champagne supper at the hotel this evening at eight o'clock.' This announcement was also met with applause, everyone knowing that Coleman kept an excellent hotel cellar.

'Congratulations, Miss Calhoun,' Captain Fairlie escorted her back to Crispin's waiting arm. 'Your horse ran an exceptional race and is certainly a credit to the rider's abilities as well as the Calhoun Stables. We'll have a lot to talk about at dinner.'

'Perhaps I could impose on you, Captain Fairlie,' Crispin jumped in. 'Could you see Miss Calhoun back to the hotel? I have to see someone off. His carriage is waiting to take him back to his home.' Crispin winked at Aurora. 'Windham sends his congratulations. He regrets he won't be able to join us tonight for the celebrations.' She could imagine Crispin bundling Windham into a carriage and sending it off, ridding them of the man's odious presence for a little while.

* * *

Dinner was a lavish affair complete with white linen tablecloths and champagne flutes. 'The place is utterly transformed.' Becher laughed, taking his seat at the large round table where Crispin and Aurora sat surrounded by the other winners. He winked at Aurora. 'Miss Calhoun, in the course of an ordinary day this place is usually just a watering hole for all of us ex-military men. We shoot billiards, talk horses, and drink Coleman's excellent wines and ales. But tonight, ah, tonight, it is revealed in its full glory. Perhaps it is your beauty that makes the transformation so utterly complete,' he complimented gallantly.

Aurora blushed prettily at the comment. 'You do me a great honour, Captain.' She was doing her best not to feel self-conscious in the gown Tessa had sent. It was a lovely confection of pale cream silk trimmed in celery-coloured ribbons and lace. The neckline was a bit of a plunge, showing off far more of her cleavage than she could ever remember Tessa showing, but Crispin had taken one look at her upstairs and convinced her it was perfect for her victory dinner, chivalrously offering to help her out of the gown later.

Aurora reached for her champagne flute and sipped, covering up the little smile that played about her lips, a smile she wouldn't be able to explain to anyone at the table without extreme embarrassment. Dressing for dinner had proved quite the experience. Between Crispin's sore ribs, her achy muscles from riding and the complexity of Tessa's gown, neither one of them had been able to dress themselves, which had resulted in some creative manoeuvres.

Her smile threatened again at the mental of image of Crispin, unable to bend over and put on his own trousers, lying prone on the bed while she slipped his dark evening trousers up his legs, his buttocks flexing while she slid the fabric up over his hips, her hands stopping to sightsee as she worked the fastenings.

Of course, he'd got his revenge the moment she stepped into Tessa's cream gown and realised she couldn't possibly do it up on her own. She giggled and put a hand over her mouth, trying to refocus her attentions on the conversation at the table. She looked up to catch Crispin's eyes on her, hot and bold, and knew she hadn't fooled him. He knew precisely what she was thinking.

'What do you think it is about the Irish? Irish-bred hunters seem to outperform English stock on a regular basis,' John Elmore mused aloud to the table.

Everyone shook their heads. 'It's a mystery,' Becher said jovially. 'It's probably the water,' he joked.

'Oh, no, it's not the water.' Aurora gave full vent to her smile, glad to have an excuse for it. 'It's the grass. There's more lime content in it,' she said matter of factly.

'You are not jesting?' Weston leaned forwards, intrigued.

'Seriously.'

Becher slapped his hand on his knee and whooped. 'She's a keeper, Ramsden. I'd give anything to find a woman who knew as much about horses as Miss Calhoun.' He reached for his own flute and raised it. 'A toast, everyone, to the beautiful, knowledgeable, incomparable Miss Calhoun.'

With good grace Aurora accepted the toast, savouring the moment. She'd never be an incomparable on the stage of the London *ton*, might never be openly acknowledged for her horse training beyond this table, but this moment was enough. She'd raced and she'd won on her own merits and these men recognised her talent for what it was.

The evening was the stuff of dreams. On her right, Captain Fairlie talked about breeding a stallion of his with one of her mares. On her left, Mr Weston talked about training techniques and sending a few two year olds to her who had not shown promise in flat racing, but showed signs of being jumpers. Across the table, Crispin was engaged in his own conversations, but his gaze was never far from her, his desire unveiled, promising all the pleasure he could deliver later back in their rooms, sore ribs notwithstanding. If she knew Crispin, they'd manage well enough. God, how she loved him.

Her mind tripped at the realisation, losing track momentarily of her conversation with Captain Fairlie. *She loved Crispin Ramsden.* For better or for worse, she'd come to love the arrogant man who'd kissed a stranger in the Dursley Road, who'd danced with the gypsies, who championed her right down to every last unconventional eccentricity she possessed. Her heart was in dangerous territory, but not tonight.

Tonight, she could not ask for more. If history conveniently forgot to list Becher's win on Norma as a tie, if her newfound love foundered against the tides of reality, so be it. Tonight, she had her victory. Her horses had been recognised for their quality, she had her reputation established, and she had a man she loved for however long it lasted.

Chapter Seventeen

The next day was a market day and like many of the race participants, she and Crispin elected to stay the extra day to rest the horses before travelling home. She was determined to savour every minute of it. Time was suspended and Aurora refused think of the realities that lay outside the cocoon of St Albans.

What choice did she have? she reflected as she dressed in another of Tessa's lovely walking dresses. The revelation of the night prior would be for her alone. She could no more tell Crispin Ramsden she loved him than she could hold back the tides. She shot a look at the bed and found him awake, hands behind his head, watching her intently as she moved through her morning *toilette*.

'Are you going to dress me next?' he drawled.

'Still too sore to put your own pants on?' She smiled and moved to the bed, hips deliberately swaying.

'Still too hard,' he parried wickedly, reaching for her.

'You're a lusty man, Ramsden.' She laughed as he hauled her down, his hands already under her skirts. How did a woman tame a stallion such as this man? Was such a thing even possible? What would she do with a tamed Crispin? She wasn't even sure that was what she wanted.

Dressing Crispin took rather longer than it needed to, but it was clear from his vigorous antics that his ribs, while still tender, were bothering him less. Aurora sat astride his now trousered legs and finished tying his cravat.

'I would never have guessed you'd do so well as a valet.' Crispin's blue eyes twinkled. He sat up and let her help him into a paisley-patterned blue-on-blue waistcoat. He swung his legs over the bed, grunting a bit at the effort, and reached for her hands. He gave her a look of boyish expectation. 'Now, Aurora, what shall we do today?'

'Let's be tourists.' She smiled impishly, catching his enthusiasm. Today would be their own private holiday, a day off from horses, a day off from Windham, a day off from the future.

There was breakfast in the hotel dining room, featuring plates piled high with rashers of bacon and eggs. People stopped by their table. There were invitations to impromptu events planned by those who were staying the extra day. With a quick glance at Aurora and a knowing smile, Crispin politely declined them all.

After breakfast, they walked the streets of St Albans, taking in the quaint sights, Crispin proving to be a veritable font of local knowledge. 'I've been here a time or two over the years.' He shrugged it off easily when she queried him.

'All right, if you're so smart then, tell me about the clock tower.' Aurora tugged at his hand and pulled him down the street to the medieval monument.

They stood in front of it, Crispin assuming the mocking stance of a guide like the type visitors might hire in London. 'This was built in the fourteen hundreds once St Albans became an established town in the medieval times, but by no means was the medieval town the first civilisation in this area. Romans settled here ages before.'

'I'm impressed.' Aurora slipped her hand back into his, revelling in the luxury of being able to do so without social concern. No one knew them. For all anyone knew they were a husband and a wife in town for the markets. While their clothes were well made, their outfits didn't particularly mark them as nobility—well, Crispin at least as nobility. Today they could be anonymous and hold hands if they wanted. And she wanted.

'If you'd like to be truly impressed, I know some far more interesting facts about St Albans than the bell tower,' Crispin whispered close to her ear, conspiratorially.

They moved on down the narrow streets, Crispin keeping up a chatter of trivia. 'There's Ye Olde Fighting Cocks, the inn where Sir Walter Raleigh stayed.'

Aurora looked around. 'I'm amazed how anyone makes a profit with so many inns competing for business.'

Crispin chuckled. 'It's on the main road to London, there's plenty of traffic. If you ask a resident, they'll tell you St Albans has the most public houses of any town in the country.'

Aurora threw Crispin a saucy look. 'Is it true?'

'Well, from personal experience I would say so. I have taken a pint in at least all of the pubs on one occasion or another,' Crispin admitted with a wry grin.

'Bashing around town with Becher?' Aurora probed.

'Not Becher. I've not known him that long, but some of the others. We'd come out during the Season when London got too boring, which it often did.'

Aurora tilted her head up and studied the man

beside her. 'I'm trying to picture you as a young buck on the town.'

'Having some difficulty?'

'Difficulty in picturing you being happy about it,' Aurora confessed. Outwardly, she could easily see Crispin dressed in a lord's clothes, commanding the attention of every young lady in the ballroom, tall and handsome and possessed of a wildness no tailor could disguise behind fashion. He'd proven to be quite a chameleon. A costume could change him utterly; he could even manage the behaviours that went with the costume. She'd seen it at the gypsy camp, at her stables, at Peyton's dinner table, here at the races among his military acquaintances. No wonder he was so valuable to the government.

But inwardly she could not imagine him being happy amid the games of London. The more she knew about Crispin Ramsden, the more she found it easy to believe he'd come looking for a place like St Albans, a bustling market town full of middle-class citizens and a transient population that didn't look twice, didn't ask questions, didn't hold expectations.

'Well, you'd be right. I preferred the military to the ballrooms of London.'

Crispin led them around a corner. 'Ah, there it is, just as I remember, the Peter's Square Market.' It was one of two markets in town, full of people shopping from food stalls. In early March there wasn't much to choose from in the way of fresh fruit, but Crispin bought a basket from a basket weaver and set to work with a wink, saying only, 'I've got an idea.'

They wove through the stalls, collecting the makings of a picnic. She laughingly bargained with the baker for a loaf of dark country bread. Crispin charmed a cheese merchant for a wedge of Cheshire cheese and a wedge of Stilton in spite of Aurora's protest they couldn't eat that much. Crispin only grinned and said, 'that's not the point.'

A farmer sold them Bosc pears, the fresh fruit a delightful luxury for Aurora. Taking up the last bit of space in their basket was a skin of wine and two glasses Crispin persuaded an innkeeper to part with.

'Ready for a walk?' Crispin asked, looping the basket over his arm.

'Where are we going?'

'Holywell Hill. The original site of the town. We have more sightseeing to do.'

The walk was more like a hike. 'Are you sure you're up to it?' Aurora eyed the upward slope east of the current town speculatively. 'You'd better let me carry the basket. I won't have you hurting your ribs. You can carry it on the way down.'

'It'll be practically empty then,' Crispin noted.

'Precisely my point. You'll thank me tomorrow when you have to sit in a bouncing carriage all day.'

Crispin dismissed her concern with a shrug. 'That's tomorrow. I'd never live it down if any of my acquaintances saw you carrying our basket up the hill and me with my hands empty.'

Aurora relented, but she kept a close watch on him and made sure they took a slow pace. There was no rush anyway. They had all day.

'Holywell Hill used to be lined with inns, but these days only a few remain, such as the White Stag over there,' Crispin commented. 'Ah, here we are. At last.'

He was slightly winded, Aurora noted. It appeared even the redoubtable Crispin Ramsden was human after all.

'Here' was a circle of crumbling ruins of what used to be the St Albans Abbey, built by the Benedictine monks. From the hill Aurora could see the plains spread beneath them for miles. The weather was different up here, too, windier. The breeze blew at her hair and she could appreciate the warmth of Crispin's body where he stood behind her, his hand at her back, the other hand gesturing to the silver strip of river in the distance.

'Before medieval settlers built up here, the Romans built in the valley over there by the Ver River—Verulamium, I think it was called.' He turned her slightly, directing her attention to the opposite hill. 'Before the Romans, the Celts built on that hill over there.' He pointed to the west. 'Prae Hill.'

His voice was close to her ear, low and private although there was no one to hear. 'It has always struck me as interesting how culture never leaves you. The peoples of Italy long preferred to build by rivers, choosing commerce and trade and the lifeblood a river provides a town over the defences of a hill. Even thousands of miles from Rome, the Romans replicated a city based on what they knew. And Englishmen have long preferred the benefits of defence on a hill to a river when it came to building early towns. Have you seen the ruins at Sarum?'

'No,' Aurora said sadly. She'd travelled, but never *to* anything, always *from* something. But Crispin had the advantages of status and wealth. He could travel by choice, yet another difference that separated them, but not today. She firmly pushed those ideas away.

'Sarum was built on a hill. Legend has it the Bishop and the knights stationed at the ring fort fought over the well. The Bishop had had enough so he shot an arrow into the air and declared he would build his own city wherever it landed.' Crispin nuzzled her neck, pushing the windblown strands of hair out of the way.

'Where did it land?'

'The arrow? Apparently where Salisbury is located today, if legend is to be believed. Hungry?'

They ate in the shelter of a crumbling stone wall, the wind passing over them as they lounged on the blanket Crispin had procured from the market. 'Here, try this. Open your mouth.' Crispin leaned over with a slice of pear adorned with Stilton and popped it into her mouth.

Aurora bit into the treat carefully, slowly tasting the mix of flavours, the tangy blue-veined white cheese with the fruity sweetness of the pear. 'Divine, absolutely divine,' she murmured.

'Now, try this.' Crispin sliced a piece of the thick bread with his knife and served it to her with a hunk of the Cheshire cheese. 'If we had a fire, I'd show you how well it melts. But it's still good cold.'

Aurora bit and ate. 'This is no ploughman's lunch. I see now why you wanted two different types of cheeses. I would have pegged you as more practical.'

'I'm practical when I must be and that's been much of the time during my travels. But I love food.' Crispin stretched his long body out the length of the blanket, wincing a little while he shifted into a more comfortable position, his head propped on his hand. 'Most of my warmest memories of travelling come from around a table, a simple table with simple food well prepared. Up in the mountains in eastern Europe, food is life. To eat is to live. The table becomes a source of vital hospitality.'

Aurora nodded, remembering how carefully he'd eaten the stew the first night they'd shared a meal.

He passed her the wineskin and she took a mouthful of the full-bodied red wine inside. 'You are a conundrum to me, Crispin. You're a lord, with lordly connections. You've demonstrated that amply enough throughout this trip. Yet, you thrive on simple pleasures. Who are you, really? What is it that you want?' Aurora dared to ask. In the intimacy of their lonely camp on the hillside, such confidences seemed to flourish.

'If I knew that, I'd have the world by a chain.' Crispin studied her with equal determination. 'What about you? What do you want?'

I want you, Crispin Ramsden, body, mind and soul, Aurora thought silently. What would he do if she voiced such sentiments out loud? Probably run screaming down the hill. They had promised not to make such claims, to hold such expectations, hadn't they? She opted for the safe route of a half-truth. 'I want you, Crispin.'

'Then come and get me,' he growled appreciatively, desire rising in his eyes, turning the sapphires to hot coals.

He'd done plenty of the seducing over the last few days. Now it was her turn. She playfully pushed him back, her hands making quick work of his cravat and shirt. She kissed him hard on the mouth, tasting the flavours of wine and pear on his lips. 'I wonder if you taste this good everywhere,' she murmured in sensual tones.

His eyes burned as he divined her intentions. Her eyes held his, unwavering in their promise. Her hands dropped to his trousers, working of their own accord to free him from the fabric. She took his freed member in her hand, stroking its length, caressing the tender head with the pad of her thumb, watching his eyes darken impossibly as his pleasure mounted. 'God, Aurora, what you do to me.' He groaned, arching into her hand, his tip giving up a bead of moisture coaxed by her touch. She'd been waiting for that, a sign that he was ready for what came next.

Aurora bent to his shaft, kissing it reverently, letting the glistening drop wet her lips. 'Temptress!' Crispin cried out, both pleased by her boldness and aroused beyond all sanity. Encouraged, Aurora held the wineskin over him and dribbled a few drops on to his phallus before moving to take him completely, taste him completely; the tang of the wine mingling with the salt of a man's essence. She thrilled in her own power to bring him such enjoyment, thrilling in the intimacy she could share unabashedly with this man alone. Never had she dared so much.

'Careful, I will not last much longer,' Crispin cautioned hoarsely.

Aurora could feel his body tightening in agreement with his warning. She repositioned herself to take him inside her, riding him slowly out of deference for his ribs. The deliberate pace of her motions brought an exquisite friction all their own, building into a pinnacle of ecstasy that shattered at its apex into a thousand shards of pleasure.

She kept him inside her long afterwards, unwilling to relinquish the moment and all that went with it. Even after she'd taken up residence in the crook of his arm, cuddled carefully and closely to his side, they lay together in abject stillness, neither of them speaking. She closed her eyes and drank in the presence of him, the feel of his hard, muscled body against hers, the smell of him; a gentleman's soap mixed with the musk of a lover's scent intoxicating and as potent as the man himself. She willed herself to remember all of it, saving it all up against the inevitable.

Crispin pushed hair out of Aurora's face, studying the soft curve of her profile in the fading light. The shadows were lengthening and their alcove was losing its heat. They'd have to go back down the hill. Back to reality. 'I don't want to go back,' he said aloud with a sigh, wondering at the words. Did he mean back to St Albans or back to Dursley Park, back to whatever awaited them there?

True, there would be four days on the road before then, but it wouldn't be the same, knowing that each mile took them closer to the unpleasantness of reality. There was Windham to deal with, the unbreakable entail and its myriad of issues to untangle, and the problem of 'then what': When Windham and the entail were resolved, as they most certainly would be, then what? When the next assignment came from London calling him back to his former life, then what?

Aurora found her courage first. 'You're cold.' She pulled at the flaps of his shirt, dragging them across his chest. 'We have to go. The others will be waiting for us at dinner. We've avoided them all day, we owe them at least our presence at supper.' She rose and began straightening her clothes. Crispin wondered if she'd tell Tessa what she'd done in that dress. Irrationally, he wished Aurora had her own clothes, her own gowns, even though he preferred her in her trousers and cut-down shirts. Aurora shouldn't have to rely on borrowed finery. Maybe he'd do something about that when he got home.

It was a husband's right, a husband's duty, to see his wife clothed.

A husband.

That was how he thought of himself when he thought of Aurora. Crispin hid a small smile. How ironic—he realised he wanted to make the most significant commitment of his life by thinking of one of the most mundane duties that commitment entailed. He wanted that right and all the others that went with it. Complications aside, he wanted to be Aurora's husband.

He had never thought to arrive at this point with

anyone. He must go slowly. He could imagine what Aurora would say. He could imagine what Peyton would say, what society would say. There was plenty to work out, not the least being the direction of his future. Aurora wasn't the only one with issues to settle. This deed would require all nature of sacrifice, from personal to social. There would be dragons aplenty to fight before he'd see the goal accomplished. But for now, he wanted to savour the elation of having reached this momentous decision.

'Why are you smiling?' Aurora queried, absently arranging her skirts.

Ah, he hadn't been successful in hiding it. Crispin gave his grin full rein. No sense to hide it now. 'I am smiling because I have found the answer,' he replied cryptically. 'I know what I want.'

'Are you going to tell me?'

'Yes, but not yet.' Crispin clambered to his feet and began to pick up the detritus of their feast, distracting Aurora with the task of packing.

Predictably the basket was much lighter with the food eaten. The trip downhill was predictably quicker too. In no time at all they entered the warren of streets that made up St Albans.

'The adventure is over,' Aurora said at his side.

'Dinner will be festive,' Crispin reminded her. 'There's still four days until we're home. Who knows what will happen on the road?' He tried for levity, but he felt it too. The adventure was slipping slowly away. He talked of the gaslights that lit the town at night, chatting of their instalment in 1824 to keep the gloom away.

They checked the horses, pleased to see Kildare in rested spirits. They dressed for dinner in a more subdued manner than that in which they'd dressed for breakfast, when the day had spread before them like an eternity.

* * *

Downstairs in the hotel dining room, Becher and the others beckoned them to a table. They ate, they drank, they exchanged stories and laughed loudly over each other's escapades. But Crispin sensed the underlying desperation that permeated the edge of the group's good humour. The excitement was over. They would all go back to the mundane. Becher would go back to his post as Captain of the yeoman guard in his quiet hamlet, coming to town occasionally to conspire with Coleman on the next great event. The others would drift back to their country estates and country lives. Some of them would endeavour to go up to London for a while once the Season started. All of them would wait for next year. For them, the only season that mattered was over. The hunt and steeplechase season lasted until March. Then it was flat racing and thoroughbreds and the Jockey Club's obsessive stud book until October when they could start all over again.

Someone brought out a fiddle and Aurora danced gaily with Weston. 'Will you be back next year, Ramsden?' Elmore asked while Crispin watched Weston do a funny jig around Aurora.

'Hard to say,' Crispin replied evasively.

'And Miss Calhoun? Will she be back? Those stables have talent and goodness knows I've never seen a rider the likes of her.'

'Again, hard to say.'

Elmore fixed him with a hard gaze. 'There is no brother, no father, no male relative behind the scenes of Calhoun Stables, is there? Other than you, of course, for whatever that's worth.'

'There is me,' Crispin said staunchly. He would not lie outright to John Elmore or to the others who'd backed him unerringly this week, making so much possible in an impossible world.

'I see,' John Elmore said cryptically, withdrawing back into his chair. 'It's a large gamble she takes, Ramsden. Surely you know that? For her to succeed, men of power and influence will need to make exceptions.'

'I think they will,' Crispin answered evenly. 'You're willing, Dursley's willing, all of us this week were willing. If those are any indicators of her ability to persuade, she stands a chance.'

He watched Aurora make an exaggerated curtsy to a laughing Weston and he felt his earlier elation surge. For whatever else was unclear about the future, he wanted her. He wanted her far beyond the pleasure of her company in bed. He wanted her for ever. For once, the word did not fill him with its usual dread.

Chapter Eighteen

Crispin's mind was made up. *He wanted to marry Aurora.* But he was not so foolish to believe in 'ask and you shall receive'. When it came to the concept of long-term commitment, Aurora was as skittish as he was. Or rather as skittish as he *had* been, he amended silently. He'd made his mind up. There were only the details to work out. He reasoned he would do better to work through them on his own first so that when Aurora threw up barriers to his proposal, he'd have his answers ready.

For that reason, they skirted London on the way home, electing to stay at an inn outside town the end of the first day instead of going to the town house. The last thing Crispin wanted was Aunt Lily and Eva going on about society, a reminder of the social barrier between them. Not that it mattered to Crispin. He moved in society only when need mandated such a choice. But Aurora would not see it that way. He didn't need any more reminders of his title, honorific as it was, or of the family wealth. Nor did he relish the idea of running into anyone from the Foreign Office who might have a new mission for him. Aurora would never see his proposal as sincere if she thought he'd be leaving for far-off parts for an indeterminate length of time.

Those were two loose ends he'd have to wrap up. He'd send a letter to the Foreign Office, stating his resignation. He'd halt inquiries into breaking the entail. They would live simply at Woodbrook if she chose, although he had wealth aplenty to live in whatever style she desired. Aurora could move her stables to Woodbrook, develop the farm as she wanted with the courtesy of his name behind her. Surely, Aurora would see that marriage to him would free her in ways that were currently beyond her reach. As it had freed him.

The journey home gave him all the freedom he wished to explore the new revelations that had dawned on him during the course of their trip. He'd originally loathed the idea of marriage because it would confine him, but there were no limits with Aurora. He did not have to work to keep up a conversation, he'd not had to play the usual courtship games with trinkets and poetry under the watchful eye of matchmaking mamas who studied his every move, wondering if one of their daughters would be the one to bring the wild Crispin Ramsden up to scratch.

That was not to say there hadn't been a courtship of sorts or that he didn't want to shower her with gifts. He did. He wanted to buy her dresses of her own. He'd wanted her to have Dandy that day at the horse fair. He was thinking of having a saddle commissioned for her as a wedding gift. If she wanted diamonds and emeralds, she could have those too.

'You're smiling again.' Aurora nudged his boot with her foot. She was sitting across from him in the carriage, the light drizzle outside having called a halt to riding outdoors. Beside her, Cousin Beth looked up briefly from her reading to study him.

'I suppose I am.'

'Are you going to tell me what has caused you to smile this time?'

'Not yet.' Crispin continued to grin. He'd become quite relaxed on the journey home now that he was convinced he could change enough of his life to satisfy Aurora. Perhaps he'd settled enough to test the waters.

She leaned forwards now and peered out the window. 'We're nearly there.' Familiar landmarks of Dursley land passed outside.

'It's awkward, isn't it?' she said, her hands folded in her lap, tightly locked together. 'The moment my feet touch the ground it will seem like these last two weeks have never happened. Already, I am thinking what I should do first; walk through the stables and check on the horses, go up to Dursley Park and return Tessa's things.'

'They won't seem like a fantasy if you don't let them become that,' Crispin broke in.

Aurora eyed him sharply. She was trying to read his mind with those green eyes of hers that missed nothing, noted everything. She was suspicious and her suspicions made her cautious. He could see it in the rigidness of her posture, the tight grip of her hands. She was wary.

'You know what I mean, Crispin. It's not the events that are hard to come home from.' She was making an effort to choose her words carefully so as not to embarrass Beth. 'It's pretending that we belonged together, being Miss Calhoun and Captain Crispin Ramsden.'

Crispin leaned back against the cushions of his seat, arms folded across his chest. 'I don't pretend. Have you thought that we do belong together?'

Beth looked up in abject shock, the announcement

stunning her out of her well-cultivated aura of complacency.

'Perhaps "pretend" isn't quite the right word,' Aurora answered, doggedly clinging to her argument. 'None the less, our intimacy has occurred in a social vacuum.'

'Nature abhors a vacuum,' Crispin recited absently from some old science lesson of his youth. He knew what she meant. It would do him no credit to affect otherwise. He'd been able to conveniently avoid being a peer of any significant standing among the crowds in St Albans. She'd been able to put on the mantle of respectability there as easily as she'd been able to put on a gown. The social strictures were less severe than in London. In St Albans nothing had mattered in the group of friends they'd carved out except the mutual love of horses.

Perhaps nothing had mattered because everyone had been the same. There were several captains among their group. A few honorific peers too, like himself, who bore the title only out of social deference. A pretty, respectable 'Miss' was an acceptable prospect for the men who'd flocked to St Albans: squires, captains, men of some military standing and country gentry. Respectable, but certainly not *ton*nish. Amongst the *ton*, such an association would be shunned a hundredfold. Especially when one was a Ramsden. Yet it occurred to him that both of his brothers had overcome such a standard. Neither of their wives came with impeccable social credentials. Julia had been the niece of a struggling viscount. Tessa had been the oldest daughter of a diplomat who'd run afoul of scandal in his last days.

Crispin stretched his legs out, crossing them at his ankles. 'It was not all pretence. We were not lying to anyone.'

'Some people may have created expectations. You

cannot tell me your friends did not think you were a serious suitor who was all but affianced to me. There was a certain level of artifice to the image we presented.'

'Only if we allow it to become a deception.' Crispin gave her a lazy grin. 'We could live up to their expectations, Aurora. If St Albans proved anything to me, it was that there was a place for us in this world.'

It was a bold gambit and he knew it, but he wanted the seed firmly planted in her mind before the coach rocked to a stop.

'What exactly are you suggesting?' She was all caution, a skittish filly new-come to a bridle.

Crispin gave her his best wolfish smile, brash and confident. 'I am suggesting that you marry me.' Was it his imagination or was Cousin Beth flipping far too quickly through the pages of her book in a gallant attempt to be unobtrusive? She wasn't the only agitated female in the carriage. Aurora was staring at him as if he was a freak-show oddity.

She found her voice. 'You cannot mean it, Crispin. There are a hundred reasons why I should refuse you right now, not the least being whoever proposes in a carriage in front of his cousin? Honestly, there's too many reasons to refuse and only one reason to accept,' she replied with a shake of her head.

'All you need is one reason.' Crispin was all grave solemnity. Beneath the humour and the teasing, he wanted her to know he was in deadly earnest.

The coach came to a stop in Aurora's stable yard and Crispin jumped down to help her out.

Aurora looked at him archly, letting him hand her down. 'You planned this on purpose. You waited until it would be too late to argue over your ill-timed proposal.'

Crispin laughed. 'Ill-timed is a matter of perspective. I think it was timed perfectly.' He went behind the carriage to untie Dandy and Kildare. He passed the leading ropes to her. 'I noticed you didn't say no.' He winked, jumping back into the coach. The coachman was eager to be off now that he was so close to home after four days on the road and Crispin didn't want to keep him waiting.

'I'll see you tonight. I'll send the gig for you.' He leaned down and kissed her briefly. 'You can tell me what the one reason is.'

He'd managed to fluster her. 'What reason?'

'The one reason you'd said you'd marry me!' he called over the noise of the coach setting into motion.

Incorrigible. Usually it was a word she reserved for naughty village boys and their pranks, but in this case, it fit Crispin Ramsden to perfection. No one possessed of his rightful sanity proposed marriage and didn't give the prospective bride a chance to answer. But that was precisely what he'd done.

And it was brilliant.

Not as a proposal, but as a strategy.

Aurora stood in her stable yard, her small valise at her feet, two horses in hand, and she laughed. That devil! Crispin knew his proposal was preposterous. That's why he'd hedged his bets. He knew she'd never say yes readily, but he didn't want her to say no. That promptly sobered her.

Dursley men appeared from the stables to take the horses. Another one took her bag inside her apartments and she followed him inside, noting the army of men at work in the stables. Good lord, how many men had Crispin conspired to put down here? She was thankful for their efforts. In her stunned stupor, she doubted she was capable of doing the necessary chores at the moment.

He didn't want her to say no. What in blazes was he thinking? Did he think a groom's daughter from Ireland could marry an English lord without society taking cruel notice? Did he think he would be happy with a barren woman ten years from now when he looked at his nieces and nephews and realised how empty his life was destined to be? Worse, did he think he owed her? Did he feel obliged to save her stables now that he'd done so much to put them on the road to respectability and prominence? Did he understand he would be giving up his entire way of life? Did he understand she couldn't allow him to do that? She would not tolerate such a sacrifice on her behalf.

These were all the reasons she could not marry him and there were countless more to add to the list. There was only one reason to marry him—because he loved her. She already knew she loved him, but she could not marry him for her love alone. She'd done that once before, believing that her love would be enough to sustain both of them.

Aurora flopped down on to the worn sofa. She usually refused to think of Jonathon and her first marriage. Now that Crispin had proposed, it seemed impossible to avoid it. Not only was she barren and untitled without any substantial wealth to her name, she was a divorcée to boot. Surely, Crispin must understand all the reasons she couldn't marry him. It was her duty to make him see how unsuitable she'd be. Except for one thing: she wanted to say yes.

'She'll never say yes,' Peyton asserted, drumming his hands on the polished top of his desk, having listened to Crispin's account of the trip to St Albans. 'Of the two of you she's showing the most sense in this matter.'

'She just needs to be persuaded. Certainly there are obstacles that need to be overcome, but nothing insurmountable. You did it with Tessa. Paine did it with Julia.' Crispin was undaunted by Peyton's verdict. Now that he'd made his decision and laid his plans, the way forwards seemed straight and obvious. He was impatient to embrace the future. 'There's a lot of work to be done to get Woodbrook ready for inhabitants again.'

'Already filling those bedrooms?' Peyton's blue eyes glinted mischievously.

'No. I don't think there will be any children,' Crispin replied in tones that brooked no further comment, but he could see the myriad questions in Peyton's eyes. 'Your family and Paine's will be enough for us. Besides…' Crispin waved a hand to indicate a long-past conversation. Peyton would know what he meant.

Peyton shook his head. 'You're not like them. Our parents are not us. You'd make a wonderful father. I watch you with Nicholas and Alexander and I think it would be a shame if you didn't have children of your own.'

Crispin shook his head. 'And I disagree. It's simply not in me.'

Peyton's eyes narrowed in speculation. 'You once said that about becoming a landowner, just a month ago, in fact. And now you're changing your entire life for this woman. You're taking on a property, a wife, the business of a stable. I would urge you to slow down and think this through. Aurora is not the kind of wife society would expect you take. Society may very well turn its back on you for good. I do not know that you can make her acceptable. We must be realistic about her background, Cris…' Peyton waved a hand, his voice dropping off, not wanting to elucidate the issues stacked against her.

Crispin could hear the list in his head: bastard birth, illegitimate connections only to a maternal grandfather, a deceased Irish earl, her barren state, to say nothing of her behaviours.

The comment infuriated Crispin. How dare Peyton pass judgement on him and on Aurora. 'A month ago you were all but begging me to stay and do exactly that and now you doubt my ability to carry it out.' He struggled to remain calm. 'You changed for Tessa. Paine changed for Julia.'

'I cannot speak for Paine. However, I disagree. The one thing I love most about Tessa is that she's never sought to change me. Once I realised that, I realised how much I loved her. I didn't change *for* Tessa. If I've changed at all, it's *because* of Tessa. There's a big difference between "for" and "because".' Peyton opened a small drawer and pulled out an envelope. 'You should think about all you'd be giving up.' He pushed the envelope across the desk. 'This came for you while you were gone.'

Crispin recognised the seal. The Foreign Office. He gave a dry chuckle. He'd skirted London purposely for this very reason and London had still found him. From the looks of the date, his efforts had been in vain. 'You'd think they could survive without me for a few weeks.'

'They'll have to survive a lot longer than that without you if you marry Aurora,' Peyton pointed out.

'I will resign,' Crispin countered swiftly with a tenacity he didn't quite feel at his core. Arguing with Peyton was like fighting a hydra. Defeated on one issue, Peyton brought up another. It was a sensitive issue. The solution to staying at Woodbrook was a practical one, but such a change would be Crispin's largest sacrifice for the marriage he wanted.

'And stay in one spot for years on end? You were not so sure of that a few months ago.' Peyton pushed as if he sensed the seed of doubt Crispin had tried to bury deep beneath his fury over being challenged.

'Yes!' Crispin fairly roared, coming to his feet. His integrity was being questioned. If Peyton pushed him any further on this, he had no compunction about coming to fisticuffs, but Peyton remained immobile behind the desk, giving him no opening for a brawl.

'Dammit, Peyton. Stop being the earl for one god-damned minute and be my brother.'

That did it. Peyton's chair smashed into the wall and Peyton was up, lunging for him across the desk. Crispin took his weight and dragged him over the desk, the two of them tumbling noisily to the floor, the desk ornaments crashing around them.

They punched and they struggled, they kicked and they wrestled, knocking over a lamp stand in their wake. Peyton managed to get him in a headlock. 'I've always been your brother, first and foremost. Who got you that commission? I let you go away when I wanted nothing more than to keep you near so I wouldn't be so alone.'

Crispin delivered a sharp elbow to Peyton's gut and pushed out of the headlock, tripping Peyton up with a swift twist of his leg. 'You've always been too bloody perfect!'

They went down again, Peyton taking him to the floor as he fell. The fight was a long time in the making and it might have gone on indefinitely if Tessa hadn't opened the study door, the twins spilling from her skirts in glee at the sight of their uncle and father locked in combat.

'We wanna play too!' they yelled, jumping heedlessly into the scuffle.

'You most certainly will not!' Tessa's voice acted like a wet blanket on fire. 'What in heaven's name is going on in here? Peyton? Crispin?'

Crispin shot a glance at Peyton and mumbled. 'She's your wife. You tell her.'

'Ahem. Well, it's like this.' Peyton stood up and tugged at his waistcoat, never mind that it was now minus two buttons. 'We were ah, celebrating. That's it. We were celebrating. Crispin is getting married.'

That softened Tessa slightly. 'This is wonderful news. May I assume the bride is Aurora?'

'Yes,' Crispin said, scrambling to stand up beside Peyton.

'We'll celebrate tonight in a *more fitting fashion*.' She shot Peyton a glare of disapproval that nearly made Crispin laugh. He probably would have, too, if the rest of Tessa's statement hadn't garnered so much of his attention.

'Um...about that. Perhaps we could defer the celebration.'

Tessa looked at him quizzically. 'Why? This is great news. I couldn't be happier for you both.'

'Well, she hasn't said yes.' Then Crispin hastily added, 'Yet.'

'She will.' Tessa was all confident assurance. 'The sooner the better, I say. She'll need all the protection she can get once Windham hears you're home.'

Crispin nodded. 'We humiliated him thoroughly without anyone else knowing a thing. He'll be stinging from it for a while.'

Tessa flicked a quick look at Peyton. 'You didn't tell him?'

'I haven't had a chance. We've been too busy—'

'Celebrating,' Tessa finished for him, hands on her hips.

'What's going on?' Crispin's sense of foreboding was on high alert. He'd known Windham would have to be dealt with. Humiliating him at St Albans only increased tensions between Windham and Aurora and consequently himself.

Peyton bent down and scooped up one of the twins who was persistently pulling on his father's trouser leg. 'Eleanor's gone and there's no doubt about who Windham will blame.'

Chapter Nineteen

Eleanor had run. Windham's presence in St Alban's would have provided the girl with the temptation and means to leave. A *frisson* of alarm ran sharply down Crispin's spine, straight to his gut. Aurora was alone at the stables. 'How many men were left down there to watch the property while we were gone?'

'Three watchmen. We had no trouble while you were away.'

'Three?' Crispin's sense of alarm sharpened. 'There were far more than three when I dropped her off.' The stable yard had been full of men going to and fro, carrying out the business of taking care of horses. It had looked a bit over the top, now that he thought about it, but he'd brushed it off as merely being overprotective of Peyton. He'd been too caught up in the emotions of the moment; the strategic proposal, the look of shock on Aurora's face and the fact that she hadn't said no.

Now, through the distance of a couple of hours, he saw the scene more objectively. If his suspicions were right and Windham had planted his own men down there, having done away with the Dursley watch, he didn't mean to wait. He was ready to exact his revenge the moment Aurora returned.

He shot a sharp look at Peyton and did some rapid calculations in his head. It had been two hours since he'd left Aurora. A look-out would need time to deliver his message to Windham. It would be a look-out from the stables so that Windham could ascertain she was absolutely alone. Windham would not want to hazard meeting him there too. Windham would wait and deal with him separately. Then Windham would need travel time to reach the stables.

Peyton read Crispin's concerns. 'At his fastest, barring no mishaps, he would have reached the stables fifteen minutes ago. With luck, he is still en route.'

Crispin spun on his heel, shouting orders that sent footmen running. 'I'll need a fast horse! Don't bother with a saddle. Have him out front in five minutes.' His voice sounded in control, he even sounded logical as he pounded up the stairs to his chambers. He tore through his drawers, flinging clothes carelessly to the floor, extracting the weapons that lay beneath the once neatly pressed garments. He shoved a pistol in his belt, checking to see that it was loaded. He buckled a knife sheathe around his waist. He bent to assure himself his other knife was still hidden in his boot.

'It's a veritable arsenal up here,' Peyton said tightly from the door, but he was no less armed when Crispin turned around. 'I'm coming with you.'

Crispin shook his head. 'No, it's too risky. We didn't know Windham had amassed an army. This won't be two on one.'

'All the more reason I should go,' Peyton replied.

'You're the earl,' Crispin protested. He could not live with himself if anything happened to Peyton. How would he ever face Tessa and the children again?

'Right now, I'm your brother.' Peyton turned from the door. 'We'd better hurry. Do you have your knife in your boot?'

Crispin gave a predatory grin. 'Always. You have yours?'

Peyton answered his grin with a wolfish one of his own. 'Always.'

Two horses pawed the ground outside, anxious to be off.

Crispin vaulted on to the barebacked mount with grim determination. 'Here's to incompetence,' he muttered under his breath, hoping against hope that by some miracle Windham would be waylaid. Crispin kicked his horse into motion and let out a wild yell, bent low over the horse's neck, letting it thunder down the drive. The race for the stables was on.

Aurora put aside thoughts of Crispin's proposal long enough to unpack the valise. She was tempted to change into trousers and a shirt, but decided against it. She'd just need to change back in a couple hours for dinner at Tessa's. Good lord, she was tired of skirts. She'd worn a dress more times in the past two weeks than she had in the whole three years she'd been in Dursley.

Three years! That brought a smile to her face; not the permanence of making a home here, but rather all that she'd accomplished. She felt at last that she'd put her life back together after her accident and Jonathon's desertion, after being driven out of other places that wouldn't tolerate her skills. All of those trials seemed worth it if they'd brought her to this place, to Crispin. Now did she dare to believe in love, in a man again? It was tempting when the man in question was Crispin.

Aurora hummed to herself, putting a few undergarments away in her trunk. A glimmer of white caught her eye when she rose. A letter stuck out, tucked between a few of her horse-care reference books kept on a high shelf. Perplexed, Aurora reached up for it.

She recognised the loopy handwriting immediately and cold dread filled her. Eleanor. Aurora sat down on the bed, reading and re-reading the short note over and over in stunned disbelief. She'd not thought the girl would leave. Apparently, she'd thought wrong. Eleanor had taken advantage of her father's trip to St Albans and made good her escape. Fleeing Windham's house could be called no less.

Aurora counted days in her head. Windham had not arrived in St Albans early. He'd only shown up the night before the race, but he'd still had to spend at least three days on the road. There was race day, and then he was sent packing. Aurora hoped Windham's early departure hadn't wreaked havoc with Eleanor's plans. The girl would have been counting on having up to eleven days to effect her disappearance. Would she have built in the possibility of her father returning earlier?

Worry over Eleanor gave way to a new concern. Windham would blame her for Eleanor. Aurora suddenly wished Tessa's gown had pockets, a place where she could keep a pistol. She was feeling very vulnerable. Windham would not let this latest development go unpunished. The thought did spike her worries, but she reasoned that in a couple of hours Crispin would drive the gig down to fetch her for dinner and she could tell him her concerns. She drew a deep breath. What could go wrong in a couple of hours? Windham couldn't possibly know yet that she was home and she had an abundant population of Dursley men in her stables.

To settle her nerves, Aurora took a walk through the

stable, stopping to stroke the horses who poked their heads out into the aisle. The stable was eerily quiet. With the exception of the occasional horse sound, the bustle of working men had died away. Everyone had disappeared. True, it was five o'clock and the work day was ending, but she'd thought someone would have come and told her their work was through and the men were off home. It seemed odd that the place could be bustling one hour and still the next.

Sheikh nuzzled her hand, pushing his nose against it, hunting for an apple. 'Your master has spoiled you.' She petted Sheikh's long face.

'He's spoiled you as well.' The cold voice behind her made her jump. She turned sharply, her back against Sheikh's stall door.

Windham!

'What are you doing here?' Aurora asked, keeping her chin up, her voice full of authority.

He continued to advance down the length of the aisle, a riding crop in one long-fingered hand. 'I'm here for you, Aurora. Let's not play games. You have made me look the fool for the last time. You have rejected my honourable suit, you've thrown your lover and his money in my face, stolen a decent steed out from under me, humiliated me in front of people whose respect I desired in St Albans, and convinced my daughter to run away from home and an advantageous marriage.'

'Those things are not my fault,' Aurora answered. 'I had a right to reject your suit. Eleanor has a right to make her own choices.'

'You are too bold to think you can argue with me.' He was nearer now, only twelve feet away. She could see the burn of irrational anger in his eyes. Hands behind her back, she worked the bolt to Sheikh's stall.

'You are the one who is overbold,' she challenged. 'There's Dursley men all over this place. All I have to do is scream.'

A malevolent grin took Windham's face. 'Go ahead. I think you'll find the men belong to me. We neatly disposed of the Dursley watchmen yesterday in case you arrived home early.'

Aurora held his gaze, searching for signs of the lie, but there were none. He was secure in the knowledge that there were no allies here. She was entirely at his mercy. On her periphery, Aurora spotted a pitchfork left propped up next to a stall door across the aisle. 'What do you want?'

'I want a little of what you've been giving to Ramsden. It's my due. My reward for all that I've suffered.'

If she meant to act, it had to be now. If he came any closer, she wouldn't have room to dart. Aurora lunged for the pitchfork. Her hand closed about the handle, but Windham was too fast. He grabbed her about the waist from behind.

'That's not nice, Aurora,' he chided, crushing her against him, half-dragging, half-pushing her towards the wall in an attempt to shake the pitchfork free of her grip.

Aurora screamed, struggling against him. She jabbed wildly with the pitchfork, hoping to jab a tine into a foot. She only had one chance before Windham managed to get an arm about her own arms, effectively impeding any motion from the elbows down. The pitchfork clattered uselessly to the floor.

She fought wildly, trying to kick a knee, trying to stomp on the instep of his foot, but his boots were too high, too thick, and, in the end, too resistant.

In his stall, Sheikh whinnied frantically at the loud noises and the scuffling. His hooves kicked against the door, once, twice and then he was free. Free and skittish. 'Go, Sheikh!' Aurora cried out, still fighting against Windham.

But Sheikh wanted to fight. He reared up on his legs, big and impressive. Shocked, and suddenly cognisant of the danger the big horse posed to him, Windham's grip slackened. Aurora felt his arm loosen and she jabbed an elbow hard against his ribcage. She darted to the side, leaving Windham in Sheikh's path.

Sheikh would trample Windham and she would swing up bareback like a circus rider as he passed. They would both be free. Aurora tensed, waiting for the moment. Time slowed, Windham drew a gun and the moment was lost. She instantly assessed what he meant to do.

'No!' She gave up her freedom and launched herself at Windham, trusting Sheikh would not trample her too, trusting that Sheikh would turn and run out the open end of the stable, run straight to Crispin.

Windham had always underestimated her and this was no different. He'd not expected her to re-engage. Caught off balance, they both went down together on the hard stone floor. The gun flew out of his hand, misfiring loudly into a hay bale. Aurora cursed her skirts. They tangled about her legs, making it difficult to wrestle a grown man. It didn't matter—the misfire brought men running to Windham's assistance. She was no match for Windham plus four.

In short order, her hands were bound and she was efficiently marched into her quarters where Windham summarily kicked the door shut, barking orders that chilled her to her core. 'Get ready to fire the building.'

'No—' Aurora whirled on him '—you can't mean to burn it! It's stone, it won't burn.'

'Enough of it will burn.' He pushed her into a chair. 'But not yet.'

'Free the horses.' Aurora fought the rise of panic that edged her voice.

Windham smugly took the chair across from her. 'You must bargain for them. How many of them are there? Twelve? Counting that beastly Kildare and the one your lover stole from me at the horse fair.' He smiled evilly and leaned the short distance to her, his face too close to hers. 'What twelve things would you be willing to bargain with?'

Aurora thought frantically through her list of meagre possessions. 'My mother's pearls.' She'd worn them the day she'd married Jonathon. They were perfectly matched and of great value to her both financially and sentimentally, all she had of a mother she'd lost when she was too young to remember her.

Windham scoffed. 'What would I do with pearls? I can buy far better gems.'

Aurora stuck to her offer. 'They're worth two horses, the mares at least.' They were likely in foal, but she wouldn't tell Windham that. He would only hold such knowledge against her.

Windham shook his head, running the ever-present riding crop down the side of her cheek. 'I'm not interested in that sort of bargain, Aurora. You have stolen my daughter from me with your radical ideas and indecent lifestyle. In doing so, you've taken something very personally valuable from me. I would take something personal from you in exchange.'

She didn't need to be told his intentions. She'd known from the start all that Windham had implied and all that he wanted. He wanted her body and her pride and she had no choice but to give it to him. It was the only guarantee she had that the horses would survive.

'Take off your dress, Aurora, and I'll let the mares

go.' His eyes burned with naked lust now that the pretence of negotiation was gone.

Aurora's hands trembled at the front buttons down the bodice. She should be thinking about a strategy, how to maximise the opportunity, but she couldn't think past the horses, past the shame he was so wantonly inflicting on her. To her dismay, she couldn't work the buttons effectively with her bound hands. She hated asking him for anything. She held out her bound hands.

A knife appeared in his hands from a coat pocket and he slit the bonds. 'Make it good,' he growled, flopping down into a chair and prepared to watch. 'Hurry up or I'll shoot something for good measure.'

Her freed hands went to the first button on the high collar of Tessa's gown. Then the next.

'Don't act like a nun,' Windham hissed. 'You're not a nun for Ramsden.' He was losing patience.

Aurora slowly pulled her arms out, one by one, from their sleeves as if they were tight gloves. Windham's pupils dilated. She'd miscalculated. She had not meant for such a movement to tease, she'd only thought to use it for a delay, but it had heightened his level of arousal.

She worked the fastenings of her skirt, finally letting it skitter to the floor, leaving her in chemise and petticoats. 'Free the mares,' she whispered huskily, finding some courage amid her fear. 'My dress is off. I want Dandy out next.' Three horses down, nine to go. She wanted to know Kildare was safe, but he was the prize. Windham would not let him go without a large forfeit from her. She rather hoped things would not get that far, that Crispin would come before they reached that point.

'Take down your hair and I'll let Dandy go.' Windham gestured to the man in the doorway awaiting orders.

Aurora raised her arms, reaching for the pins holding

the twist in place. She shook it free, letting the long fall of hair cascade around her shoulders. Windham rose and came to her, seizing a length of hair, bringing it to his nostrils and inhaling deeply. 'Lavender. Such a delicate, womanly smell.'

Aurora cringed and instinctively tried to step away. He captured her with an arm and dragged her against him. 'I'll be touching a lot more than your hair before we're through,' Windham answered. 'How well you play the innocent with me, such a potent aphrodisiac. Does Ramsden know what a consummate whore you are? What will he think when I tell him what we've done in here, in the very bed where he did the same thing?'

'It won't be the same thing.'

Windham made her pay for the retort. His hands fisted in the cloth of her chemise and ripped the fabric. Aurora gasped in terror. The nightmare got worse by the moment. She felt naked in her petticoats and shredded chemise in a way she'd never felt naked with Crispin even when she'd not worn a stitch. Instinctively, she crossed an arm over her chest, a futile shield against Windham's glittering eyes.

'The horses, I'll want two of the stallions,' she braved, trying to slow him down, but Windham had had enough of negotiating.

Windham sneered. He crowded her until he'd backed her into the bed frame. 'I find I grow weary of bargaining. I'll make one last bargain. Get on the bed and Kildare goes free.' He pushed her and she fell back on to the mattress. Sure of her compliance, Windham took a moment to undo his flap. Aurora seized the opportunity. She rolled to the other side of the bed and inelegantly scrambled off it, putting the bed between her and a furious Windham.

His eyes narrowed. 'Perhaps we'll have a lesson in discipline first. I will enjoy taking the crop to you.'

This was it. She'd have to fight, but with what? The bed and Windham stood between her and the door into the other room. Where was Crispin? Had a rampaging Sheikh raised any sort of alarm?

Windham smacked the crop against his hand and confidently moved around the foot of the bed. Aurora took the only avenue open to her and dived across the bed. If she was fast enough, she could gain the door.

She dived.

Windham lunged. Bigger, stronger, he felled her, his body effectively pinning her to the mattress. Aurora kicked and struggled, her efforts only serving to frustrate Wickham. He delivered a hard, stinging blow to her cheek, dazing her, subduing her. She clung to awareness with the last of her tenacity. She had to remain alert. She could not protect the horses unconscious.

There was nothing left to do but beg. Perhaps he'd planned it that way, knew it would be the final blow to what remained of her dignity. He'd taken her clothes, he'd rendered her helpless. He'd put her at his mercy. Surely that was enough. Aurora felt a tear of desperation slip out of the corner of her eye. 'Please, please don't do this. You've already humbled me.'

'Save your pathetic efforts. Pretend I'm Ramsden.'

Aurora clenched her jaw, felt his hand snake up her leg, bunching the petticoats as it went, felt the intimate press and hardness of his body, of the phallus that had risen so thoroughly in response to his crude requests. She shut her eyes, feeling each tear. Never had she been so helpless. Never had she had so little recourse. Not even her body was hers to control.

'Mr Windham!' A man dashed into the room. Her mortification sank to new lows at the thought of onlookers witnessing the débâcle. Windham made no move to ease from her, to hide her exposed body from the new arrival.

'There's riders on the horizon. If we're going to fire the place, we'd better do it now. There won't be time if we wait.'

'Damn! Throw me some rope.' Windham pressed down on her, making breathing difficult. 'I can finish with you later, Miss Calhoun. The choice is yours.'

The man returned with rope and Aurora realised what Windham intended. Unable to stop him, Aurora watched Windham loop the rope about her wrists and leash her to the bed frame. 'No, you can't mean to leave me here!' She started thrashing the moment he levered off her.

'Hush, Aurora.' Windham looked down at her, taking one last leer at her exposed breasts. 'The knot's not so tight you won't master it before the fire reaches you. If you want to escape, you will. Or perhaps you cannot live with the shame. Surely you don't expect Ramsden to want you now? There's not much to look forward to once you walk out this door, except knowing that I am waiting to finish what we've started.' He gave her a malevolent smile. 'Well, it's not for me to decide. I will leave you to your ponderings.' He took an exaggerated sniff of the air. 'Ah, smoke. Don't ponder too long.'

Aurora pulled herself up into a sitting position, the better to work the rope. Windham was right. The knot was loose enough to untie if she focused her thoughts, but it was hard to fight back her desire for haste. She had no way of knowing if Kildare had even been let out. Windham was a wholesale murderer dressed in gentlemen's coats.

She could smell smoke. She could hear the frightened neighs of the horses that were left. From the source of the sounds it seemed her captors had started at the end closest to the stable doors. The horses that were left were all in the stalls furthest from the door, with the least chance of rescue if the fire caught. Aurora struggled with the knot; it started to give. The smoke was thickening now. Dammit, they must have started the fire right outside the apartment doors, right in the centre of the stable. Fire wouldn't burn stone. It would burn the hay, the wooden stall doors, the beams that supported the roof. She had to get to the horses. The knot was almost undone.

'Smoke!' Crispin yelled, flying into a stable yard full of panicking horses, at least it seemed that way. In all likelihood there were only five horses. Their shrill calls of fright to their comrades still inside the stable lent a sense of chaos to the macabre scene. Crispin jumped down and smacked his horse on the rump, sending him out of the stable yard and away from the bedlam. Without hesitation he ran into the building, Peyton behind him. They'd come across Sheikh moments after leaving Dursley Park and they'd ridden like the devil to cover the distance.

'Aurora!' Crispin called out, raising a hand to ward off the smoke that threatened his vision.

Peyton checked the stalls they passed. 'They're empty. The remaining horses must be in the back. We'll not get to them this way. It's too far.'

Crispin nodded, still scanning the smoky interior for Aurora. Had she fallen and landed in an empty stall? Was she the one who'd freed the horses? How had they got out? 'There's a wide barn door at the other end. If you can open it from the outside, we can reach the horses. I'll check Aurora's apartments.'

Peyton nodded and dashed back towards the

entrance. Crispin knew he'd have to work fast. The flames were dangerously close to closing off any entrance to the apartments. Worse, flames licked at the beams supporting the roof. If the roof went, he'd be trapped. He had two minutes, not a second less if his judgement proved right.

A faint call reached his ears. He took one last look at the threatened beams and darted inside the apartments. 'Aurora! I'm coming!'

He found her in short order and swiftly cut away the remaining circuitry of the knot. It was obvious from the state of her that Windham had put her through an ordeal. He clutched Aurora to him, his anger soaring in primal waves of fury. How dare another attack what was his! But Windham could not be his concern now. Aurora's safety came first. She found her feet and together, they pushed their way back towards the corridor, Crispin hoping desperately the way was still clear. Ash fell from the ceiling, hot cinders flaking to the ground like snow.

He shielded her as best he could. They were lucky, it could have been worse. They would make it. He could just make out the open stable door ahead of them.

Suddenly, Aurora stiffened. Coughing and gasping, she managed one word. 'Kildare.'

Crispin shook his head frantically. 'There's no time. He may have got out.' He barely had enough voice left to utter that much. But then he heard what must have drawn Aurora's attention earlier: one last whinny in the centre of the stable. Peyton had saved all but one.

'No. Aurora, we can't. It's too risky,' he croaked with all the sternness he could muster, but Aurora jerked away from him and ran back into the inferno. He knew in the core of his being he'd never be whole again if Aurora did not survive. Crispin cursed hoarsely. Love was a damnable thing. There was no choice but to follow her.

Chapter Twenty

It was all a blur after that. Even years later, Crispin would remember little of what transpired after he followed Aurora back inside. He remembered ripping off his shirt and blindfolding Kildare; Aurora collapsing, her hands seared from handling the hot metal bolt on Kildare's stall. He remembered throwing her face down over Kildare's back like a set of saddle bags. The rest he recalled only thanks to Peyton, who caught him as he staggered out into the daylight, horse in tow. He remembered Peyton's arms about him and then nothing more. But he would never forget the fear that had drenched him; fear that he would lose her, that he would lose himself if he failed to protect her.

Physically, he'd come out of the fire remarkably unscathed with the exception of some minor burns on his chest, sustained in the last rescue. Aurora hadn't been as fortunate. Crispin glanced across the room where she lay dozing in the big bed. Three days since the fire and she was still pale, still exhausted. Her long hair was shorter now by three inches, having been singed. Her hands were wrapped in white bandages. The doctor assured him she'd recover full use of her hands, that she'd be able to hold reins again with no problem, but still the bandages were stark reminders of how close he'd come to losing her.

Of course, he wasn't surprised. Aurora obeyed no rules and was stubborn to a fault. That was why he loved her. That was why he hadn't left her side. Part of him feared he could still lose her. Not in the physical sense. She was out of danger from any subsequent ill effects of the fire. He feared he could lose her in other ways, that she'd never agree to his proposal now that the stable was gone. The loss was devastating. He'd gone down to survey the ruins, to see if there was any chance of rebuilding. He'd had nothing good to report upon his return. With that news, Aurora had seemed to slip a further from him.

Aurora stirred on the bed, deciding to wake up. 'You're still here,' she murmured at the sight of him in the window seat.

Crispin strode to the side of the bed and sat down on the edge beside her. 'Of course I'm still here.'

'I'm sure you have better things to do than sit in my room all day. You should go do them, Crispin. Tessa has a houseful of servants to wait on me.' She gave him a soft smile.

'I'd rather be the one to wait on you.' Crispin reached for a glass of water and held it for her. Her bandages made certain things difficult for the time being.

'I feel silly,' she said self-consciously, water dribbling down her chin.

'You're just used to being independent.' He set the glass back down. 'The weather is good today. Why don't we walk down to the barn and check on the horses?' He wanted to get her up and moving, wanted to get her out of this room and re-engaged in life. Something uncertain flickered in her eyes, but she reluctantly agreed. Crispin smiled his relief. One step at a time.

'There's so many of them!' Aurora exclaimed over the crowded stables. Peyton's facilities were indeed full to capacity in order to make room for Aurora's horses, but it wouldn't last long.

'The stables at Woodbrook will be ready by the week's end. We'll move the horses then,' Crispin said, easing into the things he wanted to discuss with her.

She looked at him curiously. 'You're staying, then?'

'Did you forget I've got a wedding on the horizon?'

Aurora sat down on a hay bale. 'I don't recall actually accepting and you don't have to marry me now, Crispin. You needn't feel any obligation or pity.'

Crispin began to interrupt, but she waved him into silence with her hand. 'I know it looks like the perfect solution. I've got nothing. The Calhoun stables are irreparable. I've got nowhere to go, nowhere to put up my horses and you've got a house and a barn just waiting to be filled. But you should get married for better reasons than that.'

'I asked you to marry me before all this happened,' Crispin reminded her.

'Everything is different now.'

'Nothing is different,' Crispin countered. He could see her prevaricating. What could he tell her that would persuade her this was the right path? She should know by now that she could trust him, that he didn't seek to change her. He wanted her just the way she was.

Aurora peered up at him. There was no other man equal to Crispin Ramsden. Did he have any idea how tempting it was to say yes? To let him share in her burdens? Those broad shoulders were more than capable of doing so, but she could not allow it. He would only end up being shamed by her. Windham had promised as much. 'You're wrong, Crispin. Windham—' she began, twisting a piece of straw between her fingers.

'Windham is a snake. He will be dealt with,' Crispin cut in.

Aurora shook her head. 'You cannot go around slaying all my dragons. I've fought too hard to become independent to let a man solve all my problems. Whatever happens with Windham, I want to be part of it. I deserve that. I've earned that. But it won't stop with Windham. I'm a divorced woman, Crispin. Even if I had rank, that would be enough for society to condemn me. I am an absolute liability to you. We can't hide that from society for ever. Someone will find out.'

'Peyton has voiced these concerns as well,' Crispin said flatly. 'But I've told you more than once that I don't care. I've never been one to put much stock in society's silly rules.'

'It's not just about you, Crispin. It's about Tessa and Peyton, Petra and Thomas and Eva with her début. The scandal would affect them if you married me. I don't think they'd be as nonchalant about it as you are. You feel you have nothing to lose.'

'I could lose you, Aurora. That is unacceptable. How another man let you get away is incomprehensible to me.'

She sighed and shook her head. 'Do you see why I hesitate? I've tried marriage to a peer before, Crispin. I can't pretend to be other than I am. My mother loved foolishly and gave birth to a bastard daughter. I loved foolishly and ended up divorced.

'Those kinds of things matter in your world. It is why

I must keep you at arm's length when it comes to any long-term commitment.' *And the fact that I love you beyond reason. I could not stand to see you hate me.*

'I'm not him,' Crispin said succinctly, closing his hand over hers where it lay on the railing, careful of the bandages. 'By the time those bandages are off and I can slip a ring on your finger, you'll know I am worthy of you, Aurora. I'm not a boy wet behind the ears. I am a man who knows his full measure. If I was not capable of upholding my vows, I would not propose something as enduring as marriage. May I ask the vicar to call the banns?'

The moment stretched out endlessly. Never had a three-lettered word carried so much import. 'Yes' meant more than an acceptance of the proposal, it committed her to a new way of life, one that was shared with a partner. It committed her to some level of re-engagement with society. What that level would be remained to be seen. Along with the re-entrance came the possibility of hurt and rejection. Saying yes committed her to taking that risk for Crispin's sake and the sake of the family she'd inherit through marriage. She had no doubt Crispin knew what he was asking of her. Her life had always been about risks and she was no coward. She took risks because they were worth taking and no risk to date had been more worthy than the one Crispin was asking her to take now. Suddenly, the choice was simple.

Aurora smiled. 'If you're willing to take the chance, I am too. Yes. I'll marry you.'

Some men persuaded with words, but words were often rendered meaningless in her experience. Perhaps that was why so few men had appealed to her over the years. Crispin Ramsden persuaded with actions.

Dursley Park thrummed with vibrant purpose over

the next three weeks. Crispin took up residence in the library, commandeering the long reading table for his workspace. Correspondence flowed steadily out into the world. Aurora would leave her bedchamber each day just to see what he was up to. Petra and Tessa were giddy with excitement and apparently full of secrets that caused them to laugh whenever she walked into a room.

Crispin's energy was infectious and she recognised it did much to return her to good spirits. The loss of her stables had been difficult to face, the horror of the ordeal with Windham even more so. But all that was swept aside in the wake of Crispin's enthusiasm. He wouldn't say more about whatever grand plan he'd set in motion, only that she should trust him. And to her surprise, she did.

The horses were moved to Woodbrook and Crispin began to spend long days away from his table in the library, returning each night at sunset, a tired smile on his face. Her bandages came off the day after the banns were read for the third time. The next day, Crispin presented her with a pair of specially made riding gloves and hoisted her up on Kildare. 'We're going for a ride,' he said with a playful spark in his eye while he adjusted the girth on Kildare's saddle for her.

It was the first time she'd ridden since the fire and the day was glorious. Somehow, March had bled into early April without her notice. Green had returned to England. Roadside hedges bloomed in a profusion of colours. Aurora flexed her newly healed hands around the reins, feeling the tight skin stretch. She revelled in it. It was the feeling of health. Beneath her, Kildare protested the sedate pace, fighting for his head, and Aurora gave in, eager to taste the wind and celebrate her freedom. 'Race you!' she called to Crispin.

'Aurora, wait, you don't know where we're going!' Crispin laughed.

'Better catch me, then!' she called over her shoulder.

They were going to Woodbrook. Aurora didn't know, of course, until they turned into the lane with its freshly painted sign reading 'Woodbrook Manor and Horse Farm.'

'You couldn't break the entail?' Aurora asked, sliding off Kildare in the yard.

Crispin came around to catch her, planting a kiss on her cheek. 'Didn't *want* to break the entail, after all,' he corrected.

The place was quiet today, but Aurora could see signs of construction. Timber was piled to one side where a shed was being built. Fencing around an outdoor arena looked new and other projects were progressing from the looks of things. 'So this is where you've been spending your time.'

Crispin grinned. 'Do you like it? Come, I'll give you the tour. If I know you, you'll want to see the stables first, the house second.'

She laughed. 'How'd you guess?'

'That first day in the road, you were more worried about Sheikh than me. I knew right then who had priority with you.'

It was almost overwhelming. Aurora doubted any other woman in England would get teary-eyed over a stable, but she did. Everything was of the finest quality. Her horses could not expect better accommodations. Neither could she expect a better training facility. 'We'll win St Albans every year,' she whispered in awe.

'We'll breed champions here, Aurora. This is the start of a whole new life for us, a life together.' Crispin's grip tightened on her hand and she winced a little at the unconscious pressure. Was that a tremor she'd heard in his voice? It had been so slight as to be hardly noticeable. Perhaps he'd merely swallowed the wrong way.

He let her gape at the indoor arena a few moments longer before ushering her over to the house. 'Here, try the key,' he said solemnly, pressing the key into her hand.

Aurora fitted the key into the lock, nerves fluttering suddenly in her stomach. She pushed the door open and stared in amazement. 'This is incredible.' Now she knew what Tessa and Petra had been doing. They'd been creating a home for her. Aurora stepped inside. Walls were freshly painted a pale yellow. Braided rugs dotted the floor in cheery colours. 'And furniture, too!' Aurora exclaimed. A yellow-and-blue print sofa and matching overstuffed chairs framed a white-mantled fireplace.

She wandered from room to room. She marvelled at the kitchen, which Crispin assured her would have a cook. 'We won't have to live on toasted cheese and stew every night,' he joked.

She ran her hand along the smooth surface of the dining-room table, and commented on the dishes already arranged in the china cabinet. 'Not exactly my wooden plates, are they?'

Upstairs, guest rooms were in serviceable order. The master's suite was spotless and perfect right down to the comforter turned back on the massive carved bed. 'It looks like it's just waiting for us.' She gave Crispin a mischievous smile.

'It certainly does.' He made a sweeping gesture towards the bed. 'After you, my love.'

An afternoon spent making love did much to dispel the nerves Aurora had felt at the door. She was fully cognisant of the great gift Crispin had given her. He'd given her back her life, her dreams. With Kildare and Sheikh to stand to stud, she could breed to her heart's content. With the protection of his name and his connections, she could re-establish her riding academy for women and never worry about malice destroying it again. It was not clear if they'd ever have social acceptance outside their little part of the world, but that was of secondary concern and they would have to grapple with it later. This was not a fairy tale where the prince could magically remove all her problems, all her obstacles. That was fine with her. She didn't want the fairy tale. A woman should be able to take care of herself.

More importantly, she understood that his actions said what his words could not and they were all the more meaningful because of it. *I love you.*

For the first time since the proposal, she saw what it had cost him to commit to marriage. Her acceptance was only part of the investment being made to this relationship. When he'd said this was the beginning of a whole new life for them, he'd not meant only her. He'd meant himself. There'd be no more moving around, no more dangerous assignments from the Foreign Office. His world was changing as assuredly as hers was.

'You've laid the world at my feet, Crispin,' Aurora murmured drowsily, snuggled against him in the big bed.

'I've laid Woodbrook Manor at your feet, Aurora,' he corrected teasingly. 'But if you want the world, I'll try to give you that too.' Crispin dislodged her and sat up. He reached for his discarded jacket and rummaged through it. 'I've been waiting to give you this.' He produced a small velvet box tied prettily with a pink ribbon.

The ring. Aurora knew what it was before she opened it, but that didn't stop her from gasping. Yet another display of his thoughtfulness. The ring was a simple band of gold containing three small diamonds. It was a ring she could wear beneath riding gloves, a ring to wear every day while she worked without worrying that it would snag on a harness. 'It's perfect.'

Crispin took it from her and slid it on to her hand. 'There's another surprise for you in the wardrobe.'

Aurora tossed him a saucy look. 'You just want to watch me walk across the room naked.'

Crispin grinned and laid back against the pillows, folding his arms behind his head. 'Well, that too.'

Aurora opened the wardrobe and stared. She'd been staring all day. She'd been overwhelmed all day. Crispin had arranged everything perfectly. This was no exception. 'My wedding dress,' she said simply. 'I was going to ask Tessa for one of her dresses.'

'You'll have your own gowns from now on, starting with that dress there. Not that you need to wear them, mind you. You're welcome to your trousers, but your clothes should be your own.'

'How did you ever manage this?' Aurora stroked the soft silk of the ivory gown.

'I wrote to Eva in London. If anyone knows dresses and sizes, it's Eva. She saw to all of it. I'm glad it pleases you, as far as dresses go anyway.'

Aurora fingered the celery-coloured ribbons that trimmed the sleeves. 'I'll write to her and thank her. This has been an extraordinary day.' She hung the dress back in the wardrobe and climbed back into bed, snuggling against Crispin's warm form.

'Are you happy, Aurora?' His strong arm came around her, a hand idly fussing with a length of hair.

Oddly enough, with all the miracles of the day, she couldn't give him the answer he expected. She opted to answer with a question of her own. 'Are you?'

'I have you, don't I?' Crispin whispered, rolling her

beneath him. Aurora said nothing, but she was not easily fooled. There were a lot of questions in bed with them and very few answers.

Chapter Twenty-One

There was one more issue to wrap up before the wedding, one more loose end that needed tying: Gregory Windham. With Windham squared away, Crispin would have done all he could to ensure a smooth transition for Aurora. She had not made it easy.

True to her word, Aurora insisted on being part of the plans to serve out justice to Windham. Crispin would have spared her the discomfort. He would also have preferred to have settled the issue more decisively with his fists, but Windham needed justice that would legally cast him out of society on a more permanent basis. In this instance, naked revenge would not help Aurora's cause.

Although he would have liked to have Aurora step aside on the matter, her help proved to be invaluable in building the case against Windham. She had a familiarity with the situation that he did not. She knew who to seek out to acquire the testimonies needed to build the case, cutting down their preparation time drastically. Together, they gathered depositions from Mackey the blacksmith, who'd been more than eager to tell the earl and his brother what transpired between him and

Windham, especially the parts where Mackey had refused to contribute to Windham's scheme any longer. 'I had nothing to do with burning the barn,' he'd said contritely. 'That was all Windham's men. By that point, he wasn't using village help any more. We'd had enough.'

Mackey had put them on to his assistant, Ernie, who confessed to the night attack with a beet-coloured blush. Ernie also mentioned meeting in the tavern's private room and that led them to question the tavern owner, who recalled the names of the men who'd come to meet with Windham. Aurora immediately recognised the names as belonging to her students. There were letters and interviews exchanged until the pattern of Windham's method was clear—he'd played the concerned citizen with these parents, preying on their concern for their daughters' and wives' well-being for his own benefit, subtly encouraging them to leave the academy. These letters came with post-scripted apologies over Windham's chicanery and some even with promises to pursue lessons once they returned to the area; a small sign of hope in regards to the campaign for social acceptance.

Most significant of all, there was Eleanor's letter, saved from the fire only by luck and charred around the edges, bearing witness to her concern that, if she left, her father would extract retribution from Aurora. The letter had been dated a week before the fire.

By the time they were done, they'd built a devastating case against Windham. Crispin would have preferred that the case never be aired publicly. He hoped the visit he and Peyton paid Windham would suffice for justice.

'Do you have all the files?' Peyton asked, swinging up beside him on to a sleek grey stallion.

'Yes.' Crispin patted the saddlebags. 'The copies are in your safe. I hope Windham sees reason and we have no cause to use them, however.' Crispin was grim. He cast a parting look up at the window of Aurora's room at Dursley Park. He had not told her that he meant to confront Windham today. This was for him to settle and he feared Aurora would insist on coming along. There were times when a man had to be allowed to do things for those he loved.

A familiar voice called out from an upper window and Crispin grimaced. This was not going to be one of those times. 'Wait, Crispin, where are you going?'

He looked up to see Aurora leaning over the casement. He did not dare lie to her now. 'We're going to see Windham,' he said with straightforward seriousness.

'Not without me you aren't.' Aurora slammed the window sash down and Crispin knew she'd re-appear at the front door in two minutes, the precise time it took to gain the entrance from the upper hall.

'At least she didn't shout at you for not telling her,' Peyton offered.

'Not yet. She will.' Crispin frowned.

Aurora gained the front steps, calling for a horse and slightly out of breath. He had only a few minutes to dissuade her before a groom arrived with a mount.

'Aurora, you don't have to go,' Crispin began. 'Any obligation you have to see justice served has been fulfilled. You've gathered testimonies, listened to difficult conversations about what has been done to you all for one man's revenge. You don't need to do any more. Let me handle this.'

'I will see this through to the end, Crispin.' Aurora's determination was obvious and redoubtable. 'He attempted to debase me in the most demeaning of ways.

He meant to break my pride. He meant to break me. He has to know that he did not succeed. I want him to look me in the eye and know he failed.'

Crispin knew the argument was lost. Or won, depending on how one looked at it. A horse arrived saddled from the stables. He tossed Aurora up and they were off on what was to be the final leg of their journey before they could take the walk to the altar.

They arrived in the early part of the afternoon when Windham was sure to be home. They were readily received and ushered into Windham's office. Crispin thought Windham looked rather the worse for the wear. The man's face was haggard, pale, his eyes ringed by dark circles. Perhaps waiting to confront Windham had had its benefits. His eyes widened at the sight of Aurora with them.

'Expecting us?' Crispin asked coolly as he drew out a chair for Aurora, emphasising the courtesy due a lady. He and Peyton each took a chair on either side of her in front of Windham's desk.

'I've been expecting *you* for weeks,' Windham confirmed Crispin's suspicions. Windham had thought they'd come much earlier and the waiting had taken its toll. 'Not her.' He jabbed a finger at Aurora. 'I want her out of my house. She's a Jezebel who's brought nothing but trouble to my home.'

'She stays,' Crispin answered with steel. 'She's the reason we're here and an important witness to your crimes.'

'I know nothing of crimes. There have been no charges,' Windham growled.

Peyton intervened and redirected the conversation. 'As someone of magisterial authority in these parts, I've been been investigating the fire at Miss Calhoun's stables,' he said objectively. 'We're here because it seems you've had quite an adversarial relationship with Miss Calhoun and her own testimony puts you at the stables the day of the fire.'

'She's a whore. No court will believe her lies and I'll swear to her questionable morals. I have witnesses, too, you see. I have men who will vow they've seen you spend the night in her bed, Ramsden. I'll tell them about the divorce in Ireland,' he sneered at Aurora. 'Did you think I didn't know? I know every dirty secret about you, my dear. Miss Calhoun isn't even your legal name.'

Aurora stirred beside Crispin, meeting Windham's eyes evenly. 'No, there are grounds to claim that my legal name is Baroness Ashtonmere. Since the divorce that's become a bit muddled and I prefer to go by my maiden name. My former husband prefers it too and I am happy to oblige.'

Crispin grinned at Windham's discomfort. The man who'd craved a title, who'd put Aurora down because her lack of one, had been served a very just desert at Aurora's hand. He'd have to scold her a little later, though, for keeping that bit of information from him. Not that her title mattered. In all likelihood it was defunct as Aurora had suggested. Still, some people in society would settle for any title at all when it came to conferring acceptability.

Crispin reached for the files, ready to add injury to insult. 'As for those men who'd claim I'd spent the night, I have depositions from them regarding what they were doing on private property in the middle of the night to know such details. They and others also attest to your intense dislike of Miss Calhoun.' He pushed the file across the desk. 'Look through it carefully. There is bountiful proof that you have attempted to ruin her business in hopes of forcing her to leave the area. There is also more damaging testimony from Ernie and Mackey about putting glass in Dandy's stall. Currently, we've not mentioned the disappointing episode at St Albans, but that could always be brought up,' Crispin said in falsely congenial tones.

There was a long silence while Windham went through the files, scanning the assembled documents.

'This would be scandalous indeed if it went to a public trial. Surely that cannot be what you wish.' Windham pushed the file back towards Crispin. 'I've heard the banns called. If you mean to marry her and make her respectable, you cannot wish to see her made the centrepiece of a trial where her dubious background will become an issue.'

Crispin shrugged at the threat. 'I am not a man of convention, Windham. I do not care about scandal. It will not change my feelings for my wife. I do not live among society and their opinions matter little to me.'

Crispin leaned forwards, his stature menacing. 'I do, however, care that justice is done. I will not allow my wife to live in proximity to a man who secretly covets her body and has attempted to force himself on her in the most crude of ways. A trial is nothing to me.' Crispin leaned back in the chair, hands steepled confidently in front of him.

'But you have a daughter,' Peyton put in. 'Eleanor would be painted by the same brush that taints you. A trial cannot be what *you* wish.'

'Eleanor is gone,' Windham said with dead eyes. 'Aurora Calhoun has inspired her to flee her marriage.' Anger simmered behind his flat grey gaze.

'Regardless, wherever she is, her reputation is all she has to recommend her. I would think we all must attempt to protect her in any way possible, give her the chance to make her own way. The world is harsh for a woman alone,' Peyton said smoothly.

'To that end, because of my bride's friendship with your daughter, I wish to offer you a deal.' Crispin's gaze was cold. 'You have two weeks to organise your affairs. Then you embark for Australia, not to return upon pain of immediate arrest for arson, attempted rape and the other sundry list of crimes you've committed against the future Lady Aurora.'

Windham's reaction was not what Crispin had been hoping for, but rather the one he was prepared for. 'I will kill you for this!' Windham leapt across the desk for Aurora, a dangerous blade glinting from nowhere in his hand.

Aurora's excellent reflexes saved her the worst of it. She managed to throw herself out of her chair and catch the blade on her arm, but Windham was off balance and went down with her. She fought back with her fists, flailing and punching, anything that would keep the dangerous blade from finding purchase. Rescue was immediate. Before the blade could strike again, Windham's weight left her and the fight turned as Crispin dealt him a facer, his own blade in his left hand already drawn from his boot.

Windham grappled with Crispin, but the older man was no match for Crispin's anger or expertise. Within moments, Crispin held his blade against Windham's throat. 'Now you're bargaining for your life,' Crispin growled. 'Australia, or this knife across your throat. It's no less than you deserve.'

He could sense Windham's fear. 'Australia,' the man croaked.

Crispin released him with a shove. 'Two weeks.

You're gone before my wedding. Peyton, be sure to remind him that we know Governor Arthur quite well.'

Crispin sheathed his blade and gathered Aurora to him. He escorted her out of the room to look after her injured arm, thankful it was only a small nick. Peyton could settle the details. His own temper was running too hot to be of use, but he was relieved none the less. Aurora would be spared any scandal and Windham would be a world away, unable to harm her. There was nothing left to stand in the way of marrying Aurora and taking up life as a gentleman horse breeder. Peyton would be thrilled to have him nearby. Aurora would be delighted to re-open her school. All that was left to do was post his resignation letter to the Foreign Office and await his bride at the altar. The loose ends were wrapped up. So why did he feel something was missing?

Chapter Twenty-Two

'What is the matter with me?' Aurora stepped down from the ottoman in Tessa's rooms, carefully lifting the hem of her wedding gown so that she didn't disturb the pins Tessa's maid had used to adjust the length. She stared at the woman in the mirror, the woman who would marry Lord Crispin Ramsden in two days and take up residence at Woodbrook as Lady Ramsden. Life was a long way from the three-room cottage she'd shared with her father in County Kildare, a long way from the small apartments she'd kept at her stables.

'Wedding jitters?' Tessa ventured a guess from the *chaise* where she rocked the baby. 'Everyone gets them.'

'Did you?' Aurora stood still to let the maid unbutton the exquisite dress.

'Well, to be honest, no,' Tessa admitted, then hastily added, 'Our circumstances were different, though. Jitters or not, there was no going back. We had a baby on the way.'

The addendum didn't assure Aurora. 'If you weren't sure, you wouldn't have married Peyton no matter what the situation. I know you too well, Tess.'

'I see.' Tessa handed the baby to a maid and smoothed her skirts, gathering her thoughts. 'You have doubts about Crispin?'

'No.' Aurora was confident on that score. In the weeks since accepting Crispin's ring that afternoon at Woodbrook, she'd sorted through her feelings, her nerves, countless times, looking for the source of her anxiety. 'But something's not right.' Aurora slipped into robe and sat down next to Tessa.

'Maybe it's the ring, the idea that this is for ever?'

'No.' Aurora twisted the gold band on her hand, studying it. 'Crispin has demonstrated that he loves me as much as a man can love a woman and beyond that even. Perhaps that's what bothers me. He's given up everything that matters to him.' She shook her head. 'He didn't come home to Dursley Park looking to stay and start a life.' Her mind was whirling now. She'd known from the start how much he valued his freedom, how he'd thought he'd be bored if he stayed in Dursley too long. He was a man used to wandering. He'd put that aside for her.

'He changed himself for me, Tessa, but I never wanted that. I never asked for that.' She knew now what was wrong and she was desperate to find him. She should have questioned this earlier. 'I have to find Crispin. I won't have my happiness purchased at the price of another's freedom.'

'The gown...we're not finished,' the maid protested.

Aurora shook her head. 'It won't matter. We won't need it.'

Crispin needed fresh air. He'd promised Peyton he would spend time looking at some legal documents with him this afternoon, but he wasn't ready to go inside. In two days, he'd be a married man, finally succumbing to the parson's mousetrap like his brothers before him. His freedom would be gone. Never again would he have the freedom to do as he pleased, to wander the length of the empire, to dance at gypsy campfires high in the mountains of countries waiting to be formed. In two days, he'd become Lord Crispin Ramsden and take his place in English society, whatever that place might be. Just as he had feared he would that day months ago when Peyton had first taken him to Woodbrook.

All that he'd abhorred about commitment had come to pass with two substantial differences. It had happened far more quickly than he'd anticipated. And he had Aurora in exchange for what he was about to give up. That was far more reward than he'd imagined. For Aurora, he'd give up everything. He'd not lied when he told her he'd give her the world.

He'd have a wife and a business that would bring him pleasure. Sheikh was a fine horse with prospects and it wasn't as if Aurora wasn't giving anything up either. As Lady Ramsden, she'd never race at St Albans again. She'd have to limit her steeplechasing to hunt parties and private endeavours, but they would be together and they'd have their own world somewhat apart from society at Woodbrook. It would be enough. More than enough. Any other man would begrudge him his success. He was marrying on his own terms, something not every man in England could claim.

And yet he had not sent his resignation from the Foreign Office. He'd penned it, folded it, and put it in a dresser drawer right next to the letter containing his next assignment. As he'd expected, it was to South Carolina to monitor the growing unrest in America over the slave trade, an issue that was fast coming to a head in the British Empire as well. There was a horse farm he'd be leasing for the duration of his two-year stay, although that stay was likely to be longer.

The very thought of horses seemed to conjure Aurora out of nowhere. She was dressed in trousers and one of her cut-down man's shirts, walking with grim determination down the path towards him. He smiled at the sight of her, his blood already heating. Oh, yes, this should be enough, he thought. He would make it so.

'Crispin, we can't get married,' Aurora blurted out, taking him completely off guard.

'I don't understand.' Crispin tried to focus his thoughts. Was something wrong with her dress? With the flowers? The church? What did women worry about before a wedding?

'Don't you see? I can't have you giving up your freedom for me. I don't know why I didn't see it sooner. Maybe I just didn't want to see it.'

'Aurora, wait. Slow down. You've got cold feet.' He reached for her hand and gripped it.

'Crispin, you feel it too. At Woodbrook, I asked if you were happy and you couldn't answer me. When we walked into the house, I felt your hand tighten on mine like it is now and your voice trembled.'

Crispin gave a harsh laugh. He couldn't deny her intuitions. 'I've always wondered what it would be like to have a woman know me, to truly know and understand me. I thought I'd like it. It was always the standard by which I rejected everyone, until you. You know me too well, Aurora, and I rather wish you didn't.'

Aurora wasn't daunted. 'I know you because I know myself. We are two wild hearts, Crispin. Marriage and tradition aren't for us.' She tugged at the gold band until it came off. 'Take it, Cris. I love you too much to hold you. There are some horses that aren't meant to be tamed.'

Her eyes watered, liquid moss.

He stared at the ring in the flat of his palm. He had his freedom. She'd understood his need as clearly as he had understood himself, but she was only half-right. 'I need you too, Aurora. My freedom isn't worth much without you. Maybe we aren't cut out for tradition, but I'm sure I'm cut out for marriage to you.'

'Well, we can't have both. Take your freedom and run, Crispin. I won't be strong for ever.'

Crispin regarded her for a long moment. He could not leave her. He would regret it to the end of his days. He knew it deep in his bones just as he knew there was still something fundamentally flawed in their future plans. A bold thought came to him. It wasn't the marrying he held any reservation with. With a newfound clarity, he spoke slowly as the thoughts came to him. 'Why do we have to choose? Why does marriage have to mean tradition?'

He thought of the letter in his drawer. 'Marry me. I've got a posting to South Carolina. Come with me. I'm to be a respectable horse breeder and it's meant to be more permanent, danger free. I love you and that's all that matters as long as you love me too.'

'And leave Woodbrook?' she teased, but he could see from the dancing lights in her eyes that her relief was nearly a palpable thing.

'Petra and Thomas can put it to good use until we decide we're ready for it.' Crispin grinned, his blood humming as his improvised plans took root. He felt alive, the dread of the past few days easing from his shoulders while he spun possibilities with Aurora at the paddock fence.

'I hear America is a more open society,' Aurora ventured.

Crispin nodded, understanding the root of her concern. There was no sense in leaving England if her antecedents would make her a pariah in the New World as well. 'The people there put great stock in what a man can do instead of who he is and what family he was born into. Where we're going, there's supposed to be some fine plantation homes, but the men who built them are only a generation away from having lived in log cabins in the woods. These planters are self-made men and many of their wives are self-made women.'

Aurora smiled at his reassurance. 'A place to re-invent myself sounds good.'

'Well, I wouldn't re-invent too much. I do like you just the way you are.' Crispin reached for her, kissing her full on the mouth. 'I think we've solved the riddle of our cold feet. Rather, you've solved it, Aurora, my brave girl.' He winked. 'If you hadn't spoken up, we would have started a life we weren't meant to live.'

Two months ago he'd never have believed this moment was possible. Now, he was happily awaiting his wedding to the most vibrant, stubbornly independent woman alive. Life was an adventure once more, the only way he knew how to live it.

Aurora tilted her head to the side, studying him in earnest. 'What are you thinking, Crispin?'

'Aurora, I'm thinking that I never saw you coming.'

Two days later, Aurora entered the small stone chapel at Dursley Park on a late sunlit spring morning, radiantly turned out in ivory silk, a crown of spring flowers in her dark hair, her arm looped through the Earl of Dursley's to make her way down the aisle amid the gaze of those gathered to witness the wedding.

There were friends among those assembled: Petra and Thomas, Eva and Aunt Lily who'd journeyed from London for the occasion, along with Catherine Sykes and her parents. Letitia Osborne had come, too, confessing that she wouldn't miss a chance to see the parish's bachelor vicar perform a wedding. Who knew, she'd giggled, it might put him in a proposing mood.

Aurora knew they were there. She was grateful for their presence and all it signified, but while all eyes were on her, she had eyes only for the handsome man at the altar. Crispin Ramsden waited for her, a man of uncommon strength of character, who loved her unconditionally and was willing to be her partner in life on entirely unconventional terms. His presence in her life was a blessing she had long stopped looking for.

Aurora blinked hard against an errant tear. Characteristically prepared for any circumstance, Peyton discreetly passed her a handkerchief. 'You make him happy, my dear. Shall we?'

She would remember for the rest of her life the joy that surged in her step by step down that aisle, her happiness growing greater as the distance to Crispin diminished. By the time Peyton placed her hand in his, she was full to bursting. Crispin looked at her with blue eyes that mirrored the joy of her own and smiled.

The vicar began the service, but the words were for the others assembled. They were lost in their world, emerging to recite their vows.

'You were right, the first day we met,' Aurora whispered softly during the final prayer before the service concluded.

'About what?'

'You said there were no other men like you and you were absolutely correct.'

At that moment the vicar intoned the words that ended the ceremony. 'By the power of the Church of England, I now pronounce you man and wife. You may kiss the bride.'

'Ah, my favourite part,' Crispin murmured, moving to take her in his arms. 'I have it on good authority I kiss better than I ride.'

'Thank goodness for small miracles,' Aurora breathed as Crispin took her in a kiss that would long be remembered as the finest wedding kiss Dursley had ever seen.

Outside, an open carriage waited to take them to the wedding breakfast at Dursley Park and yet another carriage waited to take them later on the first stage of their journey to Southampton and the ship to South Carolina, the ship to their future, where Kildare and Sheikh would have first-class accommodations for the duration of the voyage.

Hand in hand, Aurora walked the aisle beside Crispin towards that future. She smiled up at her husband. Who would have thought that the best way to tame wild hearts would have been to let them run free?

Epilogue

Aurora and Crispin Ramsden stood at the rail of the sleek schooner that would take them across the Atlantic to Charleston, South Carolina and into their new life. The breeze off the water blew Crispin's dark hair back from his face as he waved to the figures on the wharf. Tessa and Peyton had come to see them off, all three of the boys gathered around them; the baby in Tessa's arms and the twins climbing on Peyton. Crispin swallowed hard. He had not anticipated such a reaction to this farewell.

'Miss them already?' Aurora asked softly by his side.

'We'll see them again,' Crispin said staunchly. 'I've already got summers planned for those scamps when they're old enough.'

'The assignment's only for a few years.' Aurora smiled up at her husband.

Crispin shrugged. 'You never know. I feel like South Carolina might be the right place for us. A new world, a new life where we can decide who we want to be.'

'I know, I feel it too.' Aurora's voice was edged with excitement.

Crispin waved one last time. It had been a whirlwind

month. Gregory Windham had kept his word and disappeared quietly to Australia before the wedding. The wedding had been perfect; small and simple in the old family chapel, attended by friends they'd made in St Albans and by family. Petra and Thomas had been thrilled to take over Woodbrook and awed, too, by the generous wedding gift of the farm. Everything had fallen into place.

'Eleanor's out there somewhere—I hope she's all right.' Aurora sighed as Peyton and Tessa finally slipped from view.

Eleanor Windham was the only loose end Crispin could do nothing about. There'd been no word or sign of her since her disappearance and he knew it weighed on Aurora's mind, that Aurora felt some responsibility for the girl.

Crispin wrapped an arm about his wife's shoulders, still marvelling that he'd found the one woman in the world that could understand and fulfil him so completely. 'She'll be fine.'

The decision to leave had been a hard one to make, but the right one. There were plenty of people in South Carolina who were only one generation away from their common roots, who were more interested in what a man could make of his life than where he was born. In South Carolina they'd have a chance.

'Shall we go check on the horses?' Aurora asked after a long silence. In the large hold below, Kildare, Sheikh and Dandy would be settling in to their new quarters for the next twenty days.

Crispin nodded. 'It's always the horses first with you, isn't it?' he teased.

Aurora cocked her head and looked up at him, her green eyes dancing. 'Unless you have something better in mind?'

'As a matter of fact I do.' Crispin caught her mouth in a full-bodied kiss. 'The horses can wait.'

Aurora laughed at him, her arms about his neck.

Crispin hugged her to him and looked out over the water to their future, fully confident that the greatest adventure was the one that lay ahead.

* * * * *

COMING NEXT MONTH FROM

HARLEQUIN® HISTORICAL

Available July 27, 2010

- **THE LAWMAN'S REDEMPTION**
  by **Pam Crooks**
  (Western)
- **THE SMUGGLER AND THE SOCIETY BRIDE**
  by **Julia Justiss**
  (Regency)
  Book 3 in the *Silk & Scandal* miniseries
- **ONE UNASHAMED NIGHT**
  by **Sophia James**
  (Regency)
- **HIGHLAND ROGUE, LONDON MISS**
  by **Margaret Moore**
  (Regency)

HHCNM0710

Spotlight on

Heart & Home

Heartwarming romances
where love can happen
right when you least expect it.

See the next page to enjoy a sneak peek
from Harlequin® American Romance®,
a Heart and Home series.

Five hunky Texas single fathers—five stories from Cathy Gillen Thacker's LONE STAR DADS *miniseries. Here's an excerpt from the latest, THE MOMMY PROPOSAL from Harlequin American Romance.*

"I hear you work miracles," Nate Hutchinson drawled. Brooke Mitchell had just stepped into his lavishly appointed office in downtown Fort Worth, Texas.

"Sometimes, I do." Brooke smiled and took the sexy financier's hand in hers, shook it briefly.

"Good." Nate looked her straight in the eye. "Because I'm in need of a home makeover—fast. The son of an old friend is coming to live with me."

She was still tingling from the feel of his warm palm. "Temporarily or permanently?"

"If all goes according to plan, I'll adopt Landry by summer's end."

Brooke had heard the founder of Nate Hutchinson Financial Services was eligible, wealthy and generous to a fault. She hadn't known he was in the market for a family, but she supposed she shouldn't be surprised. But Brooke had figured a man as successful and handsome as Nate would want one the old-fashioned way. *Not that this was any of her business...*

"So what's the child like?" she asked crisply, trying not to think how the marine-blue of Nate's dress shirt deepened the hue of his eyes.

"I don't know." Nate took a seat behind his massive antique mahogany desk. He relaxed against the smooth leather of the chair. "I've never met him."

"Yet you've invited this kid to live with you permanently?"

"It's complicated. But I'm sure it's going to be fine."

Obviously Nate Hutchinson knew as little about teenage

boys as he did about decorating. But that wasn't her problem. Finding a way to do the assignment without getting the least bit emotionally involved was.

Find out how a young boy brings Nate and Brooke together in THE MOMMY PROPOSAL, coming August 2010 from Harlequin American Romance.

HAREXP0810

Praise for Amanda Forester

"Forester blends a fast-paced adventurous plot with political and religious intrigue to form the perfect backdrop for a delightful romance. The humor and interaction between two unique characters is an ideal counterpoint."

—*RT Book Reviews* Top Pick, 4.5 Stars

"Ms. Forester's prose and attention to detail are spot-on. I loved the richness of her work, and felt that the lush and vividly created scenes added to the realism of the story… The narrative is fantastic."

—*The Long and Short of It*

"The plot never falters, and fans will appreciate Forester's devotion to historical accuracy and effortless storytelling."

—*Publishers Weekly*

"Highly entertaining… the setting adequately detailed, the era perfectly captured, and the romance expertly written."

—*Romance Fiction Suite 101*

"Thrilling… Amanda Forester has a talent for incorporating intrigue and romance in equal measure into a plot. Her language and descriptions of food, parties, beliefs, and holidays brim with credibility… Forester will capture the hearts of readers."

—*Romance Junkies*

"A radiant gem… such a wonderful story that it invaded my dreams. The author has done a better than superb job at giving us a wonderful romp."

—*Yankee Romance Reviews*

Also by Amanda Forester

The Highlander's Sword
The Highlander's Heart
True Highland Spirit

A Wedding in Springtime

Amanda Forester

Cover design by Robert Papp/Shannon and Associates
Photography by Jon Zychowski
Models: Danielle Day and Dylan Solon/Agency Galatea

Published by Sourcebooks Casablanca, an imprint of Sourcebooks, Inc.
P.O. Box 4410, Naperville, Illinois 60567-4410
(630) 961-3900
FAX: (630) 961-2168
www.sourcebooks.com

Printed and bound in Canada
WC 10 9 8 7 6 5 4 3 2 1

To my family, who is my greatest joy.
And to Ed, who remains my hero.

One

London, Spring 1810

Ten minutes into her societal debut, Eugenia Talbot was ruined.

A favorable presentation in court cannot ensure a young lady's successful launch into society, but a poor presentation can certainly ruin it. Miss Eugenia Talbot pressed her lips together in an attempt to make the laughter gurgling up inside her die in her throat. The Queen of England glared down her royal nose at Genie. Her Royal Highness, Queen Charlotte, was not amused.

Genie took a deep breath—hard to do laced so tight in her stays she feared one wrong move would crack a rib. The restrictive corset held her posture rigid, which helped keep her headdress in place, a heavy jeweled item with a monstrous, white ostrich plume. Genie knelt in a deep curtsy before the queen, a move she had practiced with a special tutor hired by her aunt to ensure her correct performance. A deep curtsy wearing the required elaborate hoop skirt of court that weighed almost two stone needed to be practiced.

Rising majestically from her curtsy, Genie was pleased she had successfully navigated that potential hazard and brought herself under control. Perhaps the queen had not noticed the stifled giggle. It was hardly Genie's fault, for when the Lord Chamberlain announced her name, he also let loose an audible bodily noise. Having the unfortunate influence of brothers in her formative years, Genie could not help but find amusement in the Lord Chamberlain's offense.

"How is your family, Miss Talbot?" asked the queen with staunch politeness.

"They are all well, Your Highness," responded Genie as coached.

"Are your parents with you in London?"

"No, Your Highness. I am staying with Lady Bremerton, my aunt." Genie glanced at Aunt Cora, whose frozen countenance betrayed her anxiety over Genie's presentation.

"And your brothers and sisters?"

"I have four brothers. Two at university, one in the regulars, and one in the Royal Navy."

"Ah, our sons, they have been ripped from our bosom. Ripped I say."

"Yes, ma'am," said Genie, pressing her lips together again. She was going to kill her brothers when they returned for teaching her deplorable cant. She could not laugh.

"It is a foul wind that blows from France," said the queen.

And the Lord Chamberlain chose that moment to blow a little foul wind himself. It was loud and long, and just when Genie thought he had finished, he gave another little toot. She clenched her jaw so tight tears formed in her eyes.

She took a calming breath, sure she had gotten herself under regulation until she spied a man silently laughing, his shoulders shaking, his smile hidden behind his hand. He caught her eye, gave her a broad smile, and winked.

The entire drawing room was silently staring at her with censure. The queen gave her a look that could blister paint. The more Genie tried to get herself under control, the more amusing the entire scene became. It could not be helped; her body started to shake.

Genie attempted to take a deep breath and a giggle escaped. She tried to squelch it, but a laugh emerged, followed by an unladylike chortle and an unfortunate snort. The more she tried to stop, the worse it became, and with a burst, Genie was laughing out loud.

The queen waved a hand to dismiss her. Instead of dissipating Genie's humor, it only made her laugh harder. Genie managed another deep bow and walked backward out of the queen's presence, giggling as she went. By some miracle, she did not trip on her gown and fall to the floor. It hardly would have mattered if she had.

The Lord Chamberlain and the laughing gentleman had conspired against her. Her debut into society was a disaster. She would surely never be admitted into the *haut ton*. She was a failure. A social pariah.

Eugenia Talbot was ruined.

People stared as they passed her. Genie never felt more self-conscious, and feared her face was as bright as her skirt. She wanted nothing more than to hide away from the malicious looks and vicious whispers. Unfortunately, wearing courtly attire with feathers that soared at least two feet above her head, she was hardly inconspicuous among the steady throng of people in the outer chambers of the drawing rooms. So she plastered on a fake smile and waited for her aunt to summon her to the coach while the minutes dragged into lifetimes.

"Uncle! I am so glad you are here," said a youthful voice. A young woman was being escorted into the royal drawing rooms. She struggled forward in a similar unwieldy hoop skirt, dyed an unfortunate shade of bright pink.

"I could not forget your presentation to court," said a male voice behind Genie.

"I shall be so much less nervous with you here," gushed the young girl.

"Trust me," said the man, "after what I just witnessed, you shall be brilliant by comparison."

"What happened?" asked the girl, forgetting herself for a moment and cocking her head to one side, which forced her to use both hands to steady the plume of white feathers rising from her head.

"A debutante with a shocking lapse of propriety, who is no doubt being banished to the outer regions of the empire as we speak."

Genie turned to face her accuser. It was none other than the laughing man.

With a flash of recognition, the man had the decency to look sheepish. He waved the young girl forward into the drawing room and stepped up to

Genie. He gave Genie a bow and came up smiling, his blue eyes sparkling. He was a handsome man; there could be no denying his appeal, with sandy blond hair and laughing eyes. His features were pleasing, with high cheekbones that gave him an impish appearance. His attire was splendid in the required royal-purple silk coat and knee breeches. Unlike others who appeared foppish in the requisite colors of the English royal court, the man before her commanded his style. It was not every gentleman who could wear purple silk britches with confidence.

"Please forgive me if I have offended you," said the man with a disarming smile.

"Forgive you? Why, there is nothing to forgive. You only spoke the truth, did you not?" Genie presented the man with a smile, the kind she kept on a shelf to feign good humor when she had none to give.

"Not at all. Merely trying to encourage my niece—timid thing, needs encouragement. Do what I can to make her feel at ease."

"You are charity itself."

"No, no I…" The man paused and gave her a guilty grin. "I'm not going to redeem myself from my careless words, am I?"

"I can forgive your words. You are no doubt correct that my aunt is at this moment trying to find a penal colony for me at the greatest distance from London. What I cannot forgive is your shocking wink that caused this trouble."

"Surely this affair is not my fault! It is my Lord Chamberlain who embarrassed himself beyond redemption."

"If you had not laughed, I would have been able to calm myself."

"How could I not be amused? Honestly, I do hope the poor man survives the night."

"But no one caught you laughing," said Genie, getting at the heart of the injustice. "They were only looking at me."

"Naturally they were looking at you. Between the two of us, there can be no comparison." The man's easy smile turned flirtatious, but Genie was accustomed to flattery regarding her appearance and considered herself immune to its charms. The magnitude of her failure weighed down her shoulders. She wished she could tear off the heavy headpiece, but she had brought upon herself enough scandal for one day—all thanks to the man before her.

"I do wish I had never seen you," said Genie in uncharacteristically clipped tones. "And since you are no doubt correct that my aunt is even now booking my passage to the Americas or Botany Bay, I will take comfort in the fact that I will never see you again. Good day, sir!"

With fortuitous timing, Genie was called to join her aunt and she practically flew into the coach on the plumes of her own headdress. Unfortunately, her sweeping exit was hindered by the logistics of maneuvering three hoop skirts belonging to herself, her aunt, and her cousin, which was done with such haste Genie feared her gown would be sadly crushed. Her aunt demanded the curtains be drawn, as if the mere sight of Eugenia Talbot was so offensive the whole of London must be protected.

"Disaster! Oh, how could you do this to me?" Lady Bremerton lay back on the plush squabs of the town coach as it jolted forward, her hand on her forehead for dramatic flair. "I should have known you needed more training, more tutelage. After all, your father's family can have no concept of what is expected in higher society, let alone what is proper in court."

Genie swallowed down a retort. She had intended to prove she was every bit as polished as the other debutantes. Acting the hoyden before the queen revealed otherwise.

"I am sorry, Aunt Cora," said Genie, her contrition a tight knot in her chest. "Sorry, Cousin Louisa." Louisa's eyes were sympathetic, but her aunt would give no quarter.

"Sorry will not do you any good, nor will speaking to a known rake," chastised her aunt.

"A known rake?"

"Mr. Grant. I saw you speaking with him. He will do you no good."

"I know that is true," said Genie with a flush.

"Oh, what is to be done? You are ruined, ruined for sure. My reputation is in tatters. There is nothing else for it; you must be married. And quick!"

Two

EUGENIA HAD NOT TAKEN MORE THAN TWO STEPS inside her aunt's Mayfair townhouse before she was given an unwanted command.

"Go change into something less conspicuous," demanded her aunt. "We must speak with the Duchess of Marchford. She will know what to do."

Genie would rather have hidden under her bed or in a wardrobe for the rest of the London season, but she had caused enough disgrace for one day and would not add to her problems by being disobedient. So an hour later, she was back in the lumbering coach with her aunt, the Lady Bremerton, and her cousin, the Lady Louisa Munthgrove.

For the outing, Genie chose a plain white muslin dress with little adornment. She hoped it would help her blend into the background. Lady Bremerton, a decidedly plump woman, made the most of her natural assets in a lilac, formfitting half dress that revealed a bit more décolletage than Genie's country sensibilities found appropriate for social calls. Lady Louisa shared her mother's dark honey hair and rosy cheeks but on a smaller frame. More modest, as befitted an unmarried lady, she wore a smart blue spencer over her white muslin dress, with a sea of ruffles and lace frills at the bottom of the skirt.

Along the short journey, Genie's aunt continued to dwell on the irreparable damage Genie had done to her social standing. Naturally, the ball in her honor would have to be canceled, and any hope of receiving invitations was lost. Such was the magnitude of Genie's offense in the eyes of her aunt, that Genie was relieved to arrive finally at their destination.

The coach came to a stop with a jerk in front of the Marchford mansion, situated prominently in Grosvenor Square. Remembering not to gape at the impressive architecture, Genie followed her aunt and cousin as they were helped out of the coach by the groomsman.

"Thank you, Sam," said Genie as the groomsman offered his arm to help her from the coach. This won her a stern look from her aunt.

"It will not do for you to appear overly friendly with the help," whispered her aunt as they climbed the stairs to Marchford mansion. "The coachman was merely doing what he is paid to do."

Since Genie had only been in London a few weeks, she understood her aunt was trying to help her appear less countrified, yet Town manners left a lot to be desired in her humble estimation.

They were ushered through the tall doorway by an imposing butler who informed them in the gravest of tones that the dowager duchess was not at home but was expected shortly.

"We will wait for the dowager in her sitting room," declared Lady Bremerton with authority.

Genie was momentarily surprised by her aunt's boldness until she remembered Louisa was engaged to be married to the Duke of Marchford. She assumed, since they were family friends, allowances for familiarity must be made, yet Louisa appeared distinctly uncomfortable, clutching her work bag of embroidery to her chest like a shield.

Louisa's engagement to the duke was a long-standing arrangement. The duke's recent return from working with the Foreign Office in Cadiz for the past three years had raised hopes that a date for the nuptials would soon be set. Indeed, Aunt Cora spoke of little else.

They were invited to sit in an elegant drawing room, lavishly appointed in blue and gold, with artwork Genie identified as an original Titian and a da Vinci hanging on the walls. Light poured in from large windows, giving the room a warm hue. The ornately carved furnishings were of obvious quality, and everything was neat and bright and polished to a gleaming shine.

"This is a lovely room. The light is good for stitching," Genie said to Louisa, who was an accomplished embroiderer. Instead of a smile, Louisa's shoulders sagged a bit and she merely nodded in response. Genie decided her shy cousin must be overwhelmed with the prospect of being mistress of this grand house, an intimidation she could well understand.

"Yes, Louisa will do quite nicely in this room, though there is also a small ladies' study upstairs which has even better light," said Lady Bremerton.

Genie nodded in response, noting that her aunt often answered for Louisa.

"I do hope we can get to the duchess before she hears the story from someone else," said Lady Bremerton, making herself comfortable on the settee. "I should hate to think that Genie's behavior should have any negative effect on you, my dear."

"How could it?" asked Louisa. "It was a little thing, soon forgot." Louisa gave Genie a tentative smile, which Genie quickly returned. Though cousins, they had never met until a few weeks ago. Louisa's naturally reserved style made growing acquainted a slow process. Her support at this moment of Genie's greatest defeat meant a lot.

"Soon forgot?" Aunt Cora tsked at Louisa like a naughty child. "I should think not. Why, this story will circle London before the day is done, mark my words. I only hope it should not make the duke think ill of you."

"Do you think he would break the engagement over this incident?" Louisa's eyes went wide.

"No chance of that," replied her mother. "I saw to the engagement contract myself. He will not be wiggling out of it no matter what he should like to do."

"I should not like to marry a man who does not wish to marry me," murmured Louisa.

"It makes very little difference either way," retorted Lady Bremerton. "What would you do? Follow your own fickle fancy of the moment? We have seen today the fruits of that decision."

Genie let out a whoosh of air as if she had been punched in the gut. Aunt Cora could never forget that her sister, Genie's mother, the infamous Lady Mary, had gone against the wishes of her family, broke an arranged engagement, and *eloped* with a gentleman farmer. In her aunt's eyes, Genie would always be the result of the unholy union between an earl's daughter and a lowly commoner. Genie's presentation at court was supposed to redeem her, but she had only confirmed the whispers of her *bad blood*.

Men's voices were suddenly heard in the hall, and a tall man in a superbly cut dark blue coat entered the drawing room, instantly commanding attention. His broad shoulders, aristocratic nose, and assured presence gave Genie no doubt that she was in the presence of the Duke of Marchford.

"Marchford, my dear!" exclaimed Lady Bremerton, rising from the settee. "It is wonderful to see you. You have been so busy lately we have had hardly any time together."

"Yes, sorry. So busy, just getting back in Town, you can hardly imagine," said the duke, slightly taken aback to find Lady Bremerton and his intended in his drawing room.

"Certainly, we understand, do we not, Louisa? But we hope to see you much more often in the future." Lady Bremerton beamed in a manner not shared by the stoic Marchford nor the shy Louisa. They acknowledged each other in silence.

"Marchford, have you visitors?" Another well-dressed man sauntered into the drawing room. He had changed his silk breeches for a nankeen pair that so hugged his muscular thighs Genie averted her eyes. It was none other than Mr. Grant.

"Hello! We meet again!" Much to her horror, Mr. Grant walked up to Genie directly. "I cannot tell you how relieved I am to see you are not on your way to Botany Bay," said Mr. Grant, his impish silver-blue eyes gleaming. "Marchford, I insist you introduce me to this divine creature at once!"

Marchford, having yet to meet Genie, confessed he was at a loss, and Lady Bremerton was forced to make the introductions, though her reluctance was clear.

"Miss Talbot." Grant bowed over Genie's hand. "How much better you look without your plumage."

"I could say the same for your purple britches," Genie said sweetly. She had endured enough jabs for one day.

"Just so, just so!" laughed Grant. "You have a real spitfire for a niece, Lady Bremerton."

"Yes, how true," agreed Lady Bremerton with a smile that was not so sweet.

"Have you come to visit my grandmother?" asked Marchford, businesslike and direct. He took a seat farthest from his intended, who for her part focused on her embroidery and never raised her eyes.

"Yes," answered Lady Bremerton. "Your butler informed us she was expected shortly."

Marchford nodded in agreement and gave a quick glance at the door. "She was attending a wedding this morning. I trust she will return soon."

"Perhaps she is attending the breakfast afterward."

"No, she does not care much for the groom's family. I wrote my cousin to escort her from the church."

"You don't mean Jonathan, do you?" asked Grant. "I heard this morning he was dreadful sick. His mother was going on about how she hoped it was not contagious, but unless you can catch it from that bottle of blue ruin he was nursing last night, I expect he shall be right as rain by the morrow."

The duke frowned, dark eyebrows clamping down over his eyes in a manner most intimidating. "Jonny is in the sick room?"

"He is, shall we say, indisposed." Grant's silver-blue eyes danced with a natural merriment. "Not sure where that leaves your dear grandmamma."

The Duke of Marchford muttered something under his breath Genie pretended not to hear. "I apologize, but I must see to my grandmother. If she has been waiting all this time…" The duke made a strangled sound.

Grant shook his head. "Best run for the Continent. It's your only hope. Perhaps you can join Miss Talbot on her expedition to the colonies."

"Grant, please keep these ladies company while I see to the dowager," said Marchford.

"Yes of course, fly, my friend!" Grant stood to usher his friend out the door, and the Duke of Marchford did exit the room with more haste than a strict adherence to decorum would allow.

"Such excitement, eh, ladies?" Mr. Grant sat himself next to Genie on the couch, which earned Genie a stern glance from Lady Bremerton. Genie could not but think this unfair, since she could hardly control where the man sat.

"We are perfectly comfortable waiting in the drawing room, Mr. Grant," said Lady Bremerton. "You need not stay to keep us company."

"I would not dream of leaving you alone, not when Marchford has specifically asked me to act as host. Besides, I have not yet had the chance to become acquainted with the lovely Miss Talbot."

"Genie, ring the bell for tea, please," said Lady Bremerton, interrupting Grant.

Genie dutifully stood to ring the bell. Catching her aunt's glare, she sat back down on another chair, far from Grant.

"Well played, Lady Bremerton," said Grant. "I see I have crossed swords with an expert. Miss Talbot, you are safe from me for the moment."

Grant easily turned the conversation to safer topics, but the quiver of excitement in the air every time he glanced at her told Genie that, with Mr. Grant, she was far from safe.

"So, Lady Louisa, is this your remarkable embroidery in hand? Do tell me about your latest project." Grant had little natural interest in needlework but listened attentively to Louisa's description of her ambitious project embroidering the Greek goddess Aphrodite running away with her lover Ares. Grant needed to play the charming host to win time with his latest prize. Miss Talbot was a delightful bundle, fresh as daisies in a simple white muslin dress.

Lady Bremerton was a devoted chaperone, with a reserved nature, but Grant was able to soften her demeanor by sharing his secret for where to find silks at only seven shillings and sixpence a yard. Lady Bremerton may not care for his flirtatious manner with Genie, but she was not above taking his advice on fashion.

After a lengthy conversation of the latest trends and the comfort of tea and cakes, Lady Bremerton took up a book, Lady Louisa moved farther away to sit in the light for her stitching, and Grant seized on the moment of complacency by offering in as offhand a manner as possible to show Genie some artwork, naturally leading Genie to a far end of the large drawing room to admire a Renaissance treasure.

Titian may have been a master at his craft, but Grant's admiration was solely given to Miss Talbot. In the sunlight, her golden curls shimmered. Her face was lovely; she was truly a great beauty. Gowned in white muslin, her form was perfect, slender, and curvy in all the right places. She flashed azure eyes at him with a warm smile. He smiled in return, unable and unwilling to stop himself.

"Beautiful," said Grant.

Genie nodded. "The art collection is amazing."

"The pictures are quite fine too," said Grant with a smile guaranteed to raise the blood pressure of any eligible (or ineligible) female.

But Eugenia Talbot returned his gaze without so much as a blush. "Mr. Grant, I can see you are quite incorrigible and take pains to live up to your reputation."

"My reputation? My dear girl, you have been in London only a handful of weeks at best. How can you possibly know my reputation?"

"I know what my aunt has told me," said Genie in a soft tone, so her relatives could not hear.

Grant motioned for Genie to sit on a settee at the

far end of the drawing room. Genie glanced around, but Louisa and her aunt were still within sight, though paying them no mind.

"Now tell me, of what has your aunt to accuse me?" asked Grant in a similarly hushed tone.

"Only that you are a notorious rake and that I can in no way amend my tattered reputation by boasting an acquaintance with you."

"Your aunt is correct, I fear. I shall not be accused of misleading you in the matter."

"Your honesty is commendable. I also expect you would not wish an association with me."

"You intrigue me. Whyever not?"

"I believe I am now considered a social leper. I only say so to warn you against forming an unwise acquaintance."

Grant stifled a laugh. No woman had ever warned him against her. "Surely it cannot be as bad as all that."

"Oh, but it is. At least, according to my aunt, nothing could be worse. I am considering getting a bell to ring and shouting 'unclean, unclean' whenever I enter a room so as not to catch unsuspecting persons in my web of social ruin."

At this pronouncement, Grant laughed heartily, causing Lady Bremerton to give them a sharp look before returning to her engaging gothic novel. "You do make me laugh," he whispered when he had better control of himself.

"Yes, I have a great enjoyment of laughing, as well you know. Though perhaps my humor can be ill-timed when provoked!" Genie whispered in return, her eyebrows frowned into a little pucker Grant found adorable.

"Ah, yes, again let me convey my sincere apologies for my role in your..."

"Ruin?" suggested Genie.

"In the unfortunate incident. I was having difficulty restraining myself."

"So I noticed, but unfortunately, no one noticed it was you who laughed first." Miss Talbot crossed her arms in front of her.

Despite her good humor, Grant could tell he had unwittingly caused her pain and a rarely used sense of chivalry surged within him. She was correct, he had laughed first, which he did not consider his fault in the least; however he was conscious that the wink might be considered poor form.

"Surely it is not as bad as all that. It is a moment's *on-dit*. In a few days, the gossip columns will be on to a new topic and you will be all forgot."

"You think it will be in the papers?" Genie's eyebrows raised, her eyes a terrifying deep blue.

The news of Miss Talbot's disastrous presentation would no doubt be splashed across the morning papers, a detail Miss Talbot did not need to know. "I... that is to say..." Grant wished he was a more convincing liar and had an uncharacteristic desire to win her good opinion.

Miss Talbot sighed and looked away. "Then you had best stay away lest you become tainted by association."

"I believe my reputation can withstand a short *tête-à-tête*. I am glad to have found you are not a missish little thing."

"If I were missish, I would not be in this trouble."

"But then you would not have had the pleasure of

making my acquaintance, since I avoid debutantes as a general rule," confessed Grant.

"Are you one of those men who think nothing of riding neck-or-nothing to win some ill-conceived bet, but tremble at the thought of a debutante ball?"

"William Grant, Esquire, at your service, Miss Talbot."

"At least you can have no fear of a debutante ball in my honor. It is all to be canceled now according to my aunt, for who would come? I fear I shall be packed back to the farm with all due haste. I am disappointed I could not better represent my family. We have not been close, and I had not expected my aunt to sponsor my debut into society."

"She brings you out because you are a diamond of the first water, and she wishes you to add to her own social standing by sponsoring the most beautiful debutante of the season."

"You are funning with me."

"Indeed, I am in earnest."

Miss Talbot gave him a discerning gaze, so open and blunt he was inclined to squirm like an errant schoolboy. "I do not believe you are unfamiliar with giving a lady a compliment. Your sweet words flow from well-practiced lips."

"My word! I would not think a person so young as yourself to be so jaded!"

"I have four brothers, sir. I fear I was cured of naive notions regarding men at an early age."

"Ah, with you, I can get away with nothing. And here I was trying to make a good impression. I'm a shocking rake; it's true. Despite this, I can say with complete honesty that though I have seen many a pretty girl, you are the most beautiful creature I have ever beheld."

Grant had on more than one occasion flattered without thought, but as he spoke, he realized this time his words were true. In response, he had the pleasure of seeing Miss Talbot's cheeks grow pink at last.

"Stop trying to gammon me. I can see you are quite a rogue."

"True, but now that your reputation is ruined, you can dance with me at the next ball."

"But you do not go to balls attended by debutantes," reminded Miss Talbot. "Besides, I find it very unlikely I will receive any invitations after my shocking lack of propriety."

"Leave it to me. My fault you're in this fix. Must set it right!" Grant took her gloved hand and held it between his hands, delighting in the way her slender fingers naturally curled around his. "I hereby claim the first dance, and I will have it."

"I do believe we have waited long enough for Marchford's return," called Louisa. She may have appeared to be engrossed in her work, but nothing escaped her notice.

"Yes," agreed Lady Bremerton, breaking from her novel. "I think it is time to return home."

"Ah, dear Marchford, poor boy, he has been gone long," said Grant. "Wonder if he has survived abandoning his grandmother."

Three

PENELOPE ROSE HAD MASTERED THE ART OF WEDDINGS. After standing up four times with each of her sisters, Pen had perfected a look of doleful reverence while watching the happy couple exchange their vows. This fine Saturday morning was her youngest sister Julia's turn to stand before the altar. The momentous occasion also marked the day Penelope officially became a spinster.

As the only Rose sister still unmarried, Penelope followed her sisters out of the church. Now that her youngest sister, six years her junior, had wed, it was definitely time to start wearing frilly caps and sitting with the chaperones and other old maids.

"Oh, Pen, is it not wonderful?" Julia turned her energetic embrace to Penelope. "I am the youngest but not the last to marry!"

"Yes, quite the glad event," said Pen, valiantly trying to keep the sarcasm from her voice.

"I am so happy!" Julia clasped her hands in front of her and smiled like an angel. "Oh, Pen, I think I left my reticule in the ladies' retiring room, but we must leave now. See? They are waiting. What am I to do?"

Penelope gave a small sigh. "You go now, and I will go back for the reticule. Send the coach back for me after you are delivered to the reception." She had taken care of the details for her sisters for so long, it was simply expected she would be the one to run errands and fix problems.

Pen returned to the church and hustled down to the dressing area for the brides. They had to stick to a tight time frame, as another wedding party would arrive soon. It was wedding season in Mayfair, and St. James was booked by the hour. Within the dressing area, Pen located the missing reticule and scooped the spilled contents back into the bag. Turning to leave, she noted an elderly lady sleeping in a chair in the far corner.

Pen looked around the room, but no one else was visible. The sleeping woman was not familiar to her, but her silk gown and ruby necklace proclaimed her a lady of means. Pen remembered the lady being there in the confusion before the wedding, when women from the previous nuptials were in the room.

"Hello? Is anyone else here?" Pen called to the area of the room that was curtained for privacy. The only sound that greeted her was the soft snoring of the elderly lady. Who was she?

"Excuse me, ma'am," said Pen softly. No response. She drew closer. The elderly woman's mouth was slightly ajar as she snored. "Pardon me," said Pen, giving the woman's arm a slight shake.

"Oh!" The elderly lady woke up with a start. "What are you doing, gel? You wish to give me a fright?"

Pen took a good step back. The woman who had been peacefully snoring a moment ago now appeared ready for battle, her bright blue eyes gleaming.

"I beg your pardon, ma'am, but the wedding is concluded. May I help you to your coach?"

"Thank you, no," said the white-haired woman with grave politeness. "They should return soon to let me know the carriage is ready."

"Are you with the groom's family?" asked Penelope, trying to find to whom this lady belonged.

"Gracious no!" She stopped short and gave Pen a polite smile. "Are you from the groom's side, dear?"

"N-no. I am the bride's sister."

The lady arched one eyebrow. "You claim to be the sister of Lady Beatrice?"

"Lady Beatrice? No, I am Penelope Rose. Lady Beatrice was the wedding before ours."

The elderly lady grew still, a look of pained dignity taking hold.

"Oh," said Penelope softly. "I see." She fiddled awkwardly with the reticule in her hands. Had this poor woman been abandoned by her family? Pen glanced around the room, which, despite the yellow wallpaper, managed to look drab. Here is where her unremarkable time on the marriage mart would end, stranded in the ladies' retiring room with the rest of society's discards. Pen sighed. She could not in good conscience leave an elderly lady in distress.

"Please, allow me the pleasure of conveying you home," Penelope said to the elderly lady, who somehow managed to exude a royal aura despite being stranded in the ladies' retiring room.

"Thank you. I am pleased to accept." Her voice was smooth but the rigidity in her manner showed she was anything but pleased. She stood slowly, leaning heavily on a pearl-handled cane.

Penelope walked with the elderly lady, who had still not identified herself, back to the front of the church. Their pace was a considerably slower pace than the one in which Pen had entered the church.

"So, your sister was married today?" the lady asked.

"Yes, my youngest sister married Sir William Aubrey. We are frequent visitors here as my three other sisters have also taken their turns at the altar before her," said Penelope.

"And do you have a date with the altar?"

"No, ma'am," said Pen simply. No use in belaboring that point.

The lady gave her a warm smile. "Next season will be yours."

"Unfortunately, I have been here three seasons already, and I fear my time in London will shortly come to a close. We have been sponsored by my aunt, and she plans to close her London house and retire to the country."

"And do you return to the country too?"

"My plans are not quite settled." Pen had wrestled silently with her future for many months since learning that Julia was to be married. Her aunt had hinted broadly at retiring to the country alone, leaving Pen in need of a new living situation.

The lady gave a sly grin. "Care little for country life? I cannot stand it myself. Find yourself a Town man as your sister has."

"My sisters have been fortunate in finding excellent husbands." Pen put on a tight smile, the one that hurt her face if she wore it too long. She was tired of pretending not to notice the contrast between her beautiful blond sisters and her own plain features topped with mousy brown hair. "My sisters are all quite pretty, you understand. I have found that men are primarily interested in the essentials when choosing a wife, which are of course her beauty and her dowry. Having little of either, I find a long and dreary future as an old maid before me."

The lady raised her eyebrows, and Penelope flushed at what had just come out of her mouth. A deplorable tendency to speak her mind was yet another item on the long list of reasons why no offers of marriage had been directed her way.

The lady laughed and rapped her cane on the marble floor, causing a sharp staccato snap to echo through the hall. "You forget family, my dear. More than one marriage has been based on the greedy aspirations of a social climber."

It was Penelope's turn to laugh. "Then, as a daughter of a country parson, my matrimonial prospects are decidedly negligible."

"You have wit, child, and that more than makes up for anything else you might lack."

"You may be right, but I have yet to find a man who courted a woman based on the size of her… er… wit."

The lady beside her laughed again, her bright blue eyes twinkling. Pen smiled in return, happy her own sorry circumstances at least served as an amusement to others.

"I fear, after three seasons in London and the marriage of my youngest sister, I am officially on the shelf," said Penelope with a shrug. "Since I must find a new living situation, I was considering taking a post as a lady's companion or perhaps a governess."

The elderly lady gasped. "Surely your sisters would not abandon you!"

"Oh no, any one of my sisters would be glad to have me live with them. I have no brothers, you see. But I…" Pen paused. She had not vocalized this to anyone. The lady waited attentively, and Pen found it was easy to talk to this stranger about topics she would never broach with her sisters. "I do not wish to burden them when they are so newly married. The thought of being passed around from sister to sister like an old gown does not appeal."

The lady nodded in understanding, the smile wilting from her face. "I understand not wishing to be a burden, easily put aside and forgot." Her eyes slid past Penelope to the open door of the church. "Ah, look, my grandson has seen fit to remember this poor old woman."

A man jumped up the few steps and passed through the tall, white columns, toward the main doors. Pen's pulse quickened with real anger at the man who had abandoned his grandmother, just like every other man who had pushed past Penelope to be introduced to her more attractive sisters.

Penelope stepped outside and beyond the hearing of her new friend to intercept the gentleman. The man was an imposing figure in a dark blue coat and formfitting breeches, revealing a muscular physique.

His cravat was tied in a crisp knot and instead of swimming in the current fashion of high collar points, he managed to command the style to his proportions, not be overcome by its dictates. His dark, wavy hair was combed back in an efficient fashion. He had a straight nose, square jaw, and gray-green eyes, which would have been more handsome had they not appeared cold and aloof.

His aristocratic manner only fueled Pen's anger. He most likely thought only of himself, like so many other self-absorbed rich gentlemen who could not be troubled to acknowledge her existence. But how could he possibly neglect his own grandmother?

"Good morning, sir," Penelope greeted the gentleman with deceptive mildness. She did not make it a point to speak to men to whom she had not been introduced, but she made an exception in this case. "Did you forget something at church this morning?"

The gentleman slowed his step, his face a condescending mask, showing his displeasure at being accosted by an unknown female. It was all Penelope could do to prevent her eyes from rolling. Who did he think he was?

"Or perhaps I should say someone?" Penelope continued.

That stopped the man. He looked down at her, a frown marring an otherwise handsome face. His fine looks only heightened her anger. He had everything yet could not be bothered to show one scrap of common decency toward his own family.

"My grandmother. Do you know where she is? Is she well?" At least he could pretend to show concern.

"She is fine, no thanks to you. Forgive me, it is not my place to say, but I find it reprehensible that your entire wedding party could leave behind an elderly lady such as your grandmother. She has been here for hours. Have you only now noticed she was missing?"

"A most unfortunate miscommunication." The man waved his hand dismissing her concerns. Pampered rich aristocrat, he probably never spared a thought beyond how much he could stake at cards or whether his damned cravat was tied in the latest mode.

"How you could neglect your own grandmother is beyond my comprehension. Do you have any consideration for how confused and rejected she must have felt when she awoke to find she had been abandoned by her own flesh and blood?"

"I did not intend—"

"No, of course not. You simply assumed someone else would look after your responsibilities and continued pondering the progress of the war or whether the wine was to your liking or whatever topic rich men consider fashionable."

"You are an expert on male thought patterns?" He raised one eyebrow in a manner characteristic of his grandmother. His eyes might have sparkled too, but she was in no mood to be charmed.

"N-no," Penelope flushed at his manner, which had taken a lazy, almost seductive tone. If he thought he could sweet-talk her into a giggling miss, he had mistaken her for the rest of the simpering debutantes on the marriage market. "You stray from the topic. I simply wanted to state that you would oblige me greatly if you would take better care of your grandmother in the future. She may never tell you because she is a kindly woman, but your actions have caused her great pain."

"And for that I am truly sorry, Grandmamma," he said, looking beyond her.

Pen turned to find the elderly woman standing behind her.

"You most certainly should be," retorted the lady.

The gentleman turned his gaze back to Penelope. "You are correct that my action or inaction today was inexcusable; however, you are sadly mistaken if you believe I will not be hearing about this for the foreseeable future. I can only assure you that I will certainly suffer for my misdeeds."

"Bah! What would you know of suffering?" His grandmother dismissed his comment with a negligent wave of her hand. "James, this is Miss Penelope Rose. Would you be so good as to introduce us?"

"My pleasure. Grandmamma, may I present Miss Penelope Rose. Miss Rose, Her Grace, the Dowager Duchess of Marchford."

Penelope froze. Dowager duchess? Had she been conversing in a most familiar way to a *duchess*? "Your Grace," Penelope managed and dropped a curtsy.

"And this"—the dowager waved her hand toward her grandson—"is the current Duke of Marchford."

Of course he was. Penelope took a sharp breath before dropping another curtsy. Now she was not only a spinster but would probably be banned from London proper. Could a duke banish you from England entirely? After her shocking lapse in propriety, she might have to start a new life on the Continent.

"James, we will take Miss Rose home. How long will it take you to pack, child?"

Penelope looked up and realized the dowager was speaking to her. Was she being ousted from the country immediately?

"Pack?" Penelope choked on the word.

"Yes, dear, pack to come live with me. James, see to it that her things are removed from wherever she lives and placed in the blue bedroom. Or are you more partial to yellow?"

Penelope opened her mouth but no sound emerged. She turned to the duke who returned her open-mouthed gaze.

"She is to stay with us?" The duke found his voice first.

"Yes. Please welcome my new companion!"

Four

MR. WILLIAM GRANT ENTERED THE HALLS OF WHITE'S flanked by his friends, James Lockton, the Duke of Marchford, and Duncan Maclachlan, the Earl of Thornton.

"I was of the understanding you were trying to separate yourself from female company, not add to their ranks in your household," said Mr. Grant with a drawl only one as fashionably attired as he could deliver. In a long-tailed coat of claret superfine, he could have put any dandy to shame, had it not been for his rebellious blond curls, which were a bit too natural for a true aficionado of fashion.

"If you are referring to the opera singer, I was merely enjoying the view, not offering a *carte blanche*," replied Marchford, taking his customary seat in the hallowed halls of White's gentlemen's club.

"I ken he is referring to the companion yer grand-mother recently employed," explained Thornton with a slight lilt to his voice, even though the Scottish lord had been educated in England. More somber in appearance, with his short, black hair and gray eyes,

Thornton's olive green coat and gray waistcoat were a drab contrast to Grant's colorful attire.

"If I recall correctly, you said not days after you returned that Granny would be removed to the dowager house within a week," said Grant with a smirk.

Marchford was spared the indignity of replying by the timely arrival of his burgundy, served to the Duke and Lord Thornton. Mr. Grant, naturally, was offered his preferred whiskey, the fault, he had claimed, of a Scottish ancestor. Though Marchford may have wished it, Grant was not inclined to drop the topic.

"Not that I mind your inefficiencies. I made a bit of brass on your tardiness," said Mr. Grant.

Marchford paused, his burgundy halfway to his lips. "You bet against me, old friend?"

"You cannot expect me to pass on the prospect of easy blunt," said Grant with an unapologetic smile. "You have been away too long. Your grandmother has ruled London society and the Marchford household for how many years now? Why ever since—"

Marchford's eyes flashed, and Grant exchanged a glance with Thornton.

"Give or take the past four decades," Grant amended vaguely. "If you think the Dowager Duchess of Marchford is going to pack up and leave London in the middle of the season, you must have bats in your attic."

"I am only asking her to do what she demanded of me. Has she not written me often asking me to return and take up my responsibilities? I cannot bring a wife into the house with grandmother reigning supreme."

"I doubt yer grandmother thought yer marriage would require her to leave London," observed Thornton.

"Lady Louisa cannot possibly manage the household with grandmother there. You have met the lady. A more timid creature I have never beheld. I fear she will be bullied by the housemaids, let alone the dowager," said Marchford.

"Perhaps yer bride and the dowager could forge an alliance," suggested Thornton, always one to promote a steady course.

The duke shook his head. "No. My grandmother will not share the reins. I will not do that again."

Having been his friends since their Eton days, Thornton and Grant knew well the fights between Marchford's mother and grandmother, which eventually led to his mother's demise. The men became engrossed with their respective drinks, and the subject was dropped.

"Ye visited yer intended?" asked Thornton, breaking the silence.

"Just yesterday," said Marchford.

"I am a witness that you were not in the room with her for more than a minute. Even you cannot qualify that as a 'visit,'" said Grant.

"I did visit her upon my return," defended the duke.

"But that was almost three weeks ago. Have ye not visited her since?" asked Thornton.

"I doubt Lady Louisa has changed much in the passing weeks. Indeed, I find she was not significantly different since the last time I saw her three years ago."

"Your affection for her astounds me," drawled Grant, a smile in his blue eyes.

"Is it quite impossible to break the arrangement?" asked Thornton.

"The Duke of Marchford is obligated to marry the Lady Louisa. And so he shall." Marchford spoke without emotion and took another sip of his wine. His friends were well aware of the long-standing arrangement. The longer it stood, the clearer Marchford's ambivalence toward the match became.

"What a romantic you are, my friend," mocked Grant. "A toast then, to your impending nuptials." He raised his glass in salute. "I don't envy you. With the burden of titles comes the expectation of a legitimate heir only a wife can provide. Now me, I am most blessed to be unencumbered by the burden of producing an heir. M'sisters have produced enough nephews to take on my estate once I quit this earth, and I have no embarrassment of means which necessitates the hunt for an heiress."

"So, ye have quite decided not to marry?" asked Thornton.

"I cannot fathom a state more fatally dull than that of marriage. Have not the temperament for it, I fear. I'll leave the heiresses to you, my friend. I shall live quite comfortably without the burden of a wife. Think I'll write a new will every year naming a different nephew as heir and watch them fall over themselves to win my affection. What an amusing diversion it shall be."

"When you become a mean-spirited old man, remind me to cut our acquaintance," said the duke.

Far from being offended, Grant merely laughed. "Speaking of mean-spirited, when and how do you propose to remove your grandmother from London? You are aware her bringing in a companion is a direct attack on your authority."

"No, no," disagreed Thornton, "merely a shot across the bow, warning ye to proceed no further."

"Who is this companion? Perhaps I could seduce her away for you." Grant laughed at his friend's raised eyebrows, adding, "Always at the service of a friend."

"The companion is a Miss Penelope Rose," reported Marchford. "I met her yesterday and she had no compunction in accosting me with her sharp tongue. As for being seduced, she does not appear to be prone to that particular vice."

"It is becoming more and more clear why yer grandmother invited her into yer home," observed Thornton.

"The Rose sisters." Grant swirled his drink and looked up at the ceiling. "Pretty things the lot of them—golden hair, sparkling blue eyes, took London by storm about three seasons ago. Though being the daughters of a deceased country clergyman in no way recommended them, they had faces that made one forget. I confess even I, only for the briefest of moments, considered making an offer to the eldest, but fortunately Lord Stanton got there before me."

"A narrow escape," commented Marchford.

"To be sure. Not aware there were any Rose sisters left to be had."

"I believe Miss Penelope Rose is the middle sister. You have been introduced to her, I am sure. She is the only brunette of the family," said Thornton.

"I do not remember her."

"Ye only remember the pretty ones."

"True." Grant eyed his drink with suspicion. "Must have something to do with the whiskey."

"Considering giving it up?" asked Thornton with a raised eyebrow.

"Goodness no! Serves its purpose well."

"So, what are ye going to do with yer grandmother's plain companion?" Thornton asked Marchford.

"I am going to do nothing with her, and with any luck, my opportunities to meet her will be few indeed. My grandmother is, naturally, welcome to take her new companion with her when she moves to the dowager house in the country."

"And how do you propose to remove your grandmother from her roost?" asked Grant.

The duke checked a smile. "In advance of her moving to the country, I have transferred her accounts to my man of business for my estate in Hertfordshire."

"Ye cut off her funds?" asked Thornton, eyebrows raised high.

"She still has the pin money that is hers," said March. "But the extra blunt I provide her every month will now only be available when she resides in Hertfordshire."

Grant shook his head and gave a low whistle. "You are a brave one, my friend. If you awake with a hatpin through your heart, don't say I didn't warn you."

"What did she say when ye told her?" asked Thornton, his eyebrows still elevated.

"I left her a note."

"Coward," accused Grant.

"True," acknowledged Marchford. "I would rather face down Napoleon's army than take on a straight fight with my grandmother. I fear I would not emerge the victor."

"If you would oblige me by continuing to lose, I shall continue to be flush with funds," commented Grant.

"You would oblige me by not betting against me!" demanded Marchford.

"You cannot ask me to pass a bet I cannot lose."

"You doubt my ability to be the master of my own house?"

Grant looked over his whiskey with a smile. "Easier for you to depose Napoleon from France than oust Granny from Marchford house."

Finishing their respective drinks, the men left for Tattersall's to inspect the prospect of new horseflesh.

After the men left, a gentleman in a drab coat quietly left the club and walked down the streets of Mayfair unnoticed by passersby. His appearance was so commonplace as to render him practically invisible. He turned into a fashionable house and was admitted without question.

"Good afternoon. Please enjoy some tea and tell me of your day."

The man accepted a teacup and recounted the entirety of the conversation between Marchford and his friends.

"It is not much to go on," commented the host, "but we must make what we can of this animosity between Marchford and the dowager."

The spy nodded in agreement and removed his gloves for tea, revealing hands covered in red disfiguring scars.

"Cover your hands, man!" demanded his companion. "No one cares to see those ugly burns."

The man stared at his hands, the scars from his

burns giving the appearance of melted red wax. "The night my father met his fate on the guillotine, I burned down his house. I got too close. Sentiment perhaps. I wished to put certain items into the flames myself."

"Were you not the cause of your father's death?"

"I revealed the truth about him to the tribunal; his death was his reward."

"Reward?"

The spy gave a brittle smile. "He was put to death the same day as that witch, Marie Antoinette. I am sure it gave him a sense of aristocratic pride."

"Ah, Madame Guillotine," said his companion wistfully. "Nothing can last forever, but we look forward to a future most bright. Here's to Napoleon." The companion raised a teacup.

"Here's to the reward he provides for information," countered the man.

"You are not a true believer in the cause."

"I am a true believer in the power of gold."

Five

"I CANNOT BELIEVE IT. THAT OLD WARHORSE HAS NO intention of leaving the field," muttered Lady Bremerton, eyeing the passing city streets from the comfort of her carriage.

"Warhorse?" Genie asked, genuinely confused.

"Do not be vulgar, Eugenia," said Lady Bremerton in clipped accents.

Genie was rendered mute in reply. The day before, they had left Marchford house without meeting with the dowager duchess. As soon as Aunt Cora heard that the dowager had used her time while abandoned at church to acquire a companion, she proposed a return to Marchford house. Louisa, who moments earlier appeared to be in fine health, suddenly developed a megrim and bowed out of the social call. Genie now understood the sudden illness. She was beginning to feel a little sick herself.

"The dowager must be made to leave," continued her aunt. "I will not rest until I see Louisa mistress of the Marchford household."

"So we are going to ask the dowager duchess to

leave?" asked Genie, forgetting her aunt hardly needed her input to engage in conversation.

"No, of course not. How can you be so dense? We are going to ask her help in finding a solution to your unfortunate behavior before the queen." Lady Bremerton smoothed her skirts. "And hopefully find a way to depose the dowager while we do it."

The coach stopped in front of Marchford house, saving Genie from trying to find a reply to such a speech. Genie followed her aunt out of the coach and silently mouthed the words "thank you" to Sam the groomsman, who gave her a small bow and mouthed the words "you're welcome" in reply.

A hack pulled up behind their coach and a young woman hopped out of the conveyance unaided, reaching back inside to pull out a bandbox. The driver demanded his fare, and the woman put the bandbox down by her feet so she could pull out her coin purse. While her attention was so occupied, Genie noticed a small urchin sneaking up under the wheels of a hack.

Having helped raise two younger brothers, Genie was wary and, without a thought, stepped into the street around to the other side of the hack. The diminutive thief grabbed the bandbox and ducked back under the hack, where Genie, with the experience of grabbing errant children only an elder sister can have, neatly snatched the culprit by the arm.

The urchin hollered with ferocity and twisted savagely, but Genie's experienced fingers held him fast. She marched the young thief, still holding the prized bandbox, around the hack and presented him to the woman.

"My bandbox!" exclaimed the woman. "Thank you, oh, you have no idea, thank you so much." The young woman clutched the bandbox to her like a priceless treasure.

"Genie, what are you doing?" asked Aunt Cora, whose shocked expression dampened Genie's triumph at having caught a thief. "Someone take hold of this vile thing and present him to the constable. He'll soon find his end at the Old Bailey."

The small child in Genie's grasp stopped wiggling and looked up at her with wide eyes. She bent down to look the child in the eye. He was in desperate need of a bath, barefoot, and wearing clothes better suited for the trash heap. *Whatever you did for one of the least of these…* She recalled the verse from Matthew 25:40 about serving God by showing mercy to others.

"What is your name?" asked Genie.

The brown eyes grew wider still. "Jem," whispered the child.

"Do you know that stealing is very wrong?"

"I jus' does as he tells me."

"Who tells you?" asked Genie.

"Please, miss, let go a' me. Old Bailey will hang me sure for nickn' the box." A single tear ran a streak down the grimy boy's face.

Genie shivered at the cold reality of the child's words. Surely they would not hang a child for theft, yet London was an unfamiliar and harsh place. Her aunt was busy giving instructions to the groom to find the constable.

Genie surveyed the sniffling urchin, her sympathy

heightened by the young thief's pitiful condition. He must surely qualify as being the "least" of the entirety of London. "You must never steal again, Jem. You promise?"

"Aye, milady, I swear!"

"You are a good boy, Jem," whispered Genie. "See to it you act like one. Now run!" Genie let go of the young miscreant who bolted across the street and disappeared into an alley.

"Oh, catch him, he's getting away," called her aunt.

"I'm sorry. He slipped away," said Genie.

The groom gave chase but returned empty-handed.

"What a shame he could not be brought to justice," said Lady Bremerton. She turned to walk up the stairs to the Marchford mansion, and both Genie and the young lady followed her.

"Are you also visiting the Duchess of Marchford?" Genie asked the lady with the bandbox.

"Yes," she replied. "I am Penelope Rose." She stood tall and had a direct look about her. Her hair was brown and pulled back into a serviceable knot. Her features were unremarkable, candid but plain. She wore a brown spencer over a blue gown, both of which were clean, neatly pressed, but lacking in fashion or adornment. The bandbox she held had clearly seen years of use. Her overall appearance was one of an efficient governess.

"Miss Rose?" Lady Bremerton turned and gave Penelope a critical glance. "So you are the companion. I see."

Genie winced internally at her aunt's superior tone.

"Yes, I met Her Grace yesterday," said Penelope.

She answered directly, without any hint at being cowed by Lady Bremerton's attempted set-down.

Genie gave Penelope a smile. "I am Genie Talbot. It is a pleasure to make your acquaintance."

They all were ushered into the house and their coats were taken by an efficient footman. An attempt was made to relieve Miss Rose of her bandbox, but she preferred to keep the box herself. Perhaps the near loss of the object left Miss Rose wary, or perhaps she had hidden something within of great value; Genie could only wonder as they were led to the drawing room by the formidable butler.

"Ungrateful whelp!" cried the muffled voice of the Dowager Duchess of Marchford from the other side of the closed parlor door.

The butler stopped, and the whole party stood still listening for a moment.

"Devious child. He grows more like his mother every day," said the duchess, her voice slicing through the cracks of the parlor door.

The butler turned and attempted to move the party of ladies elsewhere, and indeed, Genie was uncomfortable eavesdropping on what must be a private conversation. But Lady Bremerton's interest had been piqued and she held her ground in the corridor.

"How could he do this to me?" continued the duchess. "Unheard of in all of Christendom is a boy more ungrateful, more devious, more, more… and spineless! Has he the courage to say this to my face? No!"

"Madame, please." The butler again attempted to move the party down the hall, but short of being physically removed, Lady Bremerton refused to budge.

"Nonsense, Antonia is my dearest friend. I must see her in her time of need," said Lady Bremerton. But she made no effort to either leave the hall or enter the room, and instead waited eagerly to hear what the dowager might say next.

Genie glanced back at Penelope, who was still grasping her bandbox, her eyebrows knit tightly together. She gave a quick look behind her, as if considering making a run for it. Genie considered joining her if she did.

"Treachery is what this is," said the dowager in seething accents. "Shall this be borne? It shall not! He has—"

"Your Grace!" cried the butler, opening the door to stop his mistress. "The Countess of Bremerton, Miss Talbot, and Miss Rose."

The Dowager Duchess of Marchford froze, her eyes blazing. She was alone in the room. Clearly her tirade had been meant for her ears only. Genie wished her aunt had not chosen to intrude and wondered that Town manners could be so very different from country manners.

"Dearest Antonia," gushed Lady Bremerton, flying into the room like an exquisite bird. "Whatever is the matter?"

"Nothing, my dear. Nothing at all." The dowager attempted a smile, which came off more as a grimace. "Have you met my new companion?" said the dowager smoothly, as if nothing was amiss. While their attention was diverted she quickly stashed a paper under a book on a side table. "Let me introduce Miss Penelope Rose."

"Ah, so it is true!" announced Lady Bremerton. "I heard you had done something to give Marchford's nose a tweak. I do not blame you in the least. I hope for your sake he has given up this notion of forcing you to leave Town before the season is out."

"I have no intention of leaving Town," declared the dowager.

"Good for you, hold your ground. I could never be so bold, but I do admire a woman who can. Though one must take care not to appear odious and grasping, but you do it in such a manner, one could never say that of you! Besides, since Louisa and Marchford are not wed, there can be no reason for you to leave yet."

Genie noted the dowager stiffened at the word "yet."

"Please do sit down and introduce me to your lovely niece," said the dowager.

"May I present Miss Eugenia Talbot," said Lady Bremerton and Genie made a pretty curtsy. Lady Bremerton sat next to the duchess on the settee, while the younger ladies sat across from them, Miss Rose with her bandbox balanced on her knees.

"Are you enjoying the London season, Miss Talbot?" asked the dowager politely. "It must be a great change from the country."

"Yes, Your Grace, although the countryside is very pretty this time of year. I enjoy calving season and hayrides with my friends. We have such a jolly time. I was sad to miss it, though I suppose London has its own amusements."

"Hay rides?" The dowager's eyes widened in horror. The thought that anyone could prefer country living to Town life was inconceivable. "Cora, is it possible your niece prefers sitting in hay and birthing cows to society?"

"No, no!" insisted Lady Bremerton. "She is such a silly girl, always saying the wrong thing. Remember, Genie, to sit and look pretty. Try not to open your mouth and never, under any circumstances, mention hay!"

"Yes, Aunt Cora," said Genie, duly chastised.

"I heard Miss Talbot was recently presented in court," said the dowager with a raised eyebrow, and it was Lady Bremerton's turn to stiffen.

"I had hoped perhaps the news had not spread," murmured Lady Bremerton.

"My dear Cora, it is all over Town," replied the dowager. "The Comtesse de Marseille visited me earlier today."

"Odious gossip! Did she mention the situation?"

"She talked of little else."

Lady Bremerton wilted gracefully back in her chair and put her hand to her forehead. "This is dreadful. Simply dreadful. The comtesse will spread it like the plague. I have never been more humiliated in all my life. Genie is certainly ruined!"

"You know the Comtesse de Marseille," said the dowager.

"Yes, I do, that heartless viper! I do not dare throw Genie a ball now. Who would attend? I fear my reputation will be forever tarnished by this affair."

"What are you going to do?" asked the dowager.

"If she could marry and quickly, but who would marry her now?" asked Lady Bremerton.

Genie's cheeks burned at being the center of such

blunt conversation. “I understand, Aunt Cora, if you would prefer for me to simply return home.”

“Surely this one incident can be overcome,” said Miss Rose, joining the conversation. “I have witnessed far worse breaches of etiquette tolerated in society.”

“But one must first be established in society before one can break the rules,” observed the dowager.

“You also heard of the incident?” Genie asked Miss Rose.

“It was in the papers,” the girl explained with an apologetic shrug.

“It was?” asked Genie. Did not London have anything better to talk about than her terrible gaffe?

Lady Bremerton leaned back in her chair and groaned softly. “No wonder the butler said the papers had not been delivered. My dearest Antonia, I am relying on you to help us!”

“She is young,” said the dowager. “Surely some allowances can be made. If you handle it correctly, she could be known as an original. Of course, she must have an offer soon.”

Lady Bremerton shook her head. “But who? I doubt Genie will be receiving any invitations now.”

“Is she well dowered?” asked the dowager in her straightforward manner.

“She has twenty thousand pounds for a dowry, but I would be willing to add to it if only she could be respectably taken off my hands.”

“Would you now?”

“I could not ask that of you, Aunt Cora,” said Genie. “I think it would be best if I leave for home.”

“Yes, perhaps there is nothing else to do,” sighed

Lady Bremerton. "Mayhap Antonia can give you a ride out of London when she moves to the country."

"I have no plans to leave London," repeated the dowager crisply.

"Is there nothing that can repair Miss Talbot's reputation?" asked Penelope.

The dowager gazed at Penelope as if just noticing her. "My dear Miss Rose, you must think me a cruel host, making you carry around that bandbox."

"Not at all, Your Grace," said Penelope. "I fear I arrived at an inconvenient time, when you had visitors."

"Not at all. Let me show you to your room, so you may put away your things. I believe your trunks have already arrived. Cora, dear, do you mind if I step out for a moment?"

Lady Bremerton demurred and the dowager led Miss Rose out of the room. As soon as they had quit the room, Lady Bremerton walked over to the paper the dowager had placed on the side table and snatched it out from underneath the book.

"Aunt Cora!" gasped Genie.

"Quiet! I must find out what had Antonia is such a state. Ah, it is a letter from Marchford."

"Really, Aunt, I do not think—"

"Good. Do not think. Ah, see here, Marchford has threatened to cut off her funds unless she moves to the country." Aunt Cora's eyes gleamed. "Good lad, I did not think he had it in him."

"Why would he do such a thing?" asked Genie, shocked that a grandson could be so heavy-handed with his own grandmother.

"You do not understand," said Lady Bremerton,

placing the letter back under the book and returning to her seat. "The dowager did not approve of the previous Duchess of Marchford, and while I cannot say I quite approved of the previous duke's choice of a second wife, the dowager was perfectly beastly to her. Eventually… well, the less said about that the better, but suffice to say, I will not have my daughter treated in such a dreadful manner."

Genie hoped her aunt would expound on what happened to the previous Duchess of Marchford, but her aunt apparently approved of snooping but not gossip and said nothing more. Genie clasped her hands in front of herself. What had she gotten herself into?

Six

Penelope Rose followed the duchess to her new bedroom, wondering if her decision to act as the elderly woman's companion was entirely sound. She had not anticipated being engaged with company quite so soon, and there definitely appeared to be something amiss in the Marchford household.

"Here is your room," said the dowager, sweeping into a bright room of sky blue and cream. The mahogany poster bed was draped with light blue curtains, which matched the drapes on the window. There was a delicate blue and cream flowered paper on the walls and a dressing table of the same rich mahogany wood. The drapes were pulled back to reveal large windows with a fine view of the garden in the back of the house. It was an elegant room, better than any room Pen had ever had. And it was all hers, not to be shared with one or two of her sisters.

"It is beautiful." In her excitement over the room, Pen moved her hands around the side of the bandbox, forgetting she had to hold it just so or it would…

"Oh!" exclaimed Pen as the bottom ripped out of the box and the contents spilled onto the floor.

"Your box seems to have ripped," commented the dowager.

Frantically, Pen sank to her knees to snatch her belongings off the floor and pile them next to her on the writing table. Her diary, a stack of letters tied in ribbon, a parcel of her sketches and watercolors even she had to admit were poor, her needlepoint workbag, but where was her book?

Debrett's Peerage of England had slid across the floor near the dowager. Pen made a quick grab for it, picking it up by the spine. She placed it on the table with the rest of her belongings, but multiple sheets of thin paper fell from the volume to the floor.

"What is this?" The dowager picked up one of the sheets and began to read.

Pen scrambled to grab the other pages and regained her feet, her brain racing to find some rational explanation. "It is nothing. Nothing of importance."

"Why, it has the name of Mr. Grant with an entry just like out of the peerage, his date of birth, holdings, family, connects, estimated annual income. That is not part of *Debrett's*. What is this?" For an elderly lady, she certainly had no difficulty reading the tiny script on the page.

"Please, Your Grace, it is nothing, just a bit of schoolgirl silliness," said Penelope in an octave a bit higher than her own. She had promised her sisters the precious volumes of *Debrett's* guide would not fall into enemy hands. Much to her horror the dowager walked to the table and picked up the copy of the *Peerage*.

"Why some of these entries have a good deal of writing in the margins." The dowager flipped through the pages and Pen resisted the urge to grab the book from the dowager's hands. "You have listed every man… no, every *bachelor* between here and Hadrian's Wall."

"Not every bachelor, just the ones we have met or learned about since coming to London." Pen winced at her own words. She was not helping her situation. It was unbearably hot in the room.

The duchess gave her a cold look. "I do not know what you are playing at, but we are a respectable household," said the dowager with a voice like thin ice.

"Oh no, Your Grace, it is nothing like that."

The duchess's clear suspicion compelled Penelope to explain herself further lest she be accused of keeping a book of men to arrange a less conventional sort of arrangement. "When we first came to London, my two elder sisters and I entered society first. It was hoped we could find suitable husbands. My eldest sister became quite popular. Within a month, my uncle had received ten offers for her hand. Within two months, men were coming to speak to him almost daily."

"Yes, I recall your eldest sister was the diamond of the season," said the dowager.

"My sister was flattered of course, but it all became very confusing. We needed to sort through her suitors and find the ones who were the most eligible."

"So, you naturally investigated their bank accounts and chose the one with the most blunt to spend," drawled the duchess.

"The wealthiest suitor was forty years her senior with cold hands and wet eyes. No, ma'am, we did not choose the wealthiest," said Pen.

"You chose a love match?"

Penelope paused. "My sister came to fancy a very charming man, handsome of face and well established in society. However, further inquiries into his habits revealed that he was also charming to several other ladies… married ladies. Perhaps this is customary in some circles, but it would have made my sister quite unhappy."

"So you used *Debrett's Peerage* as a guidebook for eligible marital partners?" The dowager rifled through the pages.

"Yes. Marriage is nothing to be entered lightly. We found that when men are wooing, they rarely share their true nature with their intended. We needed to look at the situation logically, soberly, to help guide affection along its proper course."

"Well, I can understand your motivations," conceded the dowager, somewhat mollified. "Look here, what do these letters mean? Is this written in code?"

"We had some abbreviations." Pen again resisted the urge to snatch her book away from prying eyes.

"So what does 'EOF' next to the Earl of Wentworth stand for?"

Another rush of heat crawled up Pen's neck. Could this first day get any worse? "It means 'embarrassed of funds.'"

"I declare! Wentworth is hardly at a standstill."

"If you say so, Your Grace," demurred Pen.

"Wait, no, I did hear just last night that he was quite

in dun territory." The dowager looked her over as if weighing her worth. "I congratulate your ingenuity."

"These few notes were only intended to help secure the happiness of my sisters," murmured Pen. She was not sure if the dowager's comments were praise or censure.

"You ought not show this to anyone. Find a suitable place here where it will not be found by a curious housemaid."

"Yes, indeed. So… you are still interested in having me serve as a companion?" asked Pen.

"Quite, my dear." She gave Pen a wicked smile. "It will take more than an index of bachelors to shock me." The dowager's eyes flashed lightning blue. "He thinks he has won, but I shall show him. I shall support myself. I will not be put out of my own home!"

"Your Grace?"

The dowager gave her a sweet smile that made Pen wary. "I propose we assist Lady Bremerton with her errant niece."

"I should like to help her," said Pen with sincerity.

"You may have overheard me earlier," said the dowager, her head held high, as if daring Pen to find fault. "I had just received a letter from my grandson, informing me that he intends to cut me off. I can hardly believe he could be so hateful, but it is quite true."

"Why, that is terrible!" Penelope gasped. Her low opinion of the Duke of Marchford was now sealed.

"Yes, yes, quite," said the dowager, pleased to have someone agree with her. "Such a hateful thing to do to one's own grandmother." She reclined morosely yet gracefully into a chair, her hand smoothing her white, precisely coiffed hair.

"I am shocked! But can he do this? I do not mean to pry into your affairs, but surely you have your own funds."

"Yes, of course, I have my pin money, but the duke, four subsequent dukes to be exact, have always supplemented my allowance. Why, without this support, I would have only fifty pounds a week. Fifty! How am I to live on such a paltry amount?"

Penelope held her tongue. Fifty pounds a week was to her a small fortune.

"If nothing can be done to increase the allowance, we shall be forced from London."

"Could it be, I mean with the strictest economy, that you could manage on fifty pounds?" asked Penelope, careful to add just a hint of anxiety to her tone, as if she truly had concern that fifty pounds would be inadequate to meet her needs.

The dowager shook her head. "No, no, it is not possible. Unless..." She paused, giving Pen a steely glance with glittering eyes. "Unless we can do something to raise our fortunes."

"But what could we do?"

"I have an idea." She rose majestically from the chair, her back as straight as a lance. "Come, Penelope, we must not keep our company waiting."

Pen followed the dowager back downstairs to the drawing room, wondering what sort of scheme the dowager was plotting. At the dowager's request, Pen rang the bell for tea.

"Cora," said the dowager in a voice smooth as

silk, "I have been thinking and I believe I may know someone who can help."

"Truly? You are my only hope."

"What if I knew a discreet lady who creates eligible matches for those in society whose prospects are few?" asked the dowager.

"A matchmaker?" asked Lady Bremerton.

"A discreet purveyor of eligible unions." The dowager gave Pen a knowing smile that made Pen quite nervous about the direction the dowager was heading. "The lady is very discreet, very exclusive, with a proven record for finding the most eligible of matches."

"Oh, that is exactly what I need. Who is this lady?"

"I cannot say, for her identity is a closely guarded secret. Please do not repeat this to anyone."

"No, of course not." Lady Bremerton lowered her voice and leaned forward.

"She has a written ledger of eligible bachelors," said the dowager in hushed tones. "Their worth, their connections and proclivities, it is all written in her secret book. She is an expert in marriage and how to extricate damsels from difficult situations."

Lady Bremerton's eyes were wide. Genie's were likewise afflicted. Pen was alarmed that the dowager was speaking about her annotated version of *Debrett's* and tried in vain to catch the dowager's eye.

"Antonia, please, you must tell me how I can contact this lady. She is precisely the miracle I have hoped for."

"I do not wish to disappoint you, but her fees are rather high. I would even call them extravagant."

"Price is of no concern."

"What would you be willing to pay?" asked the dowager, her blue eyes gleaming.

"Anything!" said Lady Bremerton recklessly.

The tea cart arrived and Pen made a point of rattling the china to disturb the conversation as much as possible with the hope of shaking the dowager off the topic. Pen could not feel comfortable with what the dowager was proposing.

"I might be willing to contact Madam X if you can tell me what you would be willing to spend to see your niece married before the end of the season," said the dowager, undeterred by Pen's clattering teacups.

Lady Bremerton's eyelids fluttered and she glanced around wildly. "If Eugenia could be married before the end of the season, oh, that would be something. I would… I would match her dowry!"

"Aunt Cora!" exclaimed Genie. "You could not possibly."

"Hold your tongue, child!" exclaimed Lady Bremerton. "'Tis nothing but a trifle in comparison to having my reputation tarnished."

"Certainly," said the dowager evenly, "a wise investment to be sure. I shall be in touch with Madam X and let you know her answer."

Pen stifled a gasp. The dowager was auctioning off Pen's questionable services in the marriage mart for a shocking amount. Pen clinked her teacup down on her saucer, trying to get the dowager's attention but in vain.

"Your Grace—" began Penelope, determined to end this farce, but the dowager interrupted her.

"Marchford? Is that you dearest?" called the duchess.

A rustle from the corridor was silenced. Penelope could imagine the duke judging whether he needed to respond or if he would best make a run for it. At length, he came to the open doorway.

"Yes, Grandmother?"

"Marchford, may I present to you Miss Talbot? She is the cousin of Lady Louisa and is lately come to London."

"Ah, yes. Louisa's cousin." The duke gave Miss Talbot a discerning look. "I have heard of her arrival." His wry smile was not shared by Lady Bremerton.

"Please be a dear and show the young people a tour of the house," continued the dowager. "I have a few things I need to discuss with Lady Bremerton. You were not on your way out, were you? You are always so considerate, so obliging, that's a dear."

Marchford, wearing a midnight blue, double-breasted, cutaway riding coat over suede breeches and top boots, was almost certainly going out for a ride. He gave a perfunctory smile and spun the riding crop in his hand. "I would be pleased to take the young ladies on a short tour of the house." He bowed politely and even though he said and acted as he ought, Pen had no question that he was displeased with this turn of events.

Pen and Genie walked toward the door to begin their tour; indeed, they had no other choice. Pen glanced back at the dowager, sure she had found a way to get the dissenting voices out of the room so the dowager could plot more efficiently with Lady Bremerton. She had a nagging suspicion she should not leave poor Lady Bremerton undefended, but there was nothing to do but follow the duke out the door.

Marchford led the two ladies through the house, showing them the briefest glance at the drawing rooms, the salon, and the library. The library appeared extensive and Pen was drawn into the room, admiring his collection. She was roused back to order by the duke standing at the door, watch in hand. She barely made it out of the room before he strode off again, rapidly commenting on fluted moldings and ionic columns.

"I would have liked to explore the library too, but I did not dare," whispered Genie, falling into step beside Pen.

Pen smiled at her. "You must come back, and we will explore it together."

Genie gave a tight smile. "Thank you. Though I warrant I will be returning soon to the country. I cannot possibly allow my aunt to pay such an amount and I know there is no way for my father to pay her back."

"Begging your pardon, but you may have some difficulty controlling what those two old campaigners do."

"You are very right," conceded Genie. "Might there be any hope for my reputation?"

"There is always hope. I have seen the most outrageous behavior tolerated by the *haut ton* from one of their favorites."

"I doubt I shall be graced with the honor of being a society favorite," said Genie, her eyes growing bluer.

Pen gave Genie a bracing smile as they followed the duke into the spacious ballroom. "You never can tell. My sisters received considerably more attention than we thought possible. I am learning the Duchess of Marchford holds her own power in society. Do not pack your gowns quite yet."

"Thank you, Penelope. I am so glad I have met you today. You have given me hope!"

A sudden silence caught the ladies' attention. The duke had ceased his rapid narration and stood before them the picture of maligned dignity, one eyebrow aristocratically raised. "I do hope I am not disturbing your conversation."

"Not at all," blurted Pen. "Your home is truly impressive." The ballroom in which they stood was well lit with windows along the far wall. Several crystal chandeliers hung from the ornately painted ceilings. Pen could only imagine the splendor it would be when lit at night. The ballroom appeared to open into a courtyard garden in the back. Pen was curious to have a peek, but Marchford was already walking back to the door.

"I do like the gold and blue wallpaper," commented Genie.

Marchford turned and glanced around at the walls as if noticing them for the first time. "Yes, I believe my grandmother had everything redecorated in my absence."

"Then Her Grace has done quite a bit," commented Pen.

"Yes. She has quite taken command of the house," replied Marchford, a slight bite to his tone.

"It shall be very hard for her to leave it," said Pen with more feeling than she ought to have.

"Indeed, I imagine it will be." This was spoken with cool disregard, and Pen could not help but be annoyed. She opened her mouth in defense of her new mistress, but Marchford stalked out of the ballroom. "The gallery is upstairs."

Pen bristled under the weight of his disregard. The Duchess of Marchford deserved more compassion than what he deigned to show, and certainly no family member should be cut off from her accustomed funds and banished to the country. Pen followed him into the entrance hall and up the white marble staircase. Marchford walked quickly with long strides and she had to hustle to keep up, with Genie trailing along behind.

At the top of a white marble staircase, the gallery was a long hall, running the length of the spacious house. Large windows illuminated the long row of portraits along the far wall and the elegant marble statues situated artistically throughout the gallery. The sun shone brightly, giving the marble a rosy hue. Marchford strode down the length of the hall, circumventing the marble statues as if an inconvenience, impatiently swatting his riding crop against his thigh.

Pen was forced to pick up her skirts and run a few steps to catch up with him. A glance behind ensured that Genie was sufficiently out of hearing distance, giving Pen the opportunity to speak her mind.

"Forgive me, for it is not my place to say," began Pen, "but I am shocked at your disregard for what your grandmother will suffer. Forcing her to leave her home, which she so carefully maintained in your absence, is a hardship no person, even such an esteemed person as yourself, should impose on his own grandmother. And leaving a note declaring your intentions to cut off her funds should she disobey you is as cowardly as it is cruel."

The duke looked down at her with cool civility. "You are right. It is not your place to say."

He turned on his heel and stalked off down the hall. She had been given the cut direct, which, considering her rather inappropriate outburst, was well deserved. She sighed and walked after him. She was always speaking her mind in a manner most unbecoming in a female. Her outburst was impolitic too, since she had rather hoped to remain in the house more than a few days. She hustled to catch up with him again, knowing what she must do.

"Please forgive my outburst, which reveals so clearly why I am the only Rose sister to remain unmarried. I shall leave your house at once if you wish it," said Penelope.

Marchford stopped, his back to her. Silence filled the hall and Pen waited on the duke's timing for when he should next speak.

"You are also right about another thing. It was cowardly." He turned back to her. "Stay her companion. She will need the company, and it is refreshing to have one not afraid to speak her mind. Perhaps she has not told you, but my grandmother has had many companions in the past. They often do not stay long. You, I am convinced, will not be so easily frightened."

"I like your grandmother very well," Pen said with a smile. "Though she can be most insistent when she wants her way."

"Yes. Quite." Marchford turned absently to the portraits before him.

"Is this family along the wall?" Pen asked, changing to a safer subject.

"Yes. A long line of Marchfords."

"And does your portrait hang among them?"

"No. Not yet, anyway. Do not, I beg you, put the idea into my grandmother's head, or I shall find my time consumed with standing for the portrait maker."

"Being a duke, I presume this fate will befall you sooner or later. I am surprised you have not been forced to sit for a portrait yet."

"I have been away since my ascension to the title."

"Is this a portrait of your father?" Pen guessed, motioning toward a man elegantly dressed in a powder blue coat with elaborate gold embroidery and a large, curled white wig.

"Yes, the seventh Duke of Marchford. And next to him his first wife, Sophia of Lincolnshire." Marchford gestured toward a portrait of a delicate creature with a hint of a smile on her rosebud mouth.

"Charming," pronounced Pen. "Was the portrait like her?"

"I am told so. I never met her."

"Oh, did she die in childbirth?"

"Yes, but not giving birth to me." Marchford pointed at the portrait next to hers of a young man. He resembled Marchford in his eyes, but he had a smaller, more delicate frame like his mother. "This is my elder brother, Frederick, the eighth Duke of Marchford."

"I did not realize you had an elder brother," said Pen.

"Yes, poor Frederick was never strong. He had scarlet fever as a boy and never entirely recovered. He died about three years ago."

"I am sorry for your loss."

Marchford stared at the portrait of his brother.

"He had been close to death so many times, I never thought he would actually die."

Despite her resolve to dislike this man, a lump developed in her throat. She remembered all too well the pain of losing her parents. "I felt the same when my parents passed away. They both contracted the fever and were gravely ill. Even after the doctor said there was no hope, I still thought they would recover."

Silence again filled the hall. Pen expected Marchford to resume his rapid tour of the house, but he remained gazing at the portrait of his brother, his expression unreadable.

"Does your mother's portrait hang here?" asked Pen, trying to move beyond the somber mood.

"No." Instead of lightening the mood, Marchford's face grew more solemn. "Grandmother would never allow it."

Pen stared at him, surprised. "Your grandmother has chosen a more suitable place?"

Marchford glanced at her, a wry smile on his lips. "According to my grandmother, the most suitable place would have been the burn pile."

Pen opened her mouth and closed it again. What could she possibly say to that pronouncement?

"If you are to best serve my grandmother, you should understand my father had two wives. One favored"—Marchford motioned toward the pretty picture of Sophia—"one not." He motioned to himself.

"After his first wife died bringing Frederick into the world," Marchford continued, "my father married again. Unlike his first marriage, it was not arranged by my grandmother, it was indeed a *love match*." He whispered the words, as if revealing a shameful family secret. "My father died in a fire at his hunting box when I was five. My mother and grandmother..." Marchford's voice trailed off and he exhaled slowly. "My mother's portrait will never be hung as long as my grandmother lives under this roof."

"I am sorry," said Pen weakly. She had been convinced Marchford was heartless for his treatment of his grandmother, but she could see there was considerable family history driving his decisions.

"The billiard room is this way in case you have the desire to play." Marchford abruptly changed the subject and led her down a side stairwell. The notion of Pen playing billiards was absurd, but she followed along, trying to arrange her thoughts enough to form words.

"The billiard room," said Marchford, entering an unlit room with rich mahogany woodwork and burgundy velvet curtains. Compared to the airy, white gallery it was a warm, intimate space.

"I believe in love matches," blurted Pen.

Marchford raised an eyebrow. "Do you now?"

"Yes. I ensured my sisters all made good matches with men who would not only be able to give them a comfortable life, but also where there was mutual affection."

Marchford took a step toward her, his eyes dark in the dimly lit room. His features were handsome but strong with a decided nose and chiseled jawline. "The Duke of Marchford is engaged to Lady Louisa. It was intended to be my brother, but with the peerage, I also inherited a bride."

"Perhaps love can grow. Affection can develop between two people who are often in each other's company."

Marchford's eyes never left hers. "Perhaps you are right."

Pen looked away, wondering why the room had suddenly grown so hot. What could she be thinking, speaking of love matches with the duke? "Thank you for the tour, Your Grace. It was most informative."

"It seems, Miss Rose, we have a problem," he drawled in a low tone.

"A-a problem?" she stammered.

"We have lost Miss Talbot."

Seven

WILLIAM GRANT BOUNDED UP THE STAIRS TO THE front door of the Duke of Marchford's grand house. "Where's Marchford?" he asked the dignified butler who answered the bell.

"I believe His Grace is conducting a tour of the house. If you would wait in the drawing room, Mr. Grant, I shall inform His Grace that you have arrived."

"No need, no need, I shall find him myself. Must dash. Already kept my horse waiting too long. Fine stepper. Not the thing to let him get chilled."

"But, Mr. Grant," called the butler, but Grant had already bounded up the marble stairs to the gallery. It is where people generally lingered on tours of the house. He recognized some of the statuary was quite fine, but not as fine as the handsome bit of horseflesh he had recently purchased at Tatt's, waiting for him outside.

Grant paused for a moment but heard and saw no one. He walked through the gallery at a quick pace, looking for Marchford and wondering if he had gone down to the billiard room. Grant strode past the statues until arrested by a compelling sight. Miss Talbot stood looking up at a marble of Athena drawing her bow.

In the sunlight, her blond curls shimmered. Gowned in all white, had it not been for her golden hair, he might have mistaken her for another marble statue of the female form in perfection. He smiled at her, unable to stop himself.

"Hallo, we meet again." Grant walked up to Genie, all thoughts of horses forgot.

Genie noted his presence but returned his smile with a frown. "Oh no, not you again."

"You wound me!" Grant clutched his heart. "Whatever have I done to win such censure?"

"What have you done?" cried Genie. "Why, I have had to endure hours of lecture about you from my aunt. She was quite disapproving of me 'whispering in the corner of the drawing room' with you."

"Your aunt has lectured you about me? You intrigue me. Whatever did she say?"

"For a woman who holds you in such low esteem, she certainly knows a great deal about you." Genie sat down on a marble bench, her arms crossed before her. She pursed her lips in a manner that showed she was quite put out, but all Grant could see was how kissable those naturally pink lips must be.

"Do tell. I am aquiver with anticipation."

"Did you know you are the enemy of every decent young woman?"

"No!" Grant sat beside her, his face a picture of mock horror.

"Yes, quite. You are a mother's worst nightmare, a handsome, well-breeched, pleasant-mannered young gentleman who has sworn off ever entering the married state. Apparently, you have caused the decline of many a foolish miss who has set her cap at you, and you are the bane of your mother's existence. Do you deny it?"

"I am well chastised indeed."

"You accept the judgment against you?"

"Well now, I'm not sure I could ever boast of putting a young miss in decline, and as for my mother..." Grant paused and pulled out an elegant snuffbox, rolling it in his fingers a few times before returning it to his pocket. "Come to think of it, I rather think I am the bane of her existence. Or must be, to hear her talk. Mothers do take it as a personal affront if their sons don't choose to marry."

"*Only* son," corrected Genie.

"Guilty as charged, only I had no choice about the *only* part. Would that my parents had produced a half dozen strapping lads."

"So no one would be bothered by your determination not to wed?"

Grant merely smiled. Truth was, if he had been blessed with brothers, he would not have felt such pressure to wed. He might have even been married now had circumstances been different. He liked ladies as a general rule. He particularly liked the one sitting beside him. "I suppose they warned you against me."

"I am not to be within a stone's throw, and then only if etiquette does not allow me to run screaming from the room when you enter."

Grant smiled, a slow, lazy smile that generally had

the effect of making women melt. "Then why are you sitting beside me?" He leaned a little closer, waiting for the swooning to commence.

Genie raised one eyebrow. "You, sir, are an incorrigible flirt."

Not exactly a swoon—he must be having an off day. "True, true. And yet you are still here beside me."

Genie waved a hand like she was swatting away a fly. "It can make very little difference at this point. I shall be leaving soon to go back home. I was raised in the country and there I shall return."

"Do not let this minor incident ruin your entire London season. Come now, you must have more spirit than that."

"It is not just that. You can have no idea, but my aunt is actually thinking of paying a matchmaker to find me a husband. A shocking amount too, I cannot fathom it."

"So you mean to run away back home."

"I am not running—oh, you are odious." Genie shook her head with an imperious frown. "You mean to quarrel with me. Well, I'll not have it. I am not the least bit quarrelsome."

Grant laughed out loud. "No indeed, you are not!" He gazed into her deep blue eyes and suddenly felt himself at sea. He should swim for the shore and let her go, but he leaned closer instead. It was of critical importance—he came to the quick realization—that Miss Genie Talbot remain in London. "But do not leave London without enjoying the season. There are many amusements to be had."

"I confess I have wanted to see the Tower and the

cathedrals. Oh, and I hear the British Museum is not to be missed."

Grant's idea of London amusements did not include touring the town with a guidebook, but he sagely kept these musings to himself. "Indeed. And of course, you must not consider leaving Town without a visit to the theater or your first ball."

"I doubt I will have any invitations to balls." Genie's shoulders sagged a little.

"But of course you will. Did I not tell you not to worry yourself on that score? I expect when you arrive home today, you will find an invitation to the coming-out ball for Miss Cassandra Devine."

"Who is she? And why would you think anyone would invite me to a ball?"

"Cassie is my niece and I have spoken to my aunt to ensure your invitation is secure."

The corners of Genie's mouth twitched up until she gave Grant a tentative smile. "How did you arrange that?"

"By promising the most gruesome thing in the world." Grant's shoulders sagged at the mere thought of his penance. "I must dance with all the debutantes."

"No!" Genie covered her mouth with her hand in shock.

"I fear it is true. So now that you know the lengths I will go to secure you an invitation, you cannot possibly be so disobliging as to leave London before the ball."

"No, indeed, of course I shall come." Her eyes shone for a moment and then a cloud passed over them once more. "But afterward, I must go home. I cannot be responsible for causing my aunt to spend such a vast amount for a matchmaker."

"But she would only have to pay anything if you entered into the married state. This seems an easy thing to avoid."

Genie graced him with a brilliant smile. "You would know best."

Grant returned her smile. "I can tutor you in the ways of avoiding matrimony."

"I would be most obliged. Does the work of a match-breaker have a fee associated with it?"

"My fee is only the pleasure I have in protecting my friends from wedded bliss."

"Is that what happened between the duke and Lady Louisa? You worked your dark arts to wither away any affection for the match?"

Grant shook his head. "Theirs is an arranged match, and you are right about a general lack of enthusiasm from either partner for the match."

"It seems a shame that two people should be bound together for life without any affection from either party."

"I should be happy if I could inspire even a decent conversation between the two," remarked Grant without thought.

"Oh yes, do let's help them!"

Grant could not recall making any such suggestion, but the angel before him lit up with excitement, and any thought to the contrary was vanquished. "Yes, let us see what we can do."

"Good, what an excellent idea. We should try to get them together, try to encourage them to make conversation."

Grant, who never once interfered with the romantic interests, or lack of interest, of his friends, found himself nodding in agreement despite himself. Genie beamed in return and Grant decided it was all worth it. Poor Marchford would have to fend for himself.

"So I am to defend you against suitors while trying to inspire romance in the duke."

"Yes! A lovely plan I think."

Grant could think of a few other words for it but said nothing. "Whatever else we do, please recall you owe me the first dance. I have paid for it dearly and I shall have it."

"Indeed, you shall," conceded Genie.

Grant took her gloved hand in his and kissed it at the edge of the glove, his lips brushing momentarily over her skin. "Until we meet on the morrow."

"Miss Talbot!" Another young woman, brunette, not at all as pretty as the lovely bundle he was sitting beside, strode down the gallery hall with purpose, Marchford trailing in her wake. He had seen that look in a matron's eye before and knew it was time to abandon his new prize.

Grant rose and greeted his friend. "Marchford. Came to find you. Kept me waiting outside."

"I do apologize," said Marchford, strolling behind the determined female. "Miss Rose, may I present Mr. William Grant. Miss Talbot, I believe you are already acquainted."

"How do you do?" said Miss Rose evenly. "I am already acquainted with Mr. Grant."

Grant merely smiled and made his bow. He did remember Miss Rose, but he would have preferred to forget. "You are to be the dowager's new companion, I understand."

"Yes, you are correct," said Miss Rose, moving between him and the lovely Miss Talbot. Not only was she utterly immune to any flirtation, but she also appeared determined to protect Miss Talbot from the same.

"Let me show you back to the drawing room, ladies," said Marchford. "I fear I must away, as I have kept Mr. Grant waiting."

"I can escort Miss Talbot back to the drawing room, Your Grace. I fear we have kept you from your appointment." Miss Rose curtsied efficiently and, linking arms with Miss Talbot, turned to leave.

"Do not forget, Miss Talbot, the first dance is mine!" declared Grant.

Miss Talbot turned back to him. "I would be most obliged," she said before she was tugged back by the militant Miss Rose.

Grant watched the retreating figures of the women, his eyes roving with pleasure over the flawless form of Miss Talbot.

"Why do I feel compelled to remind you," drawled Marchford when the ladies were out of hearing range, "that Miss Talbot is the cousin to my intended bride?"

"Merely admiring the view," said Grant.

When Marchford returned from his ride with Grant, he was informed there was a Mr. Neville waiting for him in his library. Marchford frowned. He did not recall having any business with a Mr. Neville, and curiosity getting the best of him, he decided to speak with the man before changing his clothes.

Mr. Neville was a small man with a receding hairline. What hair he had was combed forward over the barren spots in a rather futile attempt to hide what he had lost. Marchford could have no respect for the tailor who had cut the shoulders of Neville's brown coat too wide in a vain attempt to make his client appear larger. The effect, unfortunately, made the man appear not fully grown. Despite these flaws in appearance, the man surveyed him with the utmost confidence, holding a leather case to his chest with pride.

"Do I have the pleasure of addressing the Duke of Marchford?"

"Yes," replied Marchford, unaccustomed to being addressed so directly in his own home. "And I believe you are Mr. Neville? What can I do for you, sir?"

"A pleasure to make your acquaintance, Your Grace," said the man. "I have been sent by the Foreign Office to give you this." The man handed him a sealed envelope. "Please read it, Your Grace."

Marchford noted the seal with displeasure. He had served the Foreign Office for the past eight years. Some of his service he could discuss; other operations would remain forever in secret. No one understood why he had returned to Spain after his brother died. Everyone assumed he was avoiding marriage or did not wish the responsibility of the title, but those reasons would not have kept him from doing his duty.

The truth was Marchford had been in the middle of a sensitive mission and had made important contacts with the enemy. If he had not returned, the mission would have failed. It took him three years, but they finally tracked the spy back to its source and foiled an attempt to seize the city of Cadiz. Marchford turned the sealed letter over in his hands. He thought he had made it clear he was done working as a spy.

Marchford broke the seal with a small sigh and quickly read the contents. The letter contained a warning that the Foreign Office feared French agents had infiltrated London society. Marchford was warned he himself might be the target of spies trying to gain information regarding his covert work by any means possible.

"Any number of French agents know you have been working for the Foreign Office," said Mr. Neville. "I am to take any sensitive information you have and store it for safe keeping."

"If I had any such information, I assure you it is quite safe."

Mr. Neville's brows collapsed together. "I need not tell you the war with Napoleon and his coalition goes poorly. Most of Europe has already fallen under his power. It is of vital importance any information you have does not fall into enemy hands."

"It will not."

Mr. Neville chewed on his bottom lip, clearly displeased with the duke's answer. "You must be wary of those around you. Anyone could be in league with Napoleon. He pays his spies well. You have been seen in the company of a Mr. Grant and Lord Thornton."

"Friends from my days at Eton. Not spies."

"And you live with your grandmother."

Marchford cut off the man with a laugh. "My

grandmother may have her faults, but I doubt being a secret French spy is one of them."

"She recently took up a companion, a Miss Penelope Rose." The man pulled some papers from his case. "The daughter of a country parson, now deceased. She has four sisters, all married. She remains unwed." The man spoke the last words like an indictment against her.

"I see you have done your best to pry into my affairs. I must remind you that this is my business and none of your concern." Marchford let his voice drop.

"She has gained access to your house as have others who come to visit you or your grandmother. Any one of them could be a spy. The French can offer enough money for information even my own mother would be tempted to switch allegiances."

"Then you should be concerned with getting your own house in order and stop meddling in my affairs."

"Speaking of affairs, you were seen speaking with an opera singer."

"Thank you for your service to the Crown, Mr. Neville," said the duke, holding open the door. "Have a good day."

The dismissal was undeniable. Mr. Neville bowed and quit the room.

Marchford sank into a chair and stared at the dancing flames in the hearth. He had thought he had left this life behind when he returned to London, and yet here he was again, never knowing who to trust. It was ludicrous to think any of his acquaintance could turn against him, and yet the amount of money Napoleon would be willing to give for valuable information might well turn even the most loyal of hearts. That kind of money must be quite tempting to someone of Miss Rose's circumstances.

As much as he was loathe to admit it, Mr. Neville was right, Marchford needed to keep a wary eye on those around him. It was only a matter of time before he would be the target of a spy.

Eight

After their company departed, Penelope remained in the drawing room, alone with the formidable Dowager Duchess of Marchford. She was uneasy about the conversation regarding the matchmaker and sorely suspicious. Yet the dowager was a daunting woman and Pen's employer, so she understood she needed to keep her forthright manner reasonably in check.

"I am intrigued by your description of Madame X," said Pen. "Will I have the opportunity of meeting her?"

The dowager smiled. "Why of course, since you are, naturally, the infamous Madame X."

"Me?" Pen opened her mouth to say more but nothing emerged. It was not often she was at a loss for words, yet another reason she was still unwed, but now she could do little more than stammer.

"You found husbands for all your sisters. You have notes that will be particularly helpful in finding Miss Talbot a husband."

"But, Your Grace—"

"Call me Antonia," said the dowager with a wave

of her hand. "If we are going to be partners, we shall need to work together. I shall even arrange for you to receive ten percent of the payment."

"I do not think—"

"Fine, we'll split the fee eighty-twenty. With my connections and your book of peers, we can find husbands for anyone."

"Except myself," reminded Penelope. "How can I propose to find a match for Miss Talbot when I myself remain unwed?"

Antonia was quiet for a moment, her face unreadable as she studied Penelope. "I will give you twenty-five percent and that is my last offer. We both want to stay in London; this is our chance to raise the blunt we need to do it."

"But should you be charging your friend money to help?"

The dowager waved a hand. "Bremerton is one of the richest families in England. I shall not be taking bread off her table. Lady Bremerton herself would be most grateful, and it would spare her feelings not to be beholden to me. At the very least, we could give it a try."

The clock ticked softly in the quiet room as the dowager duchess waited for a reply. Try? Pen had given up trying. All it did was make one wish for something one could never have. Best to face the ugly truth directly and accept it. With a flash of insight, Pen realized she had taken the post of companion to an elderly lady to try to avoid the pressures of the marriage mart and the disappointment it had brought her.

And yet… finding husbands for other people was a skill she apparently possessed. It would be nice to live comfortably for the remainder of her life without the embarrassment of being a burden to anyone. She liked the rationale that they were sparing Lady Bremerton's feelings by creating a fictional matchmaker, though she suspected there might be a strong dose of convenient thinking. Yet Pen did not doubt Lady Bremerton was desperate to have Genie wed and it might be diverting at least to try. What did she have to lose?

"I suppose it could not hurt to try," said Pen.

"Good girl! Now, not a word to Lady Bremerton, mind you."

"Certainly not! And how did you suggest the fee be divided?"

The dowager's eyes narrowed. "I'll give you thirty percent, but that is my final offer."

"As you wish." Penelope lowered her eyes and clasped her hands neatly in her lap. It was important to know when to quit.

"Now then." The dowager cleared her throat, getting down to business. "You did say Miss Talbot told you Grant had arranged for her to be invited to the coming-out party for Miss Devine?"

"Yes, that is correct."

"Then we have no time to lose. I shall talk to James about quashing the rumors circulating about her debut. And I must help Cora pick out an appropriate gown. She is addicted to fashion but has not the figure for it anymore I fear. What was that color she was wearing today?"

"Persimmon, I believe."

"Ghastly," declared the dowager. "She has not the coloring for it. Now go fetch *Debrett's*. We must select a husband for our young Miss Talbot."

Lady and Lord Admiral Devine were the honored hosts of the coming-out ball for their niece, Miss Cassandra Devine. True to Grant's word, an invitation was extended to Miss Talbot. Lady Devine was a kind-hearted lady, generous to a fault, but her motives in inviting Genie were dominated more by the perverse humor of watching Grant dance with debutantes than an abundance of compassion. If nothing else, it guaranteed her ball would be remembered, and that was truly all a hostess could ask for.

Grant noted the exact moment of Genie's entry into the ballroom with a rush of pleasure. She wore a gown of ice blue with a gauzy overdress of silver. Her blond hair was sleeked back into a high bun with a diamond and sapphire tiara. Her deep blue eyes, pink lips, and flawless porcelain skin could leave no mistake that she was a strikingly beautiful girl.

"There she is," said the Comtesse de Marseille, who was dressed in a raiment of silk and lace fit to beggar a king. "I cannot believe she has the audacity to show her face in society."

"That is Lady Bremerton's niece," replied a man. "Pretty thing, quite pretty, too bad she has not the manners to match."

"Whatever do you mean?" asked Grant, joining the conversation.

"Did you not hear the latest *on-dits* about Miss Talbot? Apparently, she made quite a spectacle of herself before the queen."

"Ah, you speak of the presentation," said Grant. "I was there, you know."

"Do tell!" exclaimed the comtesse with a malicious glint to her eye.

"My Lord Chamberlain made an utter fool of himself by making known the painful result of ill digestion. Truly, I worry for him. The queen was quite put out at his behavior, I must say."

The Comtesse de Marseille laughed without a trace of mirth. "I heard that young chit embarrassed herself by shrieking with laughter."

"I heard she fell to the floor with hysterics," replied the man.

"Sorry to disappoint, but that's all a hum. Such a lovely girl, she shone in comparison to the other young ladies. Wonder who could benefit from spreading false rumors?" added Grant.

"Jealous mamas, no doubt," said the comtesse with authority. "They are a vicious breed."

"I heard it from a reliable source," countered the man, not ready to give up his bit of gossip.

"As did I," agreed the comtesse. "The Talbot girl made a fool of herself."

"The Talbot girl," said the Duke of Marchford, joining the conversation with stiff hauteur, "is the granddaughter of the Earl of Wainwright and the cousin of my betrothed."

The group turned to find the duke studying them with the disinterest of a noble. If anyone doubted Miss

Talbot's behavior, it was not going to be discussed before the duke.

"Good show," said Grant as he watched the gossips promenade away stately in search of safer ground. "You can give a set-down better than most."

"I fear it is a performance I shall have to repeat all evening."

"You'll enjoy that," said Grant, not at all attending to what his friend was saying. Instead, he watched Genie's entrance into the ball, the way the candlelight shone in her hair, the soft curve of her hip in the silk gown.

"Grant." The duke's voice was threaded with warning, but his companion was enthralled.

"Yes, yes, quite right. Must dash." Grant made a direct line to the object of his fancy.

"I am not supposed to dance with you," whispered Genie as she followed Mr. Grant onto the ballroom floor.

"Who told you that? The sour-faced companion to the dowager?"

"No!" insisted Genie, who felt allegiance to her new friend as one of the only people in London who would claim a friendship with her. "Well, yes," she amended. Upon reflection, she decided there was no use in denying it. "But she is hardly the only one. I do wish to thank you for securing this invitation for me, but my aunt, my cousin, oh, everyone from the chambermaid to the groomsman has warned me not to go anywhere near you."

"I am flattered to know my reputation has finally made its way into the gossip of the chambermaids."

"You are quite incorrigible."

"My dear girl, if you insist on flattering me in this manner, I fear I shall have to make you my new favorite."

"Mr. Grant, I would beg that you stop funning me. The only reason I am standing up with you is because you made it impossible for me not to." Grant had come up to Genie and her aunt alongside the Duke of Marchford. Aunt Cora could hardly cut her future son-in-law, so she watched helplessly as Grant led Genie out to the dance floor.

"Again, your flattery is too much."

"These are serious matters, Mr. Grant. After my disastrous presentation at court, my reputation is in shreds. I cannot be seen dancing with a known rake. No respectable person will speak to me."

"You should thank me then. All the respectable people I know are dreadfully dull."

Genie was prevented from making a stinging retort by the start of the music and the necessity to attend to her steps as she skipped forward for the country dance. "I am trying to be respectable," she hissed when they crossed paths for the dance.

"You greatly disappoint me."

"Good!" She twirled and skipped until she was once more standing before him. "Now please do not force me to dance with you again. Being known as a favorite of yours would be the end of my reputation."

"Whatever do you mean, Miss Talbot?" asked Grant, his silver eyes wide and innocent.

"You know exactly what I mean. A *carte blanche*. An offer without the protection of marriage."

"Miss Talbot!" exclaimed Grant with false shock.

They separated for the dance again, and Genie knew she had been nettled into speaking of things a blushing debutante should know nothing about, or at least pretend she knew nothing about.

Grant spun back to her, graceful and natural. He took her hand. It was merely part of the dance, one she had done countless times before, but never had she been more keenly aware she was holding a man's hand.

"You shock me," whispered Grant. "Are you attempting to make me an offer?"

This time, Genie knew better than to rise to the bait. "You are a rake and a rogue, Mr. Grant."

"Guilty, my dear."

Despite her best efforts, his careless words of endearment curled up warm and happy in her chest, making themselves at home. With a tingle of warning at the back of her exposed neck, she realized she might be in real danger. He was a master of flirtation, and she was just a country girl in considerably over her head.

The dance separated them again, and Genie used the time to get herself back under regulation. She might be the daughter of a country gentleman, this might be her first ball in the excitement of a London season, but she knew who she was. And she was not going to let some slick-talking rake make her doubt herself.

"I do not need your assistance, Mr. Grant," said Genie when they linked together once more.

"Is that so?"

"It seems your goal is to ruin me. Trust me, Mr. Grant, I can do that quite well on my own."

Grant burst with mirth, laughing so hard he stopped dancing despite the odd stares of assembly.

"Please, Mr. Grant. The last thing I need is to make a spectacle of myself. *Again*," hissed Genie, chastising him to move.

Grant started up the dance again, but this time his eyes never left hers. For a while they danced without speaking, but Grant's eyes followed her throughout the dance. A warm look glowed in his eyes that Genie had never seen before. Despite being in a ballroom crushed with people, she felt isolated in his attention, as if they were dancing alone.

Although her intention was to appear nonchalant and distant, she too could not see anyone but him. He was a handsome man, of average height but of near perfect form. He was everything a gentleman should be, in appearance at least. Despite her best intentions, she slid into the magic of the moment. She was a young debutante in London, dancing with the most attractive and notorious rake in all of society. She smiled with delight.

He returned the smile, slow and true. "I fear it is I who may be ruined."

Heat flushed through her, leaving her skin hot and her mouth dry. She wished for a retort but could think of nothing to say. He took her hand, sending another jolt tingling up her arm to her spine, which somehow made her ankles weak. They had stopped any pretense of dancing and were standing before each other in the middle of the ballroom.

"I believe our set is complete," said Grant in a low tone.

It was another moment before Genie could register the words. In a flash, the ballroom came back into view. The dance was completed, and the gentlemen were leading their partners off the dance floor. Genie glanced around, nervous someone had noted her odd behavior, and indeed there were a few matrons staring at her and whispering.

"Yes, thank you," said Genie briskly, gripping Grant's arm, so anxious to leave the center of attention she ended up dragging him off the floor. Genie marched with purpose back to where her aunt was standing with Penelope. Nothing to shock a body back to propriety like her aunt's sour look. "Thank you, sir," said Genie in a clipped, businesslike tone. "I hope you will enjoy the rest of your evening."

"I always do," said Grant with a wicked grin. He bowed and disappeared back into the crowd.

Nine

Genie took a deep breath, trying to steady her racing heart. The hot, stale air only made her head swim more. The crush of the ballroom and stifling air made her a little dizzy.

"You should not look so much at him when you dance," chastised her aunt. "One would think you were encouraging his advances and nothing could be more fatal. Do not think your behavior has not been noted. Vicious women these mamas are. They will not think twice about ruining your reputation so they can push their own less favored daughter. You need to… good heavens, child, are you all right?"

In truth, Genie was light-headed and swaying. The swarm of colors and tiny lights of the numerous candles in hanging chandeliers all seemed to swirl together. "I am a little hot; the room is so crowded. Perhaps a little air?"

"Yes, go to the balcony. For heaven's sake, do not faint where everyone can see you."

"I will help. Come with me." Penelope took her elbow and led her competently through the maze of people until they reached a double door that opened onto a small terrace balcony.

"Lean against the railing and take some of the night air. The coolness will do you good. I will fetch some lemonade for you," said Penelope.

"Thank you," murmured Genie, her senses revived in the cool air. She leaned against the balcony and closed her eyes. The night air functioned as an effective restorative and soon she was feeling back to herself. She was not prone to vapors or other such episodes that seemed to afflict some women. Once again, her troubles were the fault of Mr. Grant. She was not exactly sure what he had done to have such an ill effect on her, but she was certain he was to blame.

The evening was pleasant, with no moon, the only light shining through the door from the ballroom. The balcony opened onto a courtyard garden, popular for large homes in London. A few crickets started to chirp, and Genie immediately thought of home. She missed the happy sound of crickets chirping and the frogs singing. She leaned slightly over the edge and listened intently.

"Did anyone see you leave?" whispered a male voice.

Genie straighten and scanned her surroundings but saw no one.

"No, I do not believe so," whispered a familiar woman's voice in return.

Genie realized the voices were coming from the garden below. She did not wish to intrude, but if she moved, the inevitable swish of her skirts would announce her presence.

"How long do we have, my love?" asked the man.

"An hour, no longer. I told my mother I was going to dance for the next two sets. She was sitting down to play a hand or two of whist with friends, so I should not be missed. But more than that, I do not dare. I must return to her soon."

"Must you? Let us leave this place. Run away with me," said the man, his voice thick with emotion.

"You know I cannot."

"I will not let him marry you. Marriage contract be damned. I will not allow it!"

"Hush, my darling. I swear to you, I will not marry him. How could I? You know it to be impossible."

"I need you."

There was silence and Genie guessed there was kissing occurring in the darkness of the garden.

"Are you sure you wish to do this?"

"I am sure. We have waited too long."

"It cannot be undone."

"I know it."

"I care nothing for your fortune, you know that. I would give it all away. I would not compromise you."

More silence. Genie once again felt flushed. What might it be like to kiss Grant? Images came unbidden to mind. What would it feel like? Soft? Wet? Genie had seen her brother kiss a neighbor girl, shortly before her father bought him a set of colors and shipped him off to the Continent to fight Napoleon. Genie had thought it looked rather disgusting at the time, but now she found herself becoming more open-minded to the entire kissing idea. In fact, she thought she might just want to try it for herself. The closest she had ever come was a peck on the cheek. She doubted it counted.

"I am yours, wholly and completely," said the woman's voice from below. "Now and forever, I wish to be with you. I want to do this. I need to do this. I chose to live my life with you, and after tonight, no other option will be possible. I chose you."

"Here we are," said Penelope, opening the doors to the balcony wide, casting light on the garden below. From below in the garden came a little gasp. Genie did not look down in the garden. She already knew who it was.

"I brought you some lemonade," continued Penelope, oblivious to the scene below. "Sorry it took so long. It is quite the crush tonight."

Genie motioned forward, and they left the balcony to go back into the ballroom. "Too cold," explained Genie once they were safely back inside with the doors closed.

Penelope gave a furtive glance at the closed door. "I thought it felt nice after all this heat."

"Are balls always this crowded?"

"The good ones," answered Penelope, "at least in the eyes of the hostess. This is quite a crush for a girl's debut into society. Lady Devine will be thrilled. Though I think it might have something to do with a certain nephew of hers who does not usually expose himself to the machinations of matchmaking mamas."

"Matchmaking mamas? But I thought Mr. Grant was not considered a respectable man."

"Respectable? Oh yes, he is certainly respectable. The trouble with Mr. Grant is that he is not safe."

"I am not sure I understand. I thought he was a rake."

"Yes, he is but not the bad kind."

Genie sipped her lemonade, trying to make sense of this. "There are good kinds and bad?"

"Certainly. The bad kind will seduce young innocents and leave them ruined without caring two figs about them. Those kind are not invited to parties such as these nor would they be inclined to come. There are some men in society who believe women are only there to serve their needs, and if a girl is to give them attention, they feel no compunction in enjoying it at the moment and then disregarding the girl. They seduce the innocent, then have the audacity to blame the girl, even if she is frightfully young and he is much older and experienced, and he still won't offer her his name because he is a vile, hateful creature." Penelope spoke with such venom that Genie blinked.

Penelope gulped down her lemonade in a single swig. "Just for an example."

"Yes, an example," agreed Genie, not believing a word of it. At some point, Penelope must have come across the bad sort of rake. "But you said there was a good kind of rake?"

"Yes, yes, where was I? The good sort does not seduce young innocents. They avoid debutantes as a general course in life and instead associate with women of a different nature. I am speaking of professional courtesans and married women in society who feel free to have additional relationships beyond their husband."

Genie almost dropped her lemonade. In a few short sentences, Penelope had shared more of the world than she had ever gotten from her mother or brothers. She had thought herself quite wise for having two elder brothers, but none had ever spoken of such things so blatantly.

"Forgive me, I have shocked you," said Penelope in her direct manner.

"No, well, yes, a little."

"Now you can see why I remain unmarried. I have a dreadful habit of speaking plainly when I should speak in euphemisms or better yet not speak at all. Yet, I think if a woman is going to enter the married state, she would do well to go into it with her eyes open and choose wisely."

"Yes, I agree. Though I doubt I shall have to sort through the offers. But please explain to me why the good sort of rake is better than the bad sort."

"The good sort would not intentionally ruin a girl. A mother can feel safe in that. The risk is more that the girl should become unwisely attached to him only to have her heart broken when an offer of marriage was not forthcoming. You must be wary of sending a girl into a decline. Yet the good sort of rake is also well established in society with pleasing manners and a healthy income. If such a man could be made to come to the altar, any mama would happily marry their daughter to him."

"So Mr. Grant is the good sort of rake?"

"The best kind. His manners are pleasant, his actions kind, his wallet plump, and he is handsome too. He would make a very nice sort of husband, if he could ever be made to come up to scratch."

"What would it take to do that?"

Penelope's brow scrunched into a look of concern. "Please tell me you are not developing a *tendre* for

Mr. Grant. We wish to help you be married, but you must understand, Mr. Grant is not the sort who is going to offer."

"Yes, of course," said Genie airily, as if it was of no concern. "I am still just trying to understand London society. It is quite different from home."

Penelope's face relaxed. "I completely understand. When my sisters and I first arrived in London, I was sure we had traveled to a foreign country. It took a while before I understood the rules and how to break them. Now let's see if we can make some introductions for you to some eligible men."

Penelope led Genie to where the Dowager Duchess of Marchford was playing whist with Lady Bremerton and some other friends. The game concluded with the dowager the winner. Flush with her victory, the dowager turned her considerable powers toward introducing Genie to the eligible males at the ball. Penelope somehow managed to wrangle the men to visit the dowager, who then made the introductions. Penelope and the duchess must have been working with the elusive Madame X, since they kept her busy introducing her to eligible bachelors, one after the next.

"Miss Talbot, may I present Mr. Blakely," said the Dowager Duchess of Marchford.

Mr. Blakely bowed. Genie curtsied.

"It is a pleasure to make your acquaintance," said Mr. Blakely. In a dark suit of unremarkable tailoring, there was nothing about Mr. Blakely that initially either intrigued or repulsed Genie. He was a youngish man with brown hair cut in an average manner, had brown eyes, and was of average height and build.

"Have you been in London long?" asked Genie.

"No, not long. A fortnight perhaps."

Genie nodded as if she was interested and then no longer knew what to say. She had met so many men, she was growing tired of polite conversation. "Are you enjoying the ball?"

"There do seem to be a lot of people present."

"Yes, quite a crush, from what I understand," said Genie. "The hostess should be very pleased."

"I could not say."

Genie waited to see what Mr. Blakely could say, but apparently that was more than she should have hoped for, so she continued the conversation. "As a newcomer to London, I have been most intrigued to see the sights. I hear the British Museum is fascinating."

"I have never been."

"The guidebook said it was highly recommended." Which was more than she could say for the conversation.

"Thank you for that suggestion."

"You are most welcome."

And so their conversation dragged on, one of the most innocuous, dull conversations that had ever been uttered. Genie prided herself in making good conversation, but she found it difficult to determine his feelings on any topic. He seemed content to accept the most banal opinion on any subject. It was not that there was anything wrong with Mr. Blakely. His facial features were acceptable, common perhaps. In fact, there was nothing particularly remarkable about him.

And yet, he was a good potential husband. She could not identify any feature that was wrong with Mr. Blakely, and he certainly did not ask her impertinent questions or make her feel flushed and dizzy. A definite improvement, she must say.

"The next set is beginning," said Penelope, rejoining them. "I do hope, Mr. Blakely, that you enjoy dancing as much as Miss Talbot."

"I could not say," answered Mr. Blakely, but he got the broad hint. "Shall we dance?" he asked Genie, though she did not detect any sliver of interest. Yet she was learning that in society, showing strong emotions was considered gauche. If a bland demeanor was fashionable, then Mr. Grant was correct—respectable people were dull.

Ten

"THERE YOU ARE!" ACCUSED LADY DEVINE.

Grant flinched at his aunt's words—not at the caustic tone, because he knew what was coming next. He turned from his card game to his aunt, her pursed lips and raised eyebrow a clear indication of her displeasure. She was about to ring a peal over his head, and he had done nothing but deserve it.

"Have you forgotten the promises you made me?" demanded Lady Devine.

"No, no, I was just taking a moment's reprieve," soothed Grant.

"A moment? I'll have you know that moment has taken at least four sets!"

"No, surely not that long."

"Indeed you have. I am sorry to break up the loo table, but with the cards you hold, you should be thanking me."

Grant sighed and tossed his cards to the table. "Gentlemen, I thank thee. Duty calls."

"Every debutante," reminded his aunt as they proceeded back to the ballroom. "You promised to dance with every debutante if I would invite Lady Bremerton's foolish protégée."

"Have you met Miss Talbot, Aunt?" asked Grant.

"Yes, briefly. She is a pretty young thing. Exactly the kind whose company you'd enjoy." She stopped for a moment in the corridor and lowered her voice. "I should not have to warn you, but I will not have you losing your head and making that gel some indecent proposal."

"Aunt, you shock me!" said Grant in mock horror.

"I am in earnest. Miss Talbot is under the protection of Lady Bremerton, and no matter how foolish the chit is, she is not a candidate to be your next doxy."

"Dear Aunt, you amaze me. I have never preyed on young debutantes."

"That is not entirely true," said his aunt, raising her eyebrow once more. "Do you recall the incident with Lady Stockton?"

Grant smiled in return, a charming, disarming, utterly false sort of smile. This was the trouble with family—they knew your past a little too well. "She was not Lady Stockton when the offer was made," said Grant in a low voice. "Besides, it was a trifling matter, completely forgotten." It was true that few people knew it had occurred and fewer still remembered it at all. Grant himself had tried to drink the memory away but found the incident could not be forgot.

"Just see to it, my boy, that you dance with all the debutantes and give their mamas a thrill."

Grant bowed to his aunt. "I shall meet my fate with the courage of an Englishman."

"Good." She gave Grant a little pat on the shoulder and a nudge toward the ballroom. "I've met this year's crop and you are going to need it!"

"Lemonade?"

Genie turned to find Mr. Grant holding two cups of the sweet libation. "Thank you, yes. I had thought you had gone to play cards." After hours of speaking and dancing with a half-dozen eligible men of various ages and situations in life, the sight of the charming Mr. Grant was a welcome one.

"Indeed I did but was flushed out by my aunt."

"You poor dear. And now here you are, drinking lemonade."

"I believe in trying everything at least once. How bad can it be?" Grant raised his glass to her and took a hearty gulp. Instantly, he started to gag. "Good heavens, what a dreadful concoction!"

"Lemonade does not agree with you, sir?" asked Genie, taking a sip.

"Not agree? Why, who could agree with such a wretched drink? And to think they make poor, unsuspecting young ladies drink this. I am horrified." Grant put his drink down on the table and eyed it suspiciously as if it might strike back.

Genie could not help but laugh.

"There now, that is a good sight better." Grant smiled at her.

"Stop, please. My aunt has informed me that I must never laugh again. Indeed, I am to appear a very serious lady."

"How dull. Worse than the lemonade. If this is how we are raising our young people today, we might as well surrender to France."

"Indeed, sir!"

"At least they know how to enjoy some amusement."

"And you are not amused by this soiree?"

Grant's eyes met hers. "It has not been without amusement."

Genie turned back to the ballroom where a mass of people milled about, waiting for the musicians to return from their break. She was once again feeling unusually warm, a sensation that seemed to be related to the close proximity of Mr. Grant. "Have you seen Lady Louisa?" She wished to change the subject and her mind flitted naturally to her cousin, about whom she had growing concerns.

"No, not recently. Why?"

"I was wondering if we could begin trying to bring Louisa and the duke to speaking terms."

"Is Lady Louisa feeling neglected?" asked Grant.

"Not as much as she should," murmured Genie. "But Lady Bremerton certainly feels the sting."

"I am not sure what can be done," hedged Grant.

"A dance might not be inappropriate at a ball."

"Marchford rarely dances."

"Perhaps he could make this one of those special occasions?"

"I shall make the suggestion to Marchford," promised Grant.

"Would you?" Genie touched his sleeve and smiled with gratitude. "Thank you. Might there be anything else we can do to help?"

"I shall think on it, never fear. Perhaps I could arrange to bring Marchford for a visit?"

"Yes! That would be quite the thing."

"Then it shall be done! I do apologize, but I must dash. Promised for the next set!" Grant bowed and disappeared into the sea of bodies. She caught sight of him once more leading out to the floor a plump debutante with pouty lips and spots. The sight ran tingles down her spine. He was not joking when he said he had promised to dance with every debutante to secure an invitation for her. Grant covered a wince with a smile after his foot was trod upon by the graceless young lady.

"Poor man," murmured Genie. She had been wronged by him but now saw the scales had shifted and she was in his debt.

❧

What on earth had become of him? He grimaced as his footwear again suffered attack. A few days ago, he was a notorious rake, a leader of society, carefree, and easy. Now he was standing up with an adolescent who snarled at him every time she made a mistake. What had dragged him to such depths?

He caught sight of Miss Talbot and resisted the urge to wave. Blasted girl. One look at those blue eyes and angelic face and he would promise her the crown jewels and his own head on a platter. His foot again suffered attack, his punishment for taking an interest in a debutante.

At length, the dance ended and Grant slipped away, back to the card room. His conscience pricked him again, and he knew he was not going to enjoy himself, but to meddle into his friend's affairs, an occurrence so unprecedented he was forced to take some liquid courage.

Marchford was found in a dim corner of the card room, winning a game of piquet.

"So have you spoken with your prospective bride tonight?" Grant asked Marchford as he sat down to play a round with his friend.

"Plenty of time to talk after we are married."

Grant raised an eyebrow. "Spoken like your grandmother."

Marchford leveled a glare. "What are you about, Grant?"

"I know you do not wish to marry Lady Louisa," began Grant, "but do you not think you should at least be on speaking terms?"

Marchford opened his mouth for what Grant expected to be a strongly worded rebuke. Marchford had returned from war colder than he had left, and he was a tad cool to begin with. Marchford clenched his jaw and played his card. "You are correct. I have not thought much of Lady Louisa except to know that we must marry. It always seemed..." Marchford played another card. "Lady Louisa was intended for my brother. They spent years together and I know she was very kind in helping to care for him. When Frederick died, it felt unseemly to marry his intended."

"You miss your brother."

"I do. I never wished to inherit his title, his bride. I will do what I must, but I do not wish..."

"You do not wish to appear to be enjoying the privileges meant for your brother."

Marchford nodded.

"How do you think Lady Louisa feels about this?"

"I have no idea."

"Perhaps, my friend, it is time to ask her."

Marchford stared long at his cards, considering the prospect. "Yes, you are right. I have stayed away too long."

"She is here, no time to waste. Go see her now!"

Marchford narrowed his eyes. "Are you concerned with my marital prospects or are you trying to get out of a bad hand?"

"I am outraged. Of all the years of our friendship, I would not have thought you could think so low of me. I now know your true opinion of me. And here my only concern has been for your welfare." Grant somehow managed to keep a smile from his face, but he could tell Marchford was unimpressed by the performance.

"Bad run in cards?"

"Horrid. Now go talk to that bride of yours and leave me to my whiskey."

Marchford stood in a calm, fluid motion. He was like that, always thinking and revealing nothing. It was one reason Grant reasoned Marchford needed him. Who else would give him the nudge into breaking that impenetrable shell and doing something relatively human? Marchford had been a spy too long. Not that Marchford had ever told Grant the nature of his work for the Foreign Office, but Grant knew. He just did.

"Perhaps you should see that pretty face you were dancing with earlier this evening."

"Was I? Which one?" Grant asked with utter nonchalance, but he knew exactly who Marchford meant.

"Deception does not become you. Especially when you do it so poorly," Marchford observed without emotion.

Another man might be offended, but Grant merely laughed. Marchford was right as usual, but Grant was much too practiced a bachelor to fall for easy bait. He had met many a charming, pretty face. It would take more than that to catch him.

And yet, as he forced himself back to the ballroom to dance with more simpering females, he easily recognized that no woman had ever inspired him to do something so undignified. If he was a wise man, he would take care to avoid Genie in the future. Yes, indeed, his flirtation with Miss Eugenia Talbot was officially at an end.

At least, if he had any sense, it would be.

Eleven

LADY LOUISA MUNTHGROVE, ESTEEMED ONLY daughter of Lord and Lady Bremerton, was surprisingly difficult to find. Despite having ignored her completely for the past three years of their official engagement, Marchford somehow expected her to be standing patiently along the wall of the ballroom, waiting for him. She was not. Nor was she eating a brief repast or playing at cards or walking in the garden. It occurred to him that he actually knew very little about Lady Louisa, except that she was a demure girl who was challenging to find. What did she do with her time? Where did she go? Where was she now?

Marchford strolled out into the garden, a rush of cool air pleasant after the heat of the ballroom. Grant was right; he needed to at least be on speaking terms with her. They were going to be married after all, no way around that. He had looked into the contract and spoken to Louisa's father. His plan to quietly end the contract after his brother's death had been met with fierce opposition. The Earl of Bremerton wanted his only heir to marry a duke, and it really did not matter which one.

Marchford knew what he must do. He would not force the matter and bring scandal to his house and to that of Lady Louisa. Love may not be in his future, but a marriage certainly was.

Instead of returning to the ballroom, Marchford sat on a stone bench in the garden, appreciating the stillness of the moonless night. Light poured from the door of the house, dimly lighting the garden in shades of gray. Tall bushes formed walls to create different rooms in the garden, some in sight, others hidden from view. It would be a pleasant place to stroll with an interest of fancy, not that he was at leave to indulge in that sort of activity. Marchford closed his eyes and breathed in the aroma of gardenia with a hint of lilac.

His mother had been a lover of flowers and had cultivated a wild jungle of color in their garden. After his mother was gone, his grandmother ordered the flowers to be ripped from the earth and replaced with sensible hedges. Now the Marchford house garden held nothing but well-mannered bushes trimmed at neat right angles. Nothing dared look unkempt in his grandmother's garden—his garden. Perhaps it was time to bring back the flowers.

It is remarkable how the soft swish of a woman's skirts can capture the attention of a man. Marchford turned toward the sound, waiting to see who might appear. Was it a couple hiding in the garden for a few moments alone? Was it a seductress come to help him forget his marital woes? The figure that appeared was definitely female, shapely, and alone.

"Good evening," said Marchford.

The woman gave a small shriek and put her hand over her mouth. "Marchford?"

"At your service." Marchford stood and bowed.

She stepped forward into the light, revealing Miss Penelope Rose. "What are you doing here in the dark?" she asked in an accusing manner. "You gave me a fright."

"I might ask the same of you," replied Marchford. "Why would my grandmother's companion abandon her during the party and walk alone in the garden?"

"I hardly abandoned your grandmother. She is playing whist with her friends and has no current need for me. As for walking in the garden, I find the cool air a relief after the hot ballroom. Why are you here? Shall I leave before I interrupt a lovers' tryst?"

Marchford coughed slightly at her brusque, straightforward manner. It was clear why she remained unmarried. She was all social awkwardness and sharp edges. "Nothing so scandalous, I assure you."

"Yes, yes, of course not, I beg your pardon." Penelope turned slightly toward the door to the house, as if wishing to leave but not exactly sure how to extricate herself from the conversation. Marchford was not inclined to help.

"And you? Am I interrupting a lovers' tryst?"

"Me? A tryst? Certainly not!"

"And yet, you are alone in the garden. It would be a natural assumption, an assumption you in fact made."

"Did I? Yes, well, you are you and I am, well, me."

"A true statement." Marchford smothered a smile. He should not enjoy needling her as much as he did, but her abruptness brought out a little used tendency to tease.

"So you see, there is no..." Penelope broke off and narrowed her eyes. "You are teasing me."

"Perhaps."

"That is unkind."

And at once, Marchford felt it had been unkind. The power differential between them made his words appear not to be the work of a tease but of a bully. And that he could not abide. He opened his mouth to offer his apology, but Penelope spoke before he got the chance.

"Impolitic too," continued Penelope, "for it will only inspire me to answer in kind."

Marchford closed his mouth. The fact that he was a duke and she his grandmother's companion did not appear to cow Miss Rose in the least. It was refreshing. Surprising too.

"And how would you respond? Of what have you to accuse me?"

"Much! Where would you like me to start, Your Grace?"

"I had no idea I had so many flaws readily apparent to the casual observer. Pray tell me, do you find my address lacking?"

"No, your manner and address are all what they should be." Penelope pursed her lips in a way that informed Marchford she was unhappy about this admission.

"You find want with my fashion or form?"

"No, Your Grace." Despite the chill of the garden, Penelope snapped open her fan and began to wave it in a distracted manner. "Your form is... you dress quite adequately."

"What, then, do you have to accuse me of?"

"Your character!"

"My character? Do enlighten me on how you find me wanting."

"You are prone to tease unmarried and unchaperoned ladies in dark gardens at night!"

"Ah, your shaft hits home! I am guilty as charged, Miss Rose. I stand before you a humbled man. May I escort you back to the ballroom?"

"With pleasure, Your Grace."

Marchford offered his arm to Penelope and they walked into the ballroom. He was not sure who won that round or why it was they were fighting. He had, whatever the score, enjoyed himself.

After returning Miss Rose to his grandmother, Marchford toured the ballroom, dining room, and card room again to no avail. Lady Louisa was not present. He wondered if she might have gone home when suddenly she appeared, walking along the side of the ballroom. Marchford moved for an intercept and met her at the door to the card room.

"Lady Louisa." He bowed. He came up and noticed not what he thought he would see, the shy Lady Louisa, but someone quite different than he expected. It was Louisa, but this version was flushed, her hair was styled poorly, and she appeared to be, and there is no kind way to put this, rather sweaty.

Louisa stared at him with horror in her wide eyes. Her mouth was opened slightly and it took a few moments before she uttered, "Marchford."

Something was wrong. She was a shy creature, but she should not be horrified by him. "Are you quite well?"

"Yes, of course. I mean, no, not well. I was just going to my mother to beg to go home."

"I was just leaving myself. Please allow me to convey you home."

"No!"

Marchford blinked at her vehemence.

"I beg your pardon, but I need to return to my house. I am sure my mother will tend me."

"As you wish. I do hope you will feel better."

Lady Louisa dropped a quick curtsy and fled through the door to the card room.

~

"I'm not sure she appreciated your attentions," drawled Grant, coming up from behind. He had completed his dancing obligations and was longing for freedom.

"Your powers of observation amaze me," returned Marchford in a similar tone.

"Let's go rescue Thornton and head to the club," suggested Grant, noting that Lady Bremerton was taking her two charges, the lovely Miss Talbot among them, back home, which left no reason for Grant to tarry.

Their search for their friend was interrupted by a loud, female scream. Marchford and Grant ran toward the source of the sound, out of the ballroom into the main foyer. They were followed by Thornton and half the ballroom of interested guests.

Lady Devine glided down the stairs holding an empty box.

"What is wrong?" asked Grant, running up to her, with Marchford and Thornton not far behind.

"My emerald necklace, it has been stolen!"

"Stolen?" asked Grant.

"Tell me what happened," said Marchford, quickly adopting a businesslike tone.

"I slipped upstairs to freshen my face and I found this box, which usually contains my emeralds, empty on my boudoir table!"

People streamed in through the surrounding doors, including the large form of Admiral Devine.

"Dearest!" called his wife. He made his way to her side and a moment's whisper was enough to turn the admiral's red face to pale.

More people came in from the ballroom, crowding the hall with a throng of society's best, eager for scandal.

"My dear friends, nothing to worry about," called the admiral. "A simple case of a misplaced necklace, nothing more. Please return to dancing, enjoy the French wine; it cost me dear and I will not be satisfied until it is gone."

Some of the crowd ambled back into the ballroom, while the admiral, his wife, Grant, and his friends went up to investigate the scene of the disappearance.

Their hostess showed the men into the room—a more feminine domain of lace, satin, and feathers one could not imagine. The men stood like awkward oafs in the presence of so many frills and pastels, predominated by an unhealthy dose of pink.

"I found the empty box here," said the lady, standing beside her dressing table. The admiral moved forward to look, but Grant, Marchford, and Thornton remained planted by the door, overcome by the sheer pinkness of it all. "What else was taken?" Marchford stepped forward, the first of the bachelors to venture into the feminine domain.

"Oh! I had not thought of it. Let me see." The lady opened an ornately carved cabinet and began to pull out box after box, each containing the expected jewel. "No, nothing else was taken, just the emeralds. It's odd."

"Why is that?" asked Grant, overcoming the emasculating decor of the room and joining them.

"The emeralds are not my best piece. Why would the thief only steal that?"

"Yes, that is perplexing," said Marchford, examining the room.

Lady Devine wiped a tear from her eye. "Do you think the necklace will be returned soon?"

No one answered her. The emeralds were gone.

"What will they do with them? Everyone knows the setting to be mine."

"The necklace will probably be ripped apart and the jewels sold separately," said Marchford without feeling.

"It was my mother's," whispered Lady Devine as more tears began to fall. The admiral gave Marchford a glare. Grant just shook his head. For a smart man, Marchford could be thoughtless when it came to women.

Grant motioned to Marchford, who readily followed him outside the lady's domain to where Thornton was still standing. "There may be a thief downstairs. Shall we call the police?"

"And have them search the guests? I imagine Lady Devine would not care for it," said Thornton, always practical.

"I do not care for this scene," muttered the duke. "A thief would have had ample opportunity to come up to her boudoir and steal the lot of jewels. It appears to me this scene was made to look like a failed burglary, but in fact, the thief did not care for jewels or more would be taken."

"But why?" asked Grant.

"Perhaps it was created as a diversion, so the thief could steal what he really wanted."

"What could that be?" asked Admiral Devine, joining the party.

"Not sure," said Marchford. "Have you anything else of value?"

"My wife has several pieces of jewelry, but nothing else has been taken."

"What about you, Uncle. Anything in the house of particular interest to a thief?" asked Grant.

"Well, there is the silver, some artwork, an extensive, if you do not mind me saying, collection of wine, and some of the finest whiskey handed down from my father." He looked up to the ceiling in a wistful manner.

"Admiral," said Marchford, bringing him back to the matter at hand. "Have you anything else in the house. Anything perhaps of interest to a French spy?"

The wistful look vanished and the admiral snapped to attention. "My study!"

Twelve

"THE KEYS TO THE STUDY!" ADMIRAL DEVINE CALLED to his butler.

"You keep the study locked?" asked Grant, running after his uncle, Marchford and Thornton in pursuit.

"Yes, as a precaution. I have recently received some letters of a most sensitive nature."

The keys were produced by the butler and the admiral began to unlock the door.

"Wait!" called a demanding voice. "This is a matter for the Crown to investigate!" Mr. Neville pushed his way forward. "My agents report there has been a theft in this house. Admiral Devine, you received sensitive information recently, did you not?"

"Yes, yes, letters. They are in the top drawer of my desk."

"Careful now," said Mr. Neville, taking off his large coat. "Maybe we can catch this thief."

The door was unlocked and the men carefully edged into the dark room.

"There he is!" shouted Neville, and everyone rushed into the room.

"Where is he?"

"Someone bring a light!"

A loud crash shot through the room just as the butler emerged with a candle. The window curtains were flung back and the window was smashed out.

"He's made a run for it out the window!" called Marchford.

"After him!" called Neville. "I'll run around the front and try to head him off."

Marchford pulled the drapes over the broken glass and jumped through the window after the thief, Grant and Thornton right behind him.

"Which way? Did you see him?" asked Grant. They were in a dark, cramped alley between two large houses in crowded London.

"No, let's split up and find this bastard," called Marchford. "You two go toward the front, I'll check behind."

"The thief may be dangerous. You should not go alone," said Thornton.

Marchford drew a small revolver from his waistcoat. "I will not be alone."

"Remind me to talk to you about the accouterments you bring to a ball," said Grant, and he turned to run along the side of the house toward the front, Thornton following him. The passage between the two houses was dark, and the men slowed their step around blind corners and entryways, cautious for any surprise attack. They moved silently, listening for any sound.

At the front gate, they heard a scraping noise. Grant carefully lifted the latch. Taking a slow breath to calm his racing heart, he steeled himself for battle. He burst through the gate, but an alley cat merely screeched and disappeared into the night. Grant and Thornton searched around to the front of the house but found no sign of the thief.

Marchford joined them a few minutes later. He too had not found anyone, so they returned to the study, where the admiral stood before his desk. The top drawer had been wrenched open.

"Did you catch the thief?" asked Neville, joining them a few minutes later, breathless and panting.

"No," replied Marchford. "You?"

"I thought I might have seen him once, but I could not catch him." Mr. Neville gasped for breath.

"Sit, man, sit," demanded the admiral.

"Did he get the papers?" asked Mr. Neville, collapsing into a chair.

"I am afraid he did," replied the admiral.

"Demmit, man!" yelled Mr. Neville. "This is why sensitive information should not be kept in a private residence. This information should be handed over to the Foreign Office for protection."

"Not that the Foreign Office provides any more protection," snapped the admiral.

Grant shut the door against unwanted eavesdroppers and gossips, of which London society were the worst offenders. "What do you mean, Uncle?"

"Sprung a leak, my boy. The Foreign Office has been losing information faster than a leaky rowboat takes water."

"That is a slanderous untruth!" sputtered Neville.

"How else would you explain it?" asked the admiral. "Documents missing, plans known by our enemy before they are even executed, and our spies—many have been discovered or have disappeared."

"Is this true?" asked Marchford.

"The enemy does seem to have good information," conceded Neville. "But all the more reason why we must be extremely cautious. What information did those papers contain?"

"It was correspondence from spies on the coast containing plans for the naval defense of Cadiz and other places."

"Which spies? Give me the names!" demanded Neville. "They must be warned. Their very lives are in danger."

"I think we have some time," said the admiral, walking to a wall of books. He climbed up a small ladder and pulled a tome from one of the top shelves. Opening the book, he pulled out a large envelope with an elaborate red seal.

"What is that?" asked Grant.

"Why are these men here?" asked Neville, pointing at Grant and Thornton. "They are not government agents. They have no business here."

"They are my friends," said Marchford in a quiet tone that crackled with authority.

Neville glowered under bushy eyebrows but said no more.

"The letters were written in code," said the admiral. "The code is contained in this envelope. I had one made myself, did not trust the Foreign Office. Without this, those letters are useless."

"Our people should still be warned," said Neville, taking out a small notebook.

"And so they shall, but not by you," said the admiral. "These are my men. I will see to their safety."

Neville's eyebrows once again slammed down over his eyes. "But what about the code? It cannot stay here; surely you must see that."

"Yes," conceded the admiral. "I suppose you are right."

Mr. Neville stood and stretched out his hand for the envelope.

"Marchford," said the admiral. "There is no man I trust more. Will you keep this safe?"

"Yes, Admiral," said Marchford, taking the envelope, even as Neville sputtered.

"This is exactly the sort of thing that must not happen. Private residences are not a safe place for information of vital importance to the Crown."

"Plug your own leak, Neville," demanded the admiral. "Until then, I'll not trust your office."

Neville stood up straight, reaching his full, albeit diminutive height. "I will need to interview each member of your staff, and I will need a full guest list. Let us at least acknowledge the painful truth that a member of your staff or a guest in your home is a thief working for our enemy."

The admiral's shoulders sagged. The truth was undeniable. "Yes, yes, of course. Lady Devine will provide you this information."

Grant bowed his way out of the room and left with his friends.

"Such excitement!" declared Grant. "And I thought debutante balls were a bore. Why, nothing could be further from the truth!"

"I'm so glad the drama could serve for your amusement," replied Marchford.

"It does not appear to have pleased you, my friend."

"No, indeed," said Marchford lowering his voice, "for it is likely that someone on the guest list is a spy, and I will, no doubt, be the next target."

"What do you mean you do not have the code?" A delicate figurine launched through the air and smashed to slivers on the hearth.

"I brought you exactly what you asked for," the spy defended himself, stepping to the side as a vase was hurled toward his head. It smashed on the floor behind him.

"Not good enough! How am I to read this gibberish without the damned code?"

The man ducked as a plate was flung at him.

"Now get me that code. I cannot hold my patience for long!"

If this was patient, the spy was loathe to see angry, and yet getting the code would prove problematic. "The code was given to the Duke of Marchford. He runs his house like a vault. The servants are above bribery, I've tried. He has a footman on guard in the study where I suspect the code is being kept. He even has a man sleeping in the study."

"I do not care to hear your petty problems. Every man can be bribed or killed. Do not tell me that a mere footman is going to prevent Napoleon's victory."

"It is not just the footman. The butler keeps the front door locked. There is no way in!"

A red hot poker was removed from the fire and slowly raised level with the spy's eyes. "Smash the window, poison the footman, bribe a visitor, blackmail a lover, I don't care how you do it, but bring me that code!"

Thirteen

"YOU CAN DO THIS."

"Pardon?" asked Marchford.

"You look apprehensive. Thought you needed encouragement," said Grant with a sly smile.

"I am fine. We will pay a morning call on Lady Louisa and then continue to Tattersall's. Unless you would like to go there directly, I do not wish to impose on your time."

Grant laughed. "Oh no, you are not getting out of speaking with your fiancée that easily. Besides, what have I to do? I am utterly at my leisure."

"Remind me to do something about that," muttered Marchford.

They pulled up outside the Bremerton household and handed the reins of the barouche to Marchford's tiger, who had jumped down from the back in a flash. They entered the house and were ushered into a formal sitting room.

Lady Bremerton met them with a wide smile. Marchford's prospective bride barely acknowledged him. Grant easily procured a chair for himself next to the lovely Miss Talbot and abandoned Marchford to pursue awkward conversation with Lady Bremerton.

"I hope you enjoyed the ball, Miss Talbot," said Grant in a tone he knew would raise an eyebrow from his mother, or any mother, for that matter.

"It was indeed an enjoyable event," said Genie without rising to the bait of his seductive tone. "Did you have an enjoyable evening, Your Grace?" Genie asked Marchford. If Grant hoped to monopolize her conversation, he was doomed to disappointment.

"Yes, enjoyable evening," said Marchford in a flat tone that conveyed it had been anything but.

Silence fell briefly, but Genie picked up the conversation with a determined smile. "I believe you were quite successful at cards, Aunt."

"Silly girl, you ought not speak of such things," chastised Lady Bremerton. "But since we are all almost family, I will only say that I had a fine evening. Lady… well that's not important, she fancied herself quite the card player, but she left disappointed. Some of those ladies were betting deep, let me tell you. People think it is the man who is susceptible to gambling, but I have seen evidence to the contrary."

"Certainly, I can tell you often it is the lady of the house who runs afoul of her vowels," added Grant.

"Vowels?" asked Genie.

"A gambler's term for IOUs," explained Grant with a wink to Lady Bremerton.

"Honestly, Mr. Grant, you ought not speak of such things to Genie. She is backward enough as it is."

Grant glanced at Genie, but she accepted the insult without qualm. He got the distinct impression her aunt was frequently critical. He did not care for the way Genie's quiet acceptance made her eyes dim. He did not care for it at all.

"Shall we all go for a ride in the park?" he asked, surprising nobody more than himself. He could not remember the last time he did anything as flat as taking ladies for a ride in the park.

Marchford raised an eyebrow at him. "A ride in the park?"

"Why yes, it is a lovely day for it," exclaimed Lady Bremerton, ignoring the dark clouds framed in the window before her.

"I believe a ride in the park would suit me. Do let's go, Cousin," said Genie, lending support to Grant's scheme.

Lady Bremerton encouraged all the young people to go along, while bowing out of the ride herself. It was rare that Grant found himself on the same side as a marriage-minded matriarch, but in this case, his plan to provide Genie some time to escape the house coincided nicely with Lady Bremerton's goals of putting her daughter into Marchford's company.

Several minutes later, they were seated in the stylish barouche, open to the weather, trying to ignore the brisk wind and the drop in temperature. It may have been late spring, but the London weather could be unpredictable, and Grant hoped to have some time with the ladies before encroaching rain put an end to the proceedings.

During the short ride to St. James Park, it was clear Grant and Genie were going to be responsible for the majority of the conversation. Marchford responded only when directly called upon to do so, and Lady Louisa spoke not at all.

When they arrived in the park, Genie declared her interest in taking a stroll, so the entire party alighted while the groom walked the horses.

"Shall we walk the length of the canal to the ordnance?" asked Genie. "I read in a guidebook that on the north side is a Turkish piece of ordnance brought here by the British Army and I have been desirous to see it."

"It is too far," stated Louisa, revealing that she could speak after all, if only to shorten the excursion.

"Surely it cannot be as far as all that," protested Genie with a winning smile. "My guidebook also suggests venturing into the garden to see the landscaping. It says it must not be missed. Perhaps I could walk ahead, for I am a fast walker and I'm sure I could return soon."

Grant paused a moment at this speech. Fast walker? This was St. James. People came to be seen, not to rush about in an uncivilized manner. Yet for all her lack of polish, Miss Talbot was a vision to behold, so he said, "I shall walk, er, quickly with Miss Talbot, and we shall return in a trice."

Before either Marchford or Louisa could offer protest, Grant offered Genie his arm and they sallied forth, leaving the inarticulate affianced in their wake. Fortunately for Grant's sensibilities, Genie's pace was only slightly faster than was socially acceptable and she showed no tendency to scamper.

Genie cast yet another glance over her shoulder at Marchford and Louisa.

"Surely you are not wishing to return?"

"Oh no," breathed Genie. "I only wished to see if perhaps they would initiate conversation after we left."

"It appears that Lady Louisa is not much of a conversationalist."

"Oh, but she can be. We have had lovely talks. She has been very kind to me, even when my aunt, well, you know how I have been a disappointment."

"Not to me."

Genie looked up at him, her blue eyes and blond curls framed by her bonnet. "Thank you."

Grant had the sudden urge to kiss her. Her full, rosy lips drew him toward her. How could he possibly resist? Her eyes widened and her lips parted. He leaned closer and… realized what he was doing.

He pulled back and found that they had stopped in the path, Genie looking up at him wide eyed. He must have lost his mind. She was a debutante, the *marrying* kind, not his type at all. "Pardon me, your bonnet, who made this lovely creation?"

"I did. Do you like it? I thought, compared to the beautiful bonnets I've seen in London, this might seem a bit shabby. I did put on fresh ribbons."

"Quite right, very nicely done," said Grant, only now taking notice of the bonnet. Miss Talbot was right; it was a shabby thing. "Shall we press on?"

"Yes, let's. I have a guidebook here in my reticule." To his horror, she pulled out a red bound volume of *The Picture of London: A Correct Guide to All Curiosities, Amusements, Exhibitions, Public Establishments, and Remarkable Objects in and near London.*

"How… helpful." If anyone saw him leading

around a debutante holding a guidebook, his reputation would be in tatters. "No need for that, though. I can serve as guide. Here now, put that thing away. You have me to guide you."

Genie complied, but after receiving inadequate answers to her questions about the park, its management, the notable sights, she whipped out the handy guide once more. "It says the ordnance is decorated with several Egyptian devices and is 'done in great taste.'"

Fortunately, the uncertain weather kept many Londoners away and Grant was grateful not to meet any intimates along the path. They walked along the canal lined with lime trees until they reached the ordnance, where Genie was properly impressed, then ventured into the trees of the wooded park.

"This is lovely. I am glad to see it!" Genie strolled about, her eyes shining with delight.

"It is lovely indeed." But Grant was looking only at Genie.

"Oh dear." Genie looked up at the darkening sky. "I do believe it is starting to rain."

"Let us hurry back to the coach." Grant offered his arm and walked back at a faster pace, with an eye to his polished Hessian boots. His enjoyment of Genie's company did not extend to a disregard of his boots. If he returned with them ruined, his valet might weep, poor man.

The weather was indeed unstable, and the few raindrops were soon joined by others, until throngs of raindrops plagued them from above. The rain turned into a deluge, and Grant found it necessary to seek shelter or face death by drowning. He took Genie's hand, and they both ran along the path. He expected complaint, as he would get from any finely bred London female, but Genie had been raised in the country and was made of sterner stuff. She merely smiled and ran along with him.

Finding a large willow tree, he ducked under the branches, pulling Genie next to him. The space was crowded with multiple branches, forcing Grant to pull her close. This was a disaster, stuck with a debutante under a tree in the torrential rain with his boots surely ruined.

Far from seeing the horror of the situation, Genie's eyes were dancing. She screwed up her mouth, trying not to smile.

"My boots are ruined," said Grant, stating his most pressing concern.

Genie began to laugh.

"I see you have no regard for my boots!"

"I do apologize!" said Genie between giggles. "But here we are stuck under a tree and all you can think of is your boots?"

"You would too if you knew how much they cost."

"Yes, indeed. I did not realize they were so dear. I am sure my bonnet is quite ruined too."

It was no great loss, but Grant said nothing. Despite the chill, he was suddenly quite warm. Genie stood next to him, close, inches away. He could touch her merely by shifting his feet. He would not, of course, but he wanted to. When was the last time he had been so attracted to a debutante of all things? When had he last been attracted to anyone this way?

Genie started to shiver, standing still in the cold. He guessed her long pelisse was borrowed from Louisa, since it was fashionable in style, but it was also made of muslin and not intended for inclement weather.

Grant put his hands on her delicate shoulders and gave them a gentle rub. "You are soaked, poor thing. Here, take my coat."

"No, no, I couldn't. You would be too cold."

No, he wouldn't. He was not cold at all. He was practically sweating he was so hot. He unbuttoned his coat, but Genie shook her head.

"Here, we can both be warm." He opened his coat and wrapped it around her, drawing her to him.

"I do not think… is this proper?" Genie put her hands against his chest but leaned close to allow him to wrap his coat around her.

"No, not proper I fear," confessed Grant. He was truthful, even if he was a cad. Genie felt delicious. He wrapped his arms around her and drew her closer, reveling in her small frame, her gentle curves. She laid her cheek on his chest and he had to stifle a sigh. This was what he wanted. He wished he could stay under the tree forever, boots be damned.

His arms around her rubbed her back. He wished to reach further down but dared not; he could not let this get out of control. Yet in plain truth, it was already out of control. Genie sighed and melted into him. There was no other word for it. She fit with him—warm, soft, perfect.

Genie looked up at him, her blue eyes deep and inviting. "I am quite warm now, thank you."

Grant was beyond warm. He prided himself on his

ability to avoid complications with the gentler sex, but with Genie, he was a stupid schoolboy.

"I think it is letting up a bit. Perhaps we should try again to make it to the carriage?" Her voice was airy, her breathing fast, and he could feel every time she inhaled, pressing her bosom against him.

"Perhaps," murmured Grant. He did not care about the carriage or his reputation or anything except the blue of her eyes and the rose pink of her lips. He leaned down closer, slowly. This was the time she should pull away, but instead, she tipped her head up to him. This could not happen; it must not. He stopped moving and yet still drew closer. As if moving of their own accord, their lips met. For one beautiful moment, he pressed his lips to hers and a tingling shock coursed through his body, energizing, waking parts of him, stinging him to life.

He pulled back slowly, taking a gulp of cool, moist air. What was he thinking? "I should not have done that."

Genie pulled back from his embrace and turned from him so her ugly bonnet hid her face. "I do apologize." She ducked under the branches out of the protection of the tree.

"No, it was entirely my fault," said Grant, though he did not wish to apologize for doing something he enjoyed, something he felt must be done. He followed her out from under the tree, where he was greeted by brisk winds and more rain. She would not look at him, keeping the brim of her bonnet down to hide her face.

He offered his arm and they walked briskly down the path, yet something sick and uncomfortable turned in his stomach. He stopped short, holding her hand. Still she did not look at him.

"It may not have been the right thing to do, but I will never regret having done it," said Grant.

Genie turned to face him, her eyes liquid blue. "Me neither."

He smiled at her.

She smiled at him.

And they both scampered to the carriage.

Fourteen

"YOU MUST UNDERSTAND THAT THE CODE NEEDS TO BE kept safe," said Mr. Neville.

What the Duke of Marchford understood was that government agent Edmund Neville was terribly dull and fatally repetitive. Perhaps that was his training—drone on until his victim conceded just to make him go away.

"The document is safe, Mr. Neville."

"But where is it? I must know!"

"The admiral has asked me to keep it safe and so I shall."

"Is it in this study?" Mr. Neville glanced around at the mahogany paneled walls and scarlet brocade curtains until his eyes came to rest on the large mahogany desk. "At least assure me that it is kept locked."

Marchford sighed. The man would never let him be until he got the information he wanted. He was irritated, but he understood the concern. The stakes were high, Napoleon was on the move, and so far he appeared unstoppable. Information about their enemies' movements and plans could make the difference between success and defeat.

"The code is safe." Marchford showed Neville a picture on the wall of a landscape and removed it. Behind the picture was a hole in the wall in which a metal box was kept.

"But what keeps a thief from simply removing the box?"

"Give it a try." Marchford stepped back to allow Neville access to the box.

Neville cautiously gave the box a tug, but it did not move. He pulled with more force, but the box did not budge.

"Bolted to the wall," said Marchford. "Designed it myself."

"And the key? Where is it kept?" Neville examined the lock on the box.

"I keep it on my person at all times."

"Even when you are entertaining a certain opera singer?" asked Neville.

"At all times. Anything more than that is not your concern."

"Marchford, you are in the service of the Crown. I appreciate that you have done your best to protect them, but I must insist that the codes be handed over to me immediately."

Marchford stiffened at the familiarity of the man's address and the imperialist demands. He stood still, looking down at the man without speaking until the government agent squirmed in his oversized coat.

"I thank you, Mr. Neville, for your service. If I am in need of any further assistance, I will not hesitate to ask." Marchford walked to the door of his study and opened it.

Mr. Neville gritted his teeth but had no choice but to exit the room. "Your Grace," he muttered with a substandard bow.

Penelope Rose spent the morning with the dowager going over every step of the ball. Miss Talbot had been introduced to many eligible men, and Pen had taken detailed notes on their reactions. Many men appeared attracted to her beauty, but none showed a tendency to make her an object of particular regard. Genie's reputation had indeed preceded her, and despite Grant's attempt at diffusing the gossip, few people felt confident enough in their social credit to risk making her a favorite.

Mr. Grant did appear to be the one exception, dancing with her and engaging in conversation several times. Unfortunately, Pen knew all too well Mr. Grant's intentions did not run toward marriage.

"Was there anyone else who showed particular interest?" asked the dowager.

Penelope reviewed her notes once more. "I fear not. Mr. Blakely did engage in brief conversation, but it was so stilted I could not see any interest. They did dance one set. There were several young bucks who took notice of her and a few made conversation, but none stayed long."

"It is a shame her presentation was so poor. She could have made a dash through society. Her manner is pleasing, her face pretty, she has a natural grace, and she has nice teeth."

"Teeth?" Penelope looked up in surprise.

"I am an old woman, Penelope. I know the value in things you have not yet learned to appreciate."

Penelope smiled. "I am sure you are right, Your Grace."

"What of this Blakely fellow? What do you know of him?"

"Not much. He has come to London recently. It is agreed he is a gentleman, but no one seems to know much about him."

"So he is a countryman?"

"Yes, that is my understanding. He appears to have lived a quiet, respectable life and is at an age when men think of marriage. Perhaps he is looking for a dowered wife."

"Sounds like a match made in heaven," declared the duchess. "His reserve will balance her natural liveliness."

"His manner did not reveal any tendency to be smitten with Miss Talbot."

"He does not need to be smitten, now does he? He simply needs to get married. What would it take to get him to come up to scratch?"

Pen shook her head. "After four sisters on the marriage market, I've learned not to take bets on that question. Men are rather odd when it comes to a proposal. They seem to be most likely to ask for a lady's hand if they are assured the answer will be no."

"But of course, it gives the man an opportunity to appear gallant without costing him a thing." The dowager stood, leaning on her cane. "All we need to do is get that chit married. We need to keep her in the company of young men until Mr. Blakely or one of those young bucks falls for her. It's more than one young man who has made a match based on a pretty face."

"Not to mention the teeth," commented Pen with a smile.

"None of your cheek now. I will take my afternoon rest. You continue our work. And enjoy the sitting room. The one in the dowager house is not nearly so nice." With that warning, the dowager made her way to take her rest, and Penelope was left for the afternoon to puzzle out how to marry off Genie.

"Excuse me, are you Miss Rose?"

Pen looked up with surprise. She had not heard the man enter. He was a youngish man with a serious face. He gave her a smile and his face creased awkwardly, like it was unaccustomed to such an expression.

"Yes, I am Miss Rose," replied Pen. She was conscious that this was an unusual introduction and felt it odd he was so informal in the duke's house.

"Allow me to make my introduction. I am Mr. Neville, in the service of his majesty, King George. The Duke of Marchford has told me a lot about you. I understand you are to be the companion to the duchess."

"Yes," replied Pen. She wondered what kind of picture the duke had painted of her. She doubted it could be flattering. Besides, if the duke wanted Mr. Neville known to her, why didn't he introduce the man himself? Still, Mr. Neville seemed nice enough, and it was courteous to engage her in conversation rather than ignore her like most people of the male persuasion. "Won't you sit down?"

Mr. Neville sat in a chair across from her. "I do

believe today will be a welcome change from yesterday's rain."

"Yes, quite. I caught a glimpse of blue sky earlier today," agreed Pen, feeling guilty for being suspicious of a man who merely wished to comment on the weather. He appeared benign enough, though not of the same polish as the majority of the duke's acquaintances. "Did you say you were in the service of the King?"

"Yes, I have the honor of serving as a diplomat for the Foreign Office. With the threat of Napoleon, we all must do our part."

"Yes, indeed," agreed Penelope. "I have one brother in the Navy and one serving under Wellington."

"Our country needs more dedicated families such as yours, Miss Rose. Such loyal hearts are hard to find in these troubled times."

"I should hope that is not true, Mr. Neville. Perhaps not everyone is committed to serve such as yourself, but I do put my trust in the faithfulness of an Englishman."

"I wish I had your confidence. Unfortunately, in my work, I have seen too many who were not as committed such as yourself." Mr. Neville leaned forward and lowered his voice. "There are many who would trade their honor for their own gain."

"Say it is not so!"

"Indeed, I fear it is. In fact, even today in my conversation with the duke, I have been thwarted in my object to protect the empire from the invading armies of France. Can you imagine a world in which a French dictator rules over England? Why, none of us would be safe. It would be the Terror all over again, and this time the blood of the English aristocracy would run in the streets." Mr. Neville spoke with a fervor Penelope found distressing.

"Mr. Neville, you must not pursue this line of distressing imaginings. Please let us put your creative energy toward greater use."

"Yes, yes, you are right, Miss Rose. It is just that I fear…" Mr. Neville sat back in his chair and shook his head. "I should not speak of it."

"You must do what you feel is right," agreed Penelope. After his gruesome prediction, she was not sure she wanted to hear more.

"It would not be fair to you to ask you to serve your country in this way. I would not wish to make you feel inconvenienced. I am just so concerned." Mr. Neville brought out a handkerchief and wiped his eyes.

"Mr. Neville, if there is a way in which I can serve my country, of course I am willing. What is distressing you?"

"The Duke of Marchford and I have worked together for many years. He was a diplomat and spy in Cadiz, but I assume you already knew that."

Penelope shook her head.

"It is not a secret," said the man with a wave of his hand. "He has been a loyal servant to the Crown, but lately I fear he has grown proud. He feels he should be the one to hold information, codes to communications from spies abroad."

"Is that what was stolen at the ball?"

"Yes, you are quite clever. The letters were stolen, but the codes were not. Marchford holds these codes. If they should fall into enemy hands, all could be lost.

Troop movements could be known. Our fighting lads, such as your brother, could be killed because of it."

Penelope sat in stunned silence.

"Forgive me, I should not be so forthcoming with you, but I have always trusted my intuition, and I know in my heart that you are a loyal subject to the King. You would never do anything to betray secrets to the enemy, not when it could mean your brothers' lives."

"Of course not," breathed Penelope.

"You would do whatever was needed to protect your countrymen."

Penelope nodded.

"I knew you were a lady of strong understanding."

"What is it you need me to do?"

Mr. Neville moved to sit next to her on the settee and, although no one was around, lowered his voice further. "The duke has an envelope that contains information crucial to the war effort. I know he feels he can handle the situation himself, but the information is critical. If it should fall into the wrong hands, the consequences would be dire."

"But how can I help? Do you want for me to speak with him?"

"Speak? No! I have already tried that; he absolutely refuses to see reason."

"But how am I to help?"

"It is simple. I need you to bring me that envelope."

Genie gasped. "You are asking me to steal from the duke?"

"No, of course not. I am asking you to return the envelope to its rightful owner. It is in the study, behind a picture. There is a box for which you will need a key, the key Marchford keeps with him at all times. Do not take anything of value. You must only bring me the envelope."

"But, Mr. Neville, I would not feel comfortable…"

"I understand, I do. Think no more on the subject. I shall try to find another who may help me." Mr. Neville stood and gave her a bow to take his leave.

"I am sorry I could not be of more help," said Penelope, also rising from her seat.

"I would ask that you hold this conversation in strictest confidence, Miss Rose."

"Yes, of course."

"And if you know anyone who may be able to help, please let me know. The Foreign Office would be quite grateful and, naturally, a reward would be provided."

"A reward?"

"It is standard procedure, did I not tell you? For items such as this, the reward would be substantial, about ten thousand pounds."

"Ten thousand?" It was a shocking amount of money.

"It would be enough to change a person's life forever," said Neville. "Think on it, Miss Talbot. You would get ten thousand pounds in addition to knowing you acted in the service of your King."

Penelope could only stare at the man in response. "Think on it," repeated Mr. Neville with a bow and was gone.

Ten thousand pounds. Ten *thousand* pounds! It was a fortune. All her life, Penelope had been compared to her sisters and watched as they made brilliant matches while she played a supporting role. She could not fault them for being beautiful, but she had wondered why her Creator had seen fit to make her the only plain girl in a flock of beauties. Their looks had propelled them into advantageous marriages. Without the face or the fortune, Penelope watched as her sisters began lives with their husbands, started families, and glided beyond the place where Penelope would no doubt spend the rest of her life. Unmarried. A spinster. In all the world, there could not be a more useless person than the gently bred spinster.

Unmarried, Penelope had no place in society. But ten thousand pounds could change everything. First of all, she could set up her own household. With wise investments in the nine percents, she could net nine hundred pounds per annum, more than enough to live quite comfortably.

Perhaps she could, after a few years, move to Bath and invent a deceased husband to present herself as a widow. A comfortably stationed widow was the best positioned in society. She may move freely in society, without the burden of a husband governing her movements, or the censure of never having wed. A wealthy widow—yes, that would be something quite grand. She might even take a lover.

Lover? A flood of emotions rushed through her, making her oddly hot and sweaty in unmentionable places. What madness was this? She stood up and walked out of the room. She needed fresh air. She needed to leave these odd thoughts behind.

"Mr. Neville, are you still here?" Marchford's calm voice rang through the great hall like a restorative. "I thought you had left."

"I must have taken a wrong turn and accidently

took myself on a tour of the house." Neville walked down the stairs to the foyer.

"Is that so?" asked Marchford.

No, it was not so. It was a lie. *Beware men who want you to keep secrets.* Advice from her grandmother rang in her head.

"Mr. Neville, wait a moment, sir." Penelope walked down the stairs to where the men stood in the foyer.

"Miss Rose, are you acquainted with Mr. Neville?" Marchford raised an eyebrow. "I had no idea."

"He introduced himself to me just now."

"Part of your tour of the house?" asked Marchford with a sardonic drawl.

"Mr. Neville, I have no need to think on your offer. I cannot accept it," said Penelope before she could change her mind.

"Mr. Neville, have you been propositioning my grandmother's companion?" Marchford raised an eyebrow. "How enterprising of you."

"He offered a reward of ten thousand pounds for the return of a certain envelope you keep in a locked box beneath a picture frame."

Everything went silent. Marchford's features hardened into stone; his eyes drilled on Mr. Neville, who gave a small cough and shot Penelope a dark look. Instinctively, she stepped back.

"Well done, Miss Rose," said Mr. Neville, his expression turning into an approximation of a smile. "Well done indeed. I hope you will forgive my crude methods, but I needed to discover if you were susceptible to bribery."

"This was a test?" Penelope flushed with anger. He

put her through this emotional turmoil for nothing? "You said I should do this to protect England from Napoleon. You spoke of the blood of English nobility flowing through the streets! All this was to challenge my loyalty?"

"No, no, my dear, the threat is real. You may not appreciate my methods, but I will flush out all traitors to the Crown, and I will see them swing from the highest gallows!"

"Thank you, Mr. Neville, that is quite enough," said Marchford with a razor edge. "Let me disabuse you of two false notions. First, your inquiries into the loyalty of my staff and guests are no longer required. Second, Miss Rose is not your 'dear' nor anything else to you. There is no acquaintance between you; you will forget her name and never speak to her or about her ever again. Have I made myself perfectly clear?"

Marchford stepped forward and Neville stepped back.

"Yes, Your Grace. Perfectly clear. You may not appreciate my methods, but I must get results."

"Perhaps your methods would be best used cleaning your own house. Find your own traitors and leave my household alone." Marchford backed Mr. Neville to the door as he spoke, the efficient butler being on hand to open the door and remove Mr. Neville from the house, swinging the door shut behind him.

"Thank you, Peters," said Marchford to the butler. "Mr. Neville is no longer welcome in this home. Please see to it that he is never again granted admission. Miss Rose, a word." Marchford strode into his study, Pen following behind.

"Have a seat, Miss Rose."

Penelope sat obediently but bristled at the duke's brusque manner. If he thought she could be "managed," he would soon realize his error.

"Please tell me exactly what Mr. Neville said to you," said Marchford.

Penelope quickly gave him a full report. "Now, I think I deserve to know the truth. Is what Mr. Neville said true?"

Marchford sighed and sat in a chair next to hers. "I do apologize, Miss Rose, for dragging you into this. Mr. Neville had no business speaking to you at all. But yes, it is true. I worked for the Crown in Cadiz, however 'spy' is not a word I would use lightly. In fact, it is not a word I would use at all, and I sincerely hope neither will you."

"You can depend on my discretion."

Marchford nodded and continued, "Mr. Neville is correct. At the dance, some letters were stolen, letters that could reveal the identity of British spies working on the Continent. These letters are useless, however, without the code, which the admiral asked me to keep safe."

"Why not turn it over to the Foreign Office or the War Department?"

"Because there have been a series of leaks. Information has been found in the hands of the enemy that only could have come from those offices. Neville may not like to admit to it, but somewhere in his office, there is a traitor."

"But why would Neville ask me to steal it for him?"

"There are two possibilities. The first is that he is

doing exactly what he says—he is trying to get the code so he can protect it and testing persons in my household to see if they are susceptible to bribes. The second option is that he is the traitor himself and trying to get the codes, so he can pass them on to his contacts in France."

"Mr. Neville a traitor?" The skin on her arms prickled with goose bumps as with a chill. "Which do you think more likely?"

"I'd like to think he is the traitor, but that is only because I do not care for the man. However, I have found that the spies among us are generally those you do not expect, rather than those you do."

Penelope took a long breath and leaned back in her chair. "So I may have been conversing with a traitor? What would have happened if I had given him the code?"

"If he is the traitor, he would have taken the codes and given them to France. If he is what he purports to be, the codes would have been hidden away and neither of us would have ever seen them again."

"And the ten thousand? I am only wondering, you understand."

"It is understandable. If he is not the traitor, he most likely would have had you arrested for theft and sent you to Newgate. If he is the traitor, he would have more than likely taken the codes and given you a bullet through the brain."

"Oh!" Penelope covered her mouth.

"Forgive me. I am not accustomed to speaking of these things with ladies. I have said too much."

"Nonsense, I appreciate your candor. I would rather

deal with whatever business is at hand in a straightforward manner." Penelope smoothed her skirts as if brushing away the disturbing revelations.

Marchford smiled. "You are not what I expected, and I rarely am surprised by people."

Penelope took this as a compliment. "Thank you, I am glad I exceeded your expectations." Though she guessed they were dreadfully low from the start.

"So why not take the money? Ten thousand pounds would be a fortune to you."

"There are few for whom it would not be a fortune."

"True. So why not take it?" asked Marchford.

"My grandmama told me, if something was too good to be true, find another way to get what you want."

"I have heard that saying a little differently."

"My grandmother would not be considered good *ton*, but she was always amusing. And educational."

Marchford stood and poured himself a drink of some amber liquid from a carafe on a side table. "I think I'm going to need a drink. Shall I call for some Madeira for you?"

"No, thank you. I generally limit myself to tea and lemonade."

"Another piece of grandmama's advice?"

Penelope smiled. "Grandma Moira drank naught but whiskey."

Marchford raised his eyebrows.

"She was a Scot."

"Say no more. So let me see, where were we? Oh yes, you were about to tell me what it is you want."

"Was I?" asked Pen. She knew what she wanted, but it would only work if he came to the conclusion himself.

"I am almost certain of it. Perhaps you have passed up one opportunity with the eye to another?" Marchford took a sip without breaking his gaze on her.

"Would another opportunity be forthcoming? I seem to be at liberty to hear proposals today." Penelope folded her hands in her lap.

"I appreciate the information you provided today. I do, at times, employ people to keep their eyes and ears open and tell me what they see and hear."

"I do pride myself on being observant; however, I work for your grandmother. I would not like to have any conflicts with my loyalty to her."

"Perhaps my interest in your observations is limited to situations that do not involve my grandmother. I doubt I would like to know what schemes she is concocting; in fact, I know I do not."

"I feel sure you are right."

"So she is plotting revenge?" Marchford's tone revealed more anxiety at that prospect than he had shown all day.

"I defer to your better knowledge in regards to your relations," said Pen, dodging the question.

Marchford chuckled and took a sip of his drink. "You are a worthy adversary, Miss Rose. I shall see to it that your wages will reflect our new arrangement. Now, all that is left is to settle on the price."

"Oh no, sir," said Pen, rising from her seat. "A lady never haggles with a gentleman over price. Quite unseemly. You decide what you think is appropriate, and I will know how greatly you value my contribution to your work by the amount of your decision."

Marchford rose and gave her a small bow. "Please

do not take this the wrong way, but if you were a man, I'd hire you as my personal secretary immediately."

"Alas, there is nothing I can do about the disappointment of my gender, but I will try to serve you in some small way."

"Miss Rose, there is nothing about you that I find a disappointment." He gazed at her intently, his dark eyes unreadable.

Up until this moment, Penelope had felt perfectly comfortable, but now heat slithered up the back of her neck and she swallowed compulsively. She acknowledged his comment with a quick curtsy and fled the room for safer ground.

Fifteen

GENIE COULD NOT STOP SMILING. SHE HAD WORN A smile since she returned home from her walk. She had smiled through her bath, smiled through dinner, smiled through cards, and even when her aunt chastised her for smiling, she smiled back her apology. She awoke to a sunny spring day with the smile still on her face.

Everything around her was like a dream; the only thing real was Grant. He liked her. He held her. He *kissed* her. He really did—he kissed her. She had dreamed of being kissed someday. She did not count Ernie Walters, a precocious ten-year-old who caught her under the mistletoe.

Mr. Grant definitely counted. The way he held her, caressing her back, shot strange sensations through her. He was strong; she could feel the muscles beneath his perfectly tailored coat. But the best part about him was the way he smelled. It was like nothing she had ever experienced before. It drew her to him—she wanted him, needed him. He smelled like pine and musk mixed with cheroot and whiskey, which Genie recognized sounded wretched, but on him was intoxicating.

Genie floated to the sitting room, where she was expected to keep her aunt and cousin company. She chose a comfortable chair and sighed, sitting back into the cushions. Mr. Grant. Mrs. Grant. Mrs. Eugenia Grant.

"Genie!"

Genie snapped back to the room and sat straight. Her aunt was frowning at her again, nothing new there, but Louisa was looking at her with a curious expression.

"Are you acquainted with a Mrs. Grant?" asked Louisa, giving Genie a pointed look.

Had she spoken the name out loud? Heat rose to her cheeks as she faced her aunt. "Y-yes. Mrs. Grant, an old friend I was just thinking of her. What shall we be eating tonight, Aunt Cora?"

Lady Bremerton, who prided herself on her table, could not resist launching into a detailed description of the dinner, and so the topic was changed. Halfway through the description of the lobster pâté, Genie heard a slight tapping on the window behind her. She turned and glimpsed a figure in the window before it ducked from sight.

"What was that, Genie?" asked her aunt.

"I am not sure," said Genie, but something told her the rapping at the window was for her. Her aunt launched into details of braised ham, and Genie once again heard the furtive rapping. She did not turn around this time. She knew someone was trying to get her attention.

Her heart raced. Was it Grant? Perhaps he had returned to continue where they had left off under the tree? Genie politely excused herself and walked to the front door. She felt odd in doing so and realized she had actually never opened the front door herself.

She opened the door slowly, her heart pounding hard. Who was it? There on the front stoop was… no one.

"Can I help you, Miss Talbot?"

Genie turned with a start, putting her hand over her chest as if to keep her heart inside her rib cage. "You startled me."

The butler said nothing, his polished, smooth exterior revealing nothing of his true emotions. "Did you wish to go out?"

"No, I thought I heard someone at the door." It was the wrong thing to say, she knew it as soon as the words left her mouth.

The butler stood very tall and very straight, the very picture of pained pride. "I do expect I can answer the door, Miss Talbot."

"Yes, of course you can. My mistake." Genie hurried past the offended butler and headed back to her room. She needed to get herself under control. What was the matter with her? Mr. Grant was very diverting, and he might steal a kiss under a willow tree, but he had no intentions toward marriage. She needed to push him from her mind.

A tapping sound startled her out of her revelry, particularly since her bedroom was on the third floor. She peeked through the curtains cautiously and was relieved not to find someone hanging onto the window ledge.

Plink! A small rock bounced off her window. She flung back her curtains. Perhaps Mr. Grant had come to see her after all. Opening the window, she saw a small figure cloaked in shadows.

"Oi! Milady!" called the figure, a shape much too small to be Grant. "Dub the jigger fer me!"

"Jem?" asked Genie. Was it the young boy who had tried to steal Pen's bandbox? "Whatever are you doing?"

"Open the side door fer me, miss!"

Genie hustled down to the servants' entrance, being careful to stay out of sight. She opened the door and let in the errant Jem, his long hair a tangled mess, his feet still without shoes.

"I gots a message fer ya." The lad puffed out his chest.

"Who is this from and how have you come to be a messenger?"

"I don't know the swell. But he found me watching the house fer ya and tipped me a crown to give you this." The urchin handed Genie a folded letter.

"Watching for me? Whatever for?"

"Yous was right nice to me," said the lad with simple admiration in his eyes.

Genie's heart was softened instantly to the child. Had he never known kindness? She gave him a smile and turned to the letter. The note was brief and won a smile from Genie.

"Does ya have a reply? I'm supposed to wait fer a reply."

"Yes, tell your gentleman friend I shall meet him tomorrow. Now tell me Jem, have you eaten supper tonight?"

Jem's eyes got large and he licked his lips. "No, milady," he whispered.

"Let us do something about that, shall we?"

Jem followed Genie into the kitchen. At once, Genie knew she did not belong downstairs. This was the servants' territory. Yet she knew she must feed the child, so she walked bravely into the heart of the servants' domain.

The servants were sitting around the table having tea and biscuits. A fire burned cheerfully in the fireplace and a groomsman played a jaunty tune on a fiddle. Everything stopped when she walked into the room. The servants all stood swiftly to their feet.

"Please, continue, do not stand on my account," said Genie, heat rising in her cheeks.

"What can we help you with, Miss Talbot?" asked the butler with polite disregard.

"I merely wished to ask for some supper for this boy who..." Genie was about to say he had given her a message but swallowed it back down. No one was supposed to know about that, hence the importance of using a small child instead of delivering it through the post.

"He has been a help to me. Is there some supper we could provide?" asked Genie.

No one moved, but everyone eyed the filthy creature with suspicion. "This is a Christian household, Miss Talbot," said Mrs. Grady, the housekeeper. "That boy does not belong in a respectable house."

"Yes, I'm sure you are right. Jem here is hardly respectable. But since this is a Christian household, should we not do our duty to feed the hungry and clothe the needful?"

"You want us to clothe him too? It won't do no good wi' him so filthy."

"It would be nice to provide him with clothes too, thank you for that suggestion. Would there be anything that could be used for that purpose while we get him something to eat?"

Despite the looks of reproach sent her from the various members of the household staff, Genie stood firm. Eventually, the housekeeper relented and barked out succinct orders to have the miscreant fed and clothed. Genie insisted the boy wash his hands and face before being fed, and he surprised the company by being covered in freckles, which had been concealed by the general grime. His arms and legs were scrawny and hung loosely from his body like a limp marionette.

Jem was excited about the prospect of cold ham, bread, biscuits, and tea, eating more than Genie thought a young boy could inhale. He was less excited about putting on a pair of old children's shoes one of the housemaids found in the attic, but quickly accepted an old coat.

"Now what are you going to do with the little heathen?" asked the housekeeper, voicing the question Genie had rattling around in her mind.

"Do you have a place to stay, Jemmy?" asked Genie.

Jem nodded his head, then shook it, then shrugged and reached for another fistful of ham.

"Well, do you or don't you?" asked the housekeeper.

"I stay wi' Mr. Master, if'n he don't beat me. If'n he's in a drubbn' mind, I sleeps in a doorway."

"You poor dear," said Genie.

"Naught but a street urchin," muttered the housekeeper, less inclined toward sympathy.

"But could we not keep him?" asked Genie.

The housekeeper crossed her arms over her generous bosom. “You would have to get permission from his lordship and her ladyship first, and I’d bet a lifetime of Sundays they will not be so inclined. He’s just a street rat. London is full of them. ’Tis sad to be sure, but there is naught we can do for him.”

Genie was committed to the path of helping her wayward street urchin, but she had to agree that Lady Bremerton was unlikely to look on Jem with anything other than disgust. Yet Genie knew she was in the right, and once she was confident in her principles, she never backed down.

“Do you have any parents or family?” asked Genie.

The child shook his head.

“Who is this Mr. Master you speak of?”

“He pays us to do things, nick stuff mostly,” said the boy, taking another hearty bite of biscuit while stuffing a few more in his pocket.

“Well,” said Genie, thinking of what to do. “Well, there is nothing else we can do—we must speak with my aunt.”

“Your excursion to see your betrothed has cost me my coat,” accused Grant, swirling his whiskey.

“Your coat?” asked Marchford, sitting across from him in their accustomed club.

“Was left on a damp Miss Talbot. Had twelve flaps, made by Brooks. I have a mind to ask for it back.”

“You wish to see Miss Talbot again?”

“I’d like to see my coat again.”

“She is a fine article, Grant.”

"Yes, but what is she going to do with a man's coat? Can't wear it. Look demmed silly on a girl."

Marchford shook his head and went back to his newspaper. "You avoid a topic better than any man I know. Go see your Miss Talbot if you like."

"By Jove, you're right. Must get it back before the next storm hits." With that dubious justification, Grant left Marchford in the club and took his phaeton to the Bremerton town house.

The Bremerton house was a fine one as houses go. Its placement, grandeur, and distinguished marks of age all heralded an established lineage. The Earl of Bremerton boasted the bluest blood in the neighborhood.

Mr. Grant, who came from his own long line of established gentry, accepted the trappings of wealth and prestige with equanimity. He was quite at home in these surroundings, everything in order, everything managed in adherence to a strict code of conduct. It was comfortable, predictable, maybe even mundane at times, but he did not fail to recognize he had a very comfortable life.

When Grant was admitted into the drawing room, raised voices were a clear sign that something in the ordered life of the respectable Bremerton household had gone seriously awry.

"Absolutely out of the question," declared Lord Bremerton in a voice that defied response. He was an older gentleman of few words, so he expected people to heed those words once he troubled himself to utter them.

"But we cannot turn our backs on him. Why, he is only a child!" cried Miss Talbot.

Lord Bremerton was so unaccustomed to having anyone talk back to him, he opened and closed his mouth several times without saying a word.

"Yes, dear, I see that he is only a child, and these things are much too bad, but Lord Bremerton is right. We cannot allow such a creature to live in our house." Lady Bremerton fluttered a handkerchief in front of her as if to ward away such a noxious thought.

The object of such consternation was a small, scrawny boy, with a thick crop of red hair that stuck out from his head at odd angles like a flashy porcupine. Far from being disconcerted by the conversation in which he appeared to be the primary subject, the child wandered toward the tea tray and made short work of the cakes and biscuits, eating with two hands at an alarming pace, as if he was trying to stuff as much as possible into his mouth before someone shooed him away from the food.

"This child is being used by an unscrupulous man to conduct crimes. Jem says if he cannot steal enough each day, he is beaten. Surely you cannot ask me to return this boy to such a situation," said an impassioned Miss Talbot.

"If the boy is a thief, he should be locked in Newgate," growled Lord Bremerton.

"But it is not his fault. Surely we must show this child Christian charity, as we are commanded in the Bible."

At the mention of the Holy Book, Lady Bremerton put her handkerchief to her forehead and sank majestically to her couch. "Oh, Mr. Grant!" Lady Bremerton started with the sudden realization of his presence in the room. "I fear you catch us at an inopportune moment."

"I do apologize for trespassing on your privacy, Lady Bremerton. I have come merely for the return of my coat which I neglectfully left here yesterday."

"Mr. Grant!" Genie walked up to him flush and steady. If she were a prizefighter stepping into a mill, he would have laid his bets on her. "Do you not feel it is criminal to return a child to a life of unspeakable horror and misery?"

"Well, that does sound a trifle flat," conceded Grant, only to be faced with a glowering Lord Bremerton.

"Flat? Why it would be unconscionable! This innocent child must be protected," demanded Genie.

The innocent child in question was at that moment lifting the silver spoons from the tea tray and pocketing them.

"He does seem to have a tendency to steal, dear," said Lady Bremerton with a wave of her handkerchief. "We cannot allow it in the house."

"But only because he has never been instructed in the proper way. Now put those spoons back on the tea tray, Jemmy, there's a good lad." Genie beamed down at her grimy little protégé.

"He is fortunate we do not call the magistrate immediately," said Lord Bremerton.

"Surely you would not do that," gasped Genie.

"Perhaps I can be of assistance." Grant stepped forward. He was the master of any difficult social situation, though this was a scene quite unknown to him. All eyes were now on him, but the only ones he saw were Genie's bright blue ones, alive with fire and looking up at him like a hero of old.

"Perhaps I can take the lad home, find a suitable

home for him." No one was more surprised by this suggestion than Grant himself.

"Demmed fool," muttered Lord Bremerton, but it was not him whose opinion mattered to Mr. Grant.

Genie walked up to Grant and put her hand on his sleeve. "Would you?" Her eyes were wide with hope, and a smile graced her full, rose lips. He would have said yes to anything.

"Certainly. Christian duty and all, as you said."

"Christian duty?" said Lord Bremerton with a guffaw. "I never knew you to be one of those do-gooders, Grant."

"Yes, but if you are inclined to take the boy, we would be most grateful." Here, the lady of the house gave her husband a silencing glance, and his lordship caught her meaning and said no more.

"This is most kind of you," said Genie. "Most kind." Her eyes were a kind of liquid fire that would no doubt be the death of him.

"Yes, yes, most kind," said Lady Bremerton with a furtive glance at the door as if calculating how quickly she could return her sitting room to rights without the unwanted presence of a street urchin.

"Now, Jemmy," said Genie, kneeling down to speak with him eye to eye, "would you like to go with this kind gentleman? He will help take care of you."

"He does look a flash cove, miss. Is 'e the bloke wi' the racing phaeton I saw out the window there?"

"I believe I am that 'bloke,'" replied Grant.

"Can I drive them bays ye' got, guv'nor?" Jem's eyes grew large with anticipation.

"Certainly not," said Grant with a shudder. A child

drive his bays? It was too hideous even to consider. Genie looked up at him with pleading eyes, and he fell into some alternate state of existence where he wooed debutantes, cared for the needy, and let a young thief hold the reins to his new matched bays.

"Thems fine steppers," said Jem.

The sound of the boy's voice broke the spell and Grant returned to his senses. "They are at that and you're not to touch them. You may, if you are a good lad and do not squirm, sit beside me on the box."

That was enough incentive for any young thief, and he readily agreed to follow Grant wherever he might lead. Genie deftly fished the silver butter knife and a china tea plate out of Jem's pocket, and they were ready to go.

"Thank you again, Mr. Grant, for your kindness," said Genie. "I suspect you and Jem will become the best of friends."

Grant suspected that was far from the truth but smiled and said nothing. Within a few minutes, Grant was seated on his high-perch racing phaeton, a dirty child by his side. He had come for his greatcoat and to talk with a pretty girl but, through circumstances that yet eluded him, had ended up with an urchin.

Sixteen

"George!" Genie flung her arms around a well-built young man and gave him a good squeeze. "Whatever are you doing here?"

"Took a break from school and thought I'd come see you." The young man was tall, well-proportioned, and if his coat was not cut with the exacting precision of the latest mode, he at least filled it out better than most young gentlemen of the *ton*. His hair was dark and short, a contrast to his sea blue eyes.

"Do you mean you have a break from university or you are taking a break?"

George gave a guilty smile. "I needed a break. Too many books, makes me batty."

"So of course you decided to meet me at the lending library," laughed Genie. She had responded to George's note by agreeing to meet him the next day at Hookham's Lending Library.

"I suppose that was poor planning on my part."

"Does Father know you are here, Brother dear?"

"No, course not!" He took her hand and pulled her

gently into a secluded corner of the room and lowered his voice to speak privately. "What's this I hear of your debut? What happened?"

"Oh, please tell me the news has not traveled all the way to Oxford."

"Aunt Cora wrote to Mum and she wrote me concerned."

Genie sighed. She was tired of telling this story. It was good to see her brother, but she was not pleased at how her failure was becoming well known even outside of London. Had people nothing better to do? "I laughed in front of the queen."

"And?" prompted George.

"And nothing. I laughed. She did not find it amusing, and that made me laugh harder."

"You are in trouble for laughing? What an odd lot these town folk are."

Genie shrugged. "I did not make a positive impression with the queen and that is apparently enough to become a social pariah."

"So go back home. You're in no need of anyone's good opinion."

"Go home after only a few weeks here? After the way Mama was forced to leave London? She was so hoping I could restore the family name by being accepted in society. How could I possibly face her?"

"Got a point there. Tell you what, I'll think on it for you."

Genie gave her younger brother another little hug. His presence was comforting, even if he could hardly do anything to repair the damage she had done.

"Shall we walk back to Bremerton house for tea?"

asked Genie. "I should like to introduce you to our cousin Louisa whom you have never met."

"No, no, and I'll thank you not to let anyone know I am here. If Aunt Cora sees me, she'll write Mother before the tea gets cold."

"I suppose you are right," conceded Genie. "But where are you going to stay? What are you going to do?"

"I came down with some friends from school. They know some places for amusement."

"Please tell me you are not going to visit one of those filthy gaming"—Genie searched for a word that was not a synonym of Hades—"a gaming establishment."

"Don't worry about me. I know what I'm about."

But Genie did worry. Particularly if her baby brother—he would always be that to her—was going into one of those gambling hells, known for preying on young men.

"I have heard horrible things that happen in those places," said Genie.

"Yes, I've heard that too. Why else would I want to go?"

"George!"

George smiled, looking all the more endearing for being naughty. "I'll be careful, but I must be allowed some fun. I'm going about as Mr. Smythe—isn't it a famous scheme? No one will know I am here. I'll get to have a lark and return to Oxford before anyone is the wiser."

Genie sighed. "I miss the time when a rocking horse was all you needed for amusement."

"Maybe if you made me a big one." George smiled. "Maybe I can help you too."

"How would you do that?"

"Don't know. But I should think myself quite flat if I didn't at least make an effort to help my favorite sister."

"I am your only sister."

"See? Your place in my heart is forever secure!"

Brother and sister talked for a while longer before George offered to hail Genie a hack to take her back home. When they left the library, the Comtesse de Marseille looked up from a particularly large volume with a particularly wicked smile.

"Must I be present?" asked the duke the next day over tea.

"Yes." The dowager unlocked the tea caddy and carefully mixed a blend of teas to suit her.

"There is no option?"

"We have invited Lord and Lady Bremerton, Lady Louisa, and Miss Talbot. Of course you must be present." The dowager poured hot water into the teapot to warm the vessel.

"And who else will be at the table?"

"A few gentlemen, no one for you to be concerned about." As part of the plot to find Genie a husband, the dowager and Penelope had planned a dinner party of eligible men. The dowager had waited until teatime to let her grandson know his presence was required.

"Do I need to keep guessing or are you going to tell me what plot you are hatching?" Marchford glanced between the dowager and Penelope, but neither spoke. The dowager appeared consumed in her duties as hostess, sprinkling the tea into the teapot and pouring fresh hot water over the top.

"Grandmother..." ground out Marchford.

"Do not 'Grandmother' me with such a tone," rebuked the Dowager Duchess of Marchford. "After all I am only trying to help the family of your betrothed. You know that Eugenia's presentation was less than optimal."

Marchford raised an eyebrow. "Less than optimal indeed."

"You needn't be cruel," chastised the dowager. "We must do what we can to help the family. If she can form an attachment soon, her reputation can be salvaged."

Marchford nodded his head in understanding. "How do you two pick these young men to the slaughter? I beg you would indulge my curiosity."

"We try to find young men who showed an interest in Miss Talbot or at least spoke to her," said Penelope. "We look for men who are respectable, appear to have the qualities of a good husband, and might appreciate the dowry she brings. Also, considering her debut, a gentleman who lived primarily in the country might be a good fit."

"I should not have asked. It is quite a business for you, is it not?" asked Marchford.

It was more business than he realized, but Penelope said nothing more. She was generally honest to a fault, but several years in Town had taught her to keep her own counsel when the situation called for it.

Penelope had expected a large fight over the lapse in the dowager's funds, but she was mistaken. In person, the dowager and her grandson were perfectly civil and polite. They certainly never gave the servants any material for gossip. After the unfortunate incident where her rant was overheard by Lady Bremerton, the dowager had not spoken about money again. She had, however, exchanged a series of written messages with her grandson that often resulted in her exclaiming "bah!" and throwing the missive in the fire.

"I cannot be a bridegroom for Miss Talbot. Perhaps you can make my excuses," suggested Marchford.

"I certainly cannot!" declared the dowager, placing a strainer over a teacup. "How would it look if Louisa were to come to dinner and you not be here? Besides, it will give you an opportunity to speak with her. A date must be set." She poured the tea into the cup, straining away the tea leaves.

Marchford accepted a cup of tea from his grandmother and took a slow sip. "I recognize the understanding between Lady Louisa and the Duke of Marchford is of long standing, but even you must concede that the lady does not appear interested in the relationship. Would it be unacceptable to end the betrothal?"

"James!" The dowager clanked the teapot down on the table. "This marriage has been planned since before you were born. Louisa has been waiting for your return for three years. You cannot back out now. You are honor bound!"

"Even though the relationship would cause misery to the parties involved?"

"Misery? How could it cause misery unless you make it so? If you are displeased with the relationship, change it. Be charming. Crumpet?"

"Yes, please," replied the duke, accepting the buttered crumpet. "She does not appear interested in my charm, such as it is."

"What would you suggest? Can you imagine any situation in which you could honorably dissolve the understanding between you?"

Marchford took a deep breath and exhaled slowly. His posture diminished slightly, the only sign that he had been defeated. Penelope watched the pair of aristocrats from her vantage point over tea and cake. Although she was new to the dilemma, one thing was perfectly clear—it was not within Marchford's power to end the contract.

"Have another slice of seed cake." The dowager offered Marchford the platter. "I also had cook make some ham sandwiches. I know you often get hungry before dinner."

Marchford accepted the sandwich but not without suspicion. "What is it you want?"

"Can I not offer refreshments without accusation? Are you going out this afternoon?"

"Yes, I am going with Grant to Tattersall's. Our trip yesterday was postponed."

"Good, then you won't mind delivering this finalized guest list to Lady Bremerton."

Marchford finished his tea. "I should have known I could not enjoy a ham sandwich without the expectation of repaying the favor."

"I am merely giving you an excuse to visit Louisa. Did you not suggest you needed to charm her?"

"As you wish." Marchford accepted the list.

"And another thing," continued the dowager in a

businesslike tone. "I was thinking about why Louisa might be put out. You know you have made her wait for marriage three long years. She is considerably past the age where most girls are wed. You need to make a formal announcement, set a date, and hold a ball to celebrate."

Marchford eyed his meal. "That is a lot to ask for a sandwich."

"James, it is time to commit."

Marchford was spared making a reply by the announcement that Mr. Grant had arrived. Marchford bowed out of the room and met his friend in the foyer. Grant appeared less than his normal resplendent self. His hair was out of place, his cravat sadly crushed.

"I have been tasked to give this to Lady Bremerton. Would you mind stopping by on our way to Tatt's?" asked Marchford.

Grant groaned.

"You mind telling me what is wrong?"

The men climbed onto Marchford's curricle and Grant proceeded to tell him how he had acquired a child. The story was so remarkable, prompting Marchford to ask multiple questions, that Grant was unable to complete the tale before they arrived at the Bremerton household and were required to make an appearance.

Marchford discharged his duty, handing Lady Bremerton the guest list. Naturally they were invited to visit, and naturally they obliged. Despite the presence of Miss Talbot and Lady Louisa in the parlor, Lady Bremerton dominated the conversation. "I hear you are considering making some changes to your garden," said Lady Bremerton.

Marchford acknowledged this was true.

"Why don't you take a stroll through our garden, so you can get some ideas? Louisa has been instrumental in the placement of our new rose bushes."

It was a clear ploy to get Marchford and Louisa to spend time together, but despite the apparent disinterest from either of the primary parties, the plan was accepted. Lady Bremerton bowed out of the excursion and so the young people went out into the garden.

The garden was quite beautiful with straight, manicured shrubs in neat lines and occasional rows of flowers, also neat and well manicured. After a few prods from Grant, Marchford took the hint and became more verbose, asking Louisa about the garden and describing his plans for his own garden expansion. Louisa responded infrequently, with hardly more than monosyllabic replies.

Genie and Grant held back to allow the betrothed time to foster their relationship, such as it was.

"I must thank you for encouraging Marchford to develop an acquaintance with his future wife," said Genie when the dubious couple was out of hearing range.

"I believe the honor of this visit belongs to the scheming of the dowager duchess and Lady Bremerton."

"Then I thank you for being one of the party. I am anxious to know how things are going with little Jem."

Grant knew she would ask him and he was going to have to make a reply. He took her gloved hand and led her to a stone bench where they both sat down. He should release the dainty hand, but he did not, holding it loosely for fear he might crush her hand.

"Jem is quite a scamp. A more incurable heathen I

have never met, which is saying quite a bit since I was educated at Eton," added Grant.

Genie shook her head. "That is very bad. One can only hope he grows out of it."

"Maybe he is growing. It would explain the appetite. Despite being fed here, he declared himself hungry and has been eating almost without ceasing. Must be hollow inside. He may beggar me on his board alone."

"I do apologize for getting you into this predicament. I will certainly reimburse you for any expenses you incur in his upkeep."

"Certainly not! Besides, the situation may be resolved, though perhaps not to your liking."

"Has he caused any problems?"

Grant smiled. "My entire staff from the housekeeper to the cook threatened to quit if I did not find a new home for him."

"Oh! That is very bad. Whatever did he do?"

"I put the lad in the charge of my housekeeper."

Genie nodded in approval.

"Apparently, this morning, they tried to give him a bath."

"Very reasonable," said Genie in agreement. "He did appear to be in need of it."

"He disagreed. A housemaid was bit, a footman has a black eye, and apparently the bath water was flung on François's soufflé."

"That is terribly bad!"

"Quite! You should have seen François. He brought me the soufflé, which had fallen something awful, and he was soaked through. The only one who did not take a bath today was Jem." Despite the commotion it caused in his mother's household, Grant could not think upon the incident without a smile.

Genie put her hands on her cheeks in an expression of dismay. "I am sorry I plagued you with such a child."

"A plague! Yes, that is exactly what my housekeeper called him."

"We shall definitely need to make better arrangements for him. Where is he now?"

"That is the part I fear will not please you. Jem took off running, with most of the staff in pursuit, destroying a vase in the process. Caused such a commotion I could not help but join in the fun. I chased the miscreant into the garden and over a hedge, but I fear I lost him."

"You poor man! Well, that explains your cravat. I am very sorry."

"Thank you for recognizing that the true victim here is me. I fear my cravat is a hopeless case."

"You must let me at least reimburse you for the vase."

"Oh no! Did us a favor there. My mother never liked it, but it was given to her as a wedding present by her mother-in-law. Been wanting it gone for years."

"I am glad it was not of sentimental value." Genie sighed. "I suppose we did our best. I felt sure I was being led to help this child, but I suppose we cannot help him if he will not allow it."

"I'm sorry!" squeaked a small voice from under a nearby bush.

"Jem!"

Seventeen

GRANT SCANNED THE GARDEN SURROUNDING THEM, and poking out of a hedge was the red head of the errant Jem. His response was one of joy followed by disappointment with the sure knowledge that Genie would expect him to try again with the ruffian.

"Jemmy! Come here, you naughty boy!" called Genie and the lad obeyed, holding his head low and dragging his feet. "What do you have to say for yourself?"

"I'm awful sorry, miss. But they brought a giant scrub brush and said they'd scrub the skin offa me."

"Jem, I do not believe they were trying to skin you alive. They just wanted to clean you."

Jem shrugged bony shoulders. "Theys mean coves, miss. Could I not stay wi' you? Yous right nice."

"Well, thank you. But how did you get into Lord Bremerton's garden?"

"Everyone starting yelling and kickn' up a dust. Them be chasin' me and howling something fierce. Put me all in a twitter!"

"So you ran back here?"

"Slipped through the garden gate. I ain't no bigger than a bodkin."

"You are resourceful," said Genie. "But you cannot stay here. My aunt would never allow it. Mr. Grant has opened his home to you. You must be appreciative."

"I am, miss. But could you stay with me too. You could come live wi' Mr. Grant. Your aunt ain't very nice. You wouldn't miss her, I wager."

"Jem, you must not speak that way of your betters," chastised Genie.

"Even if it's true," muttered Grant. He surveyed the wide-eyed ruffian with a mixture of amusement and horror. "We can give it one more chance, little man," said Grant. "But my mother will return in a fortnight and we will both be in the suds if she comes home to a household in chaos."

"Will you come with me?" Jem looked up at Genie with large pathetic eyes.

"Oh, I do not think…"

"Certainly she can, but only for a little bit," said Grant, snatching the opportunity. He felt very sure he was going to regret giving Jem a second chance and wanted to enjoy a little more time with Genie to make it worth his while.

"My aunt would never allow it," whispered Genie to Grant.

"But I do not live far. In fact, unless I am very mistaken, our gardens are connected. Is that how you got here, Jem? Show us."

Jem led them around large, sculpted shrubs and blooming hydrangeas to a small, forgotten gate behind a gardener's shed. The hinges squeaked in complaint, but with a little muscle from Grant, the small gate swung open. It led into a small path with large hedges on either side. Coming around the corner, it opened into a lovely garden, full in bloom. Flowers were everywhere, blooming trees, lilacs, lilies, and roses. Genie came to a full stop at its beauty. Unlike the manicured precision of the Bremerton garden, this garden was more haphazard and whimsical. Sunlight broke through the clouds and a gentle breeze whispered through the trees, sending pink apple blossoms dancing through the air.

"It is beautiful," breathed Genie. "This is your garden?"

Grant shrugged. "My mother and sisters had a free hand in this. My father and I stand aside when it comes to any sort of decorating, let the ladies fight it out."

"They have done an amazing job. I would not mind spending days here. It reminds me of home."

"Do you miss it?"

"Yes. I know it is impolitic to say, but I miss it very much. The spring is beautiful on the farm, so many things in bloom. Do you enjoy the country?"

"Always go for hunting season. My parents hold a house party with that intent each year."

"Yes, but besides hunting, do you enjoy spending time at your estate?" asked Genie.

Grant had been raised on the family estate and had escaped female control as soon as he was able. He had not given it much thought other than London allowed him more amusements and ample freedom. "I suppose the country has its charms," he said with a noncommittal shrug.

"Do you have a large estate?" asked Genie. "How many families are in your dependency?"

"I don't know," answered Grant. He left the family management to his father. Since Grant planned to leave no heir, he figured one of his nephews would have to learn the business of managing the estate.

A glance at Genie told him his answer had disappointed her. "We have two dozen families in our village," said Genie. "I have always seen it as a privilege to be able to help serve them."

Grant could think of no response. Serve his tenants? What an odd idea.

"What crops are you planting this year?" asked Genie.

"I could not begin to say," answered Grant.

"I see." Genie turned away to watch Jem run through the garden, but Grant knew he had diminished in her eyes. He wanted to defend himself that no one in polite society talked of anything so provincial as farming, yet he recognized that excuse would not serve in present company.

"I do love the country," said Genie. "I know everyone expected my mother to be miserable, marrying beneath her station, but I believe she has enjoyed it a vast deal more than if she married the man intended for her."

Lady Mary's elopement was infamous. Of course, it was expected that since Genie's mother turned her back on society, she would live an isolated and miserable life.

"They had picked a groom for her?" asked Grant, unable to keep his curiosity in check.

"Lord Bremerton," said Genie with a poignant rise of her eyebrows.

"Oh! Well now. That's awkward."

"My aunt was married off to Lord Bremerton shortly after my mother left. I don't think Aunt Cora has ever forgiven my mother for leaving her in that position. Though my mother has told me many times she had no idea her parents would marry her younger sister off to Bremerton if she left."

"No, indeed!"

"My mother only wanted to live her life with the freedom to do as her conscience called her. She wanted to be able to live out her Christian ideals to tend the sick and help the needy. She has been able to serve our little community in a way she could not living within the strictures of society."

"And this makes her happy?"

"Yes, quite."

"Astonishing."

"That is why I am convinced taking in little Jem here will no doubt make you happy," said Genie with a smile.

"No doubt," mumbled Grant as he witnessed the death of a row of poppies under Jem's tireless feet. "If you miss the delights of the country, you are welcome to the garden any time you like," said Grant with a magnanimous sweep of his arm.

"But your mother and sisters..."

"My sisters are all married and my parents are in Hertfordshire for an extended stay. M'sister is expecting and my mother is in attendance, though she was put out that my youngest sister chose the middle of the season to bring her firstborn into the world."

Jem raced past them with a stick in hand, batting at the flying petals.

Grant shook his head. "Going to need help taming this creature."

"I will stand by your side," agreed Genie. "What will your mother say when she returns to find Jem?"

Jem took his stick and whacked at the tree branches to make more petals fly into the air.

"Don't want to know," answered Grant in all honesty.

"Let's see if we can get him cleaned," said Genie. "Jem?"

The boy immediately left his game and came obediently, the picture of compliance.

"Jem, you are going to need a bath if you are to stay here."

The boy shook his head violently.

"I know you are afraid, but how about if you could give yourself a bath, without anyone watching or attacking you with a scrub brush. Would that be acceptable?"

Jem nodded enthusiastically and soon the arrangements were made. The household staff were none too happy to see Jem again, but a private bathing room was provided without too much fuss. It was clear none of the staff were interested in trying to bathe him in the kitchen again.

With the organizing and managing, Genie entered Grant's home through the garden door and it seemed perfectly natural, albeit unconventional, for Grant to offer a light tea in the parlor.

"I should really return soon," said Genie, taking another bite of a scone still warm from the oven. "They will surely miss me soon."

"And I will miss you as soon as you leave."

"This cannot be proper."

"Probably not." In truth, Grant knew it was not. He had never entertained a lady in his sitting room. He had entertained ladies, surely, but he had an apartment in Town for that sort of thing. His mother's sitting room was, well, his mother's sitting room. It was not a place to bring young ladies. He was on shaky ground with Miss Talbot, but he in no way wished her to leave.

"So, your mother is with your sister?" asked Genie, taking another warm scone. It was not for nothing the Grant household employed the best chef in London.

"Yes, I have five elder sisters. All now happily married."

"I have two elder brothers and two younger. I did find it a bit difficult to be the only girl in a house of boys. Did you find this also to be the case?"

"The only boy in a world of females?" Grant gave a mischievous grin. "Never was there a boy more coddled. My parents waited fifteen years before I finally made an appearance. As the only son, considerably younger than my sisters, I was prized, spoiled, and utterly bossed about by my six mothers."

Genie smiled. "It does not sound too terribly bad."

"It was not, I confess. I was never at a loss for amusements."

"Then why, please forgive me if it is impolite to ask these things of a self-proclaimed rake, but why have you decided never to marry?"

"Ah, yes, marriage. Well, perhaps you have no understanding, since you were not raised with sisters, but in a household of five elder sisters, there was nothing more important or spoken of with more fervor or at more length than the topic of matrimony. My sisters must be wed, of course, and the prospect of their subsequent entries onto the marriage mart comprised my entire upbringing. By the time I reached my majority, I was rather tired of the whole conversation."

"Still, it seems a bit drastic to declare never to wed."

"Had to. Only thing I could do. Have you any idea how tiring it is to have six matchmakers parading potential brides before you like an auction at Tattersall's?"

Genie considered the urgent focus on finding her a husband and nodded. "I think I may understand you."

"The ladies were getting insistent. They even tried arranging situations to entrap me. My own mother even tried to force my hand to marry the daughter of a marquis. It was a sly game, I confess, but they did not expect me to jump from the balcony."

"You jumped from the balcony?"

"Indeed I did. I was trapped on the balcony with a young lady screaming that I was molesting her and tearing her own bodice. What else was I to do?"

"Were you hurt?"

"Broke my ankle but still managed to run down the street until I found Thornton. Hid at his castle in Scotland for the rest of the season."

"That is horrible. No wonder you have a fear of debutantes."

"Dreadful fear, I'm afraid."

"But what about me? You are sitting quite alone with me. Should you not be afraid that I might cry that you have made violent love to me and entrap you into marriage?"

"Might you be willing to allow me to make violent

love to you?" Grant asked, moving from his seat to sit beside her on the couch. Their clandestine kiss was still fresh in his memory. It had not been the most passionate or skilled kiss he had ever enjoyed, but at present, hers were the only lips he wished to taste again.

Genie laughed and turned away, smoothing her skirts in a nervous fashion. "Am I to be frightened? I cannot imagine that you would molest me in your mother's sitting room."

"True. You are aware of my partiality for trees."

Genie's color heightened and she deftly redirected the conversation from the dangerous topic of trees. "Seems too benign of a parlor for a scene of seduction."

"Truly? You are an expert on seduction? What are they teaching farmers' daughters these days?"

"I am somewhat an expert if you must know," said Genie, turning back to him with a sly grin. "I have secretly read many gothic novels, and I can say with every assurance that seductions do not happen in front parlors."

"You don't say. Do go on. Where must I linger for an appropriate seduction?"

"First, it must be night. Always night. Second, there must be a thick layer of mist. Third, you should really be wandering through a moor or a graveyard."

"Wait, wait, how am I going to get a young lady to go out into a graveyard at night so I can molest her properly?"

"I'm not exactly sure, but it seems to happen all the time in novels."

"Your advice does not seem particularly sensible.

How am I to put it into practice if you don't tell me how to make the thing come about? What sensible young lady lets herself be lured out into the moors at night? Seems you would only be able to seduce young things without a brain in their heads."

"I do not believe men are interested in the size of a lady's intellect. In fact, I am sure men are only concerned with appearance. The novels are quite clear on this point. Alabaster skin is apparently a temptation no dark-hearted villain can resist. Drives them to insane lengths."

"Now I must be driven insane? Really, Miss Talbot, your version of seduction is sounding less appealing by the minute."

"And, of course, the villain must come to a horrific and most dreadful end."

"Say no more!" Grant clanked down his cup for emphasis. "I hereby repent of any thoughts of seduction. Really now, running about in graveyards with brainless chits, going insane, meeting my doom. No, no, it's all too much. I'd rather play whist with my mother."

"Then I regret to inform you that you are not a true rogue."

"I am very sorry to hear it."

"Here we are," said the housekeeper, leading in a clean boy, dressed in a skeleton suit and black boots. "I found these things of yours in the attic, Mr. Grant. I assumed you would not mind. The clothes he had on were not worth keeping. I put them in the burn pile."

Jem, for Grant could now see that it was the scrawny imp they had sent to take a private bath, paraded proudly into the room. He was considerably cleaner, but his orange hair still stuck out in odd angles and he doubted very much he had washed it.

"Look, miss. Socks!" He pulled up a pant leg to show her.

"Yes, of course you must always wear your socks," agreed Genie.

"Never had any before," said Jem.

"Oh!" said Genie, touching Grant's hand with hers. She met his eyes, and he knew at that moment he would never be the same.

Never had socks. The thought stilled Grant. He had lived his entire life in comfort and privilege, his only real difficulties being the avoidance of his marriage-minded sisters and mother. How many different pairs of socks had he owned in his life. Hundreds? Thousands? Had he ever once considered them as he put them on? No, never. Not once. He doubted he would ever look at a pair of socks the same way again.

"I shall see to it you will be provided with socks," said Grant. "Now, sit here and have a scone. I need to take Miss Talbot back home. Afterward, report to the stables. They may be able to find some work for you. If you mind your manners and make yourself useful, I'll see about letting you have some trifle for dessert."

Jem's eyes grew large. "I never had no trifle. Is it as good as they say?"

Grant leaned forward and said in a conspiratorial tone, "Better!"

Jem sat down to scones and Grant offered Genie his arm, leading her back into the garden. "You have a good way with him," she said. "It is too bad you have set your mind against matrimony. You would have been a good father."

"Have you been sent here by my mother and sisters to try to change my mind? Flattery will not serve your cause," laughed Grant, yet the compliment circled around his heart and nestled in for a comfortable stay.

"Here we are at the garden gate," said Grant. "Perhaps we can meet by the moonlight to whisper our love through a crack in the garden wall, my Pyramus to your Thisbe."

Genie laughed. "I thought you had taken a dislike to romantic tragedies."

"Ah, yes. They did both fall on their sword. I was thinking more of the delightful version told by Nick Bottom."

"*Midsummer Night's Dream*? I am always game for a laugh, much to my shame, as you well know!"

"Yet there is no lady I would rather be with," said Grant much too truthfully. He leaned a shoulder on the wall that divided their gardens and took her hand in his.

She stepped closer and gazed up at him with deep blue eyes that despite the coolness of the color danced with fire. Her lips, full and pink, beckoned him. He leaned down to indulge in a kiss but realized what he was doing and pulled back with a jerk.

"Sorry. My mistake. You are so beautiful I cannot seem to resist. Yet my intentions are less than honorable, so I must forbear!"

Genie's breath came fast and her cheeks were flushed. It only added to her beauty. "So one must only kiss if one's intentions are honorable?"

"In present company, it is a must I fear."

"Then I should give you this." In a flash, Genie wrapped her hands around his neck and pressed her lips to his. Fire shot through his body and he wrapped his arms around her, holding her tight.

She broke the kiss but did not pull away from his embrace. "My intentions are honorable," she said, looking up at him through her lashes.

He could no longer resist. He kissed her. Not a chaste kiss one bestows upon a virginal debutante, but a hungry kiss of a man enflamed with lust. Her lips parted easily and he deepened the kiss, unable to stop himself from tasting the pleasures that had plagued his thoughts since he first kissed her under the tree. His hands roamed up and down her back until he cupped her backside and pressed her to him, knowing she must feel the full length of his regard for her.

"Whatcha doing?" asked the small voice of Jem.

"Oh!" exclaimed Genie and jumped away from Grant.

"Go on back to the parlor, Jem," commanded Grant, biting back a curse for the person who dared separate him from his lady.

"Do I still get a trifle?"

"If you can get there now and stay there," demanded Grant.

A rustling in the brush was the only evidence Jem had heeded the command.

"I fear we have been gone a while," said Genie, her cheeks flushed. "How will we explain our absence?"

Grant took several deep breaths to cool his ardor. He needed to get himself under control to be seen in public. "Fortunately, I am not as attached to the truth as no doubt I should be. Leave it to me."

Grant walked beside Genie back to Bremerton house, unsure how he felt. He was supposed to make young things feel confused and love struck, not the other way around. He had never been kissed by a society miss before. There had been young ladies who attempted to kiss him but only in an effort to get "caught" and thereby force a proposal. Genie had kissed him because she wanted him, not his name or his fortune.

When they entered Lady Bremerton's sitting room, it was clear their absence had been noted, but before anyone could speak, Grant took the situation in hand.

"There you are!" Grant said to Marchford in an accusatory tone. "Where have you been? We have looked everywhere for you."

"You were looking for us?" asked Marchford. "We have been looking for you! You have been missed for at least a half hour."

"But this cannot be. We saw that you and Lady Louisa were no longer in the garden and went into the lane to look for you. We even took a stroll up and down the street, but we could never find you."

"Ah, so that is where you were," sighed Lady Bremerton in relief. "I see that there is no harm done, but next time, Genie, do tell me if you plan to leave the garden."

"Yes, Aunt Cora," said Genie obediently.

The gentlemen left shortly after, leaving Genie time to think upon her adventure with Mr. Grant. What could she have been thinking to so accost him? It may not be a graveyard at midnight, but she feared she was in very real danger of seduction.

Eighteen

"Too late for Tatt's," grumbled Marchford once he and Grant left Bremerton house. "You want to tell me where you were all this time?"

"Found an urchin and gave it a bath."

Marchford gave his friend a glare. "If you do not wish to tell me, just say so. I don't want to tax your intellect by devising such a fantasy."

"Was that an insult on my limited intellectual prowess and my tenuous grasp on reality?" laughed Grant. "How did things go with Louisa?"

"Wretched. If she spoke more than five times in the entire visit, I should be surprised, and now I have to play host to them for dinner."

"I do not envy you, my friend."

"Where can I drop you?" asked Marchford, climbing onto his curricle.

Grant put his hand on the door of the curricle but paused and stepped back. "Not going far. Think I'll walk."

Marchford turned and yanked the reins so that the horses pranced and whinnied in protest. "Did you say you were going to walk?"

"Yes, yes I did. It's not far. Think I can do it if I apply myself."

"Are you well? I should hate to leave you unprotected if you are febrile or concussed."

"Am I well? Attempting to walk the streets of London!" To his friend's, and perhaps his own, astonishment, Grant strolled down the street, walking around the block back home.

The walk itself was not long, yet he was feeling ridiculously pleased with himself for making the effort when he walked in the front door. He was greeted by his butler and his housekeeper. Armed with a comb in one hand and a hairbrush in the other, the housekeeper disappeared into the parlor to tame the wild head of Jem the urchin.

As Grant handed off his greatcoat, which this time he had managed to retrieve, a knock came at the door.

"Mr. Saunders," said Grant in greeting.

"Good day, Mr. Grant," said the man of business. "I have come to collect some papers from your father's study. He wrote to me to take care of a few things."

"Yes, of course," said Grant and ushered him into his father's study. As his father's man of business, Mr. Saunders was a not uncommon visitor, yet Grant knew very little of his activities. Instead of heading to the billiard room as usual, Grant turned and followed Mr. Saunders into the study.

"Mr. Grant, is there something I can help you with?" asked the thin man with an efficient clip to his tone.

"Wondering what you did. Maybe you could enlighten me."

Mr. Saunders opened his mouth, closed it, then opened it again. Grant waited for the first wave of shock to pass.

Mr. Saunders sat heavily in the oak chair behind the desk. "What would you like to know?"

"Everything!" Grant took a seat across from the befuddled man. "Why you're here to start."

"Ah, well," said Saunders, shuffling about some papers. "We need to find new tenants for one of the estates." Several thumps from somewhere inside the house caused the man to look up.

"Nothing to be concerned about." Grant waved off the man's worried expression. "New tenants? How do we do that?"

"We put out a notice with the land agent. Of course, we must first evict the present tenants. It might be a bit awkward since they have written me repeatedly asking for their lease to be extended."

"Why not extend it?"

"They are more than six months behind on the rent. Apparently, they have taken on several orphan boys and the expenses were more than they expected."

"An orphanage?"

"No, not quite if the letters are to be believed. They are a bit odd. Quakers, you understand, though we were not aware of it at the time of rental. They apparently feel the boys must be raised in a homelike setting."

A crash came from the parlor and Mr. Saunders again looked up, alarmed.

"Think nothing of it," said Grant calmly.

"But it sounds like something broke." Mr.

Saunders's frown intensified when a howl erupted from the parlor.

"The orange cat figurine I can only hope," said Grant wistfully. "Dreadful thing. Now tell me about this home for boys. I assure you nothing you could say could be of greater interest to me."

"Well, I'm not sure what more there is to say, other than I am charged with writing to them to let them know we expect them to vacate the premises."

"Oh no, we can't have that," declared Grant. "Their lease must be renewed."

"But the rent—good heavens, sir, what is that noise?" A scream shot through the house.

"Hairbrush," said Grant sagely. "Please do write these lovely Quakers and tell them we support their efforts, want to make a contribution. Christian duty and all that."

"Hairbrush? Christian duty? Mr. Grant, is this some sort of joke?"

"No, no. You think me a heathen?"

"Well... I have not as yet seen any evidence you care to express your faith through action."

"I do now," said Grant plainly, even as another crash and a howl gave Mr. Saunders alarm.

"Mr. Grant, something is greatly amiss in your household!"

"Indeed! We must support this boys home at once!"

"Your father is a generous man and supports many causes, but this home is not one of them. I'm afraid the rent must be paid."

"Take it out of my account."

Mr. Saunders's eyebrows rose so high they disappeared into his hairline. "Your *personal* account?"

"Yes, yes," said Grant. "And write to tell them I have a new member for their family."

Another crash was followed by a loud thump. "Should check on the crystal," said Grant. "My mother does like that."

"But I don't believe the rental house has any crystal."

"Should hope not with boys infesting the place," said Grant over the sound of splintering wood. "Must dash!"

~

The Duke of Marchford arrived home to a different sort of chaos—his grandmother standing on the front step.

"Grandmother?"

"Ah, Marchford, you are home. I was looking to see if the constable had arrived. We best call a surgeon too."

"What is wrong?" Marchford swept his field of view, looking for danger.

"It is the footman. Hurry!" The dowager led him to the study.

Upon reaching the scene of the crime, Marchford stopped and scanned the room with an efficient mental sweep. A footman lay on the floor, blood covering his head. Penelope knelt beside him, applying pressure to his head wound with a thick, white bandage. One of the windows had been broken and his papers that had been on his desk were scattered across the floor. The butler stood guarding the wall safe, which appeared untouched.

"What is his condition?" asked Marchford.

"He breathes," said Penelope. "He mumbled he heard the window break and went into the study to investigate and was struck from behind."

"Send for a surgeon," Marchford instructed one of the interested staff who had gathered outside the door.

"The document?" Marchford asked the butler.

"It is safe," he answered. "I heard the commotion and came running. I saw the man leave out the window, but I did not see the face."

Marchford surveyed the scene around him with cold displeasure. One thing was for certain—the traitor would not stop until the document had been stolen.

It was time to trap a spy.

Nineteen

GENIE WALKED INTO THE DRAWING ROOM CONSCIOUS that all eyes were on her. She arrived with her aunt, uncle, and cousin, yet she appeared to be the center of attention. Within the drawing room was the Duke of Marchford, looking, as always, stiff and unapproachable; the dowager; Penelope; and five men of varying ages, all giving her a once-over like she was a prize heifer. She had to resist the urge to turn around slowly and show her teeth.

"Here, dear, have a seat." The dowager indicated a chair and the young men flocked around her like buzzards to a fresh kill.

All were solicitous. All were attentive. But she was not sure if they were interested in her beauty, her dowry, or whether she would make another social *faux pas*.

Her aunt had dressed her in virginal white for dinner, a lace sheer layered over silk with a lovely blue silk ribbon at the high waist. It was a beautiful, expensive gown, which made her feel sophisticated, but the neckline was lower than she was accustomed, revealing more décolletage than ever before. It was fortunate her father and brothers were not there to comment, for she feared they would never have let her leave the house.

Her assets, now firmly on display, were causing a minor sensation. Many of her suitors appeared to be addressing her breasts in conversation. It was, of course, everything her aunt could have hoped, but would it be enough to cause one of these lusty lads to lose his head and pop the question? And if he did, what would her answer be?

After dinner, the ladies retired to the drawing room to allow the men time to enjoy their port at the table.

"I do thank you for your efforts to help repair my damaged reputation," said Genie in a soft tone to Penelope. They sat in a stately drawing room slightly apart from the dowager, Lady Bremerton, and Lady Louisa.

"It is my pleasure to help," said Penelope. "Did any of the men meet with your approval?"

Genie smiled back the truth. Mr. Grant came unbidden to mind. He met with her definite pleasure, too bad he was considered unsuitable. "I have been introduced to many men of late, but I have not known any long enough to form an opinion. I fear people are still wary to be long in my presence."

"Give them time to forget. Never fear, another topic of gossip will emerge soon. The best way to make people forget one scandal is to have a bigger story come along. As my grandmama said, 'folks dinna care fer a coon when they can eat veal.'"

"So I need to hope someone else will have an even greater fall from grace?"

"And someone will. By tomorrow there will be a new topic of conversation."

Genie sighed and wrapped the strings of her reticule around her fingers, a nervous twitch she had never experienced before coming to London. "I know my aunt says it is quite important that I marry soon because of my disaster at my presentation, but—"

"You do not like being pressured into marriage?"

"No, indeed, I do not."

"And yet, I imagine that you came to London with the idea to find a husband." Penelope's straightforward manner of speaking and plain brown eyes peered through the social niceties to get at the heart of the matter.

"Yes, it is true," admitted Genie. "But there is a difference between being open to falling in love and agreeing to wed the next man who enters the room."

"I agree, and I must say I am relieved to hear you say it. I know the dowager and your aunt feel differently, but I feel a marriage is not a decision to enter into lightly, nor should you necessarily wed the first man who asks."

"Yes, thank you for understanding." Genie let out a big breath in relief. She did want to get married. What unmarried female did not? But to be forced into marriage with the first person who could be coerced into asking, just so she could preserve her aunt's pride, that was not appealing. "I also am concerned that my aunt has offered to pay this matchmaker a horrendous sum should I somehow manage to become betrothed."

"Yes, I admit I was surprised by that turn of events

too. However, before you decline an offer you would otherwise like just to save your aunt's pocketbook, you might wish to consider what your aunt would prefer. If the dowager is to be believed, your aunt has the money, so it will not come as a hardship. I believe she would happily part with the blunt if it meant having her protégée respectfully wed."

Genie considered the argument and nodded slowly. "I know you are right, but still I cannot feel easy with this arrangement."

"Indeed, I should not like it either, but marrying you off early may be a cost savings to her, what with the cost of gowning you. I understand from the dowager that Lady Bremerton is paying the bills."

Genie blinked at her friend's forward comment. Even though she was raised in the country, Genie knew speaking directly of money was not an acceptable topic of conversation, but now that the topic had been raised, she was interested. "Yes, my aunt is supporting me. I had never considered the cost of the gowns. Do you think they are very dear?"

Penelope surveyed the lace and silk beauty Genie wore. "Quite dear, I should say."

"Oh, I was not aware. Now I do not know what to think."

"Forget about the pressures. It simply will not help you to dwell upon it. Perhaps you will find a man with whom you will fall in love. If it comes to it, I will support you if you need to decline an offer."

"Thank you, Pen. Truly, that is very kind." The weight Genie had carried since her grave error before the queen was lightened. Penelope Rose, in her simple muslin dress, was a friend and ally. One she dearly needed and was grateful to have.

"What of Mr. Grant?" asked Genie, feeling reassured enough in Pen's friendship to speak of matters that were close to her heart. "He was the only one who was brave enough to speak with me several times at the ball, and I suspect he may have arranged with his aunt to invite me."

"To be sure he did," replied Pen. "I heard he garnered that invitation for you by promising to dance with all the young ladies at his aunt's ball."

"That was extraordinarily kind of him," said Genie, her pulse increasing. Mr. Grant had indeed inconvenienced himself on her behalf.

"Mr. Grant is quite capable of making large grand gestures. He is well liked by his friends and critics alike."

"Why do I have the feeling you are about to tell me something of him that is not good?"

Pen took a sip of her tea and shook her head. "I do not like to revisit the past, particularly in regards to my sisters, but I would not like to see you make the same mistake. It was several years ago when we first came to London. One of my sisters became well-known for her beauty, but our connections were very low, and we were snubbed by more exacting members of the *ton*. Mr. Grant was very attentive, very courteous. He even helped us gain entry into society in a way we could not have done without him, and for that I am thankful. My sister was quite taken with him, and we held hopes that the rumors about him were untrue. Surely such a charming man could not be the rake they described. We hoped for a proposal and at last one did come."

Pen stopped and took another slow sip of tea.

"Your sister refused him?" asked Genie, impatient to hear the end of the story.

"His proposal was for her to become his mistress, not his wife."

"Oh." Genie sat back in her chair, deflated. "I see."

"He is quite charming, but I thought you should know."

"Thank you," murmured Genie. She knew the warning was for the best, but Pen had poured freezing water all over her nice, warm dream.

"This story is not widely known," said Pen.

"You can be assured of my discretion," said Genie. She really did not wish to talk about it. The dream of Mr. Grant was best forgotten.

"Mr. Blakely," announced the butler at the door of the drawing room.

Mr. Blakely entered the room in a double-breasted coat of dark blue, light trousers, and tan kid gloves. He might not be as showy as Grant, but he was not an unattractive man. He bowed his apology for being late to the dowager, with an excuse of a prior engagement. His manners were polished and pleasing, Genie decided.

Penelope vacated the chair next to Genie and Mr. Blakely was drawn to it.

"I will make my apologies to you too, Miss Talbot," said Mr. Blakely, taking her hand in his gloved one and giving her a slight bow.

"Not at all," said Genie. "I am pleased you were able to come."

Mr. Blakely's mouth twitched upward, in what

Genie guessed was a smile. "I must thank you, Miss Talbot. On your advice I visited the British Museum. I can see now why you recommended it. I found the visit most educational."

"Was it? I am pleased. The guidebook said it was not to be missed."

"Have you not visited yourself?"

"No, not yet." Genie's aunt laughed at the idea of visiting the museum. It was apparently not how young ladies spent their time.

"Perhaps I could be your escort sometime," suggested Blakely. "I should like to visit the museum again soon, and I could not ask for more pleasant company."

Genie smiled and noted with pleasure that Mr. Blakely looked her in the eye, not down the front of her gown. "I should like that very much. My guidebook lists many sights in London that should not be missed."

"A guidebook sounds sensible. Perhaps I could avail myself of it?"

"By all means! I am glad to hear you say it. You cannot imagine the grief I have endured for that guidebook. My aunt threatened to burn it if she ever saw it again. I have learned it is not considered fashionable."

"I should not like to think the opinion of others should prevent me from enjoying the history or architecture of this city."

"Exactly what I think! Thank you, Mr. Blakely. I am so glad to know I am not the only one who thinks this way."

"I should go find the gentlemen and pay my respects to my host," said Mr. Blakely. "I expect to return soon." He gave her a warmer smile and bowed his exit from the room.

In his absence, Genie was the object of four knowing smiles from the ladies in the drawing room.

"That was promising," commented the dowager with a cunning grin.

"I do hope something definitive can be arranged quickly," worried Lady Bremerton. "If Genie could at least be betrothed respectably, her value would increase and perhaps we could start receiving more invitations. I do not dare ask for a voucher to Almack's for her, not with that Jersey gel as a patroness."

"An invitation to Almack's would be just the thing," said Penelope. "If the patronesses of Almack's endorse her, she must be accepted by society at large."

"But how could this miracle be made to occur?" asked Lady Bremerton. "Surely you have been in London long enough to know Almack's is the most exclusive club in London. With Genie's reputation, how could it be made to come to pass?"

"I have seen the most atrocious behavior be tolerated and even celebrated by society. The only hope is to show her as an original," said Penelope.

"Quite right!" said the dowager, rapping the floor with her cane. "Never show fear in society. The gossips will eat you alive. Confidence is what you need, gel."

"I shall certainly try," said Genie with a smile. "If only to please you."

"No need to try to win my favor," said the dowager, but she nodded in approval. "What you need is a good man."

"And here I am," stated Mr. Grant, entering the room with an air of style and grace only he could muster. "I do not know of what you are speaking, but it is a conversation in which I must have a share. Or perhaps," he said with a wicked wink to the dowager duchess, "you would prefer my absence so you can talk about me at your leisure."

"Mr. Grant, you are incorrigible as usual," said the dowager, and Genie could almost swear she winked in return.

Genie's heartbeat quickened at the unexpected arrival of Mr. Grant. He was dressed impeccably in a sage green coat of glistening superfine, a mustard waistcoat with exquisite detailing, and matching breeches so skin tight it was positively indecent. Genie could not help but drink him in with her eyes. He was a dreadful rogue to be sure, but when he entered a room, she could not look away.

"I would not dare to contradict you, Your Grace." Mr. Grant gave a bow that put every other man on the planet to shame. At least, that is how Genie saw it.

"I have come to return to you Mr. Blakely, who found me lounging in the study," continued Grant, and only now did Genie notice that Mr. Blakely stood behind him. The rest of the men chose that moment to enter the room and the dowager gave instructions for tables to be set for cards.

"We were speaking of Almack's, Mr. Grant," said Pen. "Have you been this season?"

"Ah, Almack's. I have not graced their halls this season."

"I should say not," said Marchford.

"You do not care for Almack's?" asked Penelope.

"Almack's is fine, but the matchmaking interference I could do without," said the duke. "The last time we entered those hallowed halls, Mr. Grant was accosted by a flurry of females. His arrival seemed to spark hope in the breasts of matchmaking mamas who decided his very presence in the ballroom was a sign he was searching for a wife. It was actually quite amusing."

"I found it less amusing," said Grant.

"Was it so bad they no longer issue you vouchers?" asked the dowager.

"Obtaining a voucher is not the difficult part," said Grant.

"Those vouchers are quite exclusive," said Pen. "I doubt they would issue one to Miss Talbot."

"Is it a voucher you need?" asked Grant. "I confess when you said you needed a man, I was hoping for something a little more exciting."

"I am sorry to disappoint you," said Genie.

"Not at all! Which day should you like to attend? I shall promise that your vouchers will be delivered to you. And in payment, you can offer me the first dance."

"I promise," said Genie, warming to the idea. Dancing again with Mr. Grant, being held in his arms... her ardor was cooled by a pointed glare from her aunt.

"Can you do this?" asked the dowager. "Lady Jersey will surely object."

"But I am on friendly terms with Lady Jersey and close with the princess. Leave the worries to me."

Despite Genie's interest in sitting next to Mr. Grant, she was firmly placed in the center of a group of men, while Grant was corralled into making up a fourth for whist with Lord and Lady Bremerton and the duchess.

Genie felt sorry for the man, but he accepted his fate with equanimity and even made staunch, old Lord Bremerton break forth into laughter.

Genie survived a dull game of lottery tickets. Her only consolation was in Mr. Blakely's confidence that he also was not an enthusiast of the game and would have preferred a more challenging pastime or even reading a good book, to which Genie could only agree. The game was so simple for Mr. Blakely, he did not even have to remove his gloves during the play.

After cards, Genie noted that the dowager gave the duke several pointed looks and a glare so intense she would not have been surprised to see Marchford suddenly burst into flames. With a stifled sigh, Marchford stood and asked for the attention of his family and friends. "Lady Louisa, we have long had an understanding between us. I would like now to make this betrothal official by making a formal announcement and celebrating it with a ball."

Louisa's eyes widened and her lips were pressed into a straight line.

"Oh yes!" shrieked Lady Bremerton, her excitement getting the best of her. "That would be lovely! A grand ball, how delightful!" It was a vindication to Lady Bremerton, whose friends were beginning to talk that the duke would never come up to scratch.

Lady Bremerton began to talk of dates with the dowager, with the promise they would get together soon. Marchford took Lady Louisa's hand and bestowed upon her a chaste kiss. Genie could have sworn she saw Louisa snatch her hand back.

The party began to break up and some of the men

took their leave. The coats were requested, and Genie followed her aunt and uncle into the entryway of the grand Marchford house. The rest of the potential husbands prepared to leave, with Mr. Blakely bowing over her hand.

"Perhaps we can meet again soon and you can show me this contraband guidebook," said Blakely in an undertone.

"I'd like that," she whispered back. "I shall have to smuggle it out of my room somehow."

"Perhaps a secret rendezvous?" he suggested.

"Yes, let's!" Genie agreed.

Lady Bremerton drifted closer, making the sharing of confidences impossible, so Blakely took his leave.

"Made a new friend?" asked Grant with a slight edge to his voice Genie was unaccustomed to hearing.

Genie chose to ignore the comment and replied in an undertone, "I am sorry you were stuck playing whist with my aunt."

"It was my best game of whist in years," declared Grant, but Genie was unsure it was a compliment. "Did you have a good evening?" Mr. Grant met her eye.

"I had a most respectable time," said Genie, and then realized she had chosen the wrong word. She meant to say lovely or entertaining or pleasant, not "respectable."

Grant laughed, and in the confusion brought by the arrival of their coats, he whispered, "How dreadful. You have my full sympathy."

"I meant to say it was a pleasant evening," Genie whispered back.

"Now I know what you truly mean if you ever use that word. I do hope you will never describe me as 'pleasant.'" With a wicked wink, Grant escorted her to the door. She left but not without leaving a few slivers of her heart behind.

"How was it Mr. Blakely found you?" asked Marchford after all the guests had left.

"Entered the study saying he was looking for the dining room," said Grant.

"A ruse?"

Grant shrugged. "You have a big house. He's unfamiliar with it. Get lost myself sometimes."

The men returned to the study where Lord Thornton was reading a book in a chair, his back to the wall and the entire study within view. A loaded revolver sat on an end table next to him. The broken window had been boarded up, giving the normally sophisticated study a shanty feel.

Thornton snapped the book closed when the men entered. "What's the plan?"

"To catch a thief," stated Marchford, producing a black bag and proceeding to pull out tools.

Grant picked up a handsaw and a gimlet. "Exactly what do you intend to do with this thief? Seems a bloody mess."

"These are for some renovations," said Marchford.

"What do ye plan to do?" asked Thornton.

"I intend to make some modifications, and I am hoping you both will prove to be able tradesmen to do it," said Marchford.

"What?!" cried Grant. "Too far, my friend! Remind me why I am here standing guard over this thing?"

"Because there is no one else I trust," said Marchford simply. He rolled out a scroll with some roughly drawn plans. "This is the plan. Do you think it possible?" he asked Thornton who was looking over his shoulder.

"Aye, 'tis possible, but it will ruin the paneling."

"Grandma won't like it," stated Grant.

"That is nothing new," muttered Marchford. "I will leave this project in your capable hands."

"Leave? Where are you going?" demanded Grant.

"I have a date with an opera singer."

Twenty

JEM CREPT THROUGH THE DARK ALLEY, THOUGH THE night was black as pitch. It was not his first time finding the door in the dark. He entered the cellar through a gap in a boarded window. A single candle burned on an old table, a small point of light that seemed to be swallowed whole by the dark surroundings.

"So you finally decided to join us," said the man with the burned hands.

"Sorry. I had to wait till that housekeeper went to sleep. She's a cunning one."

"The lads had to wait for you to return to be fed," said the Candyman with deceptive mildness. He gestured to a row of five-foot square cages along the wall. Locked inside were skinny children, their eyes reflecting the single flame of the candle. They were unnaturally silent.

"Tell me what you have learned, and I will tell you if they have earned any bread today," said the man.

Jem told the man his adventures with Mr. Grant and Miss Talbot. He did not tell about the kiss.

"I told you to get inside the Marchford house, what do I care for Mr. Grant," yelled the Candyman.

"But you said I should gain their trust and I did," argued Jem.

The man stood in a flash and struck Jem across the mouth with a closed fist. Jem flew back and rolled into a ball. It was not the first time he had tasted blood.

"None of your back talk. Get in the cage," demanded the man. Jem scrambled inside if only to protect himself from further abuse. The cage door locked shut with an echoing click. "No food today. If any of you are hungry, you can blame Jem, who did not do what I asked." The man held up a small key. "Fortunately, I now have the key to the safe. All I need now is to get into the Marchford house, and you, boy, are going to help me do it."

The man took the candle and went up the cellar stairs, leaving the dank basement in utter darkness. Jem began to pull scones and biscuits, ham, and lamb shank from his pockets, socks, and hat, and passed them through the bars to the boy next to him who took some and passed it along.

"Thanks, Jem," came a whispered response. Jem curled into a ball and went to sleep, trying not to hear the faint crying from one of the younger boys. The older ones knew better than to waste their tears.

The sun was shining brightly and Genie awoke with a smile on her face. She could not help it, her first thought was of Grant. She gave herself a mental shake and tried to redirect her thoughts toward Mr. Blakely. He was a kind man and not afraid of her guidebook, which could only recommend him. As her maid assisted her into a morning dress of light blue, she had to continue to remind herself which man held precedence in her thoughts. Despite her determination, it took some mental effort to direct her thoughts toward Mr. Blakely, a practice that made her weary even at the breakfast table.

Somewhere over crumpets and eggs, she saw a red head peek through the front window. "Excuse me!" she exclaimed and hustled to the garden, where she found the expected Jem. Did he have a message for her from Grant or her brother?

"Jem! Are you well?"

"Yes'm. Gots a message for you." The boy handed her a neat envelope. Jem on the other hand, was less than tidy.

"Why, Jem. What has happened to your new clothes? They are so dirty. You must take better care of yourself."

"Yes, milady." The boy hung his head.

"Now do not be discouraged. I understand it is hard for little boys to stay clean. You must try your best. Do you understand?"

The boy nodded and ground a booted toe into the dirt.

Genie opened the letter and was a bit disappointed to find it was not from Grant. The missive was from Mr. Blakely, suggesting they meet at Marchford house to discuss the guidebook without the danger of Lady Bremerton's disdain.

"Tell the man who gave you this letter that I will meet him at Marchford house during morning calls, do you understand?"

Jem nodded, but evaded her eye. "Wouldn't you rather spend time with Grant? That cove is togged in twig."

"I do not understand." Genie often struggled to understand the young urchin, but this time he had lost her.

"He's a fine dresser and nice. You do like him, don't you?"

Genie sighed. "I'm sorry you saw our, er, embrace yesterday. I do like Mr. Grant, but I need to make other friends as well."

"I says you shouldn't."

"You have a kind heart, Jem. Can you deliver the message?"

"If you wish." Jem dragged his feet walking out of the garden and Genie wondered at his apparent dejection. She shrugged to no one in particular and traipsed upstairs to find a reticule big enough to hide her guidebook.

"Lions? Does it really have lions?" Genie bent closer over the guidebook, her head close to Mr. Blakely's.

"Yes, I believe the Tower of London does have lions," answered Blakely. "I think that should go to the top of our list."

"Definitely!" Genie had easily convinced Lady Bremerton to let her visit Penelope at the Marchford house. She told Pen and the dowager of her planned meeting with Mr. Blakely, which was met with enthusiasm. As soon as Blakely arrived, the dowager suggested they visit the garden, and so Genie found herself on a bench next to him, with Penelope somewhere amongst the hedges to maintain propriety.

"Look, they list their names," exclaimed Genie, turning the page on her red, bound volume of *The Picture of London*. Genie had purchased the fat volume for five shillings and despite the grief she had endured about it, was quite enchanted with the two pullout maps and several nice engravings.

"Miss Fanny?" read Blakely. "Seems a rather tame name for a lioness."

"Look, there's a panther named 'Miss Peggy,'" giggled Genie. "I had a friend by the same name. I should like to visit her."

"Yes, let's! What a helpful guidebook this is."

"Thank you!" Genie was pleased someone finally recognized the value of her volume.

They passed an enjoyable afternoon reading about the various glories in London, including St. Paul's Cathedral, Westminster Abbey, Kensington Palace, and many other notable sites. Genie was desirous to stroll through Hyde Park, which had apparently been recently planted with trees. Blakely confessed an interest in visiting the armory at Carlton House, the residence of the Prince of Wales, which according to the guidebook was the finest in the world.

After an hour, Blakely reluctantly stood to take his leave. They walked to the front door, Penelope discreetly following behind as any good chaperone should do.

"Well, hallo there!" called a familiar voice.

Genie turned to find Grant strolling down the grand staircase. "Grant! Are you visiting the duke?" Despite her concerted effort not to care a fig for Grant, her heart beat a little faster and a smile sprung to her face.

"Just leaving," he said with a smile, but as he approached, she noted he had an unusually disheveled appearance and, if she was not very much mistaken, was wearing the same mustard waistcoat he had worn the day before. "I see you have been visiting with your new friend." Grant's smile dimmed.

"Yes, we were reviewing my guidebook."

"How… edifying."

"May I drop you back at Bremerton house, Miss Talbot?" asked Mr. Blakely.

"Actually, I was hoping to visit Hookham's library. I have arranged to be picked up there later."

"Why, Hookham's is exactly on my way!" declared Grant. "You must allow me the pleasure of taking you."

Despite a furious glare from Penelope, Grant insisted he be given the role as squire and soon Genie was sitting next to him on his phaeton.

"You seem to be on friendly terms with Mr. Blakely," said Grant in a manner slightly less than cordial.

"He seems a very nice man," said Genie, not sure what to do with the winter in Grant's tone. "Tell me how does Jem do today? I saw him earlier this morning."

"Then you have seen him more recently than I," replied Grant. "He's a squirrelly fellow. Never seems to stay where I put him."

"Little boys are like that," laughed Genie. "He needs a place to run."

"Might have found a place. Bunch of Quakers take in orphans on a country estate."

"Yes, it sounds exactly like what Jem needs, as

long as the people there will be kind to him. I believe country living is a good choice for young boys. I should have known you would find the right place for our Jemmy." A bump in the road threw her against Grant. She straightened but left her shoulder touching his. For balance, she told herself.

"Here we are." Grant pulled up in front of Hookham's Lending Library. He jumped from the phaeton and lifted Genie neatly to the ground, his hands almost encircling her small waist. He lingered a moment longer than he should have, his eyes meeting hers, his hands on her waist. Genie forgot to breathe, looking into his silver-blue eyes and unshaven face.

"Thank you again," murmured Genie, heat crawling across her face and down into unmentionable regions.

"I am always at your service." Grant walked her to the door and left her with a bow.

Grant returned slowly to the phaeton, watching Genie through the window of Hookham's. She looked around for a moment, then threw open her arms wide to give a long embrace to a handsome young man.

Twenty-one

"I THINK THESE ARE ALL GOOD CANDIDATES," SAID the dowager over tea that afternoon. She examined sorted cards Penelope had created with the names, positions, and significant information for the potential bachelors they wished to put into the running for Genie's hand.

"I agree. These five would be good potentials. I should think Mr. Blakely is the frontrunner. They had a nice visit together over that guidebook. I believe they could become good friends," replied Penelope.

"Friends? What difference does that make? She is choosing a husband not a lover." The dowager carefully chose a biscuit from the tray.

Penelope stared at the dowager.

"You needn't look so scandalized," chastised the dowager. "You young people are so much more moralistic than we were in my time."

"Should I apologize? How was it exactly in your time? Did you entertain many lovers?"

"A lady would never quote a number," said the dowager with a sly smile. "It used to be a marriage was for family name, inheritance, and breeding. Love was something reserved for other relationships, after, of course, you provided at least one or two legitimate heirs."

"I can come back later if I have interrupted a private conversation," said the duke, who was standing by the door.

"Your grandmother was telling me of her numerous lovers. I'm not certain you would quite like to hear it."

"I am sure I would not. Miss Rose, could I have a moment in the study?" They walked down the corridor to the study, where the butler was standing guard outside the door. "Thank you, Peters."

"You are leaving nothing to chance," said Pen, following the duke into the study.

"No, not after yesterday," said the duke, motioning Penelope to sit down. He sat across from her and she could see worry lines about his eyes she had not noticed before. "I expect the thief will try again, and this time I intend to be better prepared. Tell me what was that man doing here?"

"Blakely? He came to visit Genie without the watchful eye of Lady Bremerton. Genie has a guidebook she wanted to review with him without suffering her aunt's set-downs regarding the topic of guidebooks."

"A guidebook for London?" Marchford asked with a twinge of disgust.

"Exactly so."

"Anything else I should know?"

"Most of the staff have in some way been either threatened or bribed to retrieve what you are hiding in this study."

"I am aware. I've had to send agents out to protect the families of several housemaids and a few have left altogether."

"Why did I see Mr. Grant here this morning, looking like he had slept in his clothes?" asked Pen.

"We had some fun last night and he passed out on the floor. Not safe to wake Grant until afternoon, so there was nothing I could do but let him sleep."

Pen raised an eyebrow.

Marchford sighed. "That is the story you are to tell grandmother."

"Would it do me any good to ask you for the truth?"

"I needed to go out last night and I trust none but Thornton and Grant to guard the letter. The footman and any guards I could hire are vulnerable, and I'll not trust any agents from Neville's office."

"Mr. Grant offered to drive Miss Talbot to the lending library. She left in that high-perch phaeton of his." Penelope's tone was accusatory. Marchford may trust Grant to watch over his document, but she did not trust him to watch over Genie.

"You do not approve?"

"If he has no intentions of offering marriage, which I think we both know he does not, he should clear the field."

Marchford sighed. "I will speak to him. Anything else you have to report?"

"Miss Talbot has befriended a young boy, a street urchin and thief, and is trying to rehabilitate him. Lord and Lady Bremerton rejected the notion, so Mr. Grant has agreed to house the urchin."

"I confess Grant did tell me much the same,

but I thought it must be one of his jokes. And my grandmother?"

"Feisty and plotting your demise."

"Everything is normal then, capital. I must thank you, Miss Rose. I have rarely seen my grandmother in such fine fettle. Whatever you are doing to lift her spirits, please do continue."

"I shall remind you that you directed me in such a manner sometime in the future." Pen could not help but smile.

Marchford smiled in return, a rare occurrence. "I do not mind having you in the house nearly as much as I thought I would."

"Was that a compliment? I fear I may have missed it."

"It was a little backhanded, I apologize. Let me try again. I enjoy your presence, Miss Rose. I shall miss you when you leave with my grandmother to the dowager house."

"Thank you. Since we have no plans at present to leave, you shall have the pleasure of enjoying my presence for the extended future."

"I shall accept my fate with the courage that befits an Englishman," said Marchford gallantly. "I should warn you, I shall be around the house and most likely in my rooms for the next few days. I believe I will become ill."

"You are going to keep to the house to try to catch this thief."

Marchford graced her with another smile. "You are a clever one, Miss Rose. If you could pass along my apologies for tea? Tell my grandmother I told you I was feeling ill."

"As you wish," said Penelope, standing to leave.

"Oh, I almost forgot. This arrived for you." Marchford reached for something in his inside coat pocket.

"Thank you." Penelope took the letter he handed her. It was address to her, but other than originating from London, it had not return address or information. She broke the seal quickly, curiosity overtaking her. One glance inside told her she must read this particular letter in private. "I think I shall take a moment to rest and read my letter in peace."

If he had hoped her to explain the letter, he accepted her silence and merely bowed in response. Penelope proceeded upstairs to her room to open the mysterious letter without prying eyes. There was another sealed letter inside the first one. The letter within was addressed to *Madame X*.

"Why, George, whatever is the matter?" Genie frowned into her brother's formerly playful eyes. They had a dull appearance now. She took his hand and drew him to sit with her near the window of Hookham's Lending Library.

"Nothing is the matter. This has been a great lark." He rubbed his tired eyes with his hand.

"You look dreadful. Have you slept at all since we last spoke?"

"Been having too much fun to sleep," said George.

"It does not look like you have been having any fun at all," retorted Genie.

"Shows what you know. Some things are not meant for a girl. Turns out I have a knack for cards," he said proudly, puffing out his chest.

"Cards! Please do not tell me you have been gambling away your school money, George."

"All right, I won't tell you. I didn't ask you here to quarrel but to give you this." He handed her a small box. Inside were two twinkling, emerald earbobs.

"George! These are beautiful!"

"I thought they would look nice with your coloring," said George like he had been living in Town all his life.

"Why, yes, yes, they will. Thank you so much." Genie gave George a warm hug. "But how could you possibly afford them?"

"Like I said, I have had a run of good luck. The cards love me!"

"Father and Mama would not approve of you gambling."

"They would not approve of me losing money, but you see, I'm winning money. I cannot lose!"

"I do not think that is exactly what they meant by not approving of gambling."

"I told you I wanted to do something to help you. I have seen the way so many of these ladies dress, all flash and sparkle. I know you haven't a single earbob from Mama, so I thought your baby brother could come to your aid."

"Thank you, George, now please go to sleep." She could not help but feel concern over his gray complexion.

"Yes, Genie," he said with puppy dog eyes.

"And go back to school."

"One more night tonight and then I'll go."

Genie gave her brother another big hug.

Outside the window, Grant snapped the reins and drove off in his phaeton. He had seen enough.

Penelope glanced around her bedroom to ensure she was alone. The outside letter was a note asking her to direct this letter to Madame X and no one else (this last part was underlined). Inside was another sealed letter with the simple direction, Madame X. No signature accompanied the missive and no identifying marks were given. She examined the handwriting, but she did not know it. She turned the letter in her hands, wondering what to do.

Of course there was no Madame X, except herself and the dowager. She wondered if she should turn the letter over to the dowager but stopped, pondering why the letter had been addressed to her in the first place. It seemed more reasonable if someone was trying to connect with Madame X that they would ask the dowager, so why was the note addressed to Penelope? Only one way to find out.

Penelope broke the seal. When she unfolded the paper, a hundred-pound note fluttered to the floor. She stared at it as if it might jump up and bite her. She scooped it up quickly and read the note.

Dear Madame X,

I write you for I am greatly distressed and do not know where to turn for help. I have accepted an offer of marriage that is not of my parents' choosing. Unfortunately, I am already officially betrothed to another. How can I break this long-standing marriage contract and wed the man I choose?

I have included a small deposit. If you choose to

help, please send me advice through Mrs. Roberts at 7 Chandos Street, London.

Sincerely,
Desperate

Pen read the letter again and again. Who was this "Desperate" character? And who was Mrs. Roberts and how had she heard about Madame X? No, Pen could guess the answer to the second question. She had overheard Lady Bremerton whisper to the Comtesse de Marseille that she had retained the help of an infamous matchmaker, Madame X. The news must have spread.

Penelope thought about the situation for a while, then composed a response. She rubbed the crisp hundred-pound note between her fingers. She had never felt one before. There must be a rationale that would allow her not to tell the dowager but still keep the money, but alas she could not think of one. Whoever "Desperate" was, she had gone to great lengths to prevent the dowager from reading her letter, and Penelope was determined to find out why.

With a longing glance, she folded the hundred-pound note back into the letter and sealed it, addressing it simply to "Desperate." She then wrapped it in a second paper and sealed it also, addressing it to the mysterious Mrs. Roberts.

Penelope put the letter in a book to conceal it and walked downstairs to rejoin the dowager. Tomorrow, Pen planned an outing. This letter would not be franked; no, this letter she planned to deliver to Mrs. Roberts herself.

Twenty-two

"I am looking for Mrs. Roberts. Can you direct me?" Penelope Rose asked the young man at the apothecary. The day after she received the mysterious missive, she followed the direction in the letter to a storefront in a nicer part of Town. The sign on the door said "Dr. Roberts" and inside there was an apothecary with rows and rows of bottles on the wall behind a smart young man in an apron at the counter.

"No Mrs. Roberts here, ma'am. Just a Dr. Roberts."

"Perhaps Dr. Roberts has a wife or a mother?" suggested Penelope.

"No, ma'am."

"Are you sure? I received a letter from a Mrs. Roberts and I am looking for her."

"No, ma'am. No missus and both of Dr. Roberts's parents are deceased, ma'am. God rest their souls."

"Yes, quite so," answered Penelope absently. This was not the answer she expected. She wanted to find this Mrs. Roberts, but apparently she did not exist.

"Can you tell me something of Dr. Roberts? Has he been in practice long?"

"Dr. Roberts is a fine gentleman physician, ma'am. Best in London. He has been called to treat the queen and other notable persons. He is quite well known."

"I have never heard of him."

"Begging your pardon, ma'am, but it is not the healthy who need the doctors."

The sound of laughing and murmuring of happy conversation floated down from above.

"The doctor is seeing a patient," explained the lad at the counter.

More laughter could be heard. "I do not remember my visits with the doctor being so diverting," said Penelope under her breath. "I would like an appointment. May I see him next?" asked Penelope.

"Oh no, he is far too busy. He only accepts certain cases."

Penelope opened her mouth to argue, but the door upstairs opened at that moment and out walked Lady Louisa.

"Thank you very much, Dr. Roberts," she said in more sober tones. "My mother will appreciate your advice."

"Please let me know if I can be of any greater assistance," said the doctor. He was a young man, handsome and tall. His features were pleasing and his eyes were dancing and bright. If he were to be the physician, Penelope would hardly mind being sick.

"Dr. Roberts," called the man behind the counter. "This young lady was looking for a Mrs. Roberts. Do you know who she is talking about?"

Louisa froze, recognizing Penelope. Louisa appeared to grow visibly pale, but the impression lasted but a moment. With crisp determination, Louisa continued down the stairs.

"You are looking for Mrs. Roberts?" The doctor followed Louisa down the stairs, his brows knit together.

"I have a letter for her," said Penelope.

"I can take that," said the doctor briskly.

"Is she here? I would like to deliver it myself."

"No, no, she is..." Dr. Roberts glanced at the lad behind the counter, then at Louisa. "A cousin. She is a cousin of mine. She will arrive soon. I will see that she receives it."

"Forgive me, but I have been given very particular instructions to hand this to no one but Mrs. Roberts herself."

Louisa and the good doctor exchanged a glance, but neither said a word.

"Then I wish you luck in finding her," said the good doctor. "Might I suggest you send it through the post? Perhaps you would have better luck in routing it to the right person." He bowed to the ladies and caught Louisa's eye once more.

"Good day, Dr. Roberts," said Louisa.

"Good day, Lady Louisa," he said gravely and disappeared back up the stairs.

"Lady Louisa, how remarkable that we meet here," commented Pen.

"It is not terribly remarkable. My mother is a patient of Dr. Roberts. I come regularly to pick up her medication and get advice from the doctor."

"I see." Penelope was not sure she did see, but she was determined to find out. "How fortunate for me that you were here. I took a hack here, so if you would not mind, I should love to ride back to Marchford house on your way home. It is on the way, yes?"

Louisa shot her a glance that conveyed she would rather have hot pokers stabbed in her eyes than share a coach with Penelope Rose. Penelope merely smiled. She was accustomed to having that effect on people.

"Yes, please do join me." Lady Louisa's jaw was so clenched Penelope wondered that she could speak at all.

Penelope climbed into the Bremerton town coach, which was, naturally, quite nice and more than a little pretentious. Penelope took a seat across from Louisa, who averted her gaze in a feeble attempt to pretend Penelope was not there.

"Have you known Dr. Roberts long?" asked Penelope politely.

"He is our family physician," Lady Louisa said in quelling accents. My, but the aristocracy did know how to give a set-down to the commoners. Unfortunately for Louisa, Penelope was not about to take a polite hint.

"I do hope Lady Bremerton is not terribly ill."

"Nervous complaint," said Louisa, still focusing her gaze outside the carriage.

"Did the doctor come recommended?"

"Indeed, from your mistress, the Duchess of Marchford. He has even served as a consultant to the queen, so yes, Miss Rose, he does come highly recommended."

"Is that how you met him? Through the duchess?"

Louisa turned toward her, a spark of anger in her eye. "I met him because he was the personal physician to the sixth Duke of Marchford. Dr. Roberts did everything he could, brought Frederick back from death's door more times than I care to remember, and yet it was not the will of Providence for Frederick to survive. There now, Miss Rose, have you any more questions for me?"

Penelope sat quietly for a few minutes. She could be obtuse, but she tried not to be rude. Louisa turned to stare out the window. How difficult it must be for her, Penelope suddenly realized. To be engaged to be married, only to watch her fiancé slowly die and thus find oneself obligated to marry the brother. Even though the current Duke of Marchford was not a poor-looking specimen, he clearly held no particular regard for Louisa.

Penelope knew conversation was not welcomed, yet an opportunity to speak to Louisa without others overhearing may not come again soon. She had questions and she was convinced Louisa had the answers.

"It is very strange that I could not find Mrs. Roberts. I was given clear instructions to make sure this letter was delivered directly to her hands and none else." Penelope drew the letter out of her reticule and Louisa's gaze snapped to it.

"In your visits to Dr. Roberts, have you met a Mrs. Roberts?" asked Penelope, watching carefully to gauge Louisa's reply.

"On occasion I believe I may have. Would you like me to give this to her?" She leaned forward, eyes still on the letter.

"I have been tasked with finding this Mrs. Roberts. Can you help me?"

"She is… reclusive, but I can get it to her. You can trust me."

"Can I?" Penelope let the question hang and Louisa turned away. "Lady Louisa, did you write me a letter to be directed to Madam X?"

Lady Louisa said nothing.

"I can confirm the handwriting with Miss Talbot if I need to. Is that why you sent the letter to me instead of to the dowager? She no doubt would recognize your handwriting."

"What do you want? Money? Do you wish me to buy your silence, Miss Rose?"

Penelope recoiled back into the squabs as if she had been doused in cold water. "Open your letter, Mrs. Roberts." Penelope held out the letter, which Louisa took.

Louisa opened the seals and caught the hundred-pound note before it fluttered to the floorboards. She scanned the letter quickly, then put both it and the money away in her reticule. "I misjudged you. I do apologize."

"The dowager has begun plans for the wedding."

"I know. My mother has been planning for years."

"Have you tried telling your mother you do not wish to wed the Duke of Marchford?"

"How could I? Mother was forced to marry Lord Bremerton when her sister eloped. She did so to raise the future of her children. She has lived on the expectancy that I would marry a duke since I was in my cradle."

"Yes, I can see your point. But if you are determined not to wed the duke, you must be willing to stand up to your mother."

"Speaking my mind is one thing, but how do I garner her support?"

Support? Get Lady Bremerton to dissolve her daughter's engagement to the duke? Never! "You may need to recognize your parents may not support you in this. But it is always your choice whether or not you wed. They may be angry, very angry, but they cannot force you to wed. Nor will they disown you and toss you from the house; they are too proud for that and you are their only child."

"Yes, but how can I get them to support my marriage to another?"

Insight finally flashed. "Dr. Roberts? Are you in love with Dr. Roberts?" asked Penelope.

Louisa colored and evaded her eye. "I am sorry I was beastly to you. When you saw me with him, I was ready to sink."

Penelope leaned back on the squabs and pondered Louisa's predicament. This was a puzzle. Lady Louisa marry a gentleman physician instead of the duke? Penelope shook her head. It was impossible to imagine Lord and Lady Bremerton would accept that.

"We fell in love over time," said Louisa so softly Pen could hardly hear over the squeaking and jostling of the carriage. "We were in each other's company many times when Frederick was ill. I did love Frederick. I wished to marry him at his bedside, but he wanted to give me the wedding he felt I deserved. He wanted to stand next to me, not lie on some bed. So we waited for him to recover, but it was never to be."

Louisa took out a handkerchief and dabbed her eyes. "Dr. Roberts was very compassionate. Afterward, he was kind, friendly. My mother took on nerves, so he was frequently at the house. He talked to me, made me laugh. The feelings came on so gradually, we never noticed them until it was too late."

"Dr. Roberts I am sure is an excellent man, but he is far from your station."

"I know he is now, but he is also the heir to a large estate and a baronet. When his uncle passes away, he will inherit a significant fortune. He is not wooing me for the money, of that I can assure you."

"That does improve his eligibility, but a barony is rather less than a dukedom."

Louisa nodded. "I know. And I know what my mother would say. But what else can I do? We were waiting until he inherited to go before my parents and plead our case. With Marchford being gone so long, we hoped we could make a rationale for dissolving the contract."

"But Marchford returned and ruined everything."

"Yes. Quite."

"You may have to live without their approval or your inheritance."

"And flee London in disgrace? Barred from society? And what of Dr. Roberts? If the gossip spread that he had wed me against my parents' will, none of his patients would ever speak to him again. His reputation, his practice would be ruined! Why his uncle might even be led to disinherit!"

"If you are determined to walk down this road, you will need allies, people who will support you." Pen went straight for the heart of the problem. "A good solicitor will be important. And you need to find people who can encourage your parents to accept this match. I know you wish Marchford would just go away, but his being here may help you if you can get him to support you in dissolving the union."

Louisa sighed. "I suppose I do need to talk to Marchford."

"In the end, you may need to resign yourself to one of two unpleasant options. Either follow your heart and be lost to society, or follow your parents and let go of these feelings for Dr. Roberts."

"You do not understand, Miss Rose. It is impossible for me to wed the Duke of Marchford. Simply impossible."

Twenty-three

IT HAD BEEN TWO DAYS AND GENIE HAD NOT SEEN MR. Grant. Not that she expected to or wanted to or… who was she trying to fool? Of course she wanted to see him. What good it could possibly do her was a bit more vague.

Mr. Blakely, however, had been quite solicitous in his attentions. He had visited twice and a threatened thunderstorm had ruined plans to go to Hyde Park. This had brought up memories of another storm that had caught her in the arms of Mr. Grant. The thought left her restless.

"I hope the weather will clear soon," Genie sighed, sitting with her aunt and cousin in the sitting room.

"Yes, the streets become ghastly. Why, I added an inch to my pattens just for Town wear," commented Lady Bremerton.

The formal butler entered with a bow. "For you, Lady Bremerton," intoned the butler, handing her a large envelope.

She broke the seal and gasped.

"Is something wrong?" asked Genie.

"No, no, it is most wonderful!" Lady Bremerton looked up with a glorious smile. "We have all been issued vouchers to attend Almack's tomorrow night!"

Genie smiled radiantly in return. It must have been the workings of Mr. Grant.

"You do not look at death's door. I was promised a man in ghastly health, but you look well enough." Grant surveyed the duke with a critical eye. He and Thornton had decided to visit Marchford in his bedchamber since the rumor had circulated that the duke was ill. "Though that waistcoat was a mistake."

"Wrong color or cut?" asked the duke.

"Yes," replied Grant. "Brought it with you from the Continent, I can tell."

"I did indeed. I thought it well enough."

Grant shook his head sadly. "You have been gone too long, dear friend. I will give you the name of my tailor. He will set you to rights."

"You never gave me the name of your tailor," objected Thornton.

"I thought you had no concern for fashion my friend. I had always pictured your raiment as a protest against fashionable society in defense of your Scottish bloodlines."

"'Tis just a coat, Grant."

"'*Just* a coat'? And you wonder why I would not subject my tailor to you."

Thornton's brows furrowed and he turned to Marchford. "Returning to the point of the visit, we were told ye were ill. Are ye well?"

"Yes, yes, I am well, but I must keep to my room."

"If you reveal some contagion, I fear I shall run screaming from the room," said Grant, pouring himself a whiskey. "Your story appears to be a long one. I fear I may need refreshment before you are through."

"I would invite you to help yourself, but I see you have anticipated me."

"Why must ye keep to yer room?" asked Thornton, ignoring Grant's distractions.

"I am trying to catch a spy."

Grant took a hearty swig. "I was right. A drink was needed."

"I appreciate the modifications you made the other night to the study directly below. I have continued your good work. If someone tries to remove the letter in the safe, it will pull a cord and a bell will ring there." Marchford pointed to a brass bell mounted on the wall with a cord running down the wall and disappearing under the floorboards.

"I thought this might be the direction ye were going," said Thornton. "But how will ye get down in time to catch the thief?"

"See here," Marchford opened a narrow panel in the wall which revealed a spiral staircase. "It leads to the study."

"Very cloak-and-dagger," said Grant with feeling. "When did you have this made?"

"My grandfather commissioned it when the house was built. I would like to say he had nefarious intent, but apparently he did not walk well in his later years and wished to have a shorter route from his study to his bedchamber. In any event, it is useful."

"So you have been waiting to see if the letter is stolen?"

"Yes, and look here. Remember how I asked you to drill a hole in the ceiling?" Marchford motioned to a spyglass on a letter table. He slid a small panel and stepped back to let Thornton take a look.

Thornton pointed the spyglass down. "Why, I can see the whole room. Clever thought to put a spyglass here."

"So you are spending your time locked away in your room spying on your own study?" asked Grant. "How dull."

"Yes, actually it is," admitted Marchford. "I had anticipated the thief would make an attempt on the room soon, but so far I have been disappointed."

"How long do ye intend to play the role of invalid?" asked Thornton.

"Yes, well, therein lies the rub. I cannot rightly stay here too much longer without society taking notice. Already my grandmother has insisted that a physician be called. I fear my acting ability may not be up to the task."

"So get someone else to sit here and wait for the spy—really quite a simple solution. They must have people who do this sort of thing." Grant waved his hand in a dismissive manner.

"Yes, indeed. But I suspect a spy has infiltrated deep into the Foreign Office. I do not wish to use anyone from official channels."

Grant put down his drink. "I do not like where this is going."

Marchford smiled at his friends. "I know you have been wondering what you could do to help win the war against Napoleon."

Thornton raised an eyebrow and Grant reached for the decanter to refill his glass. "If you can say that with a straight face, you have nothing to fear from your acting abilities."

"I fear the thief will not strike until I am out of the house. It is imperative we find the spy. You are the only ones I trust."

Grant shook his head. "You go too far. I cannot fathom sitting here, doing nothing all day."

"I understand." Marchford nodded. "It is a dangerous assignment. I would not wish to put you in harm's way."

"What are you suggesting?" asked Grant.

"Nothing, nothing at all. It is perfectly natural, since you have been enjoying a life of ease that you would become..." Marchford looked up at the ceiling as if in thought.

"Soft? Fearful? Cowardly?" supplied Thornton. He shrugged at Grant's glare. "Just trying to help our friend find the right word."

"Let us simply say you are out of condition. I would not wish you to get hurt if you are not physically capable or do not have the mental fortitude—"

Grant put up his hand to stop Marchford. "Enough! Say no more or I shall be forced to retaliate in kind. Do you truly believe impugning my honor would entice me to sit in your bedroom, waiting for a thief?"

"Did it?" asked the duke.

Grant sighed and flopped on the couch in the sitting area of the master bedroom. "Suppose I should get comfortable. But how is the thief going to open the safe to ring the bell? I thought you had it locked."

"I do, but one of my keys was stolen."

"Stolen?" asked Thornton in alarm.

"By a sly little opera singer."

"The one you went to see the other night?" asked Thornton.

Marchford nodded.

"That little minx." Grant shook his head.

"Yes, she was—" began Marchford.

"Not her, you!" declared Grant. "You purposely allowed her to seduce you, so she could steal the key and give it to the thief!"

Marchford merely shrugged.

"All in the line of duty to King and Crown?" Thornton raised an eyebrow.

Marchford smiled. "Long live the King."

"Thank you for seeing me."

Lord Bremerton gestured for the young man to sit in one of the high-back, comfortable chairs in his study. "What can I do for you today, Mr. Blakely?"

"I have had several pleasant conversations with Miss Talbot. Am I correct that you are serving as her guardian here in London?" asked Mr. Blakely.

"That is correct."

"I understand there is interest in seeing her engaged quickly."

Lord Bremerton said nothing, neither confirming nor denying the statement but gazing at Mr. Blakely with a confident air of the aristocracy.

"Miss Talbot is a sweet girl and very pretty. I should be the happiest man alive if she would consent to be my wife. However, I have run into some financial embarrassments since coming to London."

"Been betting deep and lost," said Lord Bremerton without emotion.

"Yes. And to be honest, I haven't the blunt to repay the debt."

"And how is it you expect me to help you with this problem of yours?"

"It pains me greatly to ask you this, but the circumstances involved force me to present my case in a manner most vulgar. I fear I must ask, if a man was engaged to Miss Talbot, if her dowry might be available even before the wedding?"

"You want to become engaged to Genie and collect early on the dowry to pay off your vowels."

"You must understand how wretched I feel in even asking this of you." Blakely's voice trembled and he gripped his own hands in tan kid leather gloves.

"Once the engagement has been accepted and announced, you shall have access to the funds to discharge your embarrassments."

"I much appreciate it, Lord Bremerton."

"I would much appreciate it if you took her off my hands and let my household get back to peace." Lord Bremerton returned to his paper.

Twenty-four

ALMACK'S ASSEMBLY ROOMS. GENIE WALKED INTO the prestigious social club and was not disappointed by the lavish interior of marble inlays and gilt railings. A full orchestra provided engaging musical selections and the main attraction of the ballroom was to join the dance. Since dancing was an occupation Genie enjoyed, she entered the hallowed halls with every expectation of being pleased. Particularly if the one responsible for her voucher was here.

She smoothed her green, shimmering, silk gown with her hands in new, long, white gloves. Her brother's emeralds dangled from her ears, making her feel expensive and somehow dangerous.

"Heaven's sake, child, do not fidget," whispered her aunt. "You must do what you can to appear respectable."

Appear respectable. As if she were conducting some huge masquerade on the unsuspecting London society. Advice from so many well-intentioned people rang in her ears, mostly a long list of things she should not do. But tonight, she did not care. She was going to dance with whomever asked, laugh if she was amused, yes, and even talk about hay if she chose. Well, maybe her aunt was right about not mentioning hay, but otherwise she intended to enjoy herself.

"Whatever you do, do not dance with Mr. Grant," said her aunt.

"Aunt Cora, I do believe we have Mr. Grant to thank for the invitation tonight. I fear I must dance with him."

"Perhaps," muttered her aunt. "But don't appear to enjoy his company."

"I fear I am not that practiced of an actress." Genie scanned the room for the impeccable form of Mr. Grant, but he was not to be found. She was disappointed, for it had been her expectation that Mr. Grant would be waiting to claim the first dance as he had done before.

Instead, Mr. Blakely caught her eye and walked toward her.

"Here comes Mr. Blakely. Be nice, do not ruin this for me, Genie," whispered her aunt.

Genie sighed. Her aunt could dampen even the most ardent of lovers.

"Good evening, Lady Bremerton, Miss Talbot." Mr. Blakely gave his bow. He was dressed in a nicely cut midnight blue coat, with the required light breeches. He gave her a warm smile, and although he was no Grant, he appeared perfectly amiable.

"May I have the honor of the first dance?" he asked, holding out a white gloved hand.

"Thank you, yes," smiled Genie.

They walked out onto the dance floor, where Genie discovered Mr. Blakely was a fine stepper, his feet light, never missing a step. He was almost as good a dancer as Mr. Grant. With the number of couples present and the intricacies of the dance, it was almost impossible to have conversation, but afterward, Mr. Blakely escorted her to have some lemonade.

"So what do you think of Almack's?" he asked.

"I am enjoying myself. I do love to dance."

"It is an enjoyment we share. I think perhaps we share many interests." He smiled at her, his brown eyes inviting.

"Is that so? What other interests do we share save dancing?"

"We enjoy history, seeing the London sights, good books, and the country, and I hope you will forgive me for saying it, but we both enjoy laughing."

"Ah, you are a cruel man to bring up my ruin. And here I am trying to show myself to best advantage. Besides, I have never known you to laugh."

"Yes, I suppose that is true. It is something I would like to learn. Something I need to learn." He looked away, the smile gone from his eyes.

"Is there something the matter?"

"After the death of my father, I have not had much laughter in my life. Perhaps you can help me find it." He took her hand and led her farther into the back of the room, along the wall, where they found a cushioned bench. She took a seat and he sat beside her, taking both of her hands in his.

Genie's heart raced and she felt the room grow uncomfortably hot. Is this what love felt like or fear?

"Forgive me for being forward, for I know we have not known each other long, but I feel I must take this opportunity to speak. I understand your aunt hopes to see a wedding for you soon, and I want to make my wishes known before another speaks ahead of me. Miss Talbot—Genie, I love the way you make me smile, I love the blue of your eyes, I simply love you. I think we would suit well together, since you are accustomed to country life and that is what I have to offer. Would you consider making me the happiest man on earth and consent to be my wife?"

Genie caught her breath. It was as nice a proposal as she could ever have hoped for. Aunt Cora would be so happy. Everyone's reputation would be saved. Here was the answer to all their prayers. She should be so happy.

"Thank you, Mr. Blakely. You have quite taken my breath away. May I consider your offer and give you a response later?"

"Of course, of course. I know we have not known each other long. I was under the strong impression from your aunt that a swift proposal would be greatly appreciated."

"Yes, thank you, I know my aunt would dearly love to see me join the matrimonial ranks."

He smiled and led her back to her aunt, who was conversing with Penelope. Without further conversation Blakely bowed and left. What was she supposed to feel? Did she feel it?

"Well? Tell me what did he say to you? What did you talk about? I saw him lead you off somewhere. Tell me there is reason to hope," demanded her aunt.

"Yes, Aunt, we must not give up hope." Genie did not tell her aunt about the proposal. To do so would mean an acceptance would be demanded immediately. If her aunt found she had turned down a proposal, she would be sent back to the country—on foot most likely.

"Genie," said Penelope. "Would you mind walking with me for some refreshment? It can get so hot in a crowded ballroom."

"Yes, of course," said Genie and followed Penelope to a table of weak lemonade.

"Did Blakely propose?" asked Penelope in her blunt manner.

"Yes."

"But you did not accept?"

"I said I would think on it."

"So what do you think?" Pen offered Genie a small tea sandwich.

"He is a fine dancer," reported Genie.

"That he is."

"He seems kind."

"Indeed."

"I do like the country."

"True."

"So I suppose I should accept?"

Penelope took a bite of her own sandwich. "It does not seem as if you hold much regard for him."

"He seems a nice man."

Penelope raised an eyebrow. "But can you see yourself in his bed?"

"Penelope!" Genie snapped open her fan and fluttered it before her. When had the room gotten so unbearably hot?

"One of the primary duties of a wife is to produce

heirs. There is only one way to do that, and it begins and ends in bed."

Genie waved her fan more furiously and tried to image herself with Mr. Blakely. Heavens, she didn't even know his first name. She could hardly make love to a man she called *Mr. Blakely*. Now, *William Grant* was a name she could cry out and—she snapped the fan shut.

"I cannot begin to think about that sort of thing in a crowded ballroom."

"Truly? I can think about it anywhere."

Genie gaped at her, but Pen waved off the comment.

"Let me tell you what more I've discovered of our Mr. Blakely," continued Penelope. "It has been difficult to get good information about the man, since he has never before been to London and I cannot find he has any intimates here. The story circulating about him is he inherited a fine country estate. I imagine he came to London in search of a pleasing wife. He also has a tendency to gamble and has been betting deep lately."

"So is he marrying me for the money?"

"I cannot say that. He may need to make an advantageous match and you need to marry soon. It does not mean that he is not genuinely interested in you or that you both will not grow in affection."

"I cannot like that he gambles."

"Nor should you. I can say, though, that most of London society gambles. If you exclude all who do, you may find yourself left with a very small pool of potential mates."

"I'm not sure I know what do to with this information."

"Think on it. Sleep on it. That is my best advice. I will say nothing of the proposal until you give me the word."

"Thank you. By the way, where do you get your information?"

"You will think less of me, but I eavesdrop on conversations. Also, never underestimate the servants. They know *everything*. The footmen are the best, often present for interesting conversations and easier to bribe than the butler."

Grant strolled into Almack's late and unsure. It was not like him to feel this way. It was not like him at all. The only thing on his mind was Eugenia Talbot. Miss Talbot. Genie. The girl whose presence he had come to desire more than he should. The girl whose simple kiss still clung to his lips. The girl who was interested in another man.

It was amusing in a way. Was it not he who broke hearts by enjoying the company of many ladies? Who was he to judge behavior that so clearly reflected his own? He had thought her an innocent, but her attention was not for him alone. No, her affections were shared with others, as her embrace with a man in the lending library so clearly showed.

He should see her, talk to her. Perhaps there was an explanation. He laughed at himself as he searched through the crowd. How many times had he felt this desperation in the eyes of a young miss who came to him, hoping for some other explanation than what was plainly obvious? Grant never lied, never made false promises, but that never stopped unrealistic hopes. Genie also had not lied to him. She made it clear they sought a husband for her.

Marriage. Grant reached for his flask to swallow down the bitter taste the word left in his mouth. He had sworn he would never fall prey. The last time he had decided to break this rule his heart had been ripped out, torn asunder, and left for the dogs to eat. He had made the mistake of falling for a Rose girl. He thought them naive, defenseless, but had underestimated the power of—

"Good evening, Mr. Grant." Miss Penelope Rose. She stood before him in crisp muslin, straight and formidable as any soldier. Napoleon's army was nothing to fear compared with this quiet lady of influence and control.

"Miss Rose," Grant nodded. He didn't have the strength to pretend a smile. She wanted to tell him something; she would not have spoken to him otherwise.

"I understand you are to thank for the vouchers to Almack's. I would like to thank you on Genie's behalf."

"She can do that herself."

"Naturally, I am certain she will. Her presence here will certainly help restore her credit amongst society, and I have hopes that soon we shall hear wedding bells."

"Do not toy with me, Miss Rose. Is Genie to be married?"

"I should hope so."

"Have you picked a bridegroom yet?"

Penelope paused. "Not as yet."

"I see."

"Do you? You are a very charming man, Mr. Grant. I do not like to bring up the past, but more than one young lady has had their head turned by you only to fall prey to disappointment."

"Yes, let's not dredge up the past." All these years, Miss Rose had been under the impression his offer to her sister had been less than honorable. The cruel irony was that he had intended marriage, but before the miscommunication could be resolved, Lord Stanton proposed and effectively left Grant in the cold. Grant allowed the misconception to hide his broken heart.

"No, let us not dwell on the hopes you have dashed."

"You know I never make false promises," said Grant.

"Which is why I am unclear why you have pursued Miss Talbot. She is an impressionable young girl and fond of you. But since you have declared yourself adverse to the institution of marriage, and she is in a position where marriage is a pressing need, I cannot see what purpose further friendship between you two could serve."

"You just cannot help but to meddle in affairs which are not yours," said Grant warmly.

"The affairs of my sisters and friends are my concern," said Pen with so much frost in her tone he almost shivered from the cold.

"Thank you, madam. You have made your position clear enough." Grant left her before he lost his composure, which he never did. He took another swig of whiskey to settle his nerves. Another thing he rarely did. It was becoming a night of firsts. Perhaps he could pass out drunk on the floor of Almack's and really make a spectacle of himself.

He was more than a bit drunk, of uncertain temper, and not fit for public viewing. A wise man would go home. Instead, he took another swig.

Twenty-five

It was getting late and Genie took another wide sweep of the ballroom, looking for a familiar figure. The more she pondered the proposal from Mr. Blakely, the more she wished to speak to Grant. Perhaps she could compare how she felt when she was with Blakely to when she was with Grant.

"Looking for someone?" asked a male voice behind her.

She swirled to find the immaculate figure of Mr. Grant. His ivy-colored coat and white breeches were so formfitting and well tailored they might have been painted on. For one horrible moment, Penelope's question invaded her consciousness and she did imagine herself in bed with Grant. He wrapped his arms around her waist and drew her closer, covering her lips with kisses and her body with his own, naked, glorious—

"Miss Talbot?"

"I do apologize, Mr. Grant," said Genie, flicking open her fan and waving it before her in a vain hope to bring herself back to the present. "I was thinking of something else and did not see you standing there."

"I am sorry to have sunk so far beneath your notice."

"No, no, not at all."

"Are you enjoying Almack's?"

"Yes, thank you so much for securing me a voucher. It is more than I thought possible."

"Have you made any new friends? I hear you are becoming quite the favorite."

Genie waved her fan before her. It was dreadfully hot in the ballroom. "I suppose." She did not wish to talk about Mr. Blakely right now.

"And did you meet your friend in Hookham's? Did you have a nice time with her?"

"Yes, quite, but who can think of books when in a ballroom?" She did not feel free to tell him about her brother either.

"Certainly not me," replied Grant with a smile that did not reach his eyes. She got the impression she had disappointed him. "You look lovely tonight. Those emeralds are divine with your gown. A gift from a new suitor perhaps?"

"No, they are from…" Genie paused, not wanting to say they were from her brother.

"While you decide whom they are from, perhaps you would care to dance?" asked Grant.

"Yes, I would very much." Genie smiled at Grant, but he seemed different, distant, removed somehow.

And so they danced. They spoke not a word, but as the music played, everything else seemed to drift away. Mr. Blakely was a fine dancer, but Mr. Grant was beyond that. He did not appear to be a man performing a series of steps, but rather one with the dance, flowing through the music. With him, she felt lightweight, giddy, and free. She was connected to the music and him and all was good.

Grant stood still in the middle of the ballroom holding out his hand. She glided to him to take it. She would follow him anywhere.

"Thank you, Miss Talbot, for a lovely dance." Mr. Grant bowed and was gone. The dance was at an end.

Genie wandered back to her aunt, stunned. Grant had not spoken to her. No conversation. No repartee. Nothing. The loss of his friendship hurt; it actually hurt. But what could be wrong? She must discover the reason.

Unfortunately, her immediate plans to press after him were arrested by Penelope and the dowager, who had several other young beaux for her to dance with. With her presence at Almack's, much of her social stigma had been lifted and young men felt free to make their interests known to the pretty, young miss.

It was over an hour later before she escaped the ballroom by whispering a need to visit the ladies' retiring room. On the way back to the ballroom, Genie found Grant alone in a corridor. She had been pondering the meaning of his silence, and now here he was, sitting on a bench with a flask in his hand.

He raised the flask as he saw her approach. "Your health," he said and went to take a drink, only to look disappointed. "All gone." He held the flask upside down. "Never fear. I'll find more whiskey to drink you with."

"No, thank you. I think you've had quite enough," said Genie with disapproval.

"You're right, of course. Why are you not with your admirers? Got yourself quite a pack of them."

There was something in Grant's tone she could not like. "My aunt has been introducing me to many people tonight."

"Capital. Capital. It is not often one finds such an enterprising young lady." Grant leaned closer and she could smell the whiskey on his breath. "Go for the one with the deepest pockets; that's always the best plan."

"Mr. Grant, I do believe you are feeling the ill effects of drink."

"If that's a fancy way of saying I'm drunk, then you're right."

"Mr. Grant, is something the matter tonight? You seem not yourself." Genie was actually concerned for him. This behavior was unusual.

"Not myself, no not myself at all," mumbled Grant.

"Whatever is wrong? Your family, are they well?"

"Yes, yes, everyone is quite well. Family. Is that what you want, Genie? A family? Damned nuisance most of the time. Always telling you what it is you ought to do."

Concern wavered. Perhaps nothing was wrong with Grant that a good night's sleep wouldn't fix.

"Now, I am going to tell you what to do," said Genie, taking charge. "You are going to go home this instant and sleep it off."

"What if I don't want to?" Grant set his jaw like a pouty boy. It was not his best look.

"I did not ask what you would like. Come now." Genie stood and offered a hand. Grant took it and pulled himself up, using a bit more force than she expected. She stumbled forward as he stood, ending up in his arms.

Neither said a word. Neither moved away. Grant leaned down closer, and in his eyes, she saw a glimpse of sorrow. She reached up and put a hand on his cheek. He closed his eyes and breathed deep. He bent down closer so that Genie thought he meant to kiss her, but instead he laid his head on her shoulder. Instinctively, she put her arms around him, as if to comfort him, though from what grief she did not know.

"Will you not tell me what is wrong?" asked Genie.

As if wakened from a trance, Grant stepped back, his eyes shuttered once more. "I see what you are about. Trying to seduce me at Almack's and compromise me to force a proposal."

"Mr. Grant. You are speaking nonsense!"

"Am I?" he said with confidence and swagger, only to have his shoulders sag the next moment. "I am, aren't I? Apologize. Never take up the bottle. Makes you stupid."

"It certainly does!"

"I need to go home," said Grant, stumbling off in the wrong direction.

"No, no, you are going the wrong way." Genie sighed and took his hand. "Here, let us find a back way out. You are not fit to be seen by anyone."

"Not fit, nit fot," slurred Grant.

"Try not speaking," suggested Genie. She wandered her way through the back passages, the places that only a servant would go. She found a servants' entrance and exited onto a side street. But here, Grant stopped her.

"No, no, I can find my carriage from here. Go back to the dance. Can't be seen leaving out the back door with Mr. Grant, that would never do."

"Still worried I am trying to compromise you?"

"I am a horse's arse, Miss Talbot."

"Will you not tell me what is wrong, Mr. Grant?"

"Lost a friend tonight." Grant looked up into the dark night. Pale stars were barely visible in the small ribbon of sky visible between the buildings.

"I am so sorry. Is it someone I know?"

Grant looked back at her and smiled even as the sadness returned to his eyes. "You will marry and never again speak to me."

"We can still be friends," said Genie, but she knew the instant she spoke, the words were not true. Her feelings for Grant stretched long past friendship. When she was married, she would need to distance herself, which would not be difficult if she married Blakely, since she would leave for the country. Her friendship with Mr. Grant would end.

Neither said anything, the realization of their loss becoming real. This could be the last time she would ever speak to him alone. Genie tried to think of what she wanted to say. She wished to tell him how she felt, but considering she was about to accept another man's proposal of marriage, the declaration seemed rather inappropriate.

"I will miss our conversations, Mr. Grant," said Genie, wishing she could say more.

"I will miss your kisses," said Grant.

And there it was. The truth she was afraid to say. She would miss them too. "Perhaps we should give each other one for good-bye?"

Grant raised an eyebrow. "That is supposed to be my line." He stepped closer, and Genie's heart raced.

He stood before her for a moment, then reached up to touch her arms, tracing down from her shoulders to the skin below her short, lace sleeves to the edge of her long, white gloves. He slowly pulled off her gloves, first one, then the other. Tingles shot from her fingers to her toes at being so undressed. He lifted each hand to his lips, kissing first the back, then the palm. Shivers of energy pulsed through her at his touch.

He slowly encircled his arms around her and she returned the favor, floating in his embrace. She breathed deep and snuggled into him. This is where she had wanted to be, wrapped in his arms.

Slowly, he bent down and pressed his cheek to hers, then kissed along her jaw until he finally reached her lips. His lips were soft and warm, and she parted her lips to him. He was wet and warm and tasted of whiskey. She relaxed into his kiss, pressing closer and getting a full response in return as he deepened the kiss. She closed her eyes and was weightless and dizzy. Her knees buckled, but he held her fast.

"Run away with me," breathed Grant into her ear.

"You cannot mean that," whispered Genie.

"But I do." Grant pulled back. "I don't want to lose you. Come away from all this stupidity of society busybodies, and be with me. Leave your critical aunt and the gossiping hordes, and simply be with me. We could live in the country together."

"What are you asking?"

"I could take care of you, protect you, and it could start tonight. You would have the best of everything. No lady would ever have been pampered the way I would lavish decadence upon you!"

Genie had an odd sensation of being both hot and cold at the same time. "You wish me to be your mistress."

"I wish you to stay my friend. Come home with me tonight. I don't care about the consequences."

"That is perhaps because those consequences are not as grave for you as they are for me." Genie stepped back toward the door, her heart beating painfully. She did not want to say good-bye and swallowed the disappointment that he had offered her everything except what she really needed—his name.

Grant closed his eyes, then opened them again, his eyes dark in the pale light. "If you loved me the way I love you, it would not matter."

Everything slowed to a stop. Not a sound could be heard, not a whisper of wind could be felt, nothing made a noise. She could not speak. She could not blink. She could not breathe. Had he said *love*?

A scullery maid opened the door with a bundle of trash in hand. She stopped short, surprised to see guests, bobbed a curtsy, and continued on.

"Get back to your aunt," said Grant as he swayed. "Do not listen to me. Drunk. Vile liquor. Bad for you I am." Grant wandered down the alley in the general direction of the line of coaches.

Genie stared after him, still too stunned to move. He loved her. Yes, he was drunk, but the emotions he shared were real, honest. She could not say how she knew, but she did. And yet, he had not offered marriage.

She took a large breath and wondered how long she had been holding it. The damp night air filled her lungs, restoring her perspective. She liked Grant.

Liked him quite a bit. Maybe even—but no. That line of thinking would do her no good. What she needed was a husband, and Grant, for all his charm, for all his self-declared love, offered her everything she wanted but nothing she needed.

Twenty-six

GENIE AWOKE WITH THE SAME FLUTTERY SENSATION IN her stomach with which she had gone to sleep the night before. A decision lay before her. A proposal. She needed to give an answer to Mr. Blakely. Could she marry him? Sleep in his bed? Give him children? The thought left her… flat.

Could she reject him? Her aunt would have a severe case of the vapors, probably toss Genie from the house, and she would return to her mother in shame.

What about Grant?

She tried to forget about him. His proposal was indecent. It was one she could not accept. And yet… the sensation of his lips on hers rushed through her with a hot flush. Could she see herself sleeping in his bed? Giving him children? The thought had her reaching for a fan. Yes, she could picture it; she could almost feel his hands running down her back and up her thighs.

Genie coughed and flung off the coverlet, standing up in the cold morning. She welcomed the cold shock of reality. She needed to get control of herself, get dressed, drink some stalwart English tea to steady herself, and then make a decision about Mr. Blakely. Mr. Grant could not enter into consideration. What would her mama say? It was too awful to contemplate.

An hour later, Genie was dressed and looking respectable, even if her meditations kept slipping into forbidden territory. She must stop thinking of Grant. Blakely would be a perfect antidote to being consumed with mad, passionate, lustful thoughts. The contemplation of him brought none of these strange sensations. He was as an Englishman should be. Predictable. Steady. Dull—that is dependable! She meant dependable, which is quite a nice compliment when you think about it.

Halfway through her eggs, one of the maids handed her a twist of a note. Since no one else had yet risen, she read it at the table.

In the garden. Come with all haste.

She knew his writing. She left the table immediately and went into the garden.

"George! Whatever are you doing in Lady Bremerton's garden? The staff will think me quite naughty going to meet you like this."

"I am sorry." Her brother stumbled forward into the pale morning light and she could see he was not well.

"Whatever has happened? You look a wreck!"

George sank down onto a stone bench and put his head in his hands. His cravat was loose, his clothes crumpled, and he smelled strongly of stale smoke and liquor. "I should never have come. I am ruined now."

Genie sat beside her brother, alarmed. "Tell me what has happened. Come now, sit up, there's a good lad. It cannot be as bad as all that. You need to rest. You look like you've been up all night."

"I do believe I have been awake for days, but what of it now? I've lost everything."

"Did you lose at gambling?"

George looked up, his eyes bloodshot and wild. "I did not know the amounts we were playing for. They were saying three and four, I thought it was hundred."

"You lost four hundred?" Genie gasped.

George laughed, a mirthless tone. "I lost four, then I wanted to make it up, but I lost another three. I had good hands, Genie, I had been winning and winning with much worse hands. I panicked. I knew I didn't have the money, so I played again, trying to win it back, but every hand I lost."

"How much did you lose, George?" A cold chill seeped through the stone bench into her bones. How could her brother get himself into such trouble?

George put his head down again and shook it.

"George, tell me the truth. How much did you lose?"

"Twelve," mumbled George in a small voice.

"Twelve hundred pounds? Oh George!" Genie put her hand to her chest.

But George shook his head. "That's when they told me they were not playing for hundreds. They were playing for thousands."

Genie stood up, gaping at him. "Twelve thousand pounds?"

George nodded miserably.

Genie sat back down hard on the cold bench.

Twelve thousand pounds.

"George, that is impossible! You could never raise that kind of money. Even Father could not raise that money."

"He must never know!" George grabbed her hand with his cold one.

"George, you are freezing out here. Come inside."

He shook his head, a more miserable boy she had never seen. "Aunt Cora would send off a post to mother straightaway. Genie, I am sorry, but I'm going to need to ask for those emeralds back."

"Yes, yes of course. I'll just be a trice."

Genie stepped lightly up to her room. She grabbed the box with the emeralds and paused to take one more look. Grant had complimented her on them. She did think they looked fine. She swallowed back regret and put the lid back on the box. It was time to be responsible and do what she needed to do to save her brother. Her decision was made. She would marry Mr. Blakely. What need could she have for sparkly ornaments?

Squaring her shoulders, she returned to the garden. She was a farm girl at heart, strong and hearty. She would meet this challenge directly and take care of her family. She would be respectably married and her fiancé would no doubt help to discharge her brother's debts. Mr. Blakely was a nice sort of man. This was the best choice. This was her only choice.

Her brother took the emeralds from her without looking her in the eye. His shoulders were stooped, giving her rise to an uncharacteristic flash of anger.

"Do you know what I think, George? I think these

men set a trap for you. They allowed you to win at first and then lured you into thinking you were playing for lower stakes, getting you to bet big. You should just explain to them that there was a misunderstanding."

George let out a choking laugh that sounded more like a rasp. "You do not understand. This is a debt of honor, one I must pay."

"There must be some way to have this debt forgiven."

George turned toward her, his eyes hollow. "No, Genie. It is a debt of honor." He stepped back and faded from view, in danger of being swallowed whole by the thick morning London fog. "If I cannot pay it…"

Cold shot through her and true panic rose in her throat. Her brother was in danger. She felt it from the hairs on the back of her neck to the tips of her frozen toes. "George, you must promise me you will not do anything rash. I will not have you jumping off a bridge because someone cheated you at cards. I will help you, I promise. Let us not give up hope."

"I must go see what I can get for these emeralds," said George in a dull voice.

"Promise me, George. Promise you will keep yourself safe. You cannot even contemplate hurting Mother like that."

The fading shape in the garden bowed his head, smaller and fainter. He was disappearing. "I promise, for now. I love you, Genie. You have always been a good sister to me."

"George! Promise you will meet me here tomorrow morning." Genie heard nothing from the dense fog. "George? One day, just give me one day."

"As you wish." The metal gate creaked and he was gone.

Genie sank back down on the cold stone bench. Twelve thousand pounds. It was a fortune. She had heard the stories of young men being routed in gambling hells and then, unable to pay the debt, "putting a period to their existence." She could not and would not let that happen to her brother.

"What am I do to?" she murmured to herself.

"Your brother is under the hatches deep," said a small voice.

"Jemmy?" asked Genie.

"Aye, milady." The small form of Jem stepped out of the mist.

"Should you not be at breakfast?"

Jem shrugged. "You need a gullgroper. Only one I know can tip that kind of blunt."

"Jem dear, I haven't a clue what you are talking about."

"A gullgroper whats lends money to gamesters."

"I see," said Genie quietly. She had no idea even an hour ago that she would be in need of this type of information.

"The Candyman can tip you the blunt you need."

"Candyman? Where would I find this person?"

"Chocolate Shoppe in Piccadilly." Jem recited the address and Genie stored it away for future reference if needed.

"Thank you, though I hope this information will not be needed. Go on back to your breakfast now. You shouldn't be out in all this damp air."

"Aye, milady." Jem shuffled back into the fog but turned and scampered back.

"Don't go there, milady," he whispered. "Don't go see the Candyman. He's a mean cove."

"Thank you, Jemmy. Go on back now." Genie listened until the footsteps disappeared in the direction of Grant's house.

Grant was next door to her. Was he sleeping now? Probably. Desire to run and tell him what happened and ask for help washed over her. But she should not, could not. Mr. Grant was a shining dream, but he was not her future.

Grant could not remember when he had acted more like a horse's arse. His behavior toward Genie, Miss Talbot to him from now on, had been incorrigible. His shocking words and actions revealed clearly he had drunk too much. The fact that he remembered every painful detail proved he had not drunk enough.

Had he really asked Miss Talbot, an innocent debutante living under the protection of the Earl of Bremerton, to be his mistress? He put his aching head in his hands and groaned. So she met a man in the lending library. So she encouraged that dull boy Blakely. None of it could excuse his own behavior.

He had always been careful to avoid any situation which would force him into marriage. He had avoided schemes, entrapments, plots, and intrigues, and yet here he was, tripping over his own stupid self. If any situation ever called for an immediate proposal of marriage, this was it. All those years of trying to avoid the matrimonial noose and here he had put his head in one of his one making.

He was going to do it. He was going to ask Eugenia Talbot to marry him.

Grant waited for the usual feeling of dread that generally accompanied the mere thought of wedding bells, but instead he felt lighter, happier, and, despite the obvious contradiction, freer.

Grant sat up and rang for his valet. It was 2:00 p.m., time for an early start for the day. Today's agenda was to get dressed, look sharp, and ask a girl to marry him. And not any girl. Genie. His Genie. He could mentally call her that now that he had decided to wed her proper. Genie who made him laugh. Genie his wife. Genie in his bed.

"Hurry man," Grant demanded to his valet. "I have important business today!"

So unusual was that declaration that the valet came to a full stop, as if ascertaining whether Mr. Grant was really his employer or had been replaced by a changeling overnight.

Once Grant had been dressed to his satisfaction, he went first to his mother's rooms. Rummaging through her jewelry boxes, he found what he was looking for. His mother had once shown him a collection of rings that had been in the family. Many were beautiful and could be used as an engagement ring. There was one kept in a small, wooden box hundreds of years old. It was a simple band of braided gold, silver, and steel, symbolizing the union between God, a man, and a woman. According to his mother, it was a love ring only to be given to one's true love.

Grant held the love ring for a moment, then returned it to the wooden box and chose a stunning emerald to match the earrings Genie wore. Maybe in time he would consider the love ring, for although he liked her, maybe even loved her, he felt the need to hold something back.

He paused for a moment, considering whether or not his mother and sisters would be pleased with his choice. He shook off the question. Genie was a living, breathing female; they would be ecstatic.

Grant arrived at Bremerton house looking like a man he would have laughed at only days before. He held a bouquet of flowers from his mother's garden, a ring was in his breast pocket, and his heart was on his sleeve. How had it come to this?

And yet, for all the ridiculousness of the situation, he did not want to be anywhere but here. He was going to ask her hand in marriage. He would do it right.

Grant was shown into the drawing room where, much to his disappointment, he was met by Lady Bremerton and her daughter.

"I am here to see Miss Talbot. Is she in?" he asked politely.

"She is resting. It has been a busy morning," said Lady Bremerton. She made no movement to call her down, and Grant sat nervously in a chair. His hands starting to sweat as he awkwardly held the flowers. He had envisioned how things would proceed when he asked for her hand. He had practiced his apology; it was a good one. Then he would tell her of his love and the things about her that he admired and all the reasons why his life would not be worth living without her.

Yet in every scenario he had imagined, Genie

was at least in the room. Lady Bremerton posed an obstacle he had not considered. His reputation had not concerned him before, but it was not helping him now. Or perhaps Genie had shared with her aunt his indecent proposal? That would certainly explain the looks of hostility directed his way from Lady Bremerton.

"It was quite an evening at Almack's last night. I hope you enjoyed the vouchers." Grant smiled. No harm in reminding her of his contribution. "Did you fare well at the tables?"

"I do not gamble, Mr. Grant." In other words, she lost.

"It was terribly flat last night. Perhaps I should return later when Miss Talbot is available."

"My niece will be quite busy today," said Lady Bremerton. "We need to start making wedding plans."

"Wedding plans?" Grant echoed.

"Yes, perhaps you have not yet heard. Mr. Blakely proposed to Genie last night. She has invited him over today so she can formally accept his proposal. We expect him any minute."

Grant's stomach recoiled as if he had been sucker punched. He had to force himself to take a slow breath. "How wonderful," he said, forcing his lips upward into what he hoped looked like a smile. "Please relay to her my best wishes for a long, happy life together. I understand now how much preparation you have before you to plan the wedding. I'll not keep you any longer."

Grant somehow managed to get his feet moving and walked out of the house with the false smile still plastered on his face and the flowers in his hand. It was the smile of a man who had just had his heart ripped from his chest. Grant walked around the block back to his house. He dropped the flowers in the gutter somewhere along the way.

There was only one thing to do. Grant reached for a bottle as soon as he walked in his study. He planned, quite simply, to crawl into a bottle and never come out. Last night, he had drunk enough to become stupid, but not enough to forget. He would not make that same mistake. With any luck, if he started drinking immediately, he would forget this whole day ever happened.

He grabbed a bottle and took a large swig. This way, when the servants found him crying, he could blame it on the drink. He wiped the tears from his eyes and lifted the bottle.

Twenty-seven

"I received your message, Miss Talbot," said Mr. Blakely, entering the drawing room.

"Come, Louisa," said Lady Bremerton, abandoning Genie to her fate. "There is something I would like to speak to you about upstairs."

When Lady Bremerton and Louisa had removed themselves, Mr. Blakely sat next to Genie on the couch.

"Thank you for coming, sir," said Genie. This was the right decision. It must be. What else could she do? Mr. Blakely was a nice man and their marriage would make everyone around them happy. "I would like to speak to you about accepting your proposal."

"You have made me the happiest of men," said Mr. Blakely with a bland smile.

"I am pleased, but I do need your help. My brother has gotten into a bit of trouble."

"I am certain whatever it is he will land on his feet. Here, I was hoping you would say yes. These are for you." Blakely handed her a familiar velvet box. Inside were emerald earrings. *Her* emerald earbobs. Genie stifled a gasp.

Genie held up the jewels to the light. "Where did you get these?"

Blakely shifted in his seat. "I bought them for you."

"Did you perhaps buy them from a Mr. Smythe?"

Blakely shifted again. "How—how did you know that?"

"Mr. Smythe is actually my brother. He gave me these earlier. I wore them to Almack's. Did you not notice?"

Blakely opened his mouth but said nothing. He clearly had not noticed.

Genie put her hand on Blakely's sleeve. It was time to present her case for her brother. "My brother decided to come to London on holiday and took an assumed name because he wanted to pursue some amusements without our father discovering him. I know it sounds very foolish and he ought not to have done it, but he is young still. Mr. Blakely, is it you that he owes a great sum of money to?"

Mr. Blakely swallowed convulsively and said nothing. On his forehead, tiny beads of perspiration began to form. He gave a barely perceivable nod.

"Well, this is fortuitous! You see, my brother misunderstood the amounts of money he was gambling for. It is very silly I know, but he does not have anywhere near the money to pay the debt. It is very fortunate then that we will be married and of course you will forgive the debt."

Mr. Blakely took the emeralds back and snapped the box shut. He stood and began to pace the room.

"Mr. Blakely?" asked Genie, a pit growing in her stomach.

"It is unfortunate indeed that your brother was so foolish," said Blakely, his voice cold. "But he is responsible for his debts."

"You would demand a debt from your own brother-in-law?"

"No, indeed I will not. But from your brother I certainly shall."

"Mr. Blakely!"

"It is a debt of honor! Your brother should never have gambled more than he had to lose. I am not responsible for him, you hear me?" His face was red and he was breathing fast.

"My brother is young and naive. Surely you would not persecute him because of it. Surely there is some compassion in your heart, if not for him, then for me?"

"I am sorry, Miss Talbot, but I fear that I will not be able to serve as a husband and spare you from the social ruin your family clearly deserves. Your dowry could not make up for the loss of the debt which I fully intend to collect from your brother. Please do not take this personally; it is simply a matter of finances."

"I think it is time for you to leave," said Genie, her fists balled at her sides. She was unaccustomed to anger, so the sudden urge to do this man physical damage came as a shock.

"I wish things had transpired differently, but I do expect to be paid."

He exited the room, leaving Genie fuming. Vile, wretched man! She followed him out to the entryway, where the butler appeared with his coat, walking stick, and top hat.

"Do allow me," said Genie sweetly, taking the hat and walking stick from the butler. With all the rage within her, she balled up her fist and punched out the top of the hat.

"What are you doing?" demanded Blakely.

"Showing you the full extent of my appreciation for your kindness to my family." Genie held out the stick with both hands and slammed it down on her thigh, breaking it in half.

"Are you mad?" shouted Blakely.

"Now get out, you vile snake." Genie threw the ruined hat and the pieces of his walking stick at his feet.

"Genie!" Lady Bremerton called down from the stairs above. "What are you doing?"

"I am forcibly removing this repulsive creature from your house, Aunt Cora."

"Genie! How could you? Mr. Blakely, there has been a misunderstanding, please don't go!"

But go he did, and none too soon for Genie, who felt she might become sick if she looked at his cold eyes any longer. Her aunt continued to rail on behind her, but Genie tried to shut her ears.

"Of all the foolish, headstrong, stupid girls, you certainly are the worst, Eugenia Talbot. How, how could you treat me this way? Why did you chase Mr. Blakely from this house like a harpy?"

"Mr. Blakely is a hideous man, Aunt. He was only interested in marriage to me for the money and when he thought he would not get enough for his trouble, he rescinded the offer."

"But what did you do wrong? You must have done something wrong!"

Genie walked in a daze back to the parlor and sunk into a chair exhausted. She bit her lip trying to hold back the tears. What on earth was she going to do now?

"Answer me when I am talking to you! How

could you have ruined this for me?!" demanded Lady Bremerton.

"Stop, Mother!" interrupted Louisa.

Everyone looked at her. Had she actually spoken?

"Can you not see that Genie is terribly upset?" continued Louisa. "If she says he has done something horrid, then he must be a cruel man unworthy of our notice. She needs the full support of her family right now, and I for one am going to give it!"

Lady Bremerton gaped at her daughter. Genie dried her tears. It was more words strung together then she had ever heard Louisa utter.

"Come, Cousin," said Louisa, taking charge of the situation for once. "Let us get you up to your room for a quiet rest. Mother, I suggest you start a rumor that we found Mr. Blakely unworthy of Genie and we will no longer be admitting him into our presence."

"Yes," said her mother sliding into a chair. "Yes, of course you are right."

Genie walked upstairs, emboldened by a new ally at her side.

Louisa followed Genie into her bedroom and shut the door.

"Are you all right?" asked Genie.

"No, not quite. I have never spoken like that to my mother." Louisa put her hand to her forehead in an unconscious mirror of her imposing matriarch. "But I should be asking you if you are all right. What happened?"

Genie collapsed on her bed. "I have been entirely deceived by the character of Mr. Blakely."

"I thought him amiable."

"Me too, but he... Louisa please do not let this be widely known, but my brother has done something very stupid. He left Oxford for a lark, got taken advantage of at a gaming establishment, and now owes Mr. Blakely a vast sum of money. I thought Mr. Blakely would forgive the debt, but he rescinded his offer of marriage and is demanding to be paid."

"That is horrible! But perhaps I can help. How much does your brother owe?"

"Twelve thousand pounds."

Louisa said nothing for a painful minute.

"I am so sorry," said Louisa, "I could not even begin to raise that kind of money. You will need to go to my father."

Genie put her own hand on her forehead. It did seem to help when the moment called for dramatic despair. "Would he be inclined to help? I was not sure he had ever forgiven my mother for breaking their engagement."

"He does not speak of it," said Louisa. "But my mother has spoken of it to me much. I was always admonished never to do as Lady Mary had done. She has told me many times she married Lord Bremerton so her children could enjoy a high station in society. But I do not care for society life. I hate to be a disappointment, but I have not the temperament for it."

"Are you going to marry the Duke of Marchford?"

"I cannot." Louisa shook her head firmly.

"How are you going to tell your parents?"

Louisa sighed. "If I knew how, I would have done it already."

"Have you tried talking to the duke?"

"I tried at Almack's, but he talked at length about his determination to be a good husband. I did not know how to tell him that—"

"You are in love with somebody else?" asked Genie gently.

Louisa stilled, suspicion in her eyes. "How did you know?"

"I heard you and a man in the garden at Lord and Lady Devine's party. I confess, ever since, I have been trying to help bring you and Marchford to more friendly terms."

Louisa nodded slowly, as if processing the information. "I understand. It would be easier if I could love the current duke, but I do not. One cannot always chose whom she loves."

Genie was quiet for a moment. "Very true."

"Perhaps if it would help, I could support you when you ask Father to help pay off your brother's debts."

Genie cringed. "I should hate to do it at all, but I suppose alone would be worse. I could support you talking to him about your engagement."

"It is a plan," said Louisa with a tentative smile.

"Twelve thousand pounds?" Lord Bremerton's face grew so red Genie feared for his health. "You want me to pull your idiot brother out of debt to the tune of *twelve thousand pounds*?"

"Young people do make unwise choices. We should not fault them for it," said Louisa in a small voice.

"Yes, they do, my dear," said Lord Bremerton.

"And I can only assume asking me to dissolve the engagement to the Duke of Marchford must be one of those unwise choices. You will marry the duke as planned. And Eugenia, your brother's financial embarrassments are not my concern. Good day!"

The ladies walked from Lord Bremerton's study with shared low spirits.

"Thank you for trying," sighed Genie.

"And thank you as well," said Louisa in a soft voice. "Genie, your mother eloped with your father. Is she happy?"

"Yes, quite happy I believe."

"That is all I needed to know." Louisa gave her a warm embrace. "I am glad I got to know you."

"And I, you." A question hung on Genie's lips, unasked. She already knew the answer.

"Did you give the Talbot chit the information about the moneylender?" asked the Candyman.

"Aye, sir," said Jem.

"I do wish we'd been able to collect her dowry before walking away, but those damn emeralds tipped our hand. No matter, I shall more than make up for that disappointment. Follow her wherever she goes. Make sure she gets here."

"Maybe she'll go somewheres else?" Jem had to jump fast to avoid the Candyman's backhand.

"Just see that she gets here. I'll know what to do with her when she arrives."

Twenty-eight

NONE OF THE OPTIONS BEFORE GENIE WERE ACCEPTable. The only thing that mattered now was saving her brother. If her family could not or would not help her, it was going to be up to her. A moneylender was an unpleasant idea, particularly since she had no way to pay the money back. But if she left her brother to face his own fate, she would lose him.

She could go to this moneylender and at least discover his terms. Perhaps there might be some way? Genie could not think of any but felt it was worth attempting. She would hate to think of her brother being lost if there was anything she could have done to prevent it.

Genie told her aunt she needed to rest, an idea that met with stony approval. After a few minutes, Genie slipped out the back way and asked Sammy the groom if he would call her a hack. He insisted he take her in the town coach, and she graciously accepted. When she arrived at the address in Piccadilly, she paused at the storefront. It was not what she expected.

"Got yourself a sweet tooth, Miss Talbot?" asked the groom with a smile.

"I suppose I do." Genie mentally reviewed the address given her by the urchin. She thought this was what he said.

The storefront was little more than a door squished between two other shops. The door was painted dark brown with the words *Chocolate Shoppe* painted in gold above it. When Jem had said the money-lender was called the Candyman, she thought this was another one of his odd street euphemisms she could not understand. She had not expected an actual chocolate shop.

"I just have a few purchases to make. I won't be but a trice!" Genie kept her tone lighter than she felt.

Genie marched to the door and opened it before she could lose what little courage she had left. The shop was dark, with two small, round tables and chairs but no customers. The walls were lined with dark wooden shelves. On one side were boxes of cocoa to make hot chocolate. On the other were candy sweets displayed on platters. There were sweetmeats, bonbons, toffee, humbugs, fondant sculpted into animals, and boxes of marzipan. It was every child's dream, yet it was eerily quiet in the store.

"Good afternoon, miss," said a young boy at the counter who could not have been more than ten years old. He wore a dirty apron over his thin frame.

"Good afternoon," said Genie, walking toward him. "I am looking for the Candyman."

"You be Miss Talbot?"

"Yes," said Genie, startled the child knew her name.

"Come this way, miss. The Candyman has been expecting you."

A chill ran down her spine, but she would not allow herself to be easily cowed.

The lad led her to a side door concealed in the paneling. It opened to a dim room, even darker than the store.

"Come in," said a man with a low, gravelly voice. He was sitting at a table, almost entirely in the dark. Resembling an undertaker in appearance, he wore all black with a hat pulled low, concealing his face.

"Did a young boy tell you I was coming?" asked Genie.

"Indeed he did. Helpful lad, Jem," said the man in an oddly low tone, almost as if he was concealing his true voice.

"Then can I surmise that he informed you why I am here?"

"Yes, yes. You are to be commended to take such care of your brother. Come, sit. I am sure we can come to some sort of arrangement."

Genie did not like the way he said that word. She did not like this man at all and ventured no further into the room. "Please state your terms, Mr…"

"Candyman is what you may call me, missy. I see you are one to get down to business. No chitchat for you today, eh, missy?" His tone was not as friendly as his words and she could not like the way he rubbed his hands together.

Genie said nothing and waited. He wanted her here for a reason, and she was certain he would get to it sooner without her help.

"Yes, well, terms. It is a grievous amount of blunt your brother lost. Grievous indeed."

"Twelve thousand pounds. What are you terms?"

"Well, now, if I be giving you such a large sum of money, what's to say you will be able to pay me back? Tell me, Miss Talbot, how you intend to repay me?"

"I have some pin money I receive every week—"

"Miss Talbot! Pin money? We are speaking of twelve thousand pounds, my dear. Not even the pin money for the royal princess would be enough to repay that amount."

"So you will not lend me the money?"

"Now, now, let's not get too hasty. I see you are upset. Poor dear. Now, let me see if I can be of help. Maybe instead of money, you can pay me in service."

Genie stiffened. There was a limit to what she would do for her brother. "I am a respectable lady."

"You haven't even heard my proposal. And my but you do make some interesting assumptions. I'm not talking of that sort of arrangement, though I will say you could make a pretty penny on your back. But women, they always have it easy, just lie back and do nothing for their supper, but don't they complain about it, like you actually asked them to work."

Genie took a step backward at that pretty speech. She should not have come.

"What I want from you is a piece of paper. That's all," said the Candyman, his voice dropping even lower.

"A piece of paper?" Genie wished she could see this man, but he kept to the shadow, the hat brim concealing his features.

"See now, not so bad, not so bad. One letter is all I ask for twelve thousand pounds. You won't get better odds. You bring me the letter, and I'll pay your debt."

"Why? What letter?"

"You needn't be so nosy. You bring me the letter; I pay the debt. Do we have a deal?"

"What letter?" Genie repeated.

"In the study of the Duke of Marchford is a safe behind a picture frame. Inside the safe is a letter with a red seal. Bring it to me and all your problems are answered."

"I could not steal from the duke." She could not, could she?

"Such a little thing to ask for the life of your brother," said the Candyman in a soft low voice.

"My brother's life?"

"He will be ruined if he cannot pay a debt of honor. Only one thing left to do but to take a swim in the Thames."

"No!"

"Well now, missy, what did you expect? Only honorable thing to do if you have no hope to pay your debts, and so I told him."

"Am I to understand that you recommended my brother take his own life?" Genie swallowed hard on the lump lodged in her throat. Her stomach tightened into granite.

"Didn't recommend anything. Just saying, in certain circumstances, it is the only respectable thing to do. He asked for a loan but there was nothing *he* could do for me. Not like you. There is a way *you* can pay the debt."

"He is an impressionable young man, you have no business recommending suicide."

"There now, don't take a pet. It will all be right as rain when you bring me the letter."

"I will do no such thing."

"Remember now, it has a red seal. When you get it, bring it to the Thorn and Thistle on Salt Street."

"Not here?"

"Not here."

"When should I meet you?"

"Go to the Thorn and Thistle and say you are looking for the Candyman. They'll find me. Mind you, do not give it to anyone else. And come alone. Don't bring your driver next time."

"I cannot possibly go to a public house unchaperoned in London."

"Don't you worry. You won't be alone for long." His tone made her wish she were a lad, so she could knock him senseless. Genie blinked at the sudden violent turn her thoughts had taken. It was the second time in one day that she had wished to do harm to another person.

"I simply cannot steal and go to a public house. I cannot." Yet even as she said it, she doubted herself. What if this was the only way?

"It's your choice, of course. This key will open the safe."

Genie stared at the key he held out to her for a long moment. The man's hand was thrust out into the light from the doorway, revealing ugly red scars. She was loathe to touch anything those hands had come into contact with until she realized the scars were severe burns, not a contagion.

"'Tis your brother, deary," said the Candyman. "Only you can know what his life is worth."

Genie took the key.

"That's a good girl."

But Genie left the strange shop feeling anything but good.

Twenty-nine

DINNER HAD NOT GONE WELL. LADY BREMERTON refused to talk, Louisa never spoke as a rule, and Genie had nothing to say. The absence of female chatter created a vacuum, which her uncle surprised the company by being willing to fill. Despite the unpleasantness of the afternoon caused by a minor revolt led by the two young ladies, Lord Bremerton was in fine fettle for having taken command of his ship.

He spoke first of the weather, then of the war, and then, as if the pump had been primed, of his friend Robby, who had been a general in a war before Genie had been born. Lord Bremerton told anyone who would listen, which at the silent table was everyone, that Robby was planning on visiting London and had promised to come to the engagement ball for Louisa.

Genie kept her eyes on her meal and ignored her uncle's speech. She had less than twelve hours to find a solution for her brother. His mood had been despondent this morning. If he came back tomorrow morning and Genie could not provide him with good news, he might give up hope entirely. She needed to do something.

She considered her visit to the chocolate shop. He wanted her to steal for him, to steal sensitive documents. She may be naive, but she was not so stupid as to think stealing documents from the duke's study would be a good plan. No, that option was definitely out.

There must be another way. Genie considered the problem, turning it around in her mind, searching for answers and solutions. She retired early to her room as did the other ladies; no one seemed in the mood to hear another war story featuring her suddenly loquacious uncle and Robby.

Out her bedroom window, through the bushy branches of spring, a light was on in the Grant household. Grant. He had made an offer too. His offer was not one she would usually contemplate. It would break her mother's heart if she became a… a… she was not even sure of the right word.

Yet her mother's heart would break even more if she learned her baby boy drowned himself in the Thames over a gambling debt. Genie would be ruined—unfit for London society, unfit for country society. But this was hardly news since she had doomed herself from the beginning with her disastrous debut. She had hoped with her presence at Almack's her reputation could be restored, but now that she had so abused Mr. Blakely, she could not hope for another offer anytime soon.

Did Mr. Grant not say he would spoil her? Lavish gifts upon her? Her first request would be to discharge her brother's gambling debts. Unlike Mr. Blakely, in whose character she had been so mistaken, she knew in her heart Grant would be generous. He would protect her brother.

She would do it. Tomorrow, she would write Mr. Grant and tell him she had decided to accept his proposal. Except tomorrow, tomorrow would be too late. Her brother would return early, and she must have good news for him or goodness knows what he would do.

The light in the far window beckoned her. Grant was there. He was awake. Could she go now? She shook her head. She couldn't go traipsing through the gardens to a man's house wearing nothing but a night rail. What kind of a hoyden was she? It was not proper!

Genie laughed at herself. Of course it was not proper. That was the whole point of what she was going to do. She was going to get improper—sinfully, wretchedly, utterly improper.

Genie put on a pair of slippers and chose a gauzy wrap that was more seduction than protection. Time to be seduced, and she couldn't wait to start. She tiptoed down the hall and descended the stairs to the garden entrance. Her skin was alive, tingling.

At the door she stopped. Was she truly going to do this? Leave her life? Leave her family? Go to Grant? No, no she could not. She was a good girl. Her mother would be heartbroken. Genie would be lost to her entire family.

And yet, there were only two ways to discharge a debt of honor. Pay the debt or die. Since twelve thousand pounds was more than George could possibly pay, that left only one option.

She wrapped her gauzy wrap around her tightly

and opened the door. If by going to Grant she could save her brother's life, she would do it. It was highly improper, but her heart sang with the prospect of being with Grant. She would find happiness with him, of that she felt sure. It may not be what she pictured for herself, but it was better than becoming a spinster, knowing she had the power to save her brother's life and did nothing to protect him.

Genie plunged herself into the cold, the gauzy wrap being of no practical use against the damp chill of night. Her dainty slippers too would be no match for traipsing through the garden. She returned to the house for her coat and a pair of pattens. She may be a wanton hussy, but she was a sensible, practical, farm girl type of wanton hussy.

She slipped through her garden easily enough, but at the back where the two gardens joined, it was dark and somewhat foreboding. Telling herself not to be timid, she plunged ahead, ignoring the squeaky gate that sent shivers down her spine, picked up her skirts, and ran to Grant's house. She wouldn't turn back now and go back through the spooky garden for anything. She tried the back door and breathed a sigh of relief to find it unlocked.

She slipped in the door and paused. What now? Tiptoe through his house like a common thief? What if his servants saw her? She had imagined clandestine romances in the past, what self-respecting teenager had not? But the reality was more mundane and less romantic than anything she expected.

Genie looked back from where she came. Dark, foreboding garden or dark, foreboding house? Tough choice. Genie removed her pattens. It wouldn't do any good to go tromping through the house. She headed toward the parlor and stopped. She had no candle. It was dark. Very dark.

She had read more gothic novels than her mother would say was healthy, but none of these stories had fully prepared her for her own adventure. How was she going to get upstairs to meet her lover?

Lover?

A mental image of her shocked parents' faces floated before her. Genie turned around. She had not the stomach for it. Better a spooky garden than her mother's look of disappointment and shame.

"Come now, don't you run away from me!"

Genie jumped at the male voice and the light that followed. Afraid to move, Genie swallowed hard and turned slowly in the hall toward the light.

Mr. Grant walked, or rather stumbled, down the hall, swinging a lantern. "Here, my pretty. I need you, pretty precious."

Genie's mouth dropped. Grant was half dressed, without a coat or cravat, and his shirt unbuttoned at the collar. Grant took another two swaying steps and she realized two important things. First, he was hideously drunk. Second, he was not talking to her. Indeed, it did not appear that he even noticed her presence standing in the shadows of the corridor.

He ambled into a room and she heard a crash and a curse. She stepped closer to see what he had done, but he came back out, a bottle in his hand.

"There's my sweet girl," said Grant gazing with affection at the bottle in his hand.

"Grant?"

Grant stopped and stared at her, as if not quite comprehending who she was. He looked down at the bottle then back up at her. "I've done drunk myself mad." He pulled out the stopper of the whiskey bottle with his teeth and spat it on the ground, taking a hearty swig from the bottle. "And I hopes I never recovers."

"Hello," said Genie, helpless to know what to say. The urge to run back home had never been so great. What on earth was she thinking? This is why all those morality plays had grim outcomes for young girls who did not protect their virtue.

"Where's my manners. Care for a drink?" Grant held out the bottle, even as he swayed.

"No, thank you, sir." It was ridiculous to put on her pretty manners at a time like this. She had entered a man's house in the dead of night to find him drunk as sin and now she was refusing hard drink as if she was standing in her mother's parlor.

"I should go." Genie turned to leave.

"Don't go." Grant's voice was so bereft she turned back. "Please, I don't mind madness. Don't leave me, I pray." Grant's voice cracked, and Genie rushed to him.

"No, no of course I won't." She put an arm around him to keep him upright, for she feared he would topple over. "Let us get you to bed."

"Yeeeeesssss. Bed, bed, bed."

She walked beside him, her arm around his waist, his arm leaning heavily on her shoulders. He made a fair bit of thumping and thudding and babbling as they made their way up the steps and though Genie's heart was pounding from the exertion and the fear that a member of his staff would find them, no one came forward. She guessed the loud ramblings of Mr. Grant were not so unusual as to rouse the house.

She let him lead her up two flights of stairs, hoping he knew where he was going and would not take her to the housekeeper's room instead. He led her through a tall door to a tastefully appointed bedroom. He set the lantern down and offered to take her coat. She shrugged it off before thinking better of it. Drunk or not, Grant's eyes roamed over her person. A wicked smile indicated he was pleased with what he saw.

She should go. She should… he stepped closer and her mind went blank. He may be vilely drunk, but he was still just as handsome, and she would wager any woman would pause if Grant looked at her in quite the same manner. There was a glint in his eye, an odd mixture of wickedness and true warmth.

"You are beautiful." It was not the words he spoke, but the way he spoke them that made her catch her breath. The words were whispered reverently, with eyes closed.

"You are not even looking at me."

"Don't need to see you to know you're beautiful."

All her life Genie had been told she was beautiful, so much so that she had taken this as a plain fact. Beautiful. This moment was the first time she ever truly felt it.

"Mr. Grant, is your, err… offer still available?"

Grant cocked his head to one side, clearly not understanding the question.

"I mean do you still want me to…" Genie stumbled

over the words. She could not say the word *mistress* could she? "You spoke of spoiling me, of caring for me, if I would run away with you. Is that offer still something you wish?"

"My only wish is to be with you." Suddenly Grant did not look drunk any more. He stopped swaying and looked her directly in the eye as sober as a banker.

"Mr. Grant, I know it is highly improper to be here."

Grant shook his head. "Very proper. Good of you."

She ignored this. "I need you to understand that my brother has unfortunately been led astray and has accrued gambling debts that are extreme."

Grant shrugged and stumbled backward, landing heavily on the richly appointed bed. Genie swallowed hard on a dry throat. He was sitting on the bed. The bed!

"As—as I said. My brother's gambling debts. He ran away from school when they had a break and came to London for the first time. He pretended to be a Mr. Smythe and has been terribly taken advantage of. I fear he might do something rash if I don't find a way to raise the money."

Grant waved a hand. "All boys gamble, get in debt. Get out of it too. Don't worry yourself."

"He owes twelve thousand pounds."

Grant squinted at her as if trying to make her come into focus. "What's that now? Lot of blunt t'be sure."

"I know. I know it is. I don't know what else to do. You were the only one I could think of who may be able to help."

Genie hoped this statement would encourage Grant to do something gallant, but the blank look on Grant's face told her she was going to need to make it clear what she was asking.

"Will you help us, Mr. Grant? Will you pay his debts?" Genie boldly stepped forward until she was directly in front of him. She put her hand on his shoulder. "I would be most grateful."

His mouth opened slightly, his eyes wide. "Do whatever you want. 'Course I will."

"Will you?"

"Give you anything." Grant gently took her hand in his and studied it like a fragile object.

A flood of relief rushed through Genie. She had done it. Her brother was safe. Grant pressed her hand to his lips and another rush of something hot and powerful coursed through her. He placed his hands on her hips and drew her closer until she was standing between his knees. Her heart pounded in her chest as he wrapped his arms around her and laid his head on her chest. Her knees went weak, and she had to put her hands on his shoulders to keep from sliding to the floor. Gone were any thoughts of tomorrow; gone were any thoughts at all.

"Will you leave me now?" he mumbled into her bosom.

"No," she whispered. She might never walk again, considering her bones were now the consistency of apple jelly.

"You are madness. Rum touch madness." He grazed his lips across her exposed flesh above the top of her night rail, leaving a searing trail of heat in his wake. With a soft finger, he traced the line where his mouth had been and then slowly explored under the gown. She caught her breath when his fingers brushed over her peaking interest. Instead of pulling away, she leaned into him.

His hands circled, cupped, teased, until her breath came fast and her legs gave way. He helped her sit down on one strong thigh even as his free hand undid the ties of her night rail, exposing her breasts. She gasped at the sensation of his mouth on her breast, his tongue circling, his soft lips caressing. He suckled her until she whimpered, giving herself wholly to the experience.

He shifted around, placing her easily on the bed, and raked her up and down. Instead of wanting to cover herself, she leaned into his gaze, giving herself to him, for in his eyes she saw nothing but pure desire and awe.

"Take off your gown," he rasped. "But leave that wrap on."

It was an impossible request, but she was more than willing to comply. She removed the wrap for a moment, tossed the sensible flannel night rail aside, and slid back into her gauzy wrap that hardly hid what it should. In fact, it was more of a tease than anything, and when she met his eye again, she knew it was having a powerful effect.

He fumbled with his shirt buttons until she laughed. "Here, let me help." She began to undo the buttons of his shirt. Instead of helping, his hands went to her, smoothing down her arms to her shoulders, where he massaged away the tension she had carried with her.

When she had relieved him of his shirt, she smoothed her hands over his toned chest. He looked good in his clothes; he looked better without them. Unlike some men who used clothing to hide flaws, his clothing only hid perfection. His muscular chest and rippling abdominal muscles made her want to kiss him. So she did.

She ran her lips across his chest as he had done to her, earning her a sharp intake of breath. She trailed kisses down until she came to his trousers. With shaky fingers, she untied his trousers, fumbling with the closures which were unfamiliar to her. With a grunt of impatience, he helped her remove the last of his clothing until he was standing before her naked, giving her his full attention.

She stared at his male member, having never seen one before. She touched and he groaned. She ran her hand down his length and he trembled.

The candle in the lantern gutted, plunging them into total darkness. She welcomed it. He gently pushed her back and she moved up to the top of the comforter and snuggled down underneath, with him next to her. He opened her wrapper like she was a precious gift and ran his hand from her breast down to her thighs.

Wanton that she was, she embraced him in return. He started soft and slow until he touched her in a place that made her gasp. He moved against her, with her, until something building inside her was bubbling up to the surface. She pressed herself closer, running her hands down his back. He slowed and nuzzling closer, he kissed her. His kiss was long and deep and opened the door to a world she had only before visited in her dreams. He was everything she ever wanted and she was flushed with arousal and pounding love and a sudden flash of pain in the realization that he must have found her wanting, for he would give her all of himself, except his name.

He kissed his way slowly down her throat until he lavished his attentions onto her breasts. She arched her back, giving herself over to him. She may not have won his heart, but he had a kiss that could make a girl forget. He covered her like a warm blanket, propping himself with an elbow so as not to squish her, but never ceasing his sweet caress. He moved faster and faster until she writhed beneath him, panting, crying out in spite of herself. Something within her was building stronger and stronger until she was certain it would consume her, and she rushed headlong into it.

Waves of sensation crashed over her, flooding her with indescribable pleasure. He plunged himself inside her at that moment, mixing pleasure with a sliver of pain even as it brought a new wave of pleasure rippling through her. He moved within her and cried out.

Collapsing beside her, he was instantly asleep. She took several deep breaths, the aftershocks of pleasure and pain still rippling through her. She closed her eyes and sunk down into the soft mattress. She sighed and fell into a dreamless sleep.

Thirty

GRANT WOKE IN A GROGGY STUPOR, UNWILLING TO BE wrenched from the blank unconsciousness only whiskey, with a mixture of whatever other hard spirits he had in the house, can produce. His need overtook his reticence and he forced himself to sit upright, grabbing for the chamber pot. He heaved the roiling contents of his stomach until he feared he may have tossed an organ of some importance. His body shook involuntarily with a sudden clammy chill.

"Are you all right?" asked a woman's voice from behind him on the bed.

Grant closed his eyes and shuddered again. Had he brought a doxy back home with him? He could not remember it. Then again, he could not remember anything about the night before. He must have been truly far gone to bring back a lightskirt to his mother's house. Some things one does not do, and this was one of them.

It was still dark outside, which gave him hope. Best to get the girl out of the house before the staff awoke to tell his mother of his exploits. He would like to think they would protect his secret, but he knew better.

"Are you well?" asked the woman again.

He supposed he would have to escort her back to wherever she belonged. His head pounded, and he would have much preferred going back to the dreamless sleep alcohol provided.

"We should get you back home," said Grant, standing up to find water. His throat burned. He could not remember eating sand, but he sure felt it in his mouth.

"Home?" The female voice raised an octave. "But I thought I would stay here."

Stay here? Was the woman mad? He really needed to stay home when he drank too much. Odd though, he thought he had intended to do just that.

"No, we need to get you—" Grant turned around. Miss Talbot sat on his bed. No, not on his bed, *in* his bed. The covers were pulled over her chest, her naked shoulders clear evidence of…

The room slanted and Grant stumbled to his knees. Miss Talbot was in his bed. Genie Talbot was in his bed. How could this be? Was he mad?

Genie pulled a blanket around herself and rushed to his side. "Grant, whatever is wrong?"

"How, how is it that you are here?" he croaked.

"Do you not remember?" Genie blushed.

Blushed! That was not a good sign. His brain spun. He must remember, he must. But no, there was nothing, just a big hole where Genie Talbot was supposed to be.

"I do not know how… I must be mad." Grant ran

his hand through his hair and rubbed his eyes. "Mother said drink would land me in Bedlam someday. Guess the old gal was right."

Genie laughed, a merry sound. "You are not mad. I came to you last night. Do you truly remember nothing?"

Grant shook his head. He remembered nothing. That was the point of drinking until he could no longer find his mouth with the bottle, but he had never regretted it so wholly as he did now. The time for self-recriminations would come soon enough; now, he needed to act fast. If the scullery maid were to come and find her naked in his room, he would be forced to put a bullet through his own head and save Genie's family the trouble.

"We must get you home."

The light in her eyes died, as if he had smothered it. She clutched the blanket around her with both hands. "I would rather stay with you. I thought we had an"—she paused and took a slow breath—"an arrangement."

"No, no, we cannot." Grant stood and offered her a hand off the floor. She rose as dignified as one could without his assistance.

"I see," she said, but she stared out into nothing, her eyes dull.

He hated himself. Utterly. "I am so sorry. I must see you home before anyone can find you here."

That seemed to rouse her. "Yes, yes of course."

"I will remove myself to allow you to dress." He fled into his dressing room, giving her the privacy he was certain she needed. He could not imagine what turn of events had led her here, but now he was in a pulsing panic to try to make it right and protect her reputation by putting her back where she belonged. Maybe no one would know. Maybe no one would find out.

He dressed fast, without a care to style. Nothing mattered now but getting Genie back. He knocked on the bedroom door and opened it slowly to find Genie standing in the middle of the room dwarfed by a large coat. She was small and delicate, and silently crying.

He was a wretched man. Wretched. He must work fast and get her back. No one could see her like this. No one could find her. He had ruined her, but at least he was going to protect her from others knowing that truth.

He started toward the door, then with great forethought, particularly remarkable since he could still feel the effects of drink, he went quickly to the bed and pushed some pillows under the blankets to make it appear as if he was sleeping.

"Come," he whispered. "Quietly now." He opened the door to the hall and crept out, Genie following behind.

He walked as quietly as he could down the corridor. He did not take a light; he did not want to be seen by any of the staff. When did the scullery maids get up to light the fires? He did not know. They were always lit when he woke. He never thought about when it occurred.

Something banged behind him and he whirled around. "Genie?" he whispered.

"Found a wall," she whispered back.

Poor thing. She had not been walking these halls since she was on leading strings, how did he expect her to know her way in the dark? He felt back for her and grabbed her hand, soft and warm. Very soft. Very warm. He pushed the thought away.

They needed to get her out of the house. He felt for the banister. "Stairs," he whispered back to her. Softly they crept down the stairs and turned toward the entrance to the garden. They were almost to the door when a light glowed in the corridor from an approaching scullery maid.

Grant grabbed Genie and whisked her into the open door of his study, flattening her against the wall in the dark so as not to be seen. She was warm, and despite everything, his body responded to hers immediately. He wanted to take her back upstairs and keep her forever. He was disgusted with himself. He wanted to kiss her right now. What was wrong with him?

The light grew brighter and he sank deeper into the shadow. The scullery maid came into view carrying a pail in one hand and a candle in the other. He held his breath. If they were caught now, there was nothing he could say to explain it, and the rumor would spread across London before the morning papers arrived on his stoop.

He pressed against Genie, back into the shadows, so close he could feel her heart race, fast and angry. He had hurt her. It was not a thing that could be forgiven. He only hoped he would be given a chance to make it right. He wanted to talk to her, to apologize, but this was not the time.

The light dimmed as the maid went up the stairs. Did she really get up this early to light the fire in his grate? Remarkable.

He took up Genie's hand again and made their way into his garden and then through the rusty gate into the Bremerton garden. Close to the door of the house, he stopped. He should not go in, that much he knew.

"Mr. Grant, I must speak to you about our agreement," whispered Genie, her face pale like marble in the moonlight.

Grant winced. Agreement? What had he done? "Genie, this is my fault, mine entirely. I accept full responsibility for it. Please forgive my imprudent words of an arrangement between us. It was foolish and I regret it more than I can express."

"But last night we talked about—"

"Forget last night!" His whispered words were harsh even to his own ears. "Pretend last night never happened. Go to bed, go to sleep, and pretend it was all a bad dream. Tomorrow—"

Light shone in the window and Grant plunged to the ground scrambling out of view. Retreating the way he came, hidden by the dense foliage, he watched to ensure Genie made it back to the house. The person with the light was there when she entered the house. He hoped she would have the good sense to make up a plausible excuse.

❧

"Good morning, miss," said the maid as Genie walked into the house. The surprise in her eyes was clear. Genie needed to give her an explanation.

I was visiting Mr. Grant, where I was ruined and tossed out like refuse.

"I could not sleep, so I sat in the garden awhile,"

said Genie in a dull tone. She wished she could go to sleep and wake up at home, this entire visit to London nothing but a bad dream.

"Are you well, miss?" The young maid's face revealed concern, not censure.

"Yes." Genie paused and shook her head. "No, not really."

"Pardon me saying, miss, but all the staff think Mr. Blakely is a wretched man and you're best without him."

"It is most certain that I will do without the man."

"My mum says men ain't naught but lying bastards." The maid averted her eyes to the floor. "Pardon me saying so, miss."

"Quite right," said Genie, standing taller. "I believe your mother had the right of it."

Genie cried until the tears stopped. Not that she was no longer miserable, but eventually the tears dry up and you must move on. Her maid thought her red, swollen eyes were due to the loss of Mr. Blakely. Genie did not bother to correct the assumption. She washed in cold water, trying to erase the memory of Grant. All she accomplished was to make herself dreadfully chilled, inside and out.

Men were wretched. Brothers, however, still needed to be tended. Especially George, who was still only a child in a grown body. He must be protected so he could grow to improve the lot of mankind. Surely he would never treat a lady in such a manner.

She met with George early in the morning and gave

him every shilling she had along with a promise that she had found a way to get the money. She secured his promise not to do anything until the next day. He was sporting a black eye and a swollen jaw. He had tried to earn his fortune through boxing but failed.

There was only one card left to play. The moneylender. Genie walked to the breakfast room with heavy feet. She knew she must be hungry, but the food turned her stomach.

"Have you seen Louisa?" asked Lady Bremerton. "She has not come down for breakfast."

"No," answered Genie. It was the truth.

"Do you know where she is this morning?"

"Sorry, I don't know." Also the truth. What Genie did not say was since it was the day of the engagement ball, she was not surprised Louisa was gone. Unfortunately, Genie had her own problems.

"I thought I might visit Miss Rose now," said Genie.

"Later perhaps. It is too early to be making calls."

"But I'd like to coordinate with Penelope about the ball tonight."

"Fine," said Lady Bremerton, distracted. "But have the groom drop you off. I'll need the coach later. Marchford can send you home."

On the short ride to Marchford house, Genie considered her options again until she was resigned she had only one thing left to do. The coldness would not leave her.

Penelope was surprised to be told Miss Talbot was waiting for her in the drawing room. Why would she be visiting so early? A keen sense of dread nipped at Pen's heels as she walked to the drawing room.

"Thank you for seeing me so early," said Genie when she was seated opposite Penelope in the drawing room. The dowager, no early riser, did not join them.

"It is not too early for me, though perhaps it is a bit unusual," said Penelope. "Is there something wrong?" Pen could not help but notice Genie's red puffy eyes and overall downcast appearance.

Genie gave a weak smile. "No, just a little tired."

"You should not lose hope that things did not work out with Mr. Blakely. In fact, Madam X has another potential suitor for you."

Genie's shoulders slouched. "The last thing I need—"

"I know it is easy to be discouraged, but let us keep hopeful. You are a beautiful girl inside and out. Helping to settle you creditably should not be so difficult."

"Forgive me, but at this moment, I feel like something you would scrape off a shoe. I am not at all interested in adding another man to my troubles," declared Genie with feeling.

Penelope could understand if Genie was discouraged by the disaster Mr. Blakely turned out to be, but it only made Genie's need for a proposal that much more urgent. "This man is a nice one. He is a parson and lives not far from London, so you could enjoy the benefits of Town whenever you like."

"The benefits of Town are limited in my estimation."

"You must not be so negative. Mr. Oliver is a kind man. He should arrive soon. He is acquainted with the family and is coming for the engagement party this evening."

On cue, the door opened and the butler announced Mr. Oliver. In walked a young man with sandy hair and bright eyes.

"Good morning to you ladies." Mr. Oliver gave a bow. "I am honored to be invited to the engagement ball for the Duke of Marchford. I was quite surprised to see the carriage he sent this morning."

"Think nothing of it." Pen waved off the comment sincerely hoping he would forget to thank the duke—particularly since the duke was not the responsible party for his mode of transportation. After the disastrous situation with Blakely, Pen and the dowager had devised a swift new plan—bring in a man from the country.

"May I present Miss Eugenie Talbot?" said Penelope.

Genie gave a tepid smile and Pen could not help wishing her friend did not look quite so fatigued. She had hoped to amaze the young parson with the dazzling beauty of Miss Talbot, but Genie was more frazzle than dazzle at the moment.

"How are you acquainted with the family?" asked Genie absently after the initial pleasantries were uttered.

"Mr. Oliver took over the parsonage from my father," explained Pen. He was also young, handsome, available, and they were running out of other candidates.

"Whose shoes I can only hope to someday be able to fill," said Mr. Oliver kindly. "And yet I think we have another connection. I believe the Duke of Marchford's intended is graced with the family name of Munthgrove. I had the occasion to marry a Miss Munthgrove a few months ago. A family member I believe. I hope to see her at the ball."

Genie nodded politely, but Penelope froze. It could

not be, could it? Surely she would not have done anything so stupid. "I think I heard of the marriage," said Pen, taking care to keep her tone conversational. "She married a Dr. Roberts?"

"Yes, indeed. Will they be attending the party do you think?"

Pen held her hands tightly in her lap to refrain from jumping up. "I should hope not. That is to say," Pen amended to Mr. Oliver's startled face, "I doubt I shall see her, but I would very much like to."

She needed to excuse herself now. But how to get rid of her guests? Mr. Oliver was obliviously cheerful and Genie looked as though she might cry.

"Mr. Oliver, you must be tired from the road, especially having to rise so early. Let me show you to your room. Genie, would you be able to entertain yourself for a while?"

"Oh yes. I will show myself out. You need not worry on my account."

Pen hustled Mr. Oliver up to a bedroom, which took longer than she anticipated because he had a habit of stopping at beautiful works of art and wanting to make conversation or ask questions. Since the illustrious home of the Duke of Marchford boasted many extraordinary works of art, this process was lengthy. After answering or deflecting all his questions, she left him in the capable hands of the housekeeper.

Pen hustled off to find the duke. The ball had to be called off!

Thirty-one

THE BUTLER STARED AT HIM AS THOUGH HE WERE an apparition.

"Can you tell me where the duke is this morning?" asked Grant.

Instead of answering, Peters removed a watch from his pocket and examined the time, held it to his ear to see if it was still ticking, then inspected it again. "It is 9:42, Mr. Grant."

Grant took a great breath of air. "Morning. Haven't seen it in years. Thought I'd give it a go."

The butler's eyebrows shot up. "And how are you getting on?"

"Don't think I'll make it a habit. A bit early, these mornings, don't you think?"

"Yes, quite."

"Although I understand I am not the only one who has paid an early call on the house. Lady Bremerton told me I could find her niece here."

The butler's features relaxed, as if the puzzle was suddenly examined. "Yes, of course, Mr. Grant, Miss Talbot is with Miss Rose in the drawing room. The duke is in his dressing room."

"Suppose I should pop in on Marchford before I surprise the ladies. Propriety and all that." Grant bounded up the stairs two at a time, not caring if he looked more schoolboy than sophisticate. He needed his friend's help to gain a private audience with Genie.

"Good heavens, what is wrong?" Marchford stared at Grant as he entered the dressing room.

"Your cravat for one thing. What have you done to it?"

Marchford whipped it off his neck. "You surprised me and I crushed it. What are you doing about at this hour?" He checked his timepiece. "Do you know what time it is?"

"Yes, I do. For some reason, everyone I meet feels compelled to read me the time. Go ahead, I know you want to."

"It is 9:48 in the morning! Are you well? Your mother, sisters, they are in good health?"

"Everyone is well as far as I know."

"Then what is it? It must be something extraordinary to bring you out of your bed at this hour."

Grant flopped into an upholstered chair. "I have been forced into offering marriage."

Marchford sank into a chair himself. "Give us a moment," he murmured to the valet who discreetly left the room. "You best tell me what this is about."

"It is about women, my dear man. They are craftier than we give them credit for. I've been caught, ensnared, *compromised*, by one of those doe-eyed debutantes who looks like they'd melt like butter at a simmering gaze but all the while they are stoking up the heat for themselves."

"Are you foxed?"

Grant shrugged. "Quite possibly. Drank a lot last night."

"Could you try again, for I am feebleminded this morning? What exactly happened?"

"Quite right, can't think straight in the morning. Too early. Facts are simple enough. I've been caught by Miss Talbot and I must step forward to press my suit."

"I thought Miss Talbot was going to marry Mr. Blakely."

"So did I, but I have it from Lady Bremerton this morning that it is not to be." Grant grinned like a boy with stolen pudding.

"You do not appear terribly upset by the prospect."

"That's how crafty those ladies are. They make you want your prison."

"So, you actually wish to wed Miss Talbot?"

"Today if possible." He brandished a folded paper from his jacket pocket. "I've been to Doctors' Commons already."

Marchford's jaw dropped. "You got a special license?"

Grant grinned again.

"My dear friend, I am concerned for you. Perhaps I should keep a watch over you until you sober up. You are clearly not in your right mind."

Grant merely laughed. "Won't make a difference. I must be wed. I must. I only hope she will give her consent."

Marchford stood to tie his cravat. "Drunk. Must be."

Grant was spared a response by a jingling sound.

"Aha!" Marchford leapt to his spyglass.

"Whatever is it?" asked Grant.

"Someone has entered the study. Perhaps we shall

catch a spy today." Marchford looked for a long while into the spyglass, then turned his gaze to Grant, his face solemn.

"What is it?" asked Grant.

Marchford stepped back to allow Grant a turn with the spyglass. Grant pressed an eye to the glass. He could see the room in a rounded fishbowl view. In the corner of the room was the spy, looking behind pictures for the wall safe. Grant stepped back and closed his eyes. He had been sucker punched again.

"I am sorry," said Marchford.

Grant looked again to make sure.

It was Genie.

"She was feigning affection to get close to me. To you. To steal the spy code." Grant's mouth was suddenly coated in sand, and the words were harsh and painful to speak.

"It does appear that way." Marchford peered into the spyglass again. "She has found the safe. Now she is opening it with the key the opera singer stole."

Grant sat back down in a chair and stared unseeing at the far wall.

"Cheer up, old friend. Now you shall be excused from marrying the little spy. Consider it a near miss."

Grant shook his head. "It was a direct hit."

This is what it felt like to have a heart broken. It hurt. He had thought it was a metaphor. It wasn't. It actually hurt. "What do we do now?" he asked Marchford.

"Wait until she takes the letter, then catch her in the act."

"What will happen to her?"

Marchford gave another look like he ate bad fish.

"That bad?"

"Treason. It's not good."

Grant's stomach tightened such that he feared he might cast up his accounts. "This is what I get for trying the morning. Won't happen again."

Marchford looked again in the spyglass.

"What is she doing now?" asked Grant.

"Nothing. Folding paper. What is she doing?"

"Did she take the letter?"

"Not yet. But the safe is opened."

"Maybe she is not a traitor," said Grant hopefully. "Maybe there is an explanation."

"An explanation for sneaking into my study, opening a hidden safe with a key stolen from me by a *paramour*?"

"Do you need to put it that way?"

"And how would you describe it?"

"She is obviously being used. You cannot believe that a young girl from Sussex is a master spy."

"No, of course she is being used, though whether it is with her will or against it may make very little difference in the eyes of the law. After she grabs the letter, we get her and then convey to her the importance of telling us who she is working for."

"But if she is innocent?"

"She is rifling through my study, old friend. She is not innocent."

"What is she doing now?" asked Grant.

Marchford looked again with the spyglass. He moved it from side to side. "She's gone!"

Both men ran down the spiral staircase and opened the hidden panel door to the study. The room was vacant.

"Dammit! She has replaced the picture over the case. Why did the bell not ring?" asked Marchford.

"Did she take the letter?"

"I'll check. Go find her!"

Grant ran out the door to the hall. No Genie. "Peters!" he called for the butler.

"Yes, sir?"

"Genie, Miss Talbot. Where is she?"

"I did not see her leave. I thought she was still with Miss Rose in the drawing room."

"No, she is not with me." Pen walked quickly down the central stairs. "Where is the duke? I need a word with him."

"Not now, Miss Rose." The duke strode from the study. "The letter is still there, but she has carefully removed the seal."

"We need to find her." Grant ran out of the house, his chest pounding. For a broken heart, it certainly made quite a racket. He looked up and down the street but could see no trace of her. It was as if she had vanished. He ran back inside the house where Marchford was giving quick instructions to the staff to search the house for her. After an agonizing few minutes, it was clear she was not there.

"Where could she be?" Grant ran his hand through his hair. He ran back outside and looked up and down the street.

"You know her better than I," accused Marchford. "Where would she go?"

Grant took a slow breath and forced himself to think rationally. He would find Genie. He did not know why she had pretended to take the letter, but he did recognize that it had done nothing to reduce her hold over him.

"Let us go back to her house, search her room, look for clues, ask the servants. We must find something that can lead us to her," said Grant.

Marchford nodded in agreement.

"Wait, Your Grace, I need to speak to you," called Penelope.

"Not now, Miss Rose."

"But I would suggest most strongly that we speak immediately," said Pen.

"Not now." The duke waved off his mother's companion.

"But the letter." Grant dropped his voice. "Can we leave it in the house?"

"We cannot," replied Marchford in the same undertone. "So I will take it with us." He patted his breast coat pocket.

Since Grant's phaeton was hitched and waiting for him, they jumped into it to go to Bremerton house.

"I am going with you," declared Penelope, who appeared wearing a sensible blue wool coat.

"Get back in the house," demanded Marchford, but Penelope swung herself up beside him onto the seat of the phaeton, squishing herself next to him. Short of pushing her off, there was little Marchford could do about it.

"Can't wait for you two to fight it out," muttered Grant, and he snapped the reins, encouraging his bays to move at a fast clip.

"I really do need to speak to you alone," pressed Penelope.

"Then you will have to wait," quelled Marchford.

"As you wish," replied Penelope, and said no more.

To say that Lady Bremerton was surprised to see the three of them was an understatement. "Marchford! Your Grace! How… how did you know she had gone?" Lady Bremerton put a delicate lace handkerchief to her eyes.

"Do you know where she has gone?" asked Marchford.

"No, no, I am so sorry, I do not know. Please believe me, I had no idea that she would do this. Oh, where is she?" Lady Bremerton began to openly weep.

Grant was startled. He had not counted Lady Bremerton among those who would mourn the loss of Genie.

"You must have some idea of where she might be," pressed Marchford. "Did she speak to you of anything? Go anywhere in the past few days that was unusual?"

Lady Bremerton shook her head. "Lord Bremerton has gone after them, but I cannot trust that he will discover them in time!"

"Them?" demanded Grant. He felt a sick twisting in his stomach that was becoming all too familiar. "Who is she with?"

Lady Bremerton grew still and pursed her lips together. "No one. I do not know. I do not know where she is!"

"Did she leave a letter? Anything that might give us a hint?" asked Marchford.

Lady Bremerton tightened her grasp on a crumpled piece of paper and shook her head.

"What about her cousin? Does she have any ideas of where she is?" asked Grant.

"Oh that stupid gel," Lady Bremerton blurted. "As if I did not have enough to deal with, now Genie has gone missing too. She is not with her, for I saw Genie early this morning after Louisa had already left."

Silence filled the drawing room. Marchford sat down hard on a chair.

"Am I to understand that my fiancée is missing?" asked Marchford in a low, calm voice.

Lady Bremerton froze. "Did you not know?"

"Lady Louisa. The lady to whom I am betrothed. A lady for whom tonight I am holding a ball in her honor has run away? Is that correct?" asked Marchford in a businesslike tone.

"I thought you knew."

Marchford glanced at Penelope. "I'm guessing I should have listened to you."

"I can only agree with you, Your Grace," said Pen.

"We came to find Miss Talbot," explained Grant, finding his own chair. What he wanted right now was a stiff drink, but he refrained. Considering what drink had done to him lately, he had sworn off the bottle. No matter how much he might wish to fade off into inebriated oblivion, he was determined to stay in the game.

"You had best let me see that letter you are holding," said Marchford calmly. "Do not fear, Lady Bremerton. I am certain things will work out for the best. The letter please."

Lady Bremerton relinquished the letter with a bit of a moan and Marchford scanned it quickly.

"Well?" asked Grant.

"She has run off with another man," stated

Marchford in a flat tone, which nonetheless started Lady Bremerton crying once more.

"Is Genie with her?" asked Grant.

"No, how can she be? She was at Marchford house not a half hour ago," said Marchford. "Did you know she had left?" he asked Penelope.

"No. But I am not surprised," Pen answered.

"Lady Bremerton, I know this is difficult, but may we have permission to search the rooms of Lady Louisa and Miss Talbot?" asked Marchford. "We may be able to find clues as to where they have both gone."

"Yes, yes, of course. We have already looked, but you may as well if you think it will help. I know I can rely on your discretion?" Her chin trembled.

"Of course, Lady Bremerton," stated Marchford. "I only wish she had come to me. We might have dispensed with this unpleasantness."

The search of the ladies' rooms revealed nothing. They took their leave of the inconsolable Lady Bremerton and stood for a moment outside the house.

"I'll check with the groom to see if he knows anything," said Grant.

"But Lady Bremerton already told us Genie had not gone anywhere but Marchford house," said the duke.

"Lady Bremerton does not appear to know all that goes on in her house," commented Pen.

Grant spoke with Sammy the groom and found Genie had gone yesterday to a chocolate shop in Piccadilly, but otherwise, there were no secret travels. When Grant returned, Marchford had taken on a greenish hue.

"You all right?" asked Grant.

"I have been speaking with Miss Rose and now I have a pressing matter to attend to."

"She knows the man your bride ran off with?" guessed Grant.

"Yes. Apparently, Louisa ran off with her… husband."

Thirty-two

THINK, THINK, THINK.

It was not the time to panic and become foolish, as was common in gothic novels. It was the time to think clearly if she wished her brother, and herself, to emerge from this tangle alive.

Genie clutched her reticule tightly. Inside was the letter she had created. She had carefully removed the seal from the letter she found in the safe with the duke's own penknife and reattached the seal with sealing wax onto a blank parchment. She wanted to help her brother, but she was not about to steal secret documents to do it.

She exited the house by the front door and quickly turned along the side, cutting through the gardens to the opposite side of the block. Her conscience pricked her. She should not have sneaked into the duke's study to steal anything. Yet, her brother's life hung in the balance. Surely that gave her just cause for some license in propriety? Did it not?

She was not sure, but she was committed to the path now. She would save her brother and then return home to become a maiden aunt. After all she had been through, the prospect was more appealing than ever before. The thing she would not consider was Grant. What they shared, how he acted in the morning. *Rejected.*

Genie stopped short, took a deep breath against the surging tide of emotion, and struck out walking again. She would not be defeated. She could not change what had happened or how far she had fallen, but she could try to make things right for her brother.

The shops she passed were open for business; people passed her on the street, giving her second glances and raised eyebrows. She was walking alone on the streets of London. Not good. She would have preferred to hire a hack, but short of a few farthings, she had given every coin she had to her brother, leaving her without enough for the fare.

Despite her love for long, solitary walks in the country, she understood that in Town, a lady never walked alone. She considered for a moment returning to the chocolate shop to produce the letter but thought better of it. The store might not be safe. She was certain she did not know all the intrigue surrounding this letter, but she was wary someone may not wish her to speak of it later. No, she must meet the Candyman in a more neutral place, and it certainly was not going to be at some public house of his choosing.

A small shape caught her eye as it darted into a doorway near her.

"Jem? Is that you?"

The thin urchin emerged from the doorway, glancing around nervously.

"Have you been following me?"

Jem stepped closer to her and nodded. "What's you doing out on the streets alone, milady?"

Genie sighed. Chastised for lack of propriety by a street urchin. "I need to deliver a letter. You know the chocolate shop you recommended to me as having a moneylender?"

The boy's eyes widened and he nodded.

"Could you deliver a message to the Candyman? Tell him I have what he was looking for and I will meet him at Hookham's Lending Library. Do you understand?"

Jem's eyes remained wide, and he nodded but remained where he was.

"Oh, of course," said Genie rummaging through her reticule and pulling out one of her few farthings. "You would like a treat from the shop." She held out the coin but the boy did not take it. "Is something the matter?"

"Are you sure you want me to go to the chocolate shop?" asked the boy.

"Yes. Is something wrong?"

"I don't like the Candyman," said Jem in a low voice, head down.

"I can always go myself—"

"No! I'll go." Jem turned on his heel and raced down the street. The coin Genie had offered still rested in her hand.

Genie waited impatiently in Hookham's library. The Candyman had not come. She had thought for certain he would arrive, given how much he wanted the envelope in her reticule, but it had not come to pass. Genie began to wonder how long she should wait and how she was going to return home.

The walk to Hookham's had not been smooth. Her unchaperoned presence had drawn more attention than she wished to garner. She had drawn looks of censure from older matrons, whistles from common laborers, and rude comments from several dandies. One of these set had followed her into Hookham's and was even now sitting in plain sight with a wolfish grin on his face. She did not relish stepping outside the relative protection of the library.

The bell at the door rang softly and Genie turned her attention, hoping the Candyman would arrive to put this entire situation behind her. Genie gritted her teeth in recognition. It was Mr. Blakely.

Genie turned away and pretended to read a book, but he walked over to her.

"Good afternoon, Miss Talbot." Mr. Blakely sat in a chair next to her.

Genie did not look up or acknowledge him in any way, hoping by sheer neglect to make him somehow disappear.

"I am glad I have seen you." Blakely leaned forward, speaking softly. "I wish you to know how sorry I am for our disagreement."

Genie glanced over the top of the book at him. "Sorry enough to forgive my brother's debt?"

Blakely colored slightly. "No, I mean… it is not in my power."

"Good day, Mr. Blakely. I can have nothing more to say to you."

"Wait, you misunderstand me. I was contacted by the Candyman who indicated you had negotiated terms and he was going to pay off your brother's debt. He asked me to meet you both here and bring a letter of forgiveness for the debt."

Mr. Blakely pulled a sealed letter from his breast coat pocket. Genie's eyes followed the letter. It was everything she wanted.

"Do you know when he will arrive?" she asked, her pulse starting to quicken. She was so close to saving her brother and being done with it.

Mr. Blakely inspected his pocket watch. "He should have been here by now. I do not know what has kept him."

Genie sat primly on the edge of her seat. She wished the Candyman would arrive soon, so she could forget she ever met Mr. Blakely.

"I suppose I could stop by the shop and see what has detained him."

"Hey, gent." The ogling dandy strode up to Mr. Blakely. "I found this ladybird first. She's coming home with me if she's leaving with anyone."

Mr. Blakely rose slowly from his chair, staring down the dandy. "You have made a grave error in judgment. You will apologize immediately to the lady or I will meet you at dawn."

The smirk on the dandy's face slid into gaping fear. "I-I am sorry. I do apologize. Thought you were someone else." He retreated and left the library with due speed.

"Thank you," Genie breathed. Even though Blakely was more interested in money than her, it did appear he was still gentleman enough to have a care for her reputation.

"Think nothing of it. I cannot imagine why he would target you to suffer his rudeness."

"I walked here without my maid," admitted Genie.

"Oh, my dear girl. I do hope you have not suffered any rough language."

"I shall survive."

"Let me take you home at once." Blakely held out his arm and Genie stood and took it.

"I would like to settle our business," said Genie.

"Yes, of course. If you have whatever it is you need to give to him, let us go at once."

Genie hesitated but nodded. It would be best to get the business completed and she did not wish to walk back home by herself. Blakely had every incentive to see her deliver the letter to the Candyman. All he wanted was the money, and she was his ticket to getting paid. She figured he would be happy to keep her safe at least until he got his money. If he decided to abandon her at the chocolate shop, she could always walk herself home. It would be only slightly longer than walking home from Hookham's and at least the business would be resolved, even if she had to endure glares and the occasional lewd comment to do it.

Blakely helped her into his coach and gave the direction to his driver. Genie hoped the journey would not be long. It was impossible to make conversation with the man who was the cause of so much distress, even if he was trying to be pleasant.

"Come to think of it, there is no real need for you

to come inside," said Blakely mildly. "I can handle the details if you wish. You wait in the carriage."

"I should like to ensure everything is completed," said Genie as the coach rolled to a stop in front of the chocolate shop.

"I suggest we trade envelopes. You hold this, which declares your brother's debts cleared and I will take in your envelope to the Candyman. If everything is fine, I will take you home."

Genie hesitated. If the Candyman opened the envelope, he would certainly discover all was not fine. Yet she could not see how standing before him would improve her situation.

"Yes, all right." She accepted the letter from him and placed it in her reticule, pulling out the letter with the red seal. When she removed it from her bag, her last farthing caught on the seal and fell to the floor of the coach.

Blakely took the sealed letter with a wide grin and bent down to pick up the coin. "Here, allow me." He tried to pick up the coin but finding it too difficult with gloves, he whisked off one of the gloves and picked up the coin holding it out to her.

Genie held out her hand, but as he gave the coin to her, she noticed his hands, covered in red scars. She had seen those hands before. She stared at Blakely's face; it couldn't be, and yet, she could see it now.

Blakely narrowed his eyes. "On second thought, you had better come in with me."

Genie shook her head.

"Oh, but I insist." Blakely pulled a small, dark handkerchief from his pocket.

Genie dove for the door on the opposite side but was caught from behind and pulled back into the coach. Something went over her mouth, her lungs burned, and everything went dark.

"Wake up!"

Genie awoke in a dark place with a damp chill to the air. She lifted her head slowly, only to find she was tied to a chair. Around her was blackness, a single lantern on a table the only light.

"Where is it?" demanded Blakely. "Where is the code? I told you to bring me the letter with the red seal in the duke's safe!"

Genie tested her bounds, but she was tied securely. "You are the Candyman, the moneylender!"

"And you are too smart for your own good."

"But why? Why wear a disguise and pretend to be a moneylender. What kind of a gentleman are you?"

Blakely smiled. "I am no gentleman at all."

"What do you mean? I was assured Mr. Blakely owns a respectable estate in the country."

"He does, or shall I say did. But I am not Mr. Blakely."

Genie shuddered from the chill creeping through her. "But you… who are you?"

"I have been known by many names. I would say I was at your service, but we both know it would be a lie. All you need to know is that I am devoted to seeing my homeland thrive under the rule of Napoleon and have no scruples when it comes to achieving my goal." He smiled, but his eyes were cold.

"I don't understand."

"No, of course not. But what you think is of little value and no importance."

"You are French?"

"But of course."

French? How could she not know? "But your accent. You sound the English gentleman."

"I am the bastard son of the Duc de Vermette. He was well pleased with me, raised me to the pomp and privilege of the duke's son, until he remarried and she gave him an heir. She wanted to secure the power and fortune for her own brat, so I was packed off to an English boarding school when I was eight years old."

"So you have lived in England?"

A cruel glint flashed in his eyes. "I returned to my homeland in time to report my father to the tribunal. I was there when he, his wife, and their nasty son all met their fate courtesy of Madame Guillotine."

Genie's pulse raced and she tried to wrench her hands free. He was a monster.

"See how it all worked out for the good? It taught me to value what is truly important in life—money."

"What is it you want?" whispered Genie.

"Simple. I want the code to find the spies—the letter with the red seal. Marchford has it. I want it. I have been offered a sum of money vast enough to turn the most loyal of hearts. Which, of course, mine never was."

Blakely pulled a knife from his boot and placed it on the table. "If I am willing to put my own father's head in the guillotine, just think of what I might do to you. You will tell me what I want to know. Where is the letter with the red seal?"

Genie swallowed hard. She feared she might get caught in her deception, but she had never imagined a scenario such as this. She needed to think fast. He thought her foolish so she could use that. "I went to the duke's study and opened the safe, just as you told me to. There was only one letter with a red seal. Is this not the red seal you were looking for?"

Blakely shoved the blank paper before her. "It is blank! How do you explain it?"

"I… I did not open the seal."

"Dammit!" Blakely cursed as he paced back and forth. "I've been tricked. It was all a farce. The duke, it is his fault!"

Genie sincerely prayed he would continue to direct his anger toward the duke and away from her.

"I have done everything you asked of me. Please, let me go!" Genie's voice sounded higher, louder than normal. Fear was making her bold, even as she began to succumb to panic.

"You have seen too much."

"They will be looking for me."

"People saw you leave in a coach with Mr. Blakely. I will circulate a rumor that you and Mr. Blakely resolved their differences and eloped."

"I would never!" cried Genie, forgetting for a moment her actual actions of last night were considerably worse. Had it only been last night? It seemed ages ago that she was held in the strong arms of Grant. The thought brought tears to her eyes.

"Do not cry. I cannot stand blubbering, I warn you," growled Blakely.

Genie blinked back a retort that he had not been

the cause of her tears. She would not waste her energy thinking of him. She scanned the room for some prospect of escape, but they were in a large, dark cellar. Along the walls, she could make out what appeared to be metal cages with piles of rags and debris. In the dim light of the lantern was a hint of movement. Staring back at her through the darkness were several pairs of eyes.

Thirty-three

"LOUISA IS MARRIED?"

"Apparently," said Marchford carelessly.

Grant frowned. "And the groom?"

"A Dr. Roberts."

Grant shook his head. "Are mornings always this exciting?"

"Only when you are awake for them," answered Marchford.

"Then I am cured of ever attempting it again. What are you going to do?"

"Miss Rose has suggested we go round to the good doctor's residence and see if we can catch them before they flee. I own that I should most likely heed this advice."

Grant glanced at Miss Rose who was sitting primly on the seat of the phaeton. The two men walked a few steps away, out of earshot. "What of the letter and Miss Talbot?"

Marchford patted his breast coat pocket. "The letter is safe for now. As for Miss Talbot, I fear I am at a loss. Did the servants know anything?"

"The groom drove her to a chocolate shop yesterday, but otherwise, I do not know."

"Have you any other idea of where she would go? What she would do?" asked Marchford.

Grant shook his head. "I cannot believe she would do anything like this at all. Although..." Grant's voice trailed off. He would rather be drawn and quartered than reveal that Genie had come to him last night. But why had she come? He was irresistible of course, but he had been profoundly drunk last night. Why had she been there? Was she in some sort of trouble? Had she come to him for help?

"What is it?" asked Marchford. "If you know something..."

"She may have been in trouble," said Grant slowly. "She spoke to me, but I forget. I regret I was deep in my cups at the time."

"Try to remember," pressed Marchford.

Grant pressed his hands to his temples until it hurt, hoping the pain would clear his head. "Promise me you will shoot me if a drop of liquor ever again passes through my lips."

Marchford's eyebrows rose. "I can only surmise you are making a joke."

"No, my friend. My memory is hazy but I feel sure Genie would not be in this trouble today if I had not been so beset by drink. And now it has taken from me the only lady I ever truly cared about." Tears sprung to his eyes, unbidden and unfamiliar. Gone was the cool mask of society's upper crust. He was a broken man.

Marchford put his hand on Grant's shoulder. "Steady on. We will find her."

"Yes, yes of course." Grant gave himself a mental shake. "Forgive me, this morning thing appears not to be to my liking."

"So if Miss Talbot was in trouble, perhaps she was being blackmailed or threatened in some way," said Marchford in his direct way, getting back to the business at hand.

"Yes, considering her actions of late, I would have to agree with you," said Grant, a chill taking hold.

"She could have been pressured to steal the letter."

"But she did not. She stole only the seal."

"Then she may be in danger once the people discover she has not given them what they want," said Marchford bluntly.

A tremor like ice water ran down Grant's spine. "We need to find her," he said, his voice quavering.

Marchford studied him for a moment, as if noticing him for the first time. "I fear, dear chap, you are in love."

"Do you really think so?"

"I cannot find any other reasonable explanation. You have bought a special license, sworn off drinking, lost control of your emotions on a public street, and—most disturbing of all—done all this before noon. I would say the evidence leads me to no other conclusion."

"I suppose under the circumstances, it would be foolish to deny it. I love her madly, it's true. I need you to be honest. If she has taken this letter somewhere, what will happen to her when they find it is a fake?"

"They want the letter. They will probably hold on to her for leverage until they can get it."

"How can we find her?" asked Grant.

"Doubt we have to. I wager they will come to find me. I need to find my errant bride, then I will return home to see if a message comes."

"I would like to inspect this chocolate shop," said Grant. "It's most likely nothing, but it's our only lead." He glanced at Penelope, sitting in his phaeton. "Take my horses. I'll grab a hack."

A short while later, Grant walked into the chocolate shop, his senses bombarded by the rich aroma. It was a dark shop, so small he might have passed it many times before ever realizing it was there. A young lad stood at the back counter in a dirty apron. It hardly appeared to be a setting for intrigue.

Still, what could be a better cover than a chocolate shop in Piccadilly?

"May I help you, sir?" asked the lad as Grant approached.

"I do hope so. Found myself in some trouble. Thought perhaps coming here would help," said Grant vaguely, hoping the lad would reveal something.

"Trouble with your vowels, sir?"

"Find myself quite at a standstill. Heard this place might help," fabricated Grant.

"Candyman's busy now. Come back later perhaps."

"Could I wait for him? Pockets to let."

The lad sized him up, then nodded and led him to a small, dark room behind a door in the paneling. "Wait here."

Grant sat at the table of the dim room until he heard other customers enter the shop and figured the lad would be busy. He opened the door on the other side of the room. It could not be a coincidence that Genie had visited a chocolate shop that doubled as what appeared to be a moneylender. Did she need money? Was that why she pretended to take the letter?

He sneaked out the door on the other side of the small room and found himself in a corridor. Down the hall were the sounds of the kitchens with people chatting through their work. He supposed making the chocolate and the sweets took considerable effort.

He opened the door across from him and entered a small study. He searched the papers and found ledgers of sales, but nothing of particular interest. On a hidden shelf behind the desk, he found a ledger of monies loaned to men and women who had fallen on hard luck. He raised an eyebrow at some familiar names, but the name of Genie Talbot was not among them.

He cautiously opened the door once more and edged down the corridor closer to the kitchens. On the left was another door and he quickly dashed to it. Opening the door, he found a staircase leading down to the cellar. He closed the door behind him and slowly crept down the stairs into the gloom.

"I should thank you for interposing yourself today," said Marchford. "Your knowledge of the location of Dr. Robert's place of business is helpful."

"I would say you're welcome, but I do not think it was a compliment," said Penelope, sitting next to him on the phaeton.

"I thought we had an agreement that you would tell me relevant information. You have clearly been here before. Did you not think my fiancée's husband would be relevant to me?"

"I did not know she was *married*," Penelope defended herself. "I did know she was interested in Dr. Roberts, but I did not know the extent of the relationship. How do you feel about this turn of events?"

"I wish she had told me before I announced a ball in her honor. Going to be dashed awkward." Marchford steered deftly through the crowded London streets.

"Here we are, on the left. What is your plan now?" asked Penelope.

Marchford pulled up in front of the respectable house in a nicer part of Town. He left Penelope's question hanging in the air, since he did not know the answer himself. Inside the residence, the young man in the apothecary attempted to tell them the doctor was unavailable, but Marchford ignored him. If there was a time to break social convention, this must be it.

"I believe his living quarters are upstairs," said Penelope.

Marchford did not wait but bounded up the stairs with the shop clerk right behind, demanding he stop. Marchford burst through a door and got lucky. Dr. Roberts stood in the drawing room.

"Your Grace," said the good doctor. "It is quite all right," said the good doctor to his shop clerk, who glared at the interlopers but left the room.

Face to face with one of the doctors who had attempted to save his brother's life, memories of sickbeds, treatments, and medicine flooded Marchford, rendering him speechless.

"Dr. Roberts, I don't think we have formally met," said Penelope, noting the silence in the room and taking command. "I am Penelope Rose, the new companion to the Dowager Duchess of Marchford."

"A pleasure." Dr. Roberts bowed.

Penelope's sensible tone snapped Marchford back to the present. "Dr. Roberts, I do thank you once again for doing all you could for my brother," said Marchford, finding his voice. "But I am here on a different errand." He cleared his throat, wondering how to begin. "I understand you may know the location of Lady Louisa."

"I am sorry I cannot help," said the doctor. "I have not seen her since her last visit."

"Dr. Roberts, I think the time has passed for charade. I need to speak to Lady Louisa." Marchford spoke with the authority of a duke.

"I am sorry," said Dr. Roberts firmly.

"Dr. Roberts, I am not here to stop Louisa. I simply would like to talk to her."

"I am here," said Louisa, emerging from a side door. She appeared calm but clutched her reticule with white knuckles.

Marchford took a deep breath. "Is it true you are married to Dr. Roberts?"

Dr. Roberts stood beside her and took her hand. The answer was clear.

"I understand," said Marchford. He should feel disappointed, but the only thing flooding his heart was relief.

"We need to think strategy," said Penelope. "Running away will not enhance the social credit of either one of you."

Marchford glanced at Penelope, amused by her direct manner. It was a relief to have someone willing to state the plain truth without preamble or apology.

"Do you think there is any way my parents will accept my marriage to Dr. Roberts?" asked Louisa.

"There must be," declared Marchford. "And so we will find it."

Grant crept down the stairs. Ahead was a dim light in the cellar. He crept around the corner and found… nothing. A high, street-level window provided some light to inspect the room. It had cartons of flour and sugar and other ingredients, but otherwise there was nothing of interest.

He walked back up the stairs, not exactly sure what he was hoping to find. He opened the door slowly to find the surprised form of Mr. Blakely.

"Mr. Blakely? What are you doing here?"

"Mr. Grant!" Blakely clenched his jaw. "I could ask you the same question."

"Cards got you all rolled up?" asked Grant. Mr. Blakely's appearance was slightly less than his usual lack of polish. Had the man gambled himself out of the good sense to correctly tie a cravat?

Blakely gave a nervous smile. "Don't tell me you're run off your legs."

"Nothing like that. Looking for Miss Talbot actually. Found she had come here. Know anything about it?"

"Sorry, I don't. If she was looking for a loan, she might have gone to another lender I know about. I told her about it once. Never thought she would acquaint herself with it."

"What interesting conversations you must have had. Can you tell me where this is?"

"I'll do one better and take you there," said Blakely.

Grant followed Blakely out of the chocolate shop, across the street, and down a side alley not even wide enough for two to walk abreast. Blakely stopped at a cellar door.

"I've heard a moneylender operates in this cellar as well." Blakely paused as if nervous to continue.

"I'll give it a go," said Grant. He slowly opened the cellar door. "Hello!" he called but got no reply. He carefully crept in a few steps. "Hello!" he called again.

"Grant?" came a female voice from the darkness.

"Genie?" shouted Grant. He stumbled forward into the dark cellar. "Genie are you there?"

"Yes, only do be careful!" cried Genie.

Running forward, Grant could see her now, tied to a chair. "I have found you!" Relief to see her alive was mixed with a panic to help her escape immediately.

"Careful, there are other people in the cellar!" cried Genie.

Grant was grabbed by several pairs of hands. He prepared to strike but saw he was being attacked by children, dirty street urchins. He checked his swing and tried to push them away. He took out his penknife to cut Genie's bonds but was attacked again and so he merely put the knife in her hand.

"Let go!" he demanded. "Blakely, I've found Genie. Get help!"

More dropped on him from above, one covered his mouth with a foul smelling cloth. He was able to free himself but not before spots of light flashed before his eyes.

The room spun and he fought against the

encroaching darkness. Mr. Blakely appeared before him, holding a club.

"Don't trust him!" called Genie.

But it was too late. The club came down hard.

Grant never felt the impact.

Thirty-four

"If you would, could you inform my grandmother of the latest developments? I will be in my study," said Marchford as he pulled the phaeton into the drive of his London estate.

"I can only assume you are in jest," said Penelope.

"I do not jest."

"You expect me to break the news that your intended has married the family physician instead?" Penelope and Marchford had convinced the illicit couple not to run but to give Marchford a chance to explain the situation to Louisa's parents. They even agreed to come to the ball if the duke thought it would be helpful. Penelope was not sure how Marchford was going to manage getting Lord Bremerton to accept the marriage, but she was interested in seeing him try.

"She would take it better from you," said Marchford jumping down from the phaeton.

"No, you would take it better if you were not there when she was informed."

"As I said."

"Your Grace," ground out Penelope as she accepted Marchford's assistance from the high phaeton.

"I need to be available should a message come."

"You expect someone to contact you?" asked Penelope. They had been able to talk briefly in the phaeton and Marchford had explained that Genie, for reasons not yet ascertained, had stolen the seal to the paper Marchford had been guarding.

"I do. Once they discover the paper is blank, they will come back after me for it."

Penelope paused before the front entrance. "What will they do to Miss Talbot?"

"Nothing until they get their hands on the letter."

"And after that?" Penelope asked with some reluctance. She probably didn't want to know.

"We will find her first."

Penelope was right; she did not want to know. Considering the risks, she guessed it would be best for Marchford to focus on the many problems at hand. Of course, that left her telling the dowager about Louisa's marriage.

"My grandson has gotten himself into some kind of mischief," said the dowager when Penelope walked into the drawing room. She sat straight as a dagger, holding her cane before her like a weapon.

"How would you know?" asked Penelope.

"I know. It is in his nature. His mother was the same, nothing but mischief and intrigue, and of course you know where that got her." The dowager's eyes flashed in a manner that did not invite question.

"I wonder where Lady Bremerton has got to. She planned to come for tea to discuss the ball. Silly woman," muttered the dowager. "I shall find her tedious when Marchford and Louisa are to be wed."

"I should very much doubt they will wed," said Penelope, shifting nervously in her seat. "I fear I have news you may not like."

"What is it, gel? Speak up!"

"I fear Lady Louisa has been secretly wed to another."

The dowager was still for a moment before exhaling a large sigh. "Oh thank heaven. I am relieved Marchford will not be saddled with that missish little thing."

Penelope felt her jaw drop. "But I thought the union had your full support."

"Lady Louisa was intended for Frederick. She would have made him a lovely bride had he lived. Unfortunately, the marriage contracts were drawn up such that with his passing, Louisa was bound to marry James. But they would never have suited. Could you not see that?"

"Well, of course, anyone could see that. They were most unsuited for each other. But why did you not speak out? Why not disband the union?"

"It was not in our power to do so, even James understood that. If the contract was to be broken, it could only be so from the side of the future bride. Marchford could in no way dissolve the union and keep his honor intact."

"I wonder that Lady Louisa's parents did not dissolve the union," said Penelope.

"Louisa was engaged to a *duke*. I should wonder very much if they had broken that alliance!"

"Even if the parties involved would not make each other happy?"

"What has that got to do with anything? Honestly, Penelope, sometimes you can be so dreadfully bourgeoise. Whom did Louisa marry?" The dowager prepared the tea, speaking of the elopement as if it were commonplace.

Penelope took a breath to keep herself in check. "Your physician, Dr. Roberts."

"Well, now, a common doctor. That will give Cora's nose a tweak."

"I believe he is an extraordinary doctor," said Penelope. In her estimation, Dr. Roberts had earned more respect for his profession than society's elite, who did nothing but gamble, drink, and feel superior.

"Now don't get your hackles up, gel. I will own that I have the greatest respect for him. Though if Louisa married him behind everyone's back, she has more pluck than I gave her credit for. We will need to find a way to gammon off the gossips."

"That will be a challenge indeed." Penelope accepted the tea, feeling restored by the strong flavor. "When does James want to cancel the ball?"

"He is in his study. I believe he is engaged with another matter at present."

"Please inform him I need to speak to him about what to do tonight. You may be called upon to take ill. Something with spots and hideously contagious so we can quarantine the house."

"Must it be spots?" sighed Penelope.

"Without a doubt. Spots."

Grant woke up groggy and aching. He tried without success to open his eyes. As if coming back from a deep sleep, Grant struggled to regain consciousness.

"Grant? Grant!" said a familiar voice, followed by a persistent shake.

"Stop," mumbled Grant, sitting up. "You'll crumple my cravat."

"Thank heaven you are alive," breathed Genie.

"What happened?" Grant peered into the gloom, trying to get his bearings. He was cold and damp. The light from outside was mostly blocked by boards over a high window, but in the dim light, he discovered he was sitting on a pile of rags and damp refuse. Forgetting his company, he exclaimed something almost as ugly as his surroundings.

"Are you all right?" asked Genie.

"Sorry. Forgot. Yes, I'm well. Head hurts, but it's been hurting all day so no matter. What happened?"

"Blakely is actually a French spy who is working for Napoleon."

"Knew there was a reason I disliked the man," muttered Grant.

"He wants some letter with a red seal that Marchford has. I thought if I gave him the seal he would be satisfied, but he discovered the paper was blank."

"But why did you need to bring him anything?"

"Blakely is the one who holds George's debt."

Grant held his head with both hands, trying to make his world stop spinning. "Who's George?"

"My brother. Don't you remember? I told you about him when we, uh… talked last night."

"Remember nothing. Horribly drunk."

"Oh. Blakely tricked my brother into betting deep and George now owes him twelve thousand pounds. Is it still considered a debt of honor if you find the man you owe is a traitor?"

"Yes, but you have license to kill him."

"I am ashamed to say the man has inspired me to contemplate violence," confessed Genie.

"If I see him again, I'll do more than contemplate." Grant felt for Genie but ran into something hard and metal. Forcing his eyes to focus, he realized he was locked in a small cage. "Genie, you need to get out of here."

"I can't."

"Are you tied to the chair?" Grant could hardly see her in the dark.

"I was, but I was able to cut free with your penknife, but the cellar is locked and I cannot get out."

Grant struggled to stand and found he could not reach his full height in the cage, which was about five-feet square. "Who keeps cages in his cellar?"

"I think he keeps children in them," replied Genie. "He forces them to work for him."

"What a lovely chap. Too bad there aren't more rats. Could have been a perfect setting for seduction in one of your books."

Genie sighed. "I always wanted to have an adventure, but I fear now all I want is to go home."

"Very sensible. Where's Blakely?"

"You'll not like it. Blakely sent an urchin to give Marchford a message to meet him in Hyde Park with the letter tonight. They plan to exchange us for the letter."

Grant slammed the cage door trying to break free. There must be a way out. He was concerned for Marchford and for his own skin, but the thought of what unscrupulous people might do to Genie unleashed within him cold panic. "Genie, you must find a way out."

"I've tried. There is none."

"Try again!" he shouted in an uncharacteristic show of anger. He needed to get her to safety. He needed to know she would be well more than he needed his next breath. "I'm sorry, but I cannot live in this world without you."

The cellar was silent for a moment. "Truly?" asked Genie in a small voice.

"Truly."

"I did not expect to see you again. I thought you had taken me into dislike."

"Dislike? No, how could I?" Grant pushed against the solid bars as if it were possible to squeeze though. "I called on your house early this morning, but you had gone."

"Did you?" Genie reached out a cold hand through the bars of the cage and Grant took it and held tight. "You… you wished to speak with me?"

"Of course. This morning when I saw you, all I wanted was to put you back where you belonged. I was afraid at what I had done."

"You didn't do anything. I came to you to accept your offer and gain your support to pay my brother's debt."

"Had I been anything other than dreadfully cup-shot, I would have marched you home and still paid your brother's debts."

"Really?" It had never occurred to Genie that Grant would give away such a large amount without asking anything in return.

"Give you anything." Drunk or sober, Grant meant every word.

Grant pushed his face as far as he could between the bars and Genie met him, her soft lips blending with his until nothing else existed but her sweet, clean scent and the promise of her kiss. Despite everything, he was ready for more, the kind of more iron bars rendered impossible.

"I underestimated you. I've ruined everything." Genie pulled back.

"No, I have been the fool. Had I had my wits about me last night, things would have been different. But, Genie, you must get out of here."

Genie sat down on the chair. "I think I should pray."

"Pray?"

"Ever since my brother came to me, I've been desperate to solve this and save him. I've done everything I can think of except pray. Stupid really, since God knows what I should do, especially when I don't."

Genie sat on the chair and bowed her head. Grant watched and waited, a growing sense of panic overtaking him. He needed to get her out somehow. *Lord, I'm not one for praying, as well you know, but please get her out of here.*

A scratching sound got his attention. The dim light got darker. Someone was at the boarded-up window.

"Genie!" hissed Grant.

Genie was at his side at once.

"Hide the penknife under your glove," Grant

whispered. "When he attacks, stab him. Aim for the eyes and then run away as fast as you can."

After a few grunts, a small figure squeezed through a small crack between the boards and landed softly on the ground. The child glanced around and approached Genie, who had sat back down to pretend she was still tied to the chair.

"Milady?"

"Jem!" said Genie, forgetting to pretend to be tied and standing up to give the lad an embrace.

"Don't trust him!" yelled Grant. "He's probably been working for Blakely—or whatever the blazes his name is—this whole time." He prayed for help and got an urchin instead.

"Jem, is this true?"

"I'm sorry," said Jem in a small voice. "I didn't want to, but the Candyman would do horrible things. He's a mean cove."

"I understand," said Genie, much kinder than Grant would have been. "But now you must help us. Where is the Candyman and the other lads?"

"Gone to Hyde. Plan to fleece the duke then hush him good."

"I do not quite understand," said Genie.

"They plan to steal the letter from Marchford and then kill him. Is that the plan?" asked Grant.

"Aye, you're a cunning swell."

"Jem, you must help us get out so we can warn him," said Genie.

Jem proudly held up a key. "That's what I come for. Nicked it straight from his pocket. He always said I was a leery cull when learn'n the knuckle."

"Good boy, Jem!"

Jem unlocked the cage and Grant was never happier to hug a dirty urchin. "Did right by yourself, m'lad." And perhaps praying wasn't such a bad idea either.

Grant took Genie into his arms and kissed her right there in the cellar in front of Jem and the rats. "I love you, Eugenia Talbot."

Genie beamed back at him. "I love you too, William Grant."

"There is much I wish to say, but for now, let's be gone," said Grant.

This proved harder than expected. There were two doors to exit the cellar, but both the interior door up a rickety flight of stairs and the exterior hatch door were padlocked from the outside.

"Can't you go out Pitt's picture?" asked Jem.

"The window," explained Grant to Genie. "So named for Pitt's window tax. And no, there is no way for me to fit. Can't see how anyone could."

"I'm next to nothing," said Jem.

Genie climbed up on a crate to better see the opening between the boards. "I am too big for that I fear."

Grant helped her down, mentally reprimanding himself for enjoying putting his hands around her waist.

"Jem, can you squeeze out and go warn the Duke of Marchford not to go to Hyde Park and to come here to help us instead?"

Jem's eyes widened. "They'll have watchers on the house. They'll know if I go in. 'Sides, why would the duke believe me?"

"Tell him I said…" Grant thought for a moment

for something Marchford would recognize only Grant would know. Grant motioned to Jem and the lad came close. Grant whispered something in his ear.

"What's that?" asked Jem.

"A very important name."

"Is it secret?"

"Very!"

Thirty-five

"YOUR GRANDMOTHER REQUESTS YOUR PRESENCE TO discuss canceling the ball tonight," said Penelope. She entered Marchford's library, which had taken a militant turn, with boards across the windows and various weaponry within easy reach.

"What is our excuse?" asked Marchford.

"Apparently, I have taken ill."

"Contagious?"

"Dreadfully. Something with spots."

"I hope you will soon recover."

"Me too. Have you gotten word from the thieves?"

"Yes. This was delivered." Marchford held up a missive with a red seal. "Clever—they sent back my seal, so I'd know they were in possession of Miss Talbot. They would like to trade her for the letter code at dusk in Hyde Park."

"A trap?"

"Naturally."

Yelling and a loud bang interrupted their conversation. Marchford pulled a pistol from his coat and pushed Penelope behind him on his way to the door.

He cracked the door from his study and looked out, then opened it all the way. "What is the meaning of this?"

"Your Grace! An urchin boy has invaded!" yelled the butler, giving chase to a small boy, with two footmen and a scullery maid in tow. "Came in the kitchen window. We'll soon be rid of him."

The small boy in question ran up the stairwell, then confounded his pursuers by jumping over the railing onto a small table, which broke under his weight, shattering an expensive vase. He found his feet quickly but not fast enough to avoid the strong hand of the Duke of Marchford on his shoulder.

"You the duke?" asked the lad, glancing nervously from the duke's face to the hand holding the pistol.

"Yes."

"I gots a message from Mr. Grant."

"Do you?" The duke surveyed the young boy. "Thank you, Peters," he said to his butler. "You have earned a bonus for your efforts, and you three as well." He nodded to his staff. The duke marched the boy into the study, his hand never leaving the boy's shoulder.

Penelope followed them. She was not invited, but she could not possibly miss the excitement now that she was a part of it.

"I know this lad," said Penelope. "He is the boy who attempted to steal my bandbox outside your house."

"Is that true?" asked the duke.

"Aye, sir," said the boy, his eyes never leaving the gun.

"I believe he is also the lad Miss Talbot rescued and Mr. Grant has been housing. Goes by the name Jem."

"Yes, ma'am," said Jem.

"So what brings you to visit my home, Master Jem?" asked the duke in a mild tone.

"Mr. Grant sent me. He wants me to tell you not to go to Hyde. They means to snabble you."

"Snabble?" asked Penelope.

"To rob and murder, have I got that right?" asked Marchford in a lazy tone as if the plot was of little consequence.

"Yessir."

"And why can the illustrious Mr. Grant not tell me this himself?"

"He and milady are pitch-kettled in a cellar."

"And I suppose you would like me to follow you to this cellar?" asked Marchford.

"Aye!"

A knock on the door revealed a heavily laden Lord Thornton. He carried a rope, shovel, rifle, bucket, lantern, and a brace of pistols.

"Good heavens, Lord Thornton," exclaimed Penelope. "You look quite the adventurer."

"Aye! James requested my assistance. I have learned to come prepared," said Thornton.

"Good show!" said Marchford approvingly.

"What are we doing today?" asked Thornton.

"Trying to rescue a damsel in distress without getting killed ourselves," answered Marchford.

"Always a good plan. Especially that last part," said Thornton with feeling.

"Young Jem here was just going to tell us why I would put my life in his hands by following him into a cellar."

"Mr. Grant told me to tells you something." Jem eyed Penelope and Thornton suspiciously and motioned Marchford to lean down so he could whisper in his ear.

"Ah!" exclaimed Marchford. "There is little you could have said that would have enticed me to believe you, but I know Grant would not, even under pain of torture, ever reveal that name. Lead on, Master Jem!"

"What name?" asked Penelope and Thornton together.

"Grant's tailor!"

"Can you pry off the board?" asked Genie.

Grant had stripped off his coat and was now standing precariously on several stacked crates, attempting to remove the boards from the small window. "Could if I had something to pry it with."

"Could we squeeze out if you got the boards off?"

"Doubt I could, but you might." Grant jumped down and inspected the crates but rejected them as too flimsy to provide a pry bar.

"What about the chair?" asked Genie, reading his mind.

"Good thought!" Grant took the chair and swung it over his head bashing it on the ground. Genie jumped at the noise but thrilled at watching Grant do something physically rigorous, an activity not generally in his repertoire.

He slammed the chair down again and it broke apart. A few wrenches more and he had one of the chair legs free, a turned piece of solid oak. He tested its weight in his hand. "This may do it." He scrambled up the crates again, but before he could attempt prying off the boards, voices were heard in the alley.

"Hide!" hissed Grant as he jumped down. "And if you see an opportunity to run, do it!"

Genie crouched in a dark corner and Grant hid behind the wooden stairs leading up to the alley entrance. The door opened, bathing the cellar in light. Genie retreated further into the gloom.

"I do not care to hear your complaints," said Mr. Blakely, or the Candyman, or whatever he was calling himself today. "You made a convincing wench."

"Yessir," moped a lad wearing Genie's long coat and bonnet.

"They will have their sights on me, but they will not suspect you. That's why you will fire the fatal shot. Wait until you are close enough to put a bullet through his brain."

"Yessir," said the lad in the bonnet.

"Now remember, Marchford will no doubt bring friends, so we must be prepared to take them out as well. Of course, not all his friends will be present, will they Mr. Grant?" Blakely strode down the steps into the cellar and peered into the gloom at the cage where Grant… wasn't.

Grant jumped at Blakely from behind, knocking him to the ground. Blakely cursed brutally, kicking Grant off and drawing a pistol. Grant lunged for the gun. With an orange flash and a blast, the shot went high, the gunpowder smoke burning Grant's lungs.

Using the stock of the gun as a weapon, Blakely struck Grant hard across the jaw, but Grant would not be taken down. Grant returned the favor with a facer to Blakely's nose. Blood spurted and Grant used the distraction to knock the pistol from Blakely's hand and put him in a headlock, wrestling him to the ground.

"Stop!" cried the boy in the bonnet, pulling his own flintlock pistol from his coat. "Let 'im up," he said, aiming the gun at Grant.

Behind the boy Genie stepped out of the shadows, her face as white as her gown. All the boys were in a circle looking at him, the door to the alley still open. This was her chance to get away. Grant looked at her and slid his gaze to the cellar door, hoping she would run for it.

"Hallo there, m'lad," said Grant in a bright tone, not letting go of Blakely. "You look a bright boy. Why have you taken up with this Frenchie?"

"Didn't know he was French, did I?" defended the lad.

"You do now," retorted Grant. "I've got no quarrel with you, lad, put down the gun."

"Shoot him," gasped Blakely, but Grant pressed harder, silencing any commentary from the French spy.

"Sorry, guv'nor, but I gots to do as he says."

"But that would spoil my surprise, dear lad."

"What's that?" asked the lad suspiciously.

"Something you won't get if I'm dead I assure you."

"What is it?"

"A home!" conjured Grant. Genie was edging slowly to the door. He just needed to keep them distracted long enough for Genie to make it outside.

"I ain't going to no workhouse."

"No, not a workhouse," said Grant. "A real home in the country."

"Jus' for 'im or me too?" asked a small boy.

"For you all," said Grant.

"Sorry, guv'nor, that horse won't run. I knows when some flash cull is trying to gammon me." The boy with the pistol cocked it and aimed for Grant.

"Forgive me for intruding," said Genie as if she had walked into her aunt's drawing room.

Grant's heart sank; she had almost made it out. The boys all turned their attention now to her.

"Do you know whom you are addressing?" asked Genie. "Why, this is Mr. William Grant. If he says something is so, then you can trust his word. I know I do," she added, capturing his attention with large blue eyes. She was, to be sure, the most beautiful woman ever created.

"Is it really true?" asked the small boy.

"Of course it is!" declared Genie. "He told me of a place in the country with a nice couple to take care of you, horses to ride, streams to play in, and all the food you can eat."

"Don't care for horses. Never been to the country none." The lad in the bonnet looked from Grant to Genie, unsure.

"I've never even crossed the Thames," said one boy.

"Me neither," added another.

"Better to live in the country than work for a French spy who makes you dress like a girl and shoot men in cellars," persisted Genie.

"Aye, milady. I s'pose you're right." The boy uncocked the pistol and handed it to Genie.

"You are a very good lad," said Genie soothingly.

She cocked the pistol and leveled it at Blakely. "You will stand in my presence, Mr. Blakely.

Grant stared at his Genie in disbelief. She stood tall, chin raised, gun cocked and steady. He let go of Blakely and moved out of the line of fire. Blakely slowly got to his feet, his hands raised.

"Now, Mr. Blakely," said Genie in a calm tone. "My brother owes you a great deal of money. However, I have it on good authority that I may shoot you with impunity since you are a traitor to the Crown. Unless you would like to test my resolve, I suggest you remain perfectly still."

Blakely paled but did not move. "I thought you a biddable wench."

"You are speaking to the future Mrs. Grant, so I suggest you change your tone," declared Grant. "Darling, shall I tie him up for you?"

"That would be delightful, dearest," said Genie in an airy tone, never once taking her eyes from Blakely. "Run along now, children, and go outside. It is too nice a day to be indoors."

The urchins, wide eyed and slack jawed, filed out of the cellar with a few bows and "aye, miladys." Grant searched the floor where he had broken up the chair for the bonds that had been used to tie Genie.

Grant glanced at his future bride with a sizzle of excitement. She was brave and strong, and he could not picture one moment of his life without her. He bent down to collect the ropes.

"Drop the gun!" A figure stood in the doorway, a large pistol in hand. It was a man unknown to Grant. Had Blakely's friends come at the wrong time?

Genie turned to the intruder and Blakely pounced, slamming her to the ground and wrenching the gun from her hand. Grant lunged, but Blakely regained his feet and lowered the gun at Genie. Grant fell on her, protecting her with his body.

"Grant!" called Marchford.

A flash and a pop, and the room filled with gun smoke.

"Genie! Genie, are you all right?" called Grant.

"Yes," coughed Genie. "Slightly crushed. What happened? Are you hurt?"

Was he? Grant stood and helped Genie to her feet. Nothing in particular was ailing him. Marchford, Thornton, and the unknown man stood in the doorway, all with pistols in hand. Blakely lay crumpled on the floor.

"You shot him?" Grant asked Marchford, even as he drew Genie into his arms to hide her face from the corpse.

"No," answered Marchford.

"I did," said the man. "Mr. Neville, servant of the Crown."

"Pleasure, Mr. Neville," said Grant.

"Yes, indeed," said Genie.

"You must have got my message and brought the cavalry," Grant commented to Marchford.

"Indeed I did come, but I cannot account for Mr. Neville's presence."

"We have had the Candyman under surveillance for a while," said Neville. "Some of my operatives thought he was acting shady, so I determined to check it out for myself."

"Well, I for one am glad you did!" declared Grant. "Come, Genie, let's get you out of here."

They walked up the steps, blinking in the sunlight of the afternoon.

"Milady!" shouted Jem. The lad ran and put his arms around Genie.

"I am happy to see you! You brought Marchford and everyone is safe. Well, except the Candyman, but he was a villain," reasoned Genie.

The children all grouped around Grant. "Does we still get to go to the country?" asked the lad, taking off Genie's bonnet and coat and returning them. Genie smiled but doubted she would wear either again.

"Yes, of course. I can drive you out soon, but I will need to find a place for you until then," said Grant.

"I shall detain the urchins," said Neville.

"They saved us; they should be cared for. Some are in dreadful condition. They need to be cleaned and fed," said Genie.

"They should go to an infirmary for care," said Thornton. Despite some protests from Neville that the lads should by all rights go to a workhouse, Thornton offered to see the boys safely to the infirmary, with the promise from both Grant and Marchford not to worry about the expense.

"But what of the letter that caused this entire problem?" asked Neville. "Your Grace, surely you must see that you cannot keep sensitive documents."

"For once, Mr. Neville, you are right. I will not keep it any longer." Marchford pulled folded papers from his coat. Neville held out his hand, but Marchford shook his head. "Thornton, if you could bring the lantern from the carriage?"

Thornton nodded and returned moments later with

the lit lantern. Marchford unfolded the letter, held it up for Neville to see, then dipped it into the lantern, catching the edge on fire.

"What are you doing, man?" Neville lunged, but Marchford easily held him off, turning the page to ensure the entire document disappeared into ash.

"But now how will we communicate with our operatives?" demanded Neville.

"There is a new code. This one is obsolete," said Marchford calmly. "Now then, Thornton and I will escort the children to the infirmary. Grant, I trust you can see Miss Talbot safely home."

"We need to search Blakely's rooms," said Grant. "I assume he was the thief at Admiral Devine's house, and I imagine we should find both the papers he stole and my aunt's emeralds."

"The emerald earrings!" exclaimed Genie. "He must have reset them and then allowed my brother to win them, knowing he could get them back once he put him into debt."

"I will search his apartments with the constable after we deliver the children," said Thornton.

"I see you have no more need for me," said Neville with a scowl.

"Yes, of course we have need of you," said Marchford with a droll smile. "You can dispose of the body."

Thirty-six

"BUT I DON'T WANT TO GO WI' THE BOYS!" WAILED Jem and cleaved to Genie as immovable as a limpet.

"Very well," soothed Grant. "You can stay with me for a few more days until we all ride out to the country." He handed Genie into the hack and lifted Jem in as well. Grant sat beside Jem, wishing there was not an urchin between him and his beloved, and gave the direction to the driver.

"I suppose I must go back to my aunt's house, but really I wish I did not have to," sighed Genie.

"Did your aunt kick up a fuss when Louisa ran off?" asked Grant.

"You know?"

"Yes, and what's more she got herself hitched."

"Well, now! To whom?" asked Genie.

"Some doctor."

Genie put her hand to her head. "I feel I've been in the cellar for days. Poor Aunt Cora will be in high dudgeon."

"Got a better idea." Grant gave the direction to Marchford's house. "Get ready for the ball there. Send for your clothes."

"Are they still going to have the ball?" asked Genie.

"Don't know," said Grant in all honesty. "If not, better be there than with your aunt anyway."

"True. I suppose I will have to go back soon enough," sighed Genie.

"Why can't you live with Mr. Grant like me?" asked Jem.

Grant also planned to ask Genie the same question but thought that the presence of an urchin between them made the circumstance less than ideal, so he refrained.

"Jem, I need to go home to the country, and you also will have a new home in the country," said Genie.

"To stay with you?"

"No, dear. I will go home and you will go to your new home with the other boys."

"Don't want to!" said Jem with defiance.

"But wouldn't you like to have meadows to run in, streams to swim in, horses to ride? You could work in the stables." Genie was doing her best to conjure a picture no active boy could resist.

"I'd like to rides me a galloper, milady," said Jem with wide eyes. "But I want to stay with you!" Jem crossed his scrawny arms and set his jaw, determined.

"I promise I will visit as often as I can," said Genie, unsure how far he would be from her home. "And so will Mr. Grant," she added, cavalierly volunteering him.

"I will at that," Grant said in happy agreement. "Take you out there myself. Estate belongs to m'father. Stands to reason I'll visit often."

Despite these reassurances, the little boy shook his head defiantly. "I won't go."

"But whyever not?" asked Genie.

"Because." Jem looked around and leaned closer to whisper his secret. "Because I'm a mot."

"A mot?" asked Genie.

"A mot!" cried Grant.

Jem nodded her head.

"What's a mot?" asked Genie.

"He is a she!" exclaimed Grant.

"You're a girl?"

Jem nodded. "When the Candyman first caught me, I knew nuthing but bad would happen if'n he knew I was a girl, so I became a boy."

"Oh, my dear child!" exclaimed Genie and wrapped Jem into a warm embrace. "But what is your name?"

"Jemima Price."

"Where are your parents?"

"Dead, milady. And it's no use asking about my aunts 'cause they're dead too."

"But how did the Candyman catch you?" Genie smoothed Jem's hair out of her eyes trying valiantly to see something of a little girl.

"I was powerful hungry. He offered free sweets. Once he found there was none who'd miss me, I ended up in a cage."

"Oh, my poor darling," said Genie, giving her another hug. "How brave you have been." Genie looked up at Grant with tears in her eyes and he knew a grand gesture was very soon in his future.

"Why don't you stay with me?" he said with resignation. "I'm sure we need a maid of some sort. But you must only break the bric-a-brac I don't like."

"You would have to apply yourself, Jemima," Genie said, "and of course you must have dresses."

"I'd like me to wear some dresses," said Jemima shyly.

"I saw a calico yesterday that would be perfect for your coloring, and we'll need to get you some new boots and stockings and ribbons and bonnets!" Genie began to pour into Jemima's willing ear all the wonders of millinery while Grant counted the cost with obliging acquiescence.

"There you are!" The Duchess of Marchford rapped her cane on the marble entryway in an irritated manner. Penelope stepped to the side to make sure her toes did not fall victim to the cane.

Grant, Genie, and Jemima arrived at the house at the same time as Marchford returned.

"Did anyone consider they were keeping an old woman waiting?" continued the dowager. "But no, it is of no matter of course, as long as you all were enjoying your amusements."

"Of amusement such as those, there can never be too few," muttered Grant.

"You look a sight, the lot of you." The dowager shook her head. "And have you given any thought to the fact that in a few short hours, several hundred guests shall arrive at our house expecting a ball to celebrate a duke's betrothal."

"Can you cancel on such short notice?" asked Pen.

"We must! The prospective bride has married a commoner. It will be a scandal when it gets out. The only thing to do is put a notice on the door that we've come down with the pox and retreat to the country—or perhaps the Continent."

"Napoleon might have something to say about that, Grandmother," said Marchford.

"He doesn't have the mouth on him that the Comtesse de Marseille does. At least our woes will provide amusement for some, vile woman."

"Perhaps we can talk more about this after we have taken care of Miss Talbot," Penelope suggested. "You appear to have been through a lot today."

"I fear I look a sight," agreed Genie, trying to smooth her hair. "I thought I could impose upon you and get ready for the ball here. I wasn't feeling quite up to facing my aunt, but if you will cancel, I will bid you all farewell."

"Nonsense, child. Stay and refresh yourself. But what is this creature you have with you?" asked the dowager.

"May I present Miss Jemima Price," said Grant. "She is responsible for saving all of our lives."

"It needs a bath." The dowager called for her personal abigail and a flock of ladies' maids to attend to the needs of the weary ladies.

When Genie had withdrawn, Jemima in hand, Grant also confessed a great need for a bath. "Sorry to leave you in such a tangle with a missing bride," said Grant.

"If only Napoleon would invade or some such," said the dowager. "The best way to avoid scandal is to give the gossips something else to chew on."

"It is a shame Napoleon cannot be more obliging," said Marchford.

Grant bowed and turned to leave but stopped and searched his coat pocket. With a smile, he strode back, waving the special marriage license in his hand. "Got a plan to save all our reputations." He gave a foolish grin. "Except mine. I'm ruining myself!"

Marchford stood in front of the curtain concealing the garden, ready for the boldest performance of his life. If he failed tonight, the reputations of many would be in tatters. "Ladies and gentleman, distinguished guests."

The noise and bustle of the ball subsided and several hundred of the most notable people in the land turned their attention to the duke. This was the moment for which they had been waiting. A salacious rumor being whispered was that Lady Louisa had run away, but most in the ballroom were waiting to hear the official news from Marchford himself.

Marchford resisted the urge to adjust his cravat. He prided himself in maintaining his composure no matter what the circumstances, yet this many eyes gave him pause—especially when he was not quite sure how to express himself without inviting scandal. He decided to start with the mundane. "I have behind me a project into which I have put a great deal of personal effort and from which I have derived a great deal of personal satisfaction.

"This new garden boasts several new species that have traveled here from such remote places as Spain, Italy, and even the Far East. I am particularly pleased with the flowers which have flooded the gardens with a heavenly aroma. I do hope all of you will have an opportunity to stroll the gardens to appreciate the beauty of the natural world."

Marchford took a deep breath. It was time. "But

first, I would like to say a few words to some important guests. It is my pleasure that the Earl of Bremerton could be here with his wife and their daughter, Lady Louisa."

On cue, Penelope opened a side door and out walked Lord Bremerton and his family with expressions more appropriate for a public hanging than a society ball. Marchford had convinced them to pretend approval for their daughter to avoid scandal, but they were none too happy about it.

"As many of you are aware, our families have long been close. We have supported each other through times of great joy and great loss, and our two houses have always maintained close ties. Over the years, I have come to feel for Louisa as a brother would feel for his sister. Therefore, it gives me great joy to announce the marriage of Lady Louisa and Dr. Roberts."

A collective gasp filled the room.

Marchford smiled as if he had not just heard the stunned shock of his friends and relations. Penelope ushered Dr. Roberts out the side door and he walked to stand beside Louisa.

"I am greatly pleased with this union," said the dowager, joining the nervous couple before the crowd. "I wish them great joy."

Marchford motioned for the servers to come forward with the champagne. "If you will all charge your glasses, I would like to propose a toast to the happy couple." The guests were silent as they accepted flutes of champagne, as if waiting to see the crowd's reaction to such startling news.

"To my dear friends, Lady Louisa and Dr. Roberts.

May your union be long and prosperous. I truly wish you every happiness." Marchford saluted the tense couple with his glass and took a small sip as the crowd began to stir.

"And now, my friends," Marchford regained their focus. It would not do to let the gossips begin their commentary now. "Let me present to you the main attraction and the primary reason why I have invited you all to this ball." Marchford glanced at Pen, who gave him a small nod. Everything was ready. Marchford pasted on a smile and raised his voice. "And now for the unveiling of what I believe to be my finest work."

Marchford gave the signal and the curtain fell.

The ballroom was once again filled with a loud, collective gasp.

Thirty-seven

GENIE PREPARED FOR THE BALL IN MARCHFORD HOUSE. Runners had been sent to collect her gown and she had been handed over to efficient ladies' maids who ensured she was bathed, dressed, and sparkling (thanks to a few loaned baubles from the dowager). Genie felt she should be more tired and upset, given all she had endured that day, but instead all she could feel was relieved.

She had received a note from Grant that he had found her brother and informed him that the debt was eliminated. Her brother was safe. She was safe. Grant was safe. Those things alone were enough to convince her it had been a good day.

The guests had arrived, but she remained upstairs and out of sight. Rumors had spread fast and wide about strange goings on in the Bremerton household, and though she doubted anyone could imagine a falsehood more inconceivable than the truth, she did not look forward to her reintroduction to society.

Instead of heading down to the ballroom, Genie went up the back staircase to the servants' quarters.

Marchford had allowed Jemima to stay the night until she could be given over to Grant's housekeeper in the morning. She wanted to say good-bye to the child. Little did she know, when she showed mercy to the urchin in the street, the child would later save her life.

"Thems some nice sparklers," commented the young Miss Jemima. She was sitting up in a plain, wooden bed, unrecognizable in a white night rail after a bath and a significant scrubbing. Now that she was no longer concerned with concealing her identity, she had accepted the bath with zeal.

"The necklace is pretty. A loan for the night from Her Grace," said Genie.

"And don't you worry none. I won't nick the lob. I'm done with that lay."

"Yes, well, if I understand you correctly, it would be good of you to refrain from stealing in the future."

"No point in it anymore. Candyman's dead, right?"

"Yes, well. The less said about that unhappy incident the better."

"I'ves seen a man been killed before, but never one I wanted to be killed. I'm dang sure I'm demned for it too, but it's just hows I feel."

"No more talk of this, Miss Jemima. If you are going to improve your situation, you must learn to speak with a bit more…" Genie paused, considering the right word.

"No more thieves cant ye mean. I knowed the ways I talk ain't right. But I just don't know the right way."

"You must try to learn it from the housekeeper. Do you think you can be a quick study?"

"Oh yes, ma'am!" Jem smiled brightly, her shocking

red hair, which had emerged from the wash in bold curls, bobbing about her head for emphasis. "Why, when the Candyman teached me the art of the knuckle, I took to it real natural. Could nick a dummie and thimble off a flash cove wi'out him a'knowing what's what."

Genie gave her charge a weak smile. "That's lovely," she responded without conviction.

The orphan's smile never faded, so certain she was to please Genie.

"Now, let's get you to sleep." Genie tucked in the rescued urchin.

"Never thought I'd see the day I'd sleep in a bed. A real bed!" Jemima snuggled under the white comforter and ran her hands along the coverlet. "And a pillow too. Bless me, it's like being in heaven, yes it is. I wish my mama were alive to rest next to me. She woulda loved this, just fer one night even. I feel right set up for life!"

It was a simple bed, but scrawny Jemima was almost entirely swallowed up, her red curls in a sea of crisp white the only evidence of her presence. Genie smoothed the curls and gave the large-eyed waif a smile. "Go to sleep now."

Genie extinguished the lantern and made her way out of the room to the hall before the first tear fell. What a sad life for the poor girl, who had never even slept in a bed. She made her way quietly down the back stairs, to the corridor leading to her guest room.

"Something the matter?" Grant's voice was rich and smooth, sending shivers shimmering down her spine. He was in shadow, leaning against the wall as if he had been waiting for her.

"No, well, yes, I suppose. I was sad for that poor little girl who has known nothing but hardship. I feel I must look after her and had the thought to take her home with me, but I am not sure my parents would quite approve. I expect they were hoping I'd return with a husband, not a street urchin."

"If they thought that, they could not have known your kind heart. No one could know you and be surprised if you came home with a passel of orphans."

"Oh! Do you think I could bring home them all?"

"No, my dear. But it does you credit to consider it."

"I'm not sure it does those orphans any good."

"It has been a trying day. Perhaps we can tease ourselves with this problem later?"

Genie was flooded with a warmth that pinched at her cheeks. He had spoken of them as "we" and her response was ridiculously swift. "Yes, of course."

"Something I should like to show you," said Grant with a smile, stepping into the light and offering his arm. He was, as always, a fine figure, though more refined in his choice of color pallet, with a blue superfine, double-breasted coat and white silk waistcoat over white breeches.

Genie accepted his proffered arm. For good or ill, she would go with him anywhere. They went down the staircase together, and then, instead of turning right to descend the main stairwell into the ballroom, they turned left and Grant whisked her down the servants' stairs.

"Where are we going?" Genie had a suspicion Grant had brought her to a secluded place to exchange a kiss or perhaps something more. And why should he not suspect her willing? She was a fallen lady after all, and with Grant, she might even be convinced to fall again.

"Place I wish to show you." Despite their secluded location, Grant maintained the standard of high propriety. Grant opened the stair door into the hot bustle of the kitchen and led her through to the back door into Marchford's new garden.

A gentle breeze had blown away much of the London haze, so the moon was actually visible, wreathed in an ethereal glow. The gardens were indeed a showpiece, the flowers in bloom, a sweet scent swirling through the lush greens. New flowering plants had been added to the straight hedgerows; lavender, lilies, roses, rhododendrons, and violets brightened the garden.

Grant led her a ways through the garden until they reached the doors leading back to the ballroom. The music of a country dance floated through the garden, but thick curtains covered the windows so they remained unseen. Genie was struck at the intimacy of enjoying the delights of a ball in the privacy of their own private garden.

"Shall we?" Grant held out a hand and Genie took it. Grant led her in the steps of the dance until Genie's heart pounded with more than just the exercise.

Grant gradually moved slower, until his hands encircled her waist and they embraced, revolving in slow circles. The music had died out and Genie could no longer hear any sounds from the ball. It was as if everyone were holding their breath for this moment.

"Mr. Grant, I cannot express enough how grateful I am that you came to find me, to save me." Genie smiled. "When I was in that cellar, I feared no one would miss me or care that I had gone."

Grant smiled down at her. "I will always be there to rescue you. Though with how you handled yourself today, you may be the one rescuing me."

"Well," said Genie taking a step back. It was time to gain some distance or her heart would truly break when it came time to say good-bye. "Despite how the day started, and all the chaos that ensued, my brother was saved, and we seem to have escaped without scandal, except for Lady Louisa and the duke. I do feel sorry we were not able to help their case, but we did try."

"Indeed we did. Hopeless case from the start."

"Since Louisa was already married, yes indeed. I admit it's more gumption than I thought she had. I am sorry for the gossip, but I do wish her every happiness."

"I have a plan to help reduce the gossip."

"Do you? I wish you well in it. You are very clever."

Grant paused with a rueful smile. "I have been called many things, but clever? Not that."

"Oh, but you are!"

Grant shook his head. "Trouble with you is that you only see what you wish to see. I have never in my life met a woman as artless as you. I thought I knew women, but indeed, I either know nothing of your gender or you are a new sort of breed altogether."

Genie suppressed a grin. "I believe I can assure you I am a female."

"Yes, yes, of that we have proof, much to my enduring shame."

Genie's smile faded. "Do you regret our… err, last night?"

"Indeed I do!" Grant spoke with feeling. "If I had been anything but deeply, most vilely drunk, I would have marched you home immediately."

"I am sorry," said Genie in a small voice, her hands clasped before her.

"Well, you should be. You have ruined me. Utterly ruined. I used to have a reputation, a certain notoriety about Town, and now since meeting you, everything I once was has been wrenched from me. I can look at nothing the same way. I have feelings in my chest I cannot recognize. And now this!" Grant took a small flask from his interior coat pocket and thrust it at her.

"A flask?" asked Genie meekly.

"Drink it!" he demanded.

"But I don't drink—"

"Drink it, I say!"

Genie thought Grant in a strange humor and decided it best to oblige him. She took a sip and swirled the tart contents around her mouth. "Lemonade?"

"Lemonade!" he declared savagely. "And I lay the blame for my downfall entirely at your feet."

"I suppose I should say I am sorry?"

"But you are not, I see. You have ruined me utterly and completely and rejoice in your success." If Grant was jesting with her, he did not look it. He was agitated, perspiration on his brow. Even locked in the cellar he had not appeared in such distress.

"Do not worry yourself over me. I shall return home soon, there can be no doubt of that."

"No, no you will not. You will not be returning to your parents' home any time soon."

"What do you mean?"

"I mean..." Grant paused and wiped his brow with a handkerchief. He took a deep breath as if searching for courage and took Genie's hands in his. "What I mean is..." A candle flickered in the window, which seemed to agitate him even more. "No time. Must show you."

Grant pulled Genie into his arms and kissed her, softly at first, then harder, with more urgency. Genie wrapped her hands around his neck and leaned into him for stability when her knees turned weak. Grant may have his shortcomings, but the art of kissing did not count among them. Genie pressed closer and returned the kiss until her toes curled.

With a sudden flash, they were bathed in light and the sound of a collective gasp shattered her ears. Genie pulled back to see the shocked faces of her aunt, uncle, brother George, and a veritable who's who of London society. She had done it now. She was utterly ruined.

Grant never took his eyes from her. He got down on one knee and took her by the hand. "Miss Talbot, you are the most amazing woman of my acquaintance. I thought my life complete, but it was nothing but a mere sketch. You have given my life color. Would you do me the greatest honor and consent to be..." Grant paused and swallowed compulsively. "If you would consent to be... that is to say."

The crowd began to titter and crept closer. Grant glanced at the crowd and immediately turned his head away. "My mother and sisters have returned," he whispered to the ground.

"You do not have to do this," whispered Genie, squeezing his hand.

"Yes, yes I do." Grant looked up, meeting her eyes. He cleared his throat and said in a voice loud enough to be heard in the parlor, "Genie Talbot, will you marry me?"

A wave of something hot washed through her and wrenched her breath away. She was frozen, unable to respond, unable to breathe.

Grant squeezed her hand, concern growing in his eyes. "Say yes," he mouthed to her, "please."

Genie shook her head. "I never meant to trap you," she whispered.

Grant stood and clutched her shoulders, drawing her close. "My dear girl, it is I who have trapped you. Please be my bride."

Genie smiled; she could not help it. How could she say anything but, "Yes!"

Grant reached into his pocket and produced a ring. It was a very old and unusual ring, made of three strands of metal plaited together, gold, silver, and steel. "This ring has been handed down in my family for generations. It is only to be given to one's true love." Though his voice was strong, his fingers trembled when he put the ring on her finger. "Genie, you are my one true love."

Grant drew her close for another kiss even as the crowd began to cheer. At first, Genie clamped her jaw shut, self-conscious to be kissed before strangers, but within seconds, Grant's soft lips made her forget they were being watched.

"William, my dear boy, my dear boy!" cried a woman with emotion heavy in her voice.

Genie broke from him at the words that could only be from Grant's mother. Genie's heart raced faster with anticipation of censure. What must his mother think of her?

"Mother, may I present my soon-to-be bride, Miss Eugenia Talbot."

Mrs. Grant was an attractively plump woman with rosy cheeks. She beamed first at her son, then at Genie.

"It is a pleasure to meet you, Mrs. Grant," said Genie.

"Oh, but I must kiss you too!" Mrs. Grant gave Genie a warm hug and a kiss on the cheek. "Welcome to the family, my dear. How is it I have never met you?"

"Genie is visiting her aunt, Lady Bremerton," supplied Grant.

"How beautiful you are, my dear. Oh, I love you already!" Mrs. Grant smiled at Genie. "We must sit somewhere and you will tell me how you induced my darling boy to propose."

"Yes, but first let me make introductions." Grant introduced Genie to his father and several sisters. Genie smiled and shook hands and felt much like she was standing in the middle of a wonderful but befuddling dream.

"Genie!" George ran up and gave her a huge hug. "I am so happy for you!"

"And you? You are well?" asked Genie.

"I am now, thanks to everything you've done for me."

"George, are you not in hiding anymore?"

"No. I'm sure I'll catch it from Father, but I deserve it! I could not miss this evening, not for the world."

People pressed toward them, all talking, all wanting to

know how Genie landed the most elusive bachelor of the *haute ton*, with varying degrees of tact in their questions.

"Wait, wait!" demanded Grant, and all was still again. The crowd held their breath as if waiting to see what the next excitement would be. "My dear Genie. You have consented to be my wife. With the consent of your aunt and uncle, I would like to be wed tonight."

The lords and ladies of fashion gasped again and all heads turned to look at Lord Bremerton.

"I have no objection to the marriage, but the banns must be read, dear boy," said Lord Bremerton.

With a flourish, Grant pulled a paper from his pocket. "I present a special license. If there is a parson in the assembly, I would call upon him to come forward."

"May I?" Genie did not wait for a reply and snatched the paper from Grant's hand. She unfolded it with trembling hands. Carefully, she read the elaborate script. Though unversed in what a special license might be in appearance, she had no difficulty finding her name next to Grant's.

"You really do wish to marry me." Genie's eyes were filled with liquid emotion.

"Most passionately." Grant held her close and whispered in her ear, "Last night cannot count because I was deep in my cups. Tonight I drink nothing but the fruit of lemons and I will claim you in my bed."

Genie shivered with something that had nothing to do with cold. Grant's eyes were no longer mildly distracted; now, they were focused and intent. Her skin burned wherever his gaze went. The response of her mutinous body was instantaneous, without heed that they were the center of attention in a crowded ballroom.

"Yes, yes quite." Genie smoothed her hands on her white silk gown. "Let us be married at once!"

Grant's seductive smile turned a languid that made her almost willing to lift her skirts immediately.

"Mr. Grant, I presume." A trim, well-proportioned man stood before them. "I am Mr. Oliver, a parson, but this is all very irregular."

"You will wish to see this." Genie handed him the marriage license.

Mr. Oliver glanced it over. "Yes, well, it all seems to be in order." He looked back and forth between Grant and Genie, hesitating.

"I am ashamed to say it," Grant whispered into Oliver's ear, "but if you marry us, it would save me from sin tonight." Grant gave the parson a knowing smile.

"Well, I suppose, in that case, I must proceed."

Eugenie Talbot and William Grant were married by special license in the home of the Duke of Marchford. Several hundred guests were in attendance. The bride wore white, almost the same color as the pallor of the groom. Despite some last-minute bets made in poor taste by some of the young bucks in the room, the groom did recite his vows creditably and did not collapse in a dead faint. If his voice shook, it was only for a moment, and considering the occasion, no one could think the less of him for it.

Thirty-eight

"BREMMY, YOU SLY DOG!" AN OLDER, DISTINGUISHED man walked up to Lord and Lady Bremerton, who were stoically standing next to their daughter and new son-in-law to the side of the ballroom. The dowager and Penelope stood with them in a rather vain attempt not to look awkward.

"Robby! Good to see you!" exclaimed Lord Bremerton, and he introduced his friend to the family. "This is Sir Antony Roberts."

"What a surprise you had for me. I had no idea your daughter had married my nephew!"

"Your… nephew?" asked Bremerton.

"But of course!" Sir Antony gave Dr. Roberts a hug. "This is my great-nephew and heir. If I'd known about you getting married, I would have opened the London house for you to stay in. But of course, you must have already made your arrangements. Like to help if I can."

"Yes, thank you, Uncle," said Dr. Roberts. "But I did not know you were acquainted with Lord Bremerton."

"Acquainted? He is the only reason I survived the war! A truer friend I never had," declared Robby.

"But... well, I... this is quite..." Lord Bremerton took out a handkerchief and mopped his brow. "Well, welcome to the family dear boy." He gave Dr. Roberts, his new son-in-law, a large hug.

"And who is this ravishing creature?" asked Sir Antony, surprising the company by addressing the dowager. "I beg you would introduce me."

"This is the Dowager Duchess of Marchford. Your Grace, may I present Sir Antony," said Lord Bremerton.

"Charmed," said Sir Antony, bowing over her hand. "What an amazing hostess who has arranged for what must be the most highly talked about ball of the season!"

The dowager giggled regally, as only a duchess can do.

Lord Bremerton and Sir Antony walked off to find the card table, and the newly accepted Dr. and Mrs. Roberts took to the dance floor.

"Shall I assume you are pleased with the weddings?" the dowager asked Lady Bremerton, smug as a kitten with warm milk.

"How did you ever? Well, I never... how did Madame X arrange all this?" Lady Bremerton pulled out a silk handkerchief and blotted herself.

"Madame X has her ways," declared the dowager. "The best part of Genie's wedding is that it has completely eclipsed any loose talk about your daughter's marriage to Dr. Roberts."

"Yes, oh yes. For that I am eternally grateful."

"Madam X wanted you to know that if you are pleased, you may provide payment to my solicitor. He will know what to do with the funds."

"Yes, yes of course. This has been..." Lady Bremerton took a large swig of something Pen suspected was stronger than Madeira. "I must lie down now. My daughter married to Sir Antony's heir, my niece wed to Mr. Grant. My, my, my."

"Can we truly exact payment from her when you know we had little to do with all that transpired?" whispered Penelope.

"Fate is a fickle business, Penelope," the dowager replied in a conspiratorial tone. "One must accept the loss of her favor from time to time, just as one should always accept her gifts."

"I suppose I shall be forced to concede you are right."

The dowager linked arms with Pen. "Naturally, I am correct. How odd if you ever gave credence otherwise. Now please escort me to my room. I am tired and need to lie down. I also want to go over a letter I received asking for the assistance of Madame X for an American."

"An American? But how could anyone in America know of Madame X?"

"Lady Bremerton is known far and wide for her gossip. If you thought she could keep something like a matchmaker for the *ton* a secret, you are very much confused."

"So you wish to stay in business?"

"Business? Of course not. What a thing to say. No lady manages a business. But naturally, we will continue to support the calling of Madame X." The dowager gave her a smile. "You did well tonight, orchestrating things."

Penelope smiled in return. "Thought we pulled it off nicely. Genie is a sweet girl and deserves happiness. With your permission, I'll invite the newlyweds to stay here for their honeymoon night. Grant's family has been lovely but will not give them peace and I can't think of sending her back to her aunt."

"A good thought," agreed the dowager. "Come along now, gel, and put an old woman to bed."

"She married him in a big hurry," whispered a lady to her companion.

"Makes you wonder what they had to hide," said the Comtesse de Marseille with a knowing rise to her perfectly sculpted eyebrow.

"Indeed, why would anyone feel the need to marry with such haste?" asked another.

"Marry quickly?" asked Genie, walking up behind them and taking the gossips by surprise. "Well, if Mr. Grant proposed to you, wouldn't you?"

The gossips were left speechless.

A well-dressed, large man began to laugh, louder and louder, until the hall turned to note the laughing man. "Yes indeed, Mrs. Grant. You have done well to marry as soon as one can. With Grant, one must seal the deal as soon as can be once he has been made to come up to scratch."

"Your Highness." Grant gave a bow. "May I present my wife."

"Delighted! You are a welcome relief to my ennui. Grant, you must promise to bring her to Brighton. I hope I can rely on you to provide a diversion from these trying days." The man turned and walked away, his stomach leading the way.

"Who was that?" whispered Genie.

"Our success in society," returned Grant. "That was the Crown Prince, whose mother you so insulted at your presentation."

"So all is forgiven?"

"In my opinion, there was nothing ever to forgive," said Grant. "Come now. It is getting late. No one expects the newlyweds to be the last to leave the ball."

"I suppose I should go home to pack a bag." Genie sighed. "I do not even know where we are going."

"Not far, *Mrs.* Grant," said Grant in a slow tone, more reverent than seductive. She blushed just the same.

"I cannot believe this is true," said Genie. "I am so tired with all that has happened, I think perhaps this is a dream."

"Then by all means let's get you to bed." He led her up the main staircase by the hand, and she followed him to a grand bedroom with tall doors.

Penelope stood outside. "I have taken the liberty of requesting a bag be packed for you and brought here from your aunt's house," said Pen. "The Duke and Dowager Duchess of Marchford invite you to spend your honeymoon night as their guests."

Penelope opened the door for them and revealed a graciously appointed bedroom awash in candlelight. The large white bed was covered in red rose petals. Genie walked in with a smile, then turned back to give Penelope a warm embrace.

"I know you had a hand in this, all of this, and I thank you," said Genie.

Penelope's face relaxed into an honest smile. "You are welcome. I wish you every happiness. And, Mr. Grant, I sincerely wish you every happiness as well."

"Thank you, Miss Rose," said Grant with a bow. "I greatly appreciate your sentiment." Grant led Genie in and shut the door behind them.

One glance at the flowered bed and her stomach fluttered with nerves, which she had not anticipated, considering all they had already shared. Perhaps because this time, Grant was looking at nothing but her, his eyes black in the soft candlelight.

"This night I will not forget," he murmured. "I do hope you will be gentle with me, since it is my first time."

Genie laughed. "I am certainly not the first lady you have taken to bed."

Grant gazed at her unblinking. "But you will be the last. All this time, I was only looking for you."

Genie swallowed on a dry throat. He could elevate her pulse just by looking at her.

"And I have never been bedded by my wife," he added.

Genie smiled. Somehow knowing there was something reserved just for her made it all the more sweeter. She took off her long gloves, one finger at a time. Grant watched her with interest as if she was doing something sensual.

He opened the trunk Penelope had packed and rummaged through the gowns. "Aha!" He held up the gauzy wrap. "Put this on!"

"With what?"

"Nothing but you," he said with a mischievous grin.

"You have requested that once before."

"Did I? Must have had some wits about me."

Genie needed to remove her gown, but it was the

type of fashionable garment that could not be put on or off without assistance. Grant graciously volunteered his services. As he undid the laces, she felt ridiculously embarrassed. Grant was sober now and watching every move she made. Still, after everything she had survived that day, she would not be a coward.

Her gown hit the floor, followed by her chemise and stays. Cool air shocked her skin as she reached once more for the wrap and pulled it on.

Grant sat heavily in a chair. "I have never seen such beauty."

"Perhaps you could oblige me by doing the same."

"You want for me to wear your wrap?" asked Grant.

Genie laughed at the idea, her skin prickling with the cool air and the need to be touched.

Grant removed his coat, waistcoat, and cravat. Genie's heart skipped faster with every piece of clothing he removed. Soon, the shirt was gone, and he was naked save for his breeches. With these, Genie felt compelled to help.

"Would you care to join me on the bed, Mr. Grant?" she asked.

A dazzling smile lit his face. He walked to her and she put her hands on his hips and drew him to her as she sat on the bed. She slipped her fingers under the waistband of his breeches and slowly undid the fastenings. Grant groaned.

He closed his eyes and put his hands on her shoulders more to support himself than to caress her. He actually trembled when she slid his breeches and unmentionables down. She breathed in the power of making such a man vulnerable before her.

He opened his eyes and Genie gasped at the strength of raw desire within them. He bent down and kissed her, soft, hard, fast, tender, until her toes curled and her breath came in gasps. He raked her with his eyes, and wherever he looked, his fingers followed, caressing, smoothing, messaging, teasing, until it was simply impossible to sit up any longer.

She moved back with a smile and slipped under the soft covers. He followed with hungry eyes. He joined her under the covers and took her hand, kissing her wedding ring. "It does not have large jewels, but it is from my family. The three bands represent you and me and God."

"God?"

"Biblical. Cord of three strands. What God has joined together… something like that."

"Last time I came to you. I wanted you, but I knew in my heart it wasn't right. Tonight…" She lifted her hand with her ring and pointed to the three intertwined strands. "To be joined with you in matrimony before we are joined together in bed, that is perfect."

"The ring is only meant to be given to one's true love. That is what you are to me. My one and only love."

"I have been afraid to love you," whispered Genie. "But I confess, I have loved you ever since you made me laugh before the queen."

"Shall I ever be forgiven for that indiscretion?"

Genie shook her head. "I fear you shall have to do penance every night for life."

"And what shall my penance be?" This was the seductive Grant. He snuggled next to her on his side taking full advantage of exploring her body.

"You shall be required to make me smile every day and every night."

"Let me see what I can do to bring a smile to your face." He covered her with his own body like a blanket and kissed her until she felt a tightening in her stomach. She wanted more. With deft hands, he massaged places that brought a wide smile to her face.

"I see I am doing my job. Let me see what I can do to increase that smile." With gentle movements, he joined with her, man and wife. Her smile did increase as he gradually increased his speed and pressure.

Something coiled within her, and she moved with it, searching for release. She held him close, urging him faster. He responded with a growl and then a groan as his body clenched. The coil within her released sending waves of pleasure spinning through her.

He collapsed next to her, still holding her in his arms, unwilling to let go. "Did you smile, my love?"

"I doubt I'll stop smiling for a week," breathed Genie, still trying to catch her breath. "But do not think for a moment I will allow you to shirk your duties."

"I shall accept my fate with abandon." Grant closed his eyes and his breathing began to steady.

Genie rested her head on his shoulder. "Oh dear!"

Grant was jarred awake. "What? What is it?"

"I just thought of something. Where are we going to live? Your parents are home now, and we cannot live in bachelor's quarters. Perhaps we could rent a cottage in the country?"

Grant relaxed back into the pillow. "A cottage? My dear, my family has multiple country estates. We may visit them all and you can choose your favorite."

Genie was silent for a moment. “Are you very rich?”

“It is ‘we’ now, and I suppose so.” Grant yawned.

“Then we can provide housing for all the urchins,” said Genie happily.

“Yes, yes, I told you one of our estates actually provides a home for orphans.” Grant closed his eyes and snuggled closer. “The boys will go there.”

“Yes, but there are more orphans in London. We could take care of them all!”

Grant’s eyes flew open, and he propped himself up on an elbow. “Wait, wait. All the orphans? We can’t take care of all of them!”

“How many can there be?”

“Lots! More than I have estates to fill. Now don’t even think it. Genie, aww don’t look that way, all right, all right fine. We’ll rescue as many as we can.”

“I’m glad you decided to put God in the center of our marriage, so we can be used to provide hope to others,” said Genie.

“Don’t remember saying that.”

Genie held up her hand showing her ring.

“Didn’t know God intended me to rescue urchins,” grumbled Grant.

“You didn’t know God intended me for you either.” Genie smiled again.

“Good point,” declared Grant. “Maybe God knows what he’s doing.”

“Good night, my dear husband.” Genie snuggled up to him again and closed her eyes.

“One thing!” This time it was Grant jarring her awake. “Important. I’ll beggar myself caring for urchins, but I will not do this.”

"What is it?" asked Genie.

"Mornings. Don't do them. Tried it once, ended up locked in a cellar. Won't go there again."

"Then I shall be forced to accept your schedule and sleep until teatime." Genie closed her eyes and did just as she promised.

Pen took a deep breath of the cool night air, the scent of violets filling her lungs. "You have done a beautiful job."

"Thank you. I think it turned out well." Marchford motioned for Penelope to sit on a stone bench in the garden and sat on another bench across the path from her.

"What a night," sighed Penelope.

"Everything went according to plan," declared the duke.

Penelope raised an eyebrow.

"The revised plan," amended Marchford. "You did well, organizing things."

"You did well as the master of ceremony," praised Pen. "I am happy, and perhaps a little relieved, with how things transpired. The new Mr. and Mrs. Grant seem well pleased with each other."

"Never thought I'd see the day Grant willingly got leg shackled."

"Agreed! And Lady Louisa seems content with her choice of grooms."

"I am abundantly pleased for her."

"As well you should be, since now you do not have to be noble and marry her."

Marchford stretched out on the stone bench, breathing in the cool fragrant air of the garden. "Yes, everything went according to my plan."

"Except now you are unmarried, unattached, and in the middle of the London season," reminded Penelope.

Marchford sat bolt upright. "Good heavens! What have I done?"

"Pleasant dreams, Your Grace."

Acknowledgments

I greatly appreciate my agent, Barbara Poelle, and my editor, Deb Werksman, for encouraging me to write in another time period in this first book set in Regency England. My imagination for this time period was captured when I first read Jane Austen's *Pride and Prejudice* in the seventh grade and later sealed when I coped with being on bed rest with a difficult pregnancy by repeatedly watching the BBC's *Pride and Prejudice* miniseries more times than I can possibly count. It has been tremendously fun to try my hand at writing in my favorite time period. I also would like to thank my beta reader, Laurie Maus. Thanks also to my husband, Edward, whose support is invaluable and who serves as the inspiration for every great hero.

The Highlander's Sword

by Amanda Forester

A quiet, flame-haired beauty with secrets of her own...

Lady Aila Graham is destined for the convent, until her brother's death leaves her an heiress. Soon she is caught between a hastily arranged marriage with a Highland warrior, the Abbot's insistence that she take her vows, the Scottish Laird who kidnaps her, and the traitor from within who betrays them all.

She's nothing he expected and everything he really needs...

Padyn MacLaren, a battled-hardened knight, returns home to the Highlands after years of fighting the English in France. MacLaren bears the physical scars of battle, but it is the deeper wounds of betrayal that have rocked his faith. Arriving with only a band of war-weary knights, MacLaren finds his land pillaged and his clan scattered. Determined to restore his clan, he sees Aila's fortune as the answer to his problems...but maybe it's the woman herself.

"Plenty of intrigue keeps the reader cheering all the way."—*Publishers Weekly*

The Highlander's Heart

by Amanda Forester

She's nobody's prisoner

Lady Isabelle Tynsdale's flight over the Scottish border would have been the perfect escape, if only she hadn't run straight into the arms of a gorgeous Highland laird. Whether his plan is ransom or seduction, her only hope is to outwit him, or she'll lose herself entirely…

And he's nobody's fool

Laird David Campbell thought Lady Isabelle was going to be easy to handle and profitable too. He never imagined he'd have such a hard time keeping one enticing English countess out of trouble. And out of his heart…

"An engrossing, enthralling, and totally riveting read. Outstanding!"—Jackie Ivie, national bestselling author of *A Knight and White Satin*

For more Amanda Forester books, visit:

www.sourcebooks.com

True Highland Spirit

by Amanda Forester

Seduction is a powerful weapon...

Morrigan McNab is a Highland lady, robbed of her birthright and with no choice but to fight alongside her brothers to protect their impoverished clan. When she encounters Sir Jacques Dragonet, she discovers her fiercest opponent...

Sir Jacques Dragonet is a Noble Knight of the Hospitaller Order, willing to give his life to defend Scotland from the English. He can't stop himself from admiring the beautiful Highland lass who wields her weapons as well as he can and endangers his heart even more than his life...

Now they're racing each other to find a priceless relic. No matter who wins this heated rivalry, both will lose unless they can find a way to share the spoils.

"A masterful storyteller, Amanda Forester brings new excitement to Scottish medieval romance!"—Gerri Russell, award-winning author of *To Tempt a Knight*

Lady Vivian Defies a Duke

by Samantha Grace

The Naked Truth

Lady Vivian Worth knows perfectly well how to behave like a lady. But observing proper manners when there's no one around to impress is just silly. Why shouldn't she strip down to her chemise for a swim? When her betrothed arrives to finally meet her, Vivi will act every inch the lady—demure, polite, compliant. Everything her brother has promised the man. But until then, she's going to enjoy her freedom…

A Revealing Discovery

Luke Forest, the newly named Duke of Foxhaven, wants nothing to do with his inheritance—or the bride who comes with it. He wants adventure and excitement, like the enchanting water nymph he's just stumbled across. When he discovers the skinny-dipping minx is his intended, he reconsiders his plan to find Lady Vivian another husband. Because the idea of this vivacious woman in the arms of another man might be enough to drive him insane—or to the altar.

"An ideal choice for readers who relish smartly written, splendidly sensual Regency historicals."—Booklist

For more Samantha Grace, visit:

www.sourcebooks.com

Bite Me, Your Grace

by Brooklyn Ann

London's Lord Vampire has problems

Dr. John Polidori's tale "The Vampyre" burst upon the Regency scene along with Mary Shelley's Frankenstein after that notorious weekend spent writing ghost stories with Lord Byron.

A vampire craze broke out instantly in the haut ton.

Now Ian Ashton, the Lord Vampire of London, has to attend tedious balls, linger in front of mirrors, and eat lots of garlic in an attempt to quell the gossip.

If that weren't annoying enough, his neighbor Angelica Winthrop has literary aspirations of her own and is sneaking into his house at night just to see what she can find.]

Hungry, tired, and fed up, Ian is in no mood to humor his beautiful intruder…

New York Times and *USA Today* bestselling author

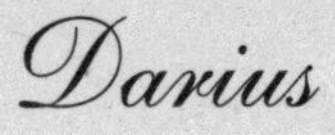

by Grace Burrowes

A story that breaks all the rules...

Darius *is a gripping and remarkable tale of desperation, devotion, and redemption from award-winning* New York Times *and* USA Today *bestselling author Grace Burrowes. Her gorgeous writing and lush Regency world will stay with you long after you turn the final page...*

With his beloved sister tainted by scandal, his widowed brother shattered by grief, and his funds cut off, Darius Lindsey sees no option but to sell himself—body and soul. Until the day he encounters lovely, beguiling Lady Vivian Longstreet, whose tenderness and understanding wrap his soul in a grace he knows he'll never deserve...

"Burrowes creates her usual intelligent characters, exciting chemistry, and flowing dialogue..."—Publishers Weekly

"Very compelling... Likable characters with enough angst to keep the story moving along."—Night Owl Reviews *Review Top Pick, 4.5 Stars*

For more Grace Burrowes, visit:

www.sourcebooks.com

New York Times and *USA Today* bestselling author

Lady Eve's Indiscretion

by Grace Burrowes

Lady Eve's got the perfect plan

Pretty, petite Evie Windham has been more indiscreet than her parents, the Duke and Duchess of Moreland, suspect. Fearing that a wedding night would reveal her past, she's running out of excuses to dodge adoring swains. Lucas Denning, the newly titled Marquis of Deene, has reasons of his own for avoiding marriage. So Evie and Deene strike a deal, each agreeing to be the other's decoy. At this rate matrimony could be avoided indefinitely… until the two are caught in a steamy kiss that no one was supposed to see.

Praise for bestselling author Grace Burrowes:

"Delicious… Burrowes delivers red-hot chemistry with a masterful mix of playfulness and sensuality."

—Publisher's Weekly *Starred Review*

"Captivating… Historical romance at its finest and rife with mystery and intrigue."

—Romance Fiction *on* Suite 101

For more Grace Burrowes, visit:

www.sourcebooks.com

If You Give a Rake a Ruby

by Shana Galen

Her mysterious past is the best revenge...

Fallon, the Marchioness of Mystery, is a celebrated courtesan with her finger on the pulse of high society. She's adored by men, hated by their wives. No one knows anything about her past, and she plans to keep it that way.

Only he can offer her a dazzling future...

Warrick Fitzhugh will do anything to protect his compatriots in the Foreign Office, including seduce Fallon, who he thinks can lead him to the deadliest crime lord in London. He knows he's putting his life on the line...

To Warrick's shock, Fallon is not who he thinks she is, and the secrets she's keeping are exactly what make her his heart's desire...

Praise for *When You Give a Duke a Diamond*:

"A lighthearted yet poignant, humorous yet touching, love story—with original characters who delight and enough sizzle to add heat to a delicious read." —*RT Book Reviews*, 4.5 stars

Geek Girl and the Scandalous Earl

by Gina Lamm

The stakes have never been higher…

An avid gamer, Jamie Marten loves to escape into online adventure. But when she falls through an antique mirror into a lavish bedchamber—200 years in the past!—she realizes she may have escaped a little too far.

Micah Axelby, Earl of Dunnington, has just kicked one mistress out of his bed and isn't looking to fill it with another—least of all this sassy, nearly naked woman who claims to be from the future. Yet something about her is undeniably enticing…

Jamie and Micah are worlds apart. He's a peer of the realm. She can barely make rent. He's horse-drawn. She's Wi-Fi. But in the game of love, these two will risk everything to win.

"Lamm's wonderfully quirky romance brings fresh humor to a familiar trope, with snappy writing and characters who share a surprising, spicy chemistry."—RT Book Reviews

"A light romance with plenty of passion and conflict."—Historical Novels Review

Once Again a Bride

by Jane Ashford

She couldn't be more alone

Widowhood has freed Charlotte Wylde from a demoralizing and miserable marriage. But when her husband's intriguing nephew and heir arrives to take over the estate, Charlotte discovers she's unsafe in her own home…

He could be her only hope…or her next victim

Alec Wylde was shocked by his uncle's untimely death, and even more shocked to encounter his uncle's beautiful young widow. Now clouds of suspicion are gathering, and charges of murder hover over Charlotte's head.

Alec and Charlotte's initial distrust of each other intensifies as they uncover devastating family secrets, and hovering underneath it all is a mutual attraction that could lead them to disaster…

The Wicked Wedding of Miss Ellie Vyne

by Jayne Fresina

When a notorious bachelor seduces a scandalous lady, it can only end in a wicked wedding

By night Ellie Vyne fleeces unsuspecting aristocrats as the dashing Count de Bonneville. By day she avoids her sisters' matchmaking attempts and dreams up inventive insults to hurl at her childhood nemesis, the arrogant, far-too-handsome-for-his-own-good James Hartley.

James finally has a lead on the villainous, thieving count, tracking him to a shady inn. He bursts in on none other than "that Vyne woman"…in a shocking state of dishabille. Convinced she is the count's mistress, James decides it's best to keep his enemies close. Very close. Seducing Ellie will be the perfect bait…

Praise for *The Most Improper Miss Sophie Valentine*:

"Ms. Fresina delivers a scintillating debut! Her sharply drawn characters and witty prose are as addictive as chocolate!"—Mia Marlowe, author of *Touch of a Rogue*

Waking Up with a Rake

by Connie Mason and Mia Marlowe

The fate of England's monarchy is in the hands of three notorious rakes.

To prevent three royal dukes from marrying their way onto the throne, heroic, selfless agents for the crown will be dispatched…to seduce the dukes' intended brides. These wickedly debauched rakes will rumple sheets and cause a scandal. But they just might fall into their own trap…

After he's blamed for a botched assignment during the war, former cavalry officer Rhys Warrick turns his back on "honor." He spends his nights in brothels doing his best to live down to the expectations of his disapproving family. But one last mission could restore the reputation he's so thoroughly sullied. All he has to do is seduce and ruin Miss Olivia Symon and his military record will be cleared. For a man with Rhys' reputation, ravishing the delectably innocent miss should be easy. But Olivia's honesty and bold curiosity stir more than Rhys' desire. Suddenly the heart he thought he left on the battlefield is about to surrender…

How to Tame a Willful Wife

by Christy English

How to Tame a Willful Wife:

1. Forbid her from riding astride
2. Hide her dueling sword
3. Burn all her breeches and buy her silk drawers
4. Frisk her for hidden daggers
5. Don't get distracted while frisking her for hidden daggers…

Anthony Carrington, Earl of Ravensbrook, expects a biddable bride. A man of fiery passion tempered by the rigors of war into steely self-control, he demands obedience from his troops and his future wife. Regardless of how fetching she looks in breeches.

Promised to the Earl of Plump Pockets by her impoverished father, Caroline Montague is no simpering miss. She rides a war stallion named Hercules, fights with a blade, and can best most men with both bow and rifle. She finds Anthony autocratic, domineering, and… ridiculously handsome.

It's a duel of wit and wills in this charming retelling of *The Taming of the Shrew*. But the question is…who's taming whom?

Wolfishly Yours

by Lydia Dare

It takes a beast...

Grayson Hadley is in his own special hell—being treated like a wayward pup by the tutor employed to turn him into a true gentleman. So when he meets a hot-blooded American beauty with the mark of a Lycan, he's only too glad to slip his leash.

To bring this lady to heel

Accustomed to running wild in the swamps of Louisiana, Miss Liviana Mayeux is shipped off to her grandfather's in London to learn a thing or two about polite society. At first she scoffs at the English Lycans' apparent tameness. Little does Livi realize how very close she is to unleashing the passion that lies just beneath the surface...

"A wonderful mix of romance and humor... Absolutely delightful and appealing."—RT Book Reviews, *4 Stars*

"A delicious treat... a sweetly romantic story and a lighthearted romp."—Night Owl Reviews

About the Author

Amanda Forester holds a PhD in psychology and worked for many years in academia before discovering that writing historical romance novels was decidedly more fun. *A Wedding in Springtime* is the first in a new Regency series combining adventure, intrigue, and romance. Her previous novels include a Highlander trilogy set in medieval Scotland. She lives in the Pacific Northwest with her supportive husband and naturally brilliant children. You can visit her at www.amandaforester.com.